DEAD TO THE WORLD

CHARLAINE HARRIS

DEAD TO THE WORLD

The right of Charlaine Harris to be identified as the author
of this work has been asserted by her in accordance with the
Copyright, Designs and Patents Act 1988.

First published in Great Britain in 2005 by
Little, Brown

This edition published in Great Britain in 2011 by
Gollancz
An imprint of the Orion Publishing Group
Orion House, 5 Upper St Martin's Lane, London WC2H 9EA
An Hachette UK Company

3 5 7 9 10 8 6 4

A CIP catalogue record for this book
is available from the British Library

ISBN 978 0 575 11705 1

Printed in Great Britain by
Clays Ltd, St Ives plc

The Orion Publishing Group's policy is to use papers that
are natural, renewable and recyclable products and made
from wood grown in sustainable forests. The logging and
manufacturing processes are expected to conform to the
environmental regulations of the country of origin.

www.charlaineharris.com
www.orionbooks.co.uk

Though they'll probably never read it, this book is dedicated to all the coaches — baseball, football, volleyball, soccer — who've worked through so many years, often for no monetary reward, to coax athletic performances out of my children and to instill in them an understanding of The Game. God bless you all, and thanks from one of the moms who crowds the stands through rain, cold, heat, and mosquitoes.

However, this mom always wonders who else might be watching the night games.

Acknowledgments

My thanks to Wiccans who answered my call for knowledge with more information than I could use – Maria Lima, Sandilee Lloyd, Holly Nelson, Jean Hontz, and M. R. 'Murv' Sellars. I owe further thanks to other experts in different fields: Kevin Ryer, who knows more about feral hogs than most people do about their own pets; Dr. D. P. Lyle, who is so gracious about answering medical questions; and, of course, Doris Ann Norris, reference librarian to the stars.

If I have made mistakes in the use of the knowledge these kind people imparted, I'll do my best to somehow blame it on them.

I found the note taped to my door when I got home from work. I'd had the lunch-to-early-evening shift at Merlotte's, but since we were at the tail end of December, the day darkened early. So Bill, my former boyfriend – that's Bill Compton, or Vampire Bill, as most of the regulars at Merlotte's call him – must have left his message within the previous hour. He can't get up until dark.

I hadn't seen Bill in over a week, and our parting hadn't been a happy one. But touching the envelope with my name written on it made me feel miserable. You'd think – though I'm twenty-six – I'd never had, and lost, a boyfriend before.

You'd be right.

Normal guys don't want to date someone as strange as I am. People have been saying I'm messed up in the head since I started school.

They're right.

That's not to say I don't get groped at the bar occasionally. Guys get drunk. I look good. They forget their misgivings about my reputation for strangeness and my ever-present smile.

But only Bill has ever gotten close to me in an intimate way. Parting from him had hurt me bad.

I waited to open the envelope until I was sitting at the old, scarred kitchen table. I still had my coat on, though I'd shucked my gloves.

Dearest Sookie – I wanted to come over to talk to you when you had somewhat recovered from the unfortunate events of earlier this month.

'Unfortunate events,' my round rear end. The bruises had finally faded, but I had a knee that still ached in the cold, and I suspected that it always would. Every injury I had incurred had been in the course of rescuing my cheating boyfriend from his imprisonment by a group of vampires that included his former flame, Lorena. I had yet to figure out why Bill had been so infatuated with Lorena that he'd answered her summons to Mississippi.

Probably, you have a lot of questions about what happened.

Damn straight.

If you'll talk to me face-to-face, come to the front door and let me in.

Yikes. I hadn't seen that one coming. I pondered for a minute. Deciding that while I didn't trust Bill anymore, I didn't believe that he would physically harm me, I went back through the house to the front door. I opened it and called, 'Okay, come on in.'

He emerged from the woods surrounding the clearing in which my old house stood. I ached at the sight of him. Bill was broad-shouldered and lean from his life of farming the land next to mine. He was hard and tough from his years as a Confederate soldier, before his death in 1867. Bill's nose was straight off a Greek vase. His hair was dark brown and clipped close to his head, and his eyes were just as dark. He looked exactly the same as he had while we were dating, and he always would.

He hesitated before he crossed the threshold, but I'd given him permission, and I moved aside so he could step past me into the living room filled with old, comfortable furniture and neat as a pin.

'Thank you,' he said in his cold, smooth voice, a voice that still gave me a twinge of sheer lust. Many things had gone wrong between us, but they hadn't started in bed. 'I wanted to talk to you before I left.'

'Where are you going?' I tried to sound as calm as he.

'To Peru. The queen's orders.'

'Still working on your, ah, database?' I knew almost nothing about computers, but Bill had studied hard to make himself computer literate.

'Yes. I've got a little more research to do. A very old vampire in Lima has a great fund of knowledge about those of our race on his continent, and I have an appointment to confer with him. I'll do some sight-seeing while I'm down there.'

I fought the urge to offer Bill a bottle of synthetic blood, which would have been the hospitable thing to do. 'Have a seat,' I said curtly, and nodded at the sofa. I sat on the edge of the old recliner catty-cornered to it. Then a silence fell, a silence that made me even more conscious of how unhappy I was.

'How's Bubba?' I asked finally.

'He's in New Orleans right now,' Bill said. 'The queen likes to keep him around from time to time, and he was so visible here over the last month that it seemed like a good idea to take him elsewhere. He'll be back soon.'

You'd recognize Bubba if you saw him; everyone knows

his face. But he hadn't been 'brought over' too successfully. Probably the morgue attendant, who happened to be a vampire, should have ignored the tiny spark of life. But since he was a great fan, he hadn't been able to resist the attempt, and now the entire southern vampire community shuffled Bubba around and tried to keep him from public view.

Another silence fell. I'd planned on taking off my shoes and uniform, putting on a cuddly robe, and watching television with a Freschetta pizza by my side. It was a humble plan, but it was my own. Instead, here I was, suffering.

'If you have something to say, you better go on and say it,' I told him.

He nodded, almost to himself. 'I have to explain,' he said. His white hands arranged themselves in his lap. 'Lorena and I—'

I flinched involuntarily. I never wanted to hear that name again. He'd dumped me for Lorena.

'I have to tell you,' he said, almost angrily. He'd seen me twitch. 'Give me this chance.' After a second, I waved a hand to tell him to continue.

'The reason I went to Jackson when she called me is that I couldn't help myself,' he said.

My eyebrows flew up. I'd heard *that* before. It means, 'I have no self-control,' or, 'It seemed worth it at the time, and I wasn't thinking north of my belt.'

'We were lovers long ago. As Eric says he told you, vampire liaisons don't tend to last long, though they're very intense while they are ongoing. However, what Eric did not tell you was that Lorena was the vampire who brought me over.'

'To the Dark Side?' I asked, and then I bit my lip. This was no subject for levity.

'Yes,' Bill agreed seriously. 'And we were together after that, as lovers, which is not always the case.'

'But you had broken up . . .'

'Yes, about eighty years ago, we came to the point where we couldn't tolerate each other any longer. I hadn't seen Lorena since, though I'd heard of her doings, of course.'

'Oh, sure,' I said expressionlessly.

'But I had to obey her summons. This is absolutely imperative. When your maker calls, you must respond.' His voice was urgent.

I nodded, trying to look understanding. I guess I didn't do too good a job.

'She *ordered* me to leave you,' he said. His dark eyes were peering into mine. 'She said she would kill you if I didn't.'

I was losing my temper. I bit the inside of my cheek, real hard, to make myself focus. 'So, without explanation or discussion with me, you decided what was best for me and for you.'

'I had to,' he said. 'I *had* to do her bidding. And I knew she was capable of harming you.'

'Well, you got that right.' In fact, Lorena had done her dead level best to harm me right into the grave. But I'd gotten her first — okay, by a fluke, but it had worked.

'And now you no longer love me,' Bill said, with the slightest of questions in his voice.

I didn't have any clear answer.

'I don't know,' I said. 'I wouldn't think you'd want to come back to me. After all, I killed your mom.' And there was the slightest of questions in my voice, too, but mostly I was bitter.

'Then we need more time apart. When I return, if you consent, we'll talk again. A kiss good-bye?'

To my shame, I would love to kiss Bill again. But it was such a bad idea, even wanting it seemed wrong. We stood, and I gave him a quick brush of lips to the cheek. His white skin shone with a little glow that distinguished vampires from humans. It had surprised me to learn that not everyone saw them like I did.

'Are you seeing the Were?' he asked, when he was nearly out the door. He sounded as though the words had been pulled out of him by their roots.

'Which one?' I asked, resisting the temptation to bat my eyelashes. He deserved no answer, and he knew it. 'How long will you be gone?' I asked more briskly, and he looked at me with some speculation.

'It's not a sure thing. Maybe two weeks,' he answered.

'We might talk then,' I said, turning my face away. 'Let me return your key.' I fished my keys out of my purse.

'No, please, keep it on your key ring,' he said. 'You might need it while I am gone. Go in the house as you will. My mail's getting held at the post office until I give them notice, and I think all my other loose ends are taken care of.'

So I was his last loose end. I damned up the trickle of anger that was all too ready to bubble out these days.

'I hope you have a safe trip,' I said coldly, and shut the door behind him. I headed back to my bedroom. I had a robe to put on and some television to watch. By golly, I was sticking to my plan.

But while I was putting my pizza in the oven, I had to blot my cheeks a few times.

Chapter 1

The New Year's Eve party at Merlotte's Bar and Grill was finally, finally, over. Though the bar owner, Sam Merlotte, had asked all his staff to work that night, Holly, Arlene, and I were the only ones who'd responded. Charlsie Tooten had said she was too old to put up with the mess we had to endure on New Year's Eve, Danielle had long-standing plans to attend a fancy party with her steady boyfriend, and a new woman couldn't start for two days. I guess Arlene and Holly and I needed the money more than we needed a good time.

And I hadn't had any invitations to do anything else. At least when I'm working at Merlotte's, I'm a part of the scenery. That's a kind of acceptance.

I was sweeping up the shredded paper, and I reminded myself again not to comment to Sam on what a poor idea the bags of confetti had been. We'd all made ourselves pretty clear about that, and even good-natured Sam was showing signs of wear and tear. It didn't seem fair to leave it all for Terry Bellefleur to clean, though sweeping and mopping the floors was his job.

Sam was counting the till money and bagging it up so he could go by the night deposit at the bank. He was looking tired but pleased.

He flicked open his cell phone. 'Kenya? You ready to take me to the bank? Okay, see you in a minute at the back door.' Kenya, a police officer, often escorted Sam to the night deposit, especially after a big take like tonight's.

I was pleased with my money take, too. I had earned a lot in tips. I thought I might have gotten three hundred dollars or more – and I needed every penny. I would have enjoyed the prospect of totting up the money when I got home, if I'd been sure I had enough brains left to do it. The noise and chaos of the party, the constant runs to and from the bar and the serving hatch, the tremendous mess we'd had to clean up, the steady cacophony of all those brains . . . it had combined to exhaust me. Toward the end I'd been too tired to keep my poor mind protected, and lots of thoughts had leaked through.

It's not easy being telepathic. Most often, it's not fun.

This evening had been worse than most. Not only had the bar patrons, almost all known to me for many years, been in uninhibited moods, but there'd been some news that lots of people were just dying to tell me.

'I hear yore boyfriend done gone to South America,' a car salesman, Chuck Beecham, had said, malice gleaming in his eyes. 'You gonna get mighty lonely out to your place without him.'

'You offering to take his place, Chuck?' the man beside him at the bar had asked, and they both had a we're-men-together guffaw.

'Naw, Terrell,' said the salesman. 'I don't care for vampire leavings.'

'You be polite, or you go out the door,' I said steadily. I felt warmth at my back, and I knew my boss, Sam Merlotte, was looking at them over my shoulder.

'Trouble?' he asked.

'They were just about to apologize,' I said, looking Chuck and Terrell in the eyes. They looked down at their beers.

'Sorry, Sookie,' Chuck mumbled, and Terrell bobbed his head in agreement. I nodded and turned to take care of another order. But they'd succeeded in hurting me.

Which was their goal.

I had an ache around my heart.

I was sure the general populace of Bon Temps, Louisiana, didn't know about our estrangement. Bill sure wasn't in the habit of blabbing his personal business around, and neither was I. Arlene and Tara knew a little about it, of course, since you have to tell your best friends when you've broken up with your guy, even if you have to leave out all the interesting details. (Like the fact that you'd killed the woman he left you for. Which I couldn't help. Really.) So anyone who told me Bill had gone out of the country, assuming I didn't know it yet, was just being malicious.

Until Bill's recent visit to my house, I'd last seen him when I'd given him the disks and computer he'd hidden with me. I'd driven up at dusk, so the machine wouldn't be sitting on his front porch for long. I'd put all his stuff up against the door in a big waterproofed box. He'd come out just as I was driving away, but I hadn't stopped.

An evil woman would have given the disks to Bill's boss, Eric. A lesser woman would have kept those disks and that computer, having rescinded Bill's (and Eric's) invitations to enter the house. I had told myself proudly that I was not an evil, or a lesser, woman.

Also, thinking practically, Bill could just have hired some human to break into my house and take them. I didn't think he would. But he needed them bad, or he'd be in trouble with his boss's boss. I've got a temper, maybe even a bad temper, once it gets provoked. But I'm not vindictive.

Arlene has often told me I am too nice for my own good, though I assure her I am not. (Tara never says that; maybe she knows me better?) I realized glumly that, sometime during this hectic evening, Arlene would hear about Bill's departure. Sure enough, within twenty minutes of Chuck and Terrell's gibing, she made her way through the crowd to pat me on the back. 'You didn't need that cold bastard anyway,' she said. 'What did he ever do for you?'

I nodded weakly at her to show how much I appreciated her support. But then a table called for two whiskey sours, two beers, and a gin and tonic, and I had to hustle, which was actually a welcome distraction. When I dropped off their drinks, I asked myself the same question. What had Bill done for me?

I delivered pitchers of beer to two tables before I could add it all up.

He'd introduced me to sex, which I really enjoyed. Introduced me to a lot of other vampires, which I didn't. Saved my life, though when you thought about it, it wouldn't have been in danger if I hadn't been dating him in the first place. But I'd saved his back once or twice, so that debt was canceled. He'd called me 'sweetheart,' and at the time he'd meant it.

'Nothing,' I muttered, as I mopped up a spilled piña colada and handed one of our last clean bar towels to the woman who'd knocked it over, since a lot of it was still in her skirt. 'He didn't do a thing for me.' She smiled and nodded, obviously thinking I was commiserating with her. The place was too noisy to hear anything anyway, which was lucky for me.

But I'd be glad when Bill got back. After all, he was my nearest neighbor. The community's older cemetery separated our properties, which lay along a parish road south of Bon Temps. I was out there all by myself, without Bill.

'Peru, I hear,' my brother Jason, said. He had his arm around his girl of the evening, a short, thin, dark twenty-one-year-old from somewhere way out in the sticks. (I'd carded her.) I gave her a close look. Jason didn't know it, but she was a shape-shifter of some kind. They're easy to spot. She was an attractive girl, but she changed into something with feathers or fur when the moon was full. I noticed Sam give her a hard glare when Jason's back was turned, to remind her to behave herself in his territory. She returned the glare, with interest. I had the feeling she didn't become a kitten, or a squirrel.

I thought of latching on to her brain and trying to read it, but shifter heads aren't easy. Shifter thoughts are kind of snarly and red, though every now and then you can get a good picture of emotions. Same with Weres.

Sam himself turns into a collie when the moon is bright and round. Sometimes he trots all the way over to my house, and I feed him a bowl of scraps and let him nap on my back porch, if the weather's good, or in my living room, if the weather's poor. I don't let him in the bedroom any-more, because he wakes up naked – in which state he looks *very* nice, but I just don't need to be tempted by my boss.

The moon wasn't full tonight, so Jason would be safe. I

decided not to say anything to him about his date. Everyone's got a secret or two. Her secret was just a little more colorful.

Besides my brother's date, and Sam of course, there were two other supernatural creatures in Merlotte's Bar that New Year's Eve. One was a magnificent woman at least six feet tall, with long rippling dark hair. Dressed to kill in a skintight long-sleeved orange dress, she'd come in by herself, and she was in the process of meeting every guy in the bar. I didn't know what she was, but I knew from her brain pattern that she was not human. The other creature was a vampire, who'd come in with a group of young people, most in their early twenties. I didn't know any of them. Only a sideways glance by a few other revelers marked the presence of a vampire. It just went to show the change in attitude in the few years since the Great Revelation.

Almost three years ago, on the night of the Great Revelation, the vampires had gone on TV in every nation to announce their existence. It had been a night in which many of the world's assumptions had been knocked sideways and rearranged for good.

This coming-out party had been prompted by the Japanese development of a synthetic blood that can keep vamps satisfied nutritionally. Since the Great Revelation, the United States has undergone numerous political and social upheavals in the bumpy process of accommodating our newest citizens, who just happen to be dead. The vampires have a public face and a public explanation for their condition – they claim an allergy to sunlight and garlic causes severe metabolic changes – but I've seen the other side of the vampire world. My eyes now see a lot of things most human beings don't ever see. Ask me if this knowledge has made me happy.

No.

But I have to admit, the world is a more interesting place to me now. I'm by myself a lot (since I'm not exactly Norma Normal), so the extra food for thought has been welcome. The fear and danger haven't. I've seen the private face of vampires, and I've learned about Weres and shifters and other stuff. Weres and shifters prefer to stay in the shadows – for now – while they watch how going public works out for the vamps.

See, I had all this to mull over while collecting tray after tray of glasses and mugs, and unloading and loading the dishwasher to help Tack, the new cook. (His real name is Alphonse Petacki. Can you be surprised he likes 'Tack' better?) When our part of the cleanup was just about finished, and this long evening was finally over, I hugged Arlene and wished her a happy New Year, and she hugged me back. Holly's boyfriend was waiting for her at the employees' entrance at the back of the building, and Holly waved to us as she pulled on her coat and hurried out.

'What're your hopes for the New Year, ladies?' Sam asked. By that time, Kenya was leaning against the bar, waiting for him, her face calm and alert. Kenya ate lunch here pretty regularly with her partner, Kevin, who was as pale and thin as she was dark and rounded. Sam was putting the chairs up on the tables so Terry Bellefleur, who came in very early in the morning, could mop the floor.

'Good health, and the right man,' Arlene said dramatically, her hands fluttering over her heart, and we laughed. Arlene has found many men – and she's been married four times – but she's still looking for Mr. Right. I could 'hear'

Arlene thinking that Tack might be the one. I was startled; I hadn't even known she'd looked at him.

The surprise showed on my face, and in an uncertain voice Arlene said, 'You think I should give up?'

'Hell, no,' I said promptly, chiding myself for not guarding my expression better. It was just that I was so tired. 'It'll be this year, for sure, Arlene.' I smiled at Bon Temp's only black female police officer. 'You have to have a wish for the New Year, Kenya. Or a resolution.'

'I always wish for peace between men and women,' Kenya said. 'Make my job a lot easier. And my resolution is to bench-press one-forty.'

'Wow,' said Arlene. Her dyed red hair contrasted violently with Sam's natural curly red-gold as she gave him a quick hug. He wasn't much taller than Arlene – though she's at least five foot eight, two inches taller than I. 'I'm going to lose ten pounds, that's my resolution.' We all laughed. That had been Arlene's resolution for the past four years. 'What about you, Sam? Wishes and resolutions?' she asked.

'I have everything I need,' he said, and I felt the blue wave of sincerity coming from him. 'I resolve to stay on this course. The bar is doing great, I like living in my double-wide, and the people here are as good as people anywhere.'

I turned to conceal my smile. That had been a pretty ambiguous statement. The people of Bon Temps were, indeed, as good as people anywhere.

'And you, Sookie?' he asked. Arlene, Kenya, and Sam were all looking at me. I hugged Arlene again, because I like to. I'm ten years younger – maybe more, since though Arlene says she's thirty-six, I have my doubts – but we've been friends ever since we started working at Merlotte's together after Sam bought the bar, maybe five years now.

'Come on,' Arlene said, coaxing me. Sam put his arm around me. Kenya smiled, but drifted away into the kitchen to have a few words with Tack.

Acting on impulse, I shared my wish. 'I just hope to not be beaten up,' I said, my weariness and the hour combining in an ill-timed burst of honesty. 'I don't want to go to the hospital. I don't want to see a doctor.' I didn't want to have to ingest any vampire blood, either, which would cure you in a hurry but had various side effects. 'So my resolution is to stay out of trouble,' I said firmly.

Arlene looked pretty startled, and Sam looked – well, I couldn't tell about Sam. But since I'd hugged Arlene, I gave him a big hug, too, and felt the strength and warmth in his body. You think Sam's slight until you see him shirtless unloading boxes of supplies. He is really strong and built really smooth, and he has a high natural body temperature. I felt him kiss my hair, and then we were all saying good night to each other and walking out the back door. Sam's truck was parked in front of his trailer, which is set up behind Merlotte's Bar but at a right angle to it, but he climbed in Kenya's patrol car to ride to the bank. She'd bring him home, and then Sam could collapse. He'd been on his feet for hours, as had we all.

As Arlene and I unlocked our cars, I noticed Tack was waiting in his old pickup; I was willing to bet he was going to follow Arlene home.

With a last 'Good night!' called through the chilly silence of the Louisiana night, we separated to begin our new years.

I turned off onto Hummingbird Road to go out to my place, which is about three miles southeast of the bar. The relief of finally being alone was immense, and I began to relax mentally. My headlights flashed past the close-packed trunks of the pines that formed the backbone of the lumber industry hereabouts.

The night was extremely dark and cold. There are no streetlights way out on the parish roads, of course. Creatures were not stirring, not by any means. Though I kept telling myself to be alert for deer crossing the road, I was driving on autopilot. My simple thoughts were filled with the plan of scrubbing my face and pulling on my warmest night-gown and climbing into my bed.

Something white appeared in the headlights of my old car.

I gasped, jolted out of my drowsy anticipation of warmth and silence.

A running man: At three in the morning on January first, he was running down the parish road, apparently running for his life.

I slowed down, trying to figure out a course of action. I was a lone unarmed woman. If something awful was pursuing him, it might get me, too. On the other hand, I couldn't let someone suffer if I could help. I had a moment to notice that the man was tall, blond, and clad only in blue jeans, before I pulled up by him. I put the car into park and leaned over to roll down the window on the passenger's side.

'Can I help you?' I called. He gave me a panicked glance and kept on running.

But in that moment I realized who he was. I leaped out of the car and took off after him.

'Eric!' I yelled. 'It's me!'

He wheeled around then, hissing, his fangs fully out. I stopped so abruptly I swayed where I stood, my hands out in front of me in a gesture of peace. Of course, if Eric decided to attack, I was a dead woman. So much for being a good Samaritan.

Why didn't Eric recognize me? I'd known him for many months. He was Bill's boss, in the complicated vampire hierarchy that I was beginning to learn. Eric was the sheriff of Area Five, and he was a vampire on the rise. He was also gorgeous and could kiss like a house afire, but that was not the most pertinent side of him right at the moment. Fangs and strong hands curved into claws were what I was seeing. Eric was in full alarm mode, but he seemed just as scared of me as I was of him. He didn't leap to attack.

'Stay back, woman,' he warned me. His voice sounded like his throat was sore, raspy and raw.

'What are you doing out here?'

'Who are you?'

'You known darn good and well who I am. What's up with you? Why are you out here without your car?' Eric drove a sleek Corvette, which was simply Eric.

'You know me? Who am I?'

Well, that knocked me for a loop. He sure didn't sound like he was joking. I said cautiously, 'Of course I know you, Eric. Unless you have an identical twin. You don't, right?'

'I don't know.' His arms dropped, his fangs seemed to be retracting, and he straightened from his crouch, so I felt there'd been a definite improvement in the atmosphere of our encounter.

'You don't know if you have a brother?' I was pretty much at sea.

'No. I don't know. Eric is my name?' In the glare of my headlights, he looked just plain pitiful.

'Wow.' I couldn't think of anything more helpful to say.

'Eric Northman is the name you go by these days. Why are you out here?'

'I don't know that, either.'

I was sensing a theme here. 'For real? You don't remember anything?' I tried to get past being sure that at any second he'd grin down at me and explain everything and laugh, embroiling me in some trouble that would end in me . . . getting beaten up.

'For real.' He took a step closer, and his bare white chest made me shiver with sympathetic goose bumps. I also realized (now that I wasn't terrified) how forlorn he looked. It was an expression I'd never seen on the confident Eric's face before, and it made me feel unaccountably sad.

'You know you're a vampire, right?'

'Yes.' He seemed surprised that I asked. 'And you are not.'

'No, I'm real human, and I have to know you won't hurt me. Though you could have by now. But believe me, even if you don't remember it, we're sort of friends.'

'I won't hurt you.'

I reminded myself that probably hundreds and thousands of people had heard those very words before Eric ripped their throats out. But the fact is, vampires don't have to kill once they're past their first year. A sip here, a sip there, that's the norm. When he looked so lost, it was hard to remember he could dismember me with his bare hands.

I'd told Bill one time that the smart thing for aliens to do (when they invaded Earth) would be to arrive in the guise of lop-eared bunnies.

'Come get in my car before you freeze,' I said. I was having that I'm-getting-sucked-in feeling again, but I didn't know what else to do.

'I do know you?' he said, as though he were hesitant about getting in a car with someone as formidable as a woman ten inches shorter, many pounds lighter, and a few centuries younger.

'Yes,' I said, not able to restrain an edge of impatience. I wasn't too happy with myself, because I still half suspected I was being tricked for some unfathomable reason. 'Now come on, Eric. I'm freezing, and so are you.' Not that vampires seemed to feel temperature extremes, as a rule; but even Eric's skin looked goosey. The dead can freeze, of course. They'll survive it – they survive almost everything – but I understand it's pretty painful. 'Oh my God, Eric, you're barefoot.' I'd just noticed.

I took his hand; he let me get close enough for that. He let me lead him back to the car and stow him in the passenger seat. I told him to roll up the window as I went around to my side, and after a long minute of studying the mechanism, he did.

I reached in the backseat for an old afghan I keep there in the winter (for football games, etc.) and wrapped it around him. He wasn't shivering, of course, because he was a vampire, but I just couldn't stand to look at all that bare flesh in this temperature. I turned the heater on full blast (which, in my old car, isn't saying much).

Eric's exposed skin had never made me feel cold before – when I'd seen this much of Eric before, I'd felt anything *but*. I was giddy enough by now to laugh out loud before I could censor my own thoughts.

He was startled, and looked at me sideways.

'You're the last person I expected to see,' I said. 'Were you coming out this way to see Bill? Because he's gone.'

'Bill?'

'The vampire who lives out here? My ex-boyfriend?'

He shook his head. He was back to being absolutely terrified.

'You don't know how you came to be here?'

He shook his head again.

I was making a big effort to think hard; but it was just that, an effort. I was worn out. Though I'd had a rush of adrenaline when I'd spotted the figure running down the dark road, that rush was wearing off fast. I reached the turnoff to my house and turned left, winding through the black and silent woods on my nice, level driveway – that, in fact, Eric had had re-graveled for me.

And that was why Eric was sitting in my car right now, instead of running through the night like a giant white rabbit. He'd had the intelligence to give me what I really wanted. (Of course, he'd also wanted me to go to bed with him for months. But he'd given me the driveway because I needed it.)

'Here we are,' I said, pulling around to the back of my old house. I switched off the car. I'd remembered to leave the outside lights on when I'd left for work that afternoon, thank goodness, so we weren't sitting there in total darkness.

'This is where you live?' He was glancing around the clearing where the old house stood, seemingly nervous about going from the car to the back door.

'Yes,' I said, exasperated.

He just gave me a look that showed white all around the blue of his eyes.

'Oh, come on,' I said, with no grace at all. I got out of the car and went up the steps to the back porch, which I don't keep locked because, hey, why lock a screened-in back porch? I do lock the inner door, and after a second's fumbling, I had it open so the light I leave on in the kitchen could spill out. 'You can come in,' I said, so he could cross the threshold. He scuttled in after me, the afghan still clutched around him.

Under the overhead light in the kitchen, Eric looked pretty pitiful. His bare feet were bleeding, which I hadn't noticed before. 'Oh, Eric,' I said sadly, and got a pan out from the cabinet, and started the hot water to running in the sink. He'd heal real quick, like vampires do, but I couldn't help but wash him clean. The blue jeans were filthy around the hem. 'Pull 'em off,' I said, knowing they'd just get wet if I soaked his feet while he was dressed.

With not a hint of a leer or any other indication that he was enjoying this development, Eric shimmied out of the jeans. I tossed them onto the back porch to wash in the morning, trying not to gape at my guest, who was now clad in underwear that was definitely over-the-top, a bright red bikini style whose stretchy quality was definitely being tested. Okay, another big surprise. I'd seen Eric's underwear only once before – which was once more than I ought to have – and he'd been a silk boxers guy. Did men change styles like that?

Without preening, and without comment, the vampire rewrapped his white body in the afghan. Hmmm. I was now convinced he wasn't himself, as no other evidence could have convinced me. Eric was way over six feet of pure magnificence (if a marble white magnificence), and he well knew it.

I pointed to one of the straight-back chairs at the kitchen table. Obediently, he pulled it out and sat. I crouched to put the pan on the floor, and I gently guided his big feet into the water. Eric groaned as the warmth touched his skin. I guess that even a vampire could feel the contrast. I got a clean rag from under the sink and some liquid soap, and I washed his feet. I took my time, because I was trying to think what to do next.

'You were out in the night,' he observed, in a tentative sort of way.

'I was coming home from work, as you can see from my clothes.' I was wearing our winter uniform, a long-sleeved white boat-neck T-shirt with 'Merlotte's Bar' embroidered over the left breast and worn tucked into black slacks.

'Women shouldn't be out alone this late at night,' he said disapprovingly.

'Tell me about it.'

'Well, women are more liable to be overwhelmed by an attack than men, so they should be more protected—'

'No, I didn't mean literally. I meant, I agree. You're preaching to the choir. I didn't want to be working this late at night.'

'Then why were you out?'

'I need the money,' I said, wiping my hand and pulling the roll of bills out of my pocket and dropping it on the table while I was thinking about it. 'I got this house to maintain, my car is old, and I have taxes and insurance to pay. Like everyone else,' I added, in case he thought I was complaining unduly. I hated to poor-mouth, but he'd asked.

'Is there no man in your family?'

Every now and then, their ages do show. 'I have a brother. I can't remember if you've ever met Jason.' A cut on his left foot looked especially bad. I put some more hot water into the basin to warm the remainder. Then I tried to get all the dirt out. He winced as I gently rubbed the wash-cloth over the margins of the wound. The smaller cuts and bruises seemed to be fading even as I watched. The hot water heater came on behind me, the familiar sound some-how reassuring.

'Your brother permits you to do this working?'

I tried to imagine Jason's face when I told him that I expected him to support me for the rest of my life because I was a woman and shouldn't work outside the home. 'Oh, for goodness sake, Eric.' I looked up at him, scowling. 'Jason's got his own problems.' Like being chronically self-ish and a true tomcat.

I eased the pan of water to the side and patted Eric dry with a dishtowel. This vampire now had clean feet. Rather stiffly, I stood. My back hurt. My feet hurt. 'Listen, I think what I better do is call Pam. She'll probably know what's going on with you.'

'Pam?'

It was like being around a particularly irritating two-year-old.

'Your second-in-command.'

He was going to ask another question, I could just tell. I held up a hand. 'Just hold on. Let me call her and find out what's happening.'

'But what if she has turned against me?'

'Then we need to know that, too. The sooner the better.'

I put my hand on the old phone that hung on the kitchen wall right by the end of the counter. A high stool sat below it. My grandmother had always sat on the stool to conduct her lengthy phone conversations, with a pad and pencil handy. I missed her every day. But at the moment I had no room in my emotional palette for grief, or even nostalgia. I looked in my little address book for the number of Fangtasia, the vampire bar in Shreveport that provided Eric's principal income and served as the base of his operations, which I understood were far wider in scope. I didn't know how wide or what these other moneymaking projects were, and I didn't especially want to know.

I'd seen in the Shreveport paper that Fangtasia, too, had planned a big bash for the evening – 'Begin Your New Year with a Bite' – so I knew someone would be there. While the phone was ringing, I swung open the refrigerator and got out a bottle of blood for Eric. I popped it in the microwave and set the timer. He followed my every move with anxious eyes.

'Fangtasia,' said an accented male voice.

'Chow?'

'Yes, how may I serve you?' He'd remembered his phone persona of sexy vampire just in the nick of time.

'It's Sookie.'

'Oh,' he said in a much more natural voice. 'Listen, Happy New Year, Sook, but we're kind of busy here.'

'Looking for someone?'

There was a long, charged silence.

'Wait a minute,' he said, and then I heard nothing.

'Pam,' said Pam. She'd picked up the receiver so silently that I jumped when I heard her voice.

'Do you still have a master?' I didn't know how much I could say over the phone. I wanted to know if she'd been the one who'd put Eric in this state, or if she still owed him loyalty.

'I do,' she said steadily, understanding what I wanted to know. 'We are under . . . we have some problems.'

I mulled that over until I was sure I'd read between the lines. Pam was telling me that she still owed Eric her allegiance, and that Eric's group of followers was under some kind of attack or in some kind of crisis.

I said, 'He's here.' Pam appreciated brevity.

'Is he alive?'

'Yep.'

'Damaged?'

'Mentally.'

A *long* pause, this time.

'Will he be a danger to you?'

Not that Pam cared a whole hell of a lot if Eric decided to drain me dry, but I guess she wondered if I would shelter Eric. 'I don't think so at the moment,' I said. 'It seems to be a matter of memory.'

'I hate witches. Humans had the right idea, burning them at the stake.'

Since the very humans who had burned witches would have been delighted to sink that same stake into vampire hearts, I found that a little amusing – but not very, considering the hour. I immediately forgot what she'd been talking about. I yawned.

'Tomorrow night, we'll come,' she said finally. 'Can you keep him this day? Dawn's in less than four hours. Do you have a safe place?'

'Yes. But you get over here at nightfall, you hear me? I don't want to get tangled up in your vampire shit again.' Normally, I don't speak so bluntly; but like I say, it was the tail end of a long night.

'We'll be there.'

We hung up simultaneously. Eric was watching me with unblinking blue eyes. His hair was a snarly tangled mess of blond waves. His hair is the exact same color as mine, and I have blue eyes, too, but that's the end of the similarities.

I thought of taking a brush to his hair, but I was just too weary.

'Okay, here's the deal,' I told him. 'You stay here the rest of the night and tomorrow, and then Pam and them'll come get you tomorrow night and let you know what's happening.'

'You won't let anyone get in?' he asked. I noticed he'd finished the blood, and he wasn't quite as drawn as he'd been, which was a relief.

'Eric, I'll do my best to keep you safe,' I said, quite gently. I rubbed my face with my hands. I was going to fall asleep on my feet. 'Come on,' I said, taking his hand. Clutching the afghan with the other hand, he trailed down the hall after me, a snow white giant in tiny red underwear.

My old house has been added onto over the years, but it hasn't ever been more than a humble farmhouse. A second story was added around the turn of the century, and two more bedrooms and a walk-in attic are upstairs, but I seldom go up there anymore. I keep it shut off, to save money on electricity. There are two bedrooms downstairs, the smaller one I'd used until my grandmother died and her large one across the hall from it. I'd moved into the large one after her death. But the hidey-hole Bill had built was in the smaller bedroom. I led Eric in there, switched on the light, and made sure the blinds were closed and the curtains drawn across them. Then I opened the door of the closet, removed its few contents, and pulled back the flap of carpet that covered the closet floor, exposing the trapdoor. Underneath was a light-tight space that Bill had built a few months before, so that he could stay over during the day or use it as a hiding place if his own home was unsafe. Bill liked having a bolt-hole, and I was sure he had some that I didn't know about. If I'd been a vampire (God forbid), I would have, myself.

I had to wipe thoughts of Bill out of my head as I showed my reluctant guest how to close the trapdoor on top of him and that the flap of carpet would fall back into place. 'When I get up, I'll put the stuff back in the closet so it'll look natural,' I reassured him, and smiled encouragingly.

'Do I have to get in now?' he asked.

Eric, making a request of me: The world was really turned upside-down. 'No,' I said, trying to sound like I was concerned. All I could think of was my bed. 'You don't have to. Just get in before sunrise. There's no way you could miss that, right? I mean, you couldn't fall asleep and wake up in the sun?'

He thought for a moment and shook his head. 'No,' he said. 'I know that can't happen. Can I stay in the room with you?'

Oh, God, *puppy dog eyes.* From a six-foot-five ancient Viking vampire. It was just too much. I didn't have enough energy to laugh, so I just gave a sad little snigger. 'Come on,' I said, my voice as limp as my legs. I turned off the light in that room, crossed the hall, and flipped on the one in my own room, yellow and white and clean and warm, and folded down the bedspread and blanket and sheet. While Eric sat forlornly in a slipper chair on the other side of the bed, I pulled off my shoes and socks, got a nightgown out of a drawer, and retreated into the bathroom. I was out in ten minutes, with clean teeth and face and swathed in a very old, very soft flannel nightgown that was cream-colored with blue flowers scattered around. Its ribbons were raveled and the ruffle around the bottom was pretty sad, but it suited me just fine. After I'd switched off the lights, I remembered my hair was still up in its usual ponytail, so I pulled out the band that held it and I shook my head to make it fall loose. Even my scalp seemed to relax, and I sighed with bliss.

As I climbed up into the high old bed, the large fly in my personal ointment did the same. Had I actually told him he could get in bed with me? Well, I decided, as I wriggled down under the soft old sheets and the blanket and the comforter, if Eric had designs on me, I was just too tired to care.

'Woman?'

'Hmmm?'

'What's your name?'

'Sookie. Sookie Stackhouse.'

'Thank you, Sookie.'

'Welcome, Eric.'

Because he sounded so lost – the Eric I knew had never been one to do anything other than assume others should serve him – I patted around under the covers for his hand. When I found it, I slid my own over it. His palm was turned up to meet my palm, and his fingers clasped mine.

And though I would not have thought it was possible to go to sleep holding hands with a vampire, that's exactly what I did.

Chapter 2

I woke up slowly. As I lay snuggled under the covers, now and then stretching an arm or a leg, I gradually remembered the surrealistic happenings of the night before.

Well, Eric wasn't in bed with me now, so I had to assume he was safely ensconced in the hidey-hole. I went across the hall. As I'd promised, I put the contents back in the closet to make it look normal. The clock told me it was noon, and outside the sun was bright, though the air was cold. For Christmas, Jason had given me a thermometer that read the outside temperature and showed it to me on a digital readout inside. He'd installed it for me, too. Now I knew two things: it was noon, and it was thirty-four degrees outside.

In the kitchen, the pan of water I'd washed Eric's feet with was still sitting on the floor. As I dumped it into the sink, I saw that at some point he'd rinsed out the bottle that had held the synthetic blood. I'd have to get some more to have around when he rose, since you didn't want a hungry vampire in your house, and it would be only polite to have extra to offer Pam and whoever else drove over from

Shreveport. They'd explain things to me – or not. They'd take Eric away and work on whatever problems were facing the Shreveport vampire community, and I would be left in peace. Or not.

Merlotte's was closed on New Year's Day until four o'clock. On New Year's Day, and the day after, Charlsie and Danielle and the new girl were on the schedule, since the rest of us had worked New Year's Eve. So I had two whole days off . . . and at least one of them I got to spend alone in a house with a mentally ill vampire. Life just didn't get any better.

I had two cups of coffee, put Eric's jeans in the washer, read a romance for a while, and studied my brand-new Word of the Day calendar, a Christmas gift from Arlene. My first word for the New Year was 'exsanguinate.' This was probably not a good omen.

Jason came by a little after four, flying down my drive in his black pickup with pink and purple flames on the side. I'd showered and dressed by then, but my hair was still wet. I'd sprayed it with detangler and I was brushing through it slowly, sitting in front of the fireplace. I'd turned on the TV to a football game to have something to watch while I brushed, but I kept the sound way down. I was pondering Eric's predicament while I luxuriated in the feel of the fire's warmth on my back.

We hadn't used the fireplace much in the past couple of years because buying a load of wood was so expensive, but Jason had cut up a lot of trees that had fallen last year after an ice storm. I was well stocked, and I was enjoying the flames.

My brother stomped up the front steps and knocked per-functorily before coming in. Like me, he had mostly grown up in this house. We'd come to live with Gran when my parents died, and she'd rented out their house until Jason said he was ready to live on his own, when he'd been twenty. Now Jason was twenty-eight and the boss of a parish road crew. This was a rapid rise for a local boy without a lot of education, and I'd thought it was enough for him until the past month or two, when he'd begun acting restless.

'Good,' he said, when he saw the fire. He stood squarely in front of it to warm his hands, incidentally blocking the warmth from me. 'What time did you get home last night?' he said over his shoulder.

'I guess I got to bed about three.'

'What did you think of that girl I was with?'

'I think you better not date her anymore.'

That wasn't what he'd expected to hear. His eyes slid sideways to meet mine. 'What did you get off her?' he asked in a subdued voice. My brother knows I am telepathic, but he would never discuss it with me, or anyone else. I've seen him get into fights with some man who accused me of being abnormal, but he knows I'm different. Everyone else does, too. They just choose not to believe it, or they believe I couldn't possibly read *their* thoughts – just someone else's. God knows, I try to act and talk like I'm not receiving an unwanted spate of ideas and emotions and regrets and accusations, but sometimes it just seeps through.

'She's not your kind,' I said, looking into the fire.

'She surely ain't a vamp,' he protested.

'No, not a vamp.'

'Well, then.' He glared at me belligerently.

'Jason, when the vampires came out – when we found

out they were real after all those decades of thinking they were just a scary legend – didn't you ever wonder if there were other tall tales that were real?'

My brother struggled with that concept for a minute. I knew (because I could 'hear' him) that Jason wanted to deny any such idea absolutely and call me a crazy woman – but he just couldn't. 'You know for a fact,' he said. It wasn't quite a question.

I made sure he was looking me in the eyes, and I nodded emphatically.

'Well, shit,' he said, disgusted. 'I really liked that girl, and she was a tiger in the sack.'

'Really?' I asked, absolutely stunned that she had changed in front of him when it wasn't the full moon. 'Are you okay?' The next second, I was chastising myself for my stupidity. Of course she hadn't.

He gaped at me for a second, before bursting out laughing. 'Sookie, you are one weird woman! You looked just like you thought she really could—' And his face froze. I could feel the idea bore a hole through the protective bubble most people inflate around their brain, the bubble that repels sights and ideas that don't jibe with their expectation of the everyday. Jason sat down heavily in Gran's recliner. 'I wish I didn't know that,' he said in a small voice.

'That may not be specifically what happens to her – the tiger thing – but believe me, something happens.'

It took a minute for his face to settle back into more familiar lines, but it did. Typical Jason behavior: There was nothing he could do about his new knowledge, so he pushed it to the back of his mind. 'Listen, did you see Hoyt's date last night? After they left the bar, Hoyt got stuck in a ditch over to Arcadia, and they had to walk two miles to get to a phone because he'd let his cell run down.'

'He did not!' I exclaimed, in a comforting and gossipy way. 'And her in those heels.' Jason's equilibrium was restored. He told me the town gossip for a few minutes, he accepted my offer of a Coke, and he asked me if I needed anything from town.

'Yes, I do.' I'd been thinking while he was talking. Most of his news I'd heard from other brains the nights before, in unguarded moments.

'Ah-oh,' he said, looking mock-frightened. 'What am I in for now?'

'I need ten bottles of synthetic blood and clothes for a big man,' I said, and I'd startled him again. Poor Jason, he deserved a silly vixen of a sister who bore nieces and nephews who called him Uncle Jase and held on to his legs. Instead, he got me.

'How big is the man, and where is he?'

'He's about six foot four or five, and he's asleep,' I said. 'I'd guess a thirty-four waist, and he's got long legs and broad shoulders.' I reminded myself to check the size label on Eric's jeans, which were still in the dryer out on the back porch.

'What kind of clothes?'

'Work clothes.'

'Anybody I know?'

'Me,' said a much deeper voice.

Jason whipped around as if he was expecting an attack, which shows his instincts aren't so bad, after all. But Eric looked as unthreatening as a vampire his size can look. And he'd obligingly put on the brown velour bathrobe that I'd left in the second bedroom. It was one I'd kept here for Bill, and it gave me a pang to see it on someone else. But I had to be practical; Eric couldn't wander around in red bikini underwear – at least, not with Jason in the house.

Jason goggled at Eric and cast a shocked glance at me. 'This is your newest man, Sookie? You didn't let any grass grow under your feet.' He didn't know whether to sound admiring or indignant. Jason still didn't realize Eric was dead. It's amazing to me that lots of people can't tell for a few minutes. 'And I need to get him clothes?'

'Yes. His shirt got torn last night, and his blue jeans are still dirty.'

'You going to introduce me?'

I took a deep breath. It would have been so much better if Jason hadn't seen Eric. 'Better not,' I said.

They both took that badly. Jason looked wounded, and the vampire looked offended.

'Eric,' he said, and stuck out a hand to Jason.

'Jason Stackhouse, this rude lady's brother,' Jason said.

They shook, and I felt like wringing both their necks.

'I'm assuming there's a reason why you two can't go out to buy him more clothes,' Jason said.

'There's a good reason,' I said. 'And there's about twenty good reasons you should forget you ever saw this guy.'

'Are you in danger?' Jason asked me directly.

'Not yet,' I said.

'If you do something that gets my sister hurt, you'll be in a world of trouble,' Jason told Eric the vampire.

'I would expect nothing less,' Eric said. 'But since you are being blunt with me, I'll be blunt with you. I think you should support her and take her into your household, so she would be better protected.'

Jason's mouth fell open again, and I had to cover my own

so I wouldn't laugh out loud. This was even better than I'd imagined.

'Ten bottles of blood and a change of clothes?' Jason asked me, and I knew by the change in his voice that he'd finally cottoned on to Eric's state.

'Right. Liquor store'll have the blood. You can get the clothes at Wal-Mart.' Eric had mostly been a jeans and T-shirt kind of guy, which was all I could afford, anyway. 'Oh, he needs some shoes, too.'

Jason went to stand by Eric and put his foot parallel to the vampire's. He whistled, which made Eric jump.

'Big feet,' Jason commented, and flashed me a look. 'Is the old saying true?'

I smiled at him. He was trying to lighten the atmosphere. 'You may not believe me, but I don't know.'

'Kind of hard to swallow . . . no joke intended. Well, I'm gone,' Jason said, nodding to Eric. In a few seconds, I heard his truck speeding around the curves in the driveway, through the dark woods. Night had fallen completely.

'I'm sorry I came out while he was here,' Eric said tentatively. 'You didn't want me to meet him, I think.' He came over to the fire and seemed to be enjoying the warmth as I had been doing.

'It's not that I'm embarrassed to have you here,' I said. 'It's that I have a feeling you're in a heap of trouble, and I don't want my brother drawn in.'

'He is your only brother?'

'Yes. And my parents are gone, my grandmother, too. He's all I have, except for a cousin who's been on drugs for years. She's lost, I guess.'

'Don't be so sad,' he said, as if he couldn't help himself.

'I'm fine.' I made my voice brisk and matter-of-fact.

'You've had my blood,' he said.

Ah-oh. I stood absolutely still.

'I wouldn't be able to tell how you feel if you hadn't had my blood,' he said. 'Are we – have we been – lovers?'

That was certainly a nice way to put it. Eric was usually pretty Anglo-Saxon about sex.

'No,' I said promptly, and I was telling the truth, though only by a narrow margin. We'd been interrupted in time, thank God. I'm not married. I have weak moments. He is gorgeous. What can I say?

But he was looking at me with intense eyes, and I felt color flooding my face.

'This is not your brother's bathrobe.'

Oh, boy. I stared into the fire as if it were going to spell out an answer for me.

'Whose, then?'

'Bill's,' I said. That was easy.

'He is your lover?'

I nodded. 'Was,' I said honestly.

'He is my friend?'

I thought that over. 'Well, not exactly. He lives in the area you're the sheriff of? Area Five?' I resumed brushing my hair and discovered it was dry. It crackled with electricity and followed the brush. I smiled at the effect in my reflection in the mirror over the mantel. I could see Eric in the reflection, too. I have no idea why the story went around that vampires can't be seen in mirrors. There was certainly plenty of Eric to see, because he was so tall and he hadn't wrapped the robe very tightly . . . I closed my eyes.

'Do you need something?' Eric asked anxiously.

More self-control.

'I'm just fine,' I said, trying not to grind my teeth. 'Your friends will be here soon. Your jeans are in the dryer, and I'm hoping Jason will be back any minute with some clothes.'

'My friends?'

'Well, the vampires who work for you. I guess Pam counts as a friend. I don't know about Chow.'

'Sookie, where do I work? Who is Pam?'

This was really an uphill conversation. I tried to explain to Eric about his position, his ownership of Fangtasia, his other business interests, but truthfully, I wasn't knowledgeable enough to brief him completely.

'You don't know much about what I do,' he observed accurately.

'Well, I only go to Fangtasia when Bill takes me, and he takes me when you make me do something.' I hit myself in the forehead with my brush. Stupid, stupid!

'How could I make you do anything? May I borrow the brush?' Eric asked. I stole a glance at him. He was looking all broody and thoughtful.

'Sure,' I said, deciding to ignore his first question. I handed over the brush. He began to use it on his own hair, making all the muscles in his chest dance around. *Oh, boy. Maybe I should get back in the shower and turn the water on cold?* I stomped into the bedroom and got an elastic band and pulled my hair back in the tightest ponytail I could manage, up at the crown of my head. I used my second-best brush to get it very smooth, and checked to make sure I'd gotten it centered by turning my head from side to side.

'You are tense,' Eric said from the doorway, and I yipped.

'Sorry, sorry!' he said hastily.

I glared at him, full of suspicion, but he seemed sincerely contrite. When he was himself, Eric would have laughed.

But darn if I didn't miss Real Eric. You knew where you were with him.

I heard a knock on the front door.

'You stay in here,' I said. He seemed pretty worried, and he sat on the chair in the corner of the room, like a good little fella. I was glad I'd picked up my discarded clothes the night before, so my room didn't seem so personal. I went through the living room to the front door, hoping for no more surprises.

'Who is it?' I asked, putting my ear to the door.

'We are here,' said Pam.

I began to turn the knob, stopped, then remembered they couldn't come in anyway, and opened the door.

Pam has pale straight hair and is as white as a magnolia petal. Other than that, she looks like a young suburban housewife who has a part-time job at a preschool.

Though I don't think you'd really ever want Pam to take care of your toddlers, I've never seen her do anything extraordinarily cruel or vicious. But she's definitely convinced that vampires are better than humans, and she's very direct and doesn't mince words. I'm sure if Pam saw that some dire action was necessary for her well-being, she'd do it without missing any sleep. She seems to be an excellent second-in-command, and not overly ambitious. If she wants to have her own bailiwick, she keeps that desire very well concealed.

Chow is a whole different kettle of fish. I don't want to know Chow any better than I already do. I don't trust him, and I've never felt comfortable around him. Chow is Asian, a small-built but powerful vampire with longish black hair. He is no more than five foot seven, but every inch of visible skin (except his face) is covered with those intricate tattoos that are true art dyed into human skin. Pam says they are yakuza tattoos. Chow acts as Fangtasia's bartender some evenings, and on other nights he just sits around to let patrons approach him. (That's the whole purpose of vampire bars, to let regular humans feel they're walking on the wild side by being in the same room with the in-the-flesh undead. It's very lucrative, Bill told me.)

Pam was wearing a fluffy cream sweater and golden-brown knit pants, and Chow was in his usual vest and slacks. He seldom wore a shirt, so the Fangtasia patrons could get the full benefit of his body art.

I called Eric, and he came into the room slowly. He was visibly wary.

'Eric,' Pam said, when she saw him. Her voice was full of relief. 'You're well?' Her eyes were fixed on Eric anxiously. She didn't bow, but she sort of gave a deep nod.

'Master,' Chow said, and bowed.

I tried not to overinterpret what I was seeing and hearing, but I assumed that the different greetings signified the relationships among the three.

Eric looked uncertain. 'I know you,' he said, trying to make it sound more statement than question.

The two other vampires exchanged a glance. 'We work for you,' Pam said. 'We owe you fealty.'

I began to ease out of the room, because they'd want to talk about secret vampire stuff, I was sure. And if there was anything I didn't want to know, it was more secrets.

'Please don't go,' Eric said to me. His voice was frightened. I froze and looked behind me. Pam and Chow were staring over Eric's shoulders at me, and they had quite different expressions. Pam looked almost amused. Chow looked openly disapproving.

I tried not to look in Eric's eyes, so I could leave him with a clear conscience, but it just didn't work. He didn't want to be left alone with his two sidekicks. I blew lots of air out, puffing up my cheeks. Well, *dammit*. I trudged back to Eric's side, glaring at Pam the whole way.

There was another knock at the door, and Pam and Chow reacted in a dramatic way. They were both ready to fight in an instant, and vampires in that readiness are very, very scary. Their fangs run out, their hands arch like claws, and their bodies are on full alert. The air seems to crackle around them.

'Yes?' I said from right inside the door. I *had* to get a peephole installed.

'It's your brother,' Jason said brusquely. He didn't know how lucky he was that he hadn't just walked in.

Something had put Jason into a foul mood, and I wondered if there was anyone with him. I almost opened the door. But I hesitated. Finally, feeling like a traitor, I turned to Pam. I silently pointed down the hall to the back door, making an opening-and-closing gesture so she could not mistake what I meant. I made a circle in the air with my finger – *Come around the house, Pam* – and pointed at the front door.

Pam nodded and ran down the hall to the back of the house. I couldn't hear her feet on the floor. Amazing.

Eric moved away from the door. Chow got in front of him. I approved. This was exactly what an underling was supposed to do.

In less than a minute, I heard Jason bellow from maybe six inches away. I jumped away from the door, startled.

Pam said, 'Open up!'

I swung the door wide to see Jason locked in Pam's arms.

She was holding him off the ground with no effort, though he was flailing wildly and making it as hard as he could, God bless him.

'You're by yourself,' I said, relief being my big emotion.

'Of course, dammit! Why'd you set her on me? Let me down!'

'It's my brother, Pam,' I said. 'Please put him down.'

Pam set Jason down, and he spun around to look at her. 'Listen, woman! You don't just sneak up on a man like that! You're lucky I didn't slap you upside the head!'

Pam looked amused all over again, and even Jason looked embarrassed. He had the grace to smile. 'I guess that might be pretty hard,' he admitted, picking up the bags he'd dropped. Pam helped him. 'It's lucky I got the blood in the big plastic bottles,' he said. 'Otherwise, this lovely lady would have to go hungry.'

He smiled at Pam engagingly. Jason loves women. With Pam, Jason was in way over his head, but didn't have the sense to know it.

'Thanks. You need to go now,' I said abruptly. I took the plastic bags from his hands. He and Pam were still in an eye-lock. She was putting the whammy on him. 'Pam,' I said sharply. 'Pam, this is my brother.'

'I know,' she said calmly. 'Jason, did you have something to tell us?'

I'd forgotten that Jason had sounded like he was barely containing himself when he'd come to the door.

'Yes,' he said, hardly able to tear his eyes away from the vampire. But when he glanced at me, he caught sight of Chow, and his eyes widened. He had enough sense to fear Chow, at least. 'Sookie?' he said. 'Are you all right?' He took a step into the room, and I could see the adrenaline left over from the fright Pam had given begin to pump through his system again.

'Yes. Everything's all right. These are just friends of Eric's who came to check on him.'

'Well, they better go take those wanted posters down.'

That got everyone's full attention. Jason enjoyed that.

'There's posters up at Wal-Mart, and Grabbit Kwik, and the Bottle Barn, and just about everywhere else in town,' he said. 'They all say, "Have you seen this man?" and they go on to tell about him being kidnapped and his friends being so anxious, and the reward for a confirmed sighting is fifty thousand dollars.'

I didn't process this too well. I was mostly thinking, *Huh?*, when Pam got the point.

'They're hoping to sight him and catch him,' she said to Chow. 'It will work.'

'We should take care of it,' he said, nodding toward Jason.

'Don't you lay one hand on my brother,' I said. I moved between Jason and Chow, and my hands itched for a stake or hammer or anything at all that would keep this vamp from touching Jason.

Pam and Chow focused on me with that unswerving attention. I didn't find it flattering, as Jason had. I found it deadly. Jason opened his mouth to speak – I could feel the anger building in him, and the impulse to confront – but my hand clamped down on his wrist, and he grunted, and I said, 'Don't say a word.' For a miracle, he didn't. He seemed to sense that events were moving forward too rapidly and in a grave direction.

'You'll have to kill me, too,' I said.

Chow shrugged. 'Big threat.'

Pam didn't say anything. If it came to a choice between upholding vamp interests and being my buddy . . . well, I guessed we were just going to have to cancel our sleepover, and here I'd been planning on French-braiding her hair.

'What is this about?' Eric asked. His voice was considerably stronger. 'Explain . . . Pam.'

A minute went by while things hung in the balance. Then Pam turned to Eric, and she may have been slightly relieved that she didn't have to kill me right at the moment. 'Sookie and this man, her brother, have seen you,' she explained. 'They're human. They need the money. They will turn you in to the witches.'

'What witches?' Jason and I said simultaneously.

'Thank you, Eric, for getting us into this shit,' Jason muttered unfairly. 'And could you let go of my wrist, Sook? You're stronger than you look.'

I was stronger than I should be because I'd had vampire blood – most recently, Eric's. The effects would last around three more weeks, maybe longer. I knew this from past experience.

Unfortunately, I'd needed that extra strength at a low point in my life. The very vampire who was now draped in my former boyfriend's bathrobe had donated that blood when I was grievously wounded but had to keep going.

'Jason,' I said in a level voice – as though the vampires couldn't hear me – 'please watch yourself.' That was as close as I could come to telling Jason to be smart for once in his life. He was way too fond of walking on the wild side.

Very slowly and cautiously, as if an uncaged lion were in the room, Jason and I went to sit on the old couch to one side of the fireplace. That notched the situation down a couple of degrees. After a brief hesitation, Eric sat on the floor and pressed himself into my legs. Pam settled on the edge of the recliner, closest to the fireplace, but Chow chose to remain standing (within what I calculated was lunging distance) near Jason. The atmosphere became less tense, though not by any means relaxed – but still, this was an improvement over the moments before.

'Your brother must stay and hear this,' Pam said. 'No matter how much you don't want him to know. He needs to learn why he mustn't try to earn that money.'

Jason and I gave quick nods. I was hardly in a position to throw them out. Wait, I could! I could tell them all that their invitation to come in was rescinded, and whoosh, out the door they'd go, walking backward. I found myself smiling. Rescinding an invitation was extremely satisfying. I'd done it once before; I'd sent both Bill and Eric zooming out of my living room, and it had felt so good I'd rescinded the entrance invite of every vampire I knew. I could feel my smile fading as I thought more carefully.

If I gave way to this impulse, I'd have to stay in my house every night for the rest of my life, because they'd return at dusk the next day and the day after that and so on, until they got me, because I had their boss. I glowered at Chow. I was willing to blame this whole thing on him.

'Several night ago, we heard – at Fangtasia,' Pam explained for Jason's benefit, 'that a group of witches had arrived in Shreveport. A human told us, one who wants Chow. She didn't know why we were so interested in that information.'

That didn't sound too threatening to me. Jason shrugged. 'So?' he said. 'Geez, you all are vampires. What can a bunch of girls in black do to you?'

'Real witches can do plenty to vampires,' Pam said, with

remarkable restraint. 'The "girls in black" you're thinking of are only poseurs. Real witches can be women or men of any age. They are very formidable, very powerful. They control magical forces, and our existence itself is rooted in magic. This group seems to have some extra . . .' She paused, casting around for a word.

'Juice?' Jason suggested helpfully.

'Juice,' she agreed. 'We haven't discovered what makes them so strong.'

'What was their purpose in coming to Shreveport?' I asked.

'A good question,' Chow said approvingly. 'A much better question.'

I frowned at him. I didn't need his damn approval.

'They wanted – they want – to take over Eric's businesses,' Pam said. 'Witches want money as much as anyone, and they figure they can either take over the businesses, or make Eric pay them to leave him alone.'

'Protection money.' This was a familiar concept to a television viewer. 'But how could they force you into anything? You guys are so powerful.'

'You have no idea how many problems a business can develop if witches want a piece of it. When we met with them for the first time, their leaders – a sister and brother team – spelled it out. Hallow made it clear she could curse our labor, turn our alcoholic drinks bad, and cause patrons to trip on the dance floor and sue us, to say nothing of plumbing problems.' Pam threw up her hands in disgust. 'It would make every night a bad dream, and our revenues would plummet, maybe to the point that the Fangtasia would become worthless.'

Jason and I gave each other cautious glances. Naturally,

vampires were heavily into the bar business, since it was most lucrative at night, and they were up then. They'd dabbled in all-night dry cleaners, all-night restaurants, all-night movie theaters . . . but the bar business paid best. If Fangtasia closed, Eric's financial base would suffer a blow.

'So they want protection money,' Jason said. He'd watched the *Godfather* trilogy maybe fifty times. I thought about asking him if he wanted to sleep with the fishes, but Chow was looking antsy, so I refrained. We were both of us just a snick and a snee away from an unpleasant death, and I knew it was no time for humor, especially humor that so nearly wasn't.

'So how did Eric end up running down the road at night without a shirt or shoes?' I asked, thinking it was time to get down to brass tacks.

Much exchanging of glances between the two subordinates. I looked down at Eric, pressed up against my legs. He seemed to be as interested in the answer as we were. His hand firmly circled my ankle. I felt like a large security blanket.

Chow decided to take a narrative turn. 'We told them we would discuss their threat. But last night, when we went to work, one of the lesser witches was waiting at Fangtasia with an alternative proposal.' He looked a little uncomfortable. 'During our initial meeting, the head of the coven, Hallow, decided she, uh, lusted after Eric. Such a coupling is very frowned upon among witches, you understand, since we are dead and witchcraft is supposed to be so . . . organic.' Chow spat the word out like it was something stuck to his shoe. 'Of course, most witches would never do what this coven was attempting. These are all people drawn to the power itself, rather than to the religion behind it.'

This was interesting, but I wanted to hear the rest of the story. So did Jason, who made a 'hurry along' gesture with his hand. With a little shake to himself, as if to rouse himself from his thoughts, Chow went on. 'This head witch, this Hallow, told Eric, through her subordinate, that if he would entertain her for seven nights, she would only demand a fifth of his business, rather than a half.'

'You must have some kind of reputation,' my brother said to Eric, his voice full of honest awe. Eric was not entirely successful at hiding his pleased expression. He was glad to hear he was such a Romeo. There was a slight difference in the way he looked up at me in the next moment, and I had a feeling of horrid inevitability – like when you see your car begin to roll downhill (though you're sure you left it in park), and you know there's no way you can catch up to it and put on the brakes, no matter how much you want to. That car is gonna crash.

'Though some of us thought he might be wise to agree, our master balked,' Chow said, shooting 'our master' a less than loving glance. 'And our master saw fit to refuse in such insulting terms that Hallow cursed him.'

Eric looked embarrassed.

'Why on earth would you turn down a deal like that?' Jason asked, honestly puzzled.

'I don't remember,' Eric said, moving fractionally closer to my legs. Fractionally was all the closer he could get. He looked relaxed, but I knew he wasn't. I could feel the tension in his body. 'I didn't know my name until this woman, Sookie, told me it.'

'And how did you come to be out in the country?'

'I don't know that either.'

'He just vanished from where he was,' Pam said. 'We

were sitting in the office with the young witch, and Chow and I were arguing with Eric about his refusal. And then we weren't.'

'Ring any bells, Eric?' I asked. I'd caught myself reaching out to stroke his hair, like I would a dog that was huddling close to me.

The vampire looked puzzled. Though Eric's English was excellent, every now and then an idiom would faze him.

'Do you recall anything about this?' I said, more plainly. 'Have any memories of it?'

'I was born the moment I was running down the road in the dark and the cold,' he said. 'Until you took me in, I was a void.'

Put that way, it sounded terrifying.

'This just doesn't track,' I said. 'This wouldn't just happen out of the blue, with no warning.'

Pam didn't look offended, but Chow tried to make the effort.

'You two did something, didn't you? You messed up. What did you do?' Both Eric's arms wrapped around my legs, so I was pinned in place. I suppressed a little ripple of panic. He was just insecure.

'Chow lost his temper with the witch,' Pam said, after a significant pause.

I closed my eyes. Even Jason seemed to grasp what Pam was saying, because his eyes got bigger. Eric turned his face to rub his cheek along my thigh. I wondered what he was making of this.

'And the minute she was attacked, Eric vanished?' I asked.

Pam nodded.

'So she was booby-trapped with a spell.'

'Apparently,' Chow said. 'Though I had never heard of such a thing, and I can't be held responsible.' His glare dared me to say anything.

I turned to Jason and rolled my eyes. Dealing with Chow's blunder was not my responsibility. I was pretty sure that if the whole story was told to the queen of Louisiana, Eric's overlord, she might have a few things to say to Chow about the incident.

There was a little silence, during which Jason got up to put another log on the fire. 'You've been in Merlotte's before, haven't you?' he asked the vampires. 'Where Sookie works?'

Eric shrugged; he didn't remember. Pam said, 'I have, but not Eric.' She looked at me to confirm, and after some thought, I nodded.

'So no one's going to instantly associate Eric with Sookie.' Jason dropped that observation casually, but he was looking very pleased and almost smug.

'No,' Pam said slowly. 'Maybe not.'

There was definitely something I ought to be worrying about right now, but I couldn't quite see the shape of it.

'So you're clear as far as Bon Temps goes,' Jason continued. 'I doubt if anyone saw him out last night, except Sookie, and I'm damned if I know why he ended up on that particular road.'

My brother had made a second excellent point. He was really operating on all his batteries tonight.

'But lots of people from here do drive to Shreveport to go to that bar, Fangtasia. I've been myself,' Jason said. This was news to me, and I gave him a narrow-eyed glare. He shrugged and looked just a tad embarrassed. 'So what's gonna happen when someone tries to claim the reward? When they call the number on the poster?'

Chow decided to contribute more to the conversation. 'Of course, the "close friend" who answers will come right away to talk to the informant firsthand. If the caller can convince the "close friend" that he saw Eric after the whore witch worked her spell on him, the witches will begin looking in a specific area. They're sure to find him. They'll try to contact the local witches, too, get them working on it.'

'No witches in Bon Temps,' Jason said, looking amazed that Chow would even suggest the idea. There my brother went again, making assumptions.

'Oh, I'll bet there are,' I said. 'Why not? Remember what I told you?' Though I'd been thinking of Weres and shifters when I'd warned him there were things in the world he wouldn't want to see.

My poor brother was getting overloaded with information this evening. 'Why not?' he repeated weakly. 'Who would they be?'

'Some women, some men,' Pam said, dusting her hands together as if she were talking about some infectious pest. 'They are like everyone else who has a secret life – most of them are quite pleasant, fairly harmless.' Though Pam didn't sound too positive when she said that. 'But the bad ones tend to contaminate the good.'

'However,' Chow said, staring thoughtfully at Pam, 'this is such a backwater that there may well be very few witches in the area. Not all of them are in covens, and getting an unattached witch to cooperate will be very difficult for Hallow and her followers.'

'Why can't the Shreveport witches just cast a spell to find Eric?' I asked.

'They can't find anything of his to use to cast such a spell,' Pam said, and she sounded as if she knew what she was talking about. 'They can't get into his daytime resting place to find a hair or clothes that bear his scent. And there's no one around who's got Eric's blood in her.'

Ah-oh. Eric and I looked at each other very briefly. There was me; and I was hoping devoutly that no one knew that but Eric.

'Besides,' Chow said, shifting from foot to foot, 'in my opinion, since we are dead, such things would not work to cast a spell.'

Pam's eyes latched on to Chow's. They were exchanging ideas again, and I didn't like it. Eric, the cause of all this message swapping, was looking back and forth between his two fellow vamps. Even to me he looked clueless.

Pam turned to me. 'Eric should stay here, where he is. Moving him will expose him to more danger. With him out of the way and in safety, we can take countermeasures against the witches.'

'Going to the mattresses,' Jason muttered in my ear, still stuck on the *Godfather* terminology.

Now that Pam had said it out loud, I could see clearly why I should have become concerned when Jason began emphasizing how impossible it was that anyone should associate Eric with me. No one would believe that a vampire of Eric's power and importance would be parked with a human barmaid.

My amnesiac guest looked bewildered. I leaned forward, gave in briefly to my impulse to stroke his hair, and then I held my hands over his ears. He permitted this, even putting his own hands on top of mine. I was going to pretend he couldn't hear what I was going to say.

'Listen, Chow, Pam. This is the worst idea of all time. I'll tell you why.' I could hardly get the words out fast enough, emphatically enough. 'How am I supposed to protect him? You know how this will end! I'll get beaten up. Or maybe even killed.'

Pam and Chow looked at me with twin blank expressions. They might as well have said, 'Your point being?'

'If my sister does this,' Jason said, disregarding me completely, 'she deserves to get paid for it.'

There was what you call a pregnant silence. I gaped at him.

Simultaneously, Pam and Chow nodded.

'At least as much as an informer would get if he called the phone number on the poster,' Jason said, his bright blue eyes going from one pale face to another. 'Fifty thousand.'

'Jason!' I finally found my voice, and I clamped my hands down even tighter over Eric's ears. I was embarrassed and humiliated, without being able to figure out exactly why. For one thing, my brother was arranging my business as though it were his.

'Ten,' Chow said.

'Forty-five,' Jason countered.

'Twenty.'

'Thirty-five.'

'Done.'

'Sookie, I'll bring you my shotgun,' Jason said.

Chapter 3

'How did this happen?' I asked the fire, when they were all gone.

All except for the big Viking vampire I was supposed to preserve and protect.

I was sitting on the rug in front of the fire. I'd just thrown in another piece of wood, and the flames were really lovely. I needed to think about something pleasant and comforting.

I saw a big bare foot out of the corner of my eye. Eric sank down to join me on the hearth rug. 'I think this happened because you have a greedy brother, and because you are the kind of woman who would stop for me even though she was afraid,' Eric said accurately.

'How are you feeling about all this?' I never would have asked the compos mentis Eric this question, but he still seemed so different, maybe not the completely terrified mess he'd been the night before, but still very un-Eric. 'I mean – it's like you're a package that they put in a storage locker, me being the locker.'

'I am glad they are afraid enough of me to take good care of me.'

'Huh,' I said intelligently. Not the answer I'd expected.

'I must be a frightening person, when I am myself. Or do I inspire so much loyalty through my good works and kind ways?'

I sniggered.

'I thought not.'

'You're okay,' I said reassuringly, though come to think of it, Eric didn't look like he needed much reassurance. However, now I was responsible for him. 'Aren't your feet cold?'

'No,' he said. But now I was in the business of taking care of Eric, who *so* didn't need taking care of. And I was being paid a staggering amount of money to do just that, I reminded myself sternly. I got the old quilt from the back of the couch and covered his legs and feet in green, blue, and yellow squares. I collapsed back onto the rug beside him.

'That's truly hideous,' Eric said.

'That's what Bill said.' I rolled over on my stomach and caught myself smiling.

'Where is this Bill?'

'He's in Peru.'

'Did he tell you he was going?'

'Yes.'

'Am I to assume that your relationship with him has waned?'

That was a pretty nice way to put it. 'We've been on the outs. It's beginning to look permanent,' I said, my voice even.

He was on his stomach beside me now, propped up on his elbows so we could talk. He was a little closer than I was comfortable with, but I didn't want to make a big issue out of scooting over. He half turned to toss the quilt over both of us.

'Tell me about him,' Eric said unexpectedly. He and Pam and Chow had all had a glass of TrueBlood before the other vampires left, and he was looking pinker.

'You know Bill,' I told him. 'He's worked for you for quite a while. I guess you can't remember, but Bill's – well, he's kind of cool and calm, and he's really protective, and he can't seem to get some things through his head.' I never thought I'd be rehashing my relationship with Bill with Eric, of all people.

'He loves you?'

I sighed, and my eyes watered, as they so often did when I thought of Bill – Weeping Willa, that was me. 'Well, he said he did,' I muttered dismally. 'But then when this vampire ho contacted him somehow, he went a-running.' For all I knew, she'd emailed him. 'He'd had an affair with her before, and she turned out to be his, I don't know what you call 'em, the one who turned him into a vampire. Brought him over, he said. So Bill took back up with her. He says he had to. And then he found out' – I looked sideways at Eric with a significant raise of the eyebrows, and Eric looked fascinated – 'that she was just trying to lure him over to the even-darker side.'

'Pardon?'

'She was trying to get him to come over to another vampire group in Mississippi and bring with him the really valuable computer data base he'd put together for your people, the Louisiana vamps,' I said, simplifying a little bit for the sake of brevity.

'What happened?'

This was as much fun as talking to Arlene. Maybe even

more, because I'd never been able to tell her the whole story. 'Well, Lorena, that's her name, she *tortured* him,' I said, and Eric's eyes widened. 'Can you believe that? She could torture someone she'd made love with? Someone she'd lived with for years?' Eric shook his head disbelievingly. 'Anyway, you told me to go to Jackson and find him, and I sort of picked up clues at this nightclub for Supes only.' Eric nodded. Evidently, I didn't have to explain that Supes meant supernatural beings. 'Its real name is Josephine's, but the Weres call it Club Dead. You told me to go there with this really nice Were who owed you a big favor, and I stayed at his place.' Alcide Herveaux still figured in my daydreams. 'But I ended up getting hurt pretty bad,' I concluded. Hurt pretty bad, as always.

'How?'

'I got staked, believe it or not.'

Eric looked properly impressed. 'Is there a scar?'

'Yeah, even though—' And here I stopped dead.

He gave every indication he was hanging on my words. 'What?'

'You got one of the Jackson vampires to work on the wound, so I'd survive for sure . . . and then you gave me blood to heal me quick, so I could look for Bill at daylight.' Remembering how Eric had given me blood made my cheeks turn red, and I could only hope Eric would attribute my flush to the heat of the fire.

'And you saved Bill?' he said, moving beyond that touchy part.

'Yes, I did,' I said proudly. 'I saved his ass.' I rolled onto my back and looked up at him. Gee, it was nice to have someone to talk to. I pulled up my T-shirt and inclined partially on my side to show Eric the scar, and he looked impressed. He touched the shiny area with a fingertip and shook his head. I rearranged myself.

'And what happened to the vampire ho?' he asked

I eyed him suspiciously, but he didn't seem to be making fun of me. 'Well,' I said, 'um, actually, I kind of . . . She came in while I was getting Bill untied, and she attacked me, and I kind of . . . killed her.'

Eric looked at me intently. I couldn't read his expression. 'Had you ever killed anyone before?' he asked.

'Of course not!' I said indignantly. 'Well, I did hurt a guy who was trying to kill me, but he didn't die. No, I'm a *human*. I don't have to kill anyone to live.'

'But humans kill other humans all the time. And they don't even need to eat them or drink their blood.'

'Not *all* humans.'

'True enough,' he said. 'We vampires are all murderers.'

'But in a way, you're like lions.'

Eric looked astonished. 'Lions?' he said weakly.

'Lions all kill stuff.' At the moment, this idea seemed like an inspiration. 'So you're predators, like lions and raptors. But you use what you kill. You have to kill to eat.'

'The catch in that comforting theory being that we look almost exactly like you. And we used to be you. And we can love you, as well as feed off you. You could hardly say the lion wanted to caress the antelope.'

Suddenly there was something in the air that hadn't been there the moment before. I felt a little like an antelope that was being stalked – by a lion that was a deviant.

I'd felt more comfortable when I was taking care of a terrified victim.

'Eric,' I said, very cautiously, 'you know you're my guest here. And you know if I tell you to leave, which I will if you're not straight with me, you'll be standing out in the middle of a field somewhere in a bathrobe that's too short for you.'

'Have I said something to make you uncomfortable?' He was (apparently) completely contrite, blue eyes blazing with sincerity. 'I'm sorry. I was just trying to continue your train of thought. Do you have some more TrueBlood? What clothes did Jason get for me? Your brother is a very clever man.' He didn't sound a hundred percent admiring when he told me this. I didn't blame him. Jason's cleverness might cost him thirty-five thousand dollars. I got up to fetch the Wal-Mart bag, hoping that Eric liked his new Louisiana Tech sweatshirt and cheap jeans.

I turned in about midnight, leaving Eric absorbed in my tapes of the first season of *Buffy the Vampire Slayer*. (Though welcome, these were actually a gag gift from Tara.) Eric thought the show was a hoot, especially the way the vampires' foreheads bulged out when they got blood-lusty. From time to time, I could hear Eric laughing all the way back in my room. But the sound didn't bother me. I found it reassuring to hear someone else in the house.

It took me a little longer than usual to fall asleep, because I was thinking over the things that had happened that day. Eric was in the witness protection program, in a way, and I was providing the safe house. No one in the world – well, except for Jason, Pam, and Chow – knew where the sheriff of Area Five actually was at this moment.

Which was, sliding into my bed.

I didn't want to open my eyes and quarrel with him. I was just at that cusp between waking and dreaming. When he'd climbed in the night before, Eric had been so afraid that I'd felt quite maternal, comfortable in holding his hand to reassure him. Tonight it didn't seem so, well, neutral, having him in the bed with me.

'Cold?' I murmured, as he huddled close.

'Um-hum,' he whispered. I was on my back, so comfortable I could not contemplate moving. He was on his side facing me, and he put an arm across my waist. But he didn't move another inch, and he relaxed completely. After a moment's tension, I did, too, and then I was dead to the world.

The next thing I knew, it was morning and the phone was ringing. Of course, I was by myself in bed, and through my open doorway I could see across the hall into the smaller bedroom. The closet door was open, as he'd had to leave it when dawn came and he'd lowered himself into the lighttight hole.

It was bright and warmer today, up in the forties and heading for the fifties. I felt much more cheerful than I'd felt upon waking the day before. I knew what was happening now; or at least I knew more or less what I was supposed to do, how the next few days would go. Or I thought I did. When I answered the phone, I discovered that I was way off.

'Where's your brother?' yelled Jason's boss, Shirley Hennessey. You thought a man named Shirley was funny only until you were face-to-face with the real deal, at which point you decided it would really be better to keep your amusement to yourself.

'How would I know?' I said reasonably. 'Probably slept over at some woman's place.' Shirley, who was universally known as Catfish, had never, ever called here before to track Jason down. In fact, I'd be surprised if he'd ever had to call anywhere. One thing Jason was good about was showing up at work on time and at least going through the motions until that time was up. In fact, Jason was pretty good at his job, which I'd never fully understood. It seemed to involve parking his fancy truck at the parish road department, getting into another truck with the Renard parish logo on the door, and driving around telling various road crews what to do. It also seemed to demand that he get out of the truck to stand with other men as they all stared into big holes in or near the road.

Catfish was knocked off balance by my frankness. 'Sookie, you shouldn't say that kind of thing,' he said, quite shocked at a single woman admitting she knew her brother wasn't a virgin.

'Are you telling me that Jason hasn't shown up at work? And you've called his house?'

'Yes and yes,' said Catfish, who in most respects was no fool. 'I even sent Dago out to his place.' Dago (road crew members had to have nicknames) was Antonio Guglielmi, who had never been farther from Louisiana than Mississippi. I was pretty sure the same could be said for his parents, and possibly his grandparents, though there was rumor they'd once been to Branson to take in the shows.

'Was his truck out there?' I was beginning to have that cold creeping feeling.

'Yes,' Catfish said. 'It was parked in front of his house, keys inside. Door hanging open.'

'The truck door or the house door?'

'What?'

'Hanging open. Which door?'

'Oh, the truck.'

'This is bad, Catfish,' I said. I was tingling all over with alarm.

'When you seen him last?'

'Just last night. He was over here visiting with me, and he left about . . . oh, let's see . . . it must have been nine-thirty or ten.'

'He have anybody with him?'

'No.' He hadn't brought anybody with him, so that was pretty much the truth.

'You think I oughta call the sheriff?' Catfish asked.

I ran a hand over my face. I wasn't ready for that yet, no matter how off the situation seemed. 'Let's give it another hour,' I suggested. 'If he hasn't dragged into work in an hour, you let me know. If he does come in, you make him call me. I guess it's me ought to tell the sheriff, if it comes to that.'

I hung up after Catfish had repeated everything he'd said several times, just because he hated to hang up and go back to worrying. No, I can't read minds over the telephone line, but I could read it in his voice. I've known Catfish Hennessey for many years. He was a buddy of my father's.

I carried the cordless phone into the bathroom with me while I took a shower to wake up. I didn't wash my hair, just in case I had to go outside right away. I got dressed, made some coffee, and braided my hair in one long braid. All the time while I performed these tasks, I was thinking, which is something that's hard for me to do when I'm sitting still.

I came up with these scenarios.

One. (This was my favorite.) Somewhere between my house and his house, my brother had met up with a woman and fallen in love so instantly and completely that he had abandoned his habit of years and forgotten all about work.

At this moment, they were in a bed somewhere, having great sex.

Two. The witches, or whatever the hell they were, had somehow found out that Jason knew where Eric was, and they'd abducted him to force the information from him. (I made a mental note to learn more about witches.) How long could Jason keep the secret of Eric's location? My brother had lots of attitude, but he actually is a brave man — or maybe stubborn is a little more accurate. He wouldn't talk easily. Maybe a witch could spell him into talking? If the witches had him, he might be dead already, since they'd had him for hours. And if he'd talked, I was in danger and Eric was doomed. They could be coming at any minute, since witches are not bound by darkness. Eric was dead for the day, defenseless. This was definitely the worst-case scenario.

Three. Jason had returned to Shreveport with Pam and Chow. Maybe they'd decided to pay him some up-front money, or maybe Jason just wanted to visit Fangtasia because it was a popular nightspot. Once there, he could have been seduced by some vamp girl and stayed up all night with her, since Jason was like Eric in that women really, really took a shine to him. If she'd taken a little too much blood, Jason could be sleeping it off. I guess number three was really a variation on number one.

If Pam and Chow knew where Jason was but hadn't phoned before they died for the day, I was real mad. My gut instinct was to go get the hatchet and start chopping some stakes.

Then I remembered what I was trying so hard to forget: how it had felt when the stake pushed into Lorena's body, the expression on her face when she'd realized her long,

long life was over. I shoved that thought away as hard as I could. You didn't kill someone (even an evil vampire) without it affecting you sooner or later: at least not unless you were a complete sociopath, which I wasn't.

Lorena would have killed me without blinking. In fact, she would have positively enjoyed it. But then, she was a vampire, and Bill never tired of telling me that vampires were different; that though they retained their human appearance (more or less), their internal functions and their personalities underwent a radical change. I believed him and took his warnings to heart, for the most part. It was just that they looked so human; it was so very easy to attribute normal human reactions and feelings to them.

The frustrating thing was, Chow and Pam wouldn't be up until dark, and I didn't know who – or what – I'd raise if I called Fangtasia during the day. I didn't think the two lived at the club. I'd gotten the impression that Pam and Chow shared a house . . . or a mausoleum . . . somewhere in Shreveport.

I was fairly sure that human employees came into the club during the day to clean, but of course a human wouldn't (couldn't) tell me anything about vampire affairs. Humans who worked for vampires learned pretty quick to keep their mouths shut, as I could attest.

On the other hand, if I went to the club I'd have a chance to talk to *someone* face-to-face. I'd have a chance to read a human mind. I couldn't read vampire minds, which had led to my initial attraction to Bill. Imagine the relief of silence after a lifetime of elevator music. (Now, why couldn't I hear vampire thoughts? Here's my big theory about that. I'm about as scientific as a Saltine, but I have read about neurons, which fire in your brain, right? When you're thinking? Since it's magic that animates vampires, not normal life force, their brains don't fire. So, nothing for me to pick up – except about once every three months, I'd get a flash from a vampire. And I took great care to conceal that, because that was a sure way to court instant death.)

Oddly enough, the only vampire I'd ever 'heard' twice was – you guessed it – Eric.

I'd been enjoying Eric's recent company so much for the same reason I'd enjoyed Bill's, quite apart from the romantic component I'd had with Bill. Even Arlene had a tendency to stop listening to me when I was talking, if she thought of something more interesting, like her children's grades or cute things they'd said. But with Eric, he could be thinking about his car needing new windshield wipers while I was pouring my heart out, and I was none the wiser.

The hour I'd asked Catfish to give me was almost up, and all my constructive thought had dwindled into the same murky maundering I'd gone through several times. Blah blah blah. This is what happens when you talk to yourself a lot.

Okay, action time.

The phone rang right at the hour, and Catfish admitted he had no news. No one had heard from Jason or seen him; but on the other hand, Dago hadn't seen anything suspicious at Jason's place except the truck's open door.

I was still reluctant to call the sheriff, but I didn't see that I had much choice. At this point, it would seem peculiar to skip calling him.

I expected a lot of hubbub and alarm, but what I got was even worse: I got benevolent indifference. Sheriff Bud Dearborn actually laughed.

'You callin' me because your tomcat of a brother is missing a day of work? Sookie Stackhouse, I'm surprised at you.' Bud Dearborn had a slow voice and the mashed-in face of a Pekinese, and it was all too easy to picture him snuffling into the phone.

'He never misses work, and his truck is at his house. The door was open,' I said.

He did grasp that significance, because Bud Dearborn is a man who knows how to appreciate a fine pickup.

'That does sound a little funny, but still, Jason is way over twenty-one and he has a reputation for . . .' *(Drilling anything that stands still,* I thought.) '. . . being real popular with the ladies,' Bud concluded carefully. 'I bet he's all shacked up with someone new, and he'll be real sorry to have caused you any worry. You call me back if you haven't heard from him by tomorrow afternoon, you hear?'

'Right,' I said in my most frozen voice.

'Now, Sookie, don't you go getting all mad at me, I'm just telling you what any lawman would tell you,' he said.

I thought, *Any lawman with lead in his butt.* But I didn't say it out loud. Bud was what I had to work with, and I had to stay on his good side, as much as possible.

I muttered something that was vaguely polite and got off the phone. After reporting back to Catfish, I decided my only course of action was to go to Shreveport. I started to call Arlene, but I remembered she'd have the kids at home since it was still the school holiday. I thought of calling Sam, but I figured he might feel like he ought to do something, and I couldn't figure out what that would be. I just wanted to share my worries with someone. I knew that wasn't right. No one could help me, but me. Having made up my mind to be brave and independent, I almost phoned

Alcide Herveaux, who is a well-to-do and hardworking guy based in Shreveport. Alcide's dad runs a surveying firm that contracts for jobs in three states, and Alcide travels a lot among the various offices. I'd mentioned him the night before to Eric; Eric had sent Alcide to Jackson with me. But Alcide and I had some man-woman issues that were still unresolved, and it would be cheating to call him when I only wanted help he couldn't give. At least, that was how I felt.

I was scared to leave the house in case there might be news of Jason, but since the sheriff wasn't looking for him, I hardly thought there would be any word soon.

Before I left, I made sure I'd arranged the closet in the smaller bedroom so that it looked natural. It would be a little harder for Eric to get out when the sun went down, but it wouldn't be extremely difficult. Leaving him a note would be a dead giveaway if someone broke in, and he was too smart to answer the phone if I called just after dark had fallen. But he was so discombobulated by his amnesia, he might be scared to wake all by himself with no explanation of my absence, I thought.

I had a brainwave. Grabbing a little square piece of paper from last year's Word of the Day calendar ('enthrallment'), *I wrote: Jason, if you should happen to drop by, call me! I am very worried about you. No one knows where you are. I'll be back this afternoon or evening. I'm going to drop by your house, and then I'll check to see if you went to Shreveport. Then, back here. Love, Sookie.* I got some tape and stuck the note to the refrigerator, just where a sister might expect her brother to head if he stopped by.

There. Eric was plenty smart enough to read between the lines. And yet every word of it was feasible, so if anyone did break in to search the house, they'd think I was taking a smart precaution.

But still, I was frightened of leaving the sleeping Eric so vulnerable. What if the witches came looking?

But why should they?

If they could have tracked Eric, they'd have been here by now, right? At least, that was the way I was reasoning. I thought of calling someone like Terry Bellefleur, who was plenty tough, to come sit in my house – I could use waiting on a call about Jason as my pretext – but it wasn't right to endanger anyone else in Eric's defense.

I called all the hospitals in the area, feeling all the while that the sheriff should be doing this little job for me. The hospitals knew the name of everyone admitted, and none of them was Jason. I called the highway patrol to ask about accidents the night before and found there had been none in the vicinity. I called a few women Jason had dated, and I received a lot of negative responses, some of them obscene.

I thought I'd covered all the bases. I was ready to go to Jason's house, and I remember I was feeling pretty proud of myself as I drove north on Hummingbird Road and then took a left onto the highway. As I headed west to the house where I'd spent my first seven years, I drove past Merlotte's to my right and then past the main turnoff into Bon Temps. I negotiated the left turn and I could see our old home, sure enough with Jason's pickup parked in front of it. There was another pickup, equally shiny, parked about twenty feet away from Jason's.

When I got out of my car, a very black man was examining the ground around the truck. I was surprised to discover that the second pickup belonged to Alcee Beck, the only African-American detective on the parish force. Alcee's presence was both reassuring and disturbing.

'Miss Stackhouse,' he said gravely. Alcee Beck was wearing a jacket and slacks and heavy scuffed boots. The boots didn't go with the rest of his clothes, and I was willing to bet he kept them in his truck for when he had to go tromping around out in the country where the ground was less than dry. Alcee (whose name was pronounced Al-SAY) was also a strong broadcaster, and I could receive his thoughts clearly when I let down my shields to listen.

I learned in short order that Alcee Beck wasn't happy to see me, didn't like me, and did think something hinky had happened to Jason. Detective Beck didn't care for Jason, but he was actually scared of me. He thought I was a deeply creepy person, and he avoided me as much as possible.

Which was okay by me, frankly.

I knew more about Alcee Beck than I was comfortable knowing, and what I knew about Alcee was really unpleasant. He was brutal to uncooperative prisoners, though he adored his wife and daughter. He was lining his own pockets whenever he got a chance, and he made sure the chances came along pretty frequently. Alcee Beck confined this practice to the African-American community, operating on the theory that they'd never report him to the other white law enforcement personnel, and so far he'd been right.

See what I mean about not wanting to know things I heard? This was a lot different from finding out that Arlene really didn't think Charlsie's husband was good enough for Charlsie, or that Hoyt Fortenberry had dented a car in the parking lot and hadn't told the owner.

And before you ask me what I do about stuff like that, I'll tell you. I don't do squat. I've found out the hard way that it almost never works out if I try to intervene. What happens is no one is happier, and my little freakishness is brought to everyone's attention, and no one is comfortable around me for a month. I've got more secrets than Fort Knox has money. And those secrets are staying locked up just as tight.

I'll admit that most of those little facts I accumulated didn't make much difference in the grand scheme of things, whereas Alcee's misbehavior actually led to human misery. But so far I hadn't seen a single way to stop Alcee. He was very clever about keeping his activities under control and hidden from anyone with the power to intervene. And I wasn't too awful sure that Bud Dearborn *didn't* know.

'Detective Beck,' I said. 'Are you looking for Jason?'

'The sheriff asked me to come by and see if I could find anything out of order.'

'And have you found anything?'

'No, ma'am, I haven't.'

'Jason's boss told you the door to his truck was open?'

'I closed it so the battery wouldn't run down. I was careful not to touch anything, of course. But I'm sure your brother will show back up any time now, and he'll be unhappy if we mess with his stuff for no reason.'

'I have a key to his house, and I'm going to ask you to go in there with me.'

'Do you suspect anything happened to your brother in his house?' Alcee Beck was being so careful to spell everything out that I wondered if he had a tape recorder rolling away in his pocket.

'Could be. He doesn't normally miss work. In fact, he never misses work. And I always know where he is. He's real good about letting me know.'

'He'd tell you if he was running off with a woman? Most brothers wouldn't do that, Miss Stackhouse.'

'He'd tell me, or he'd tell Catfish.'

Alcee Beck did his best to keep his skeptical look on his dark face, but it didn't sit there easily.

The house was still locked. I picked out the right key from the ones on my ring, and we went inside. I didn't have the feeling of homecoming when I entered, the feeling I used to have as a kid. I'd lived in Gran's house so much longer than this little place. The minute Jason had turned twenty, he'd moved over here full-time, and though I'd dropped in, I'd probably spent less than twenty-four hours total in this house in the last eight years.

Glancing around me, I realized that my brother really hadn't changed the house much in all that time. It was a small ranch-style house with small rooms, but of course it was a lot younger than Gran's house – my house – and a lot more heating- and cooling-efficient. My father had done most of the work on it, and he was a good builder.

The small living room was still filled with the maple furniture my mother had picked out at the discount furniture store, and its upholstery (cream with green and blue flowers that had never been seen in nature) was still bright, more's the pity. It had taken me a few years to realize that my mother, while a clever woman in some respects, had had no taste whatsoever. Jason had never come to that realization. He'd replaced the curtains when they frayed and faded, and he'd gotten a new rug to cover the most worn spots on the ancient blue carpet. The appliances were all new, and he'd worked hard on updating the bathroom. But my parents, if they could have entered their home, would have felt quite comfortable.

It was a shock to realize they'd been dead for nearly twenty years.

While I stood close to the doorway, praying I wouldn't see bloodstains, Alcee Beck prowled through the house, which certainly seemed orderly. After a second's indecision, I decided to follow him. There wasn't much to see; like I say, it's a small house. Three bedrooms (two of them quite cramped), the living room, a kitchen, one bathroom, a fair-sized family room, and a small dining room: a house that could be duplicated any number of times in any town in America.

The house was quite tidy. Jason had never lived like a pig, though sometimes he acted like one. Even the king-size bed that almost filled the biggest bedroom was more-or-less pulled straight, though I could see the sheets were black and shiny. They were supposed to look like silk, but I was sure they were some artificial blend. Too slithery for me; I liked percale.

'No evidence of any struggle,' the detective pointed out.

'While I'm here, I'm just going to get something,' I told him, going over to the gun cabinet that had been my dad's. It was locked, so I checked my key ring again. Yes, I had a key for that, too, and I remembered some long story Jason had told me about why I needed one – in case he was out hunting and he needed another rifle, or something. As if I'd drop everything and run to fetch another rifle for him!

Well, I might, if I wasn't due at work, or something.

All Jason's rifles, and my father's, were in the gun cabi-net – all the requisite ammunition, too.

'All present?' The detective was shifting around impa-tiently in the doorway to the dining room.

'Yes. I'm just going to take one of them home with me.'

'You expecting trouble at your place?' Beck looked interested for the first time.

'If Jason is gone, who knows what it means?' I said, hoping that was ambiguous enough. Beck had a very low opinion of my intelligence, anyway, despite the fact that he feared me. Jason had said he would bring me the shotgun, and I knew I would feel the better for having it. So I got out the Benelli and found its shells. Jason had very carefully taught me how to load and fire the shotgun, which was his pride and joy. There were two different boxes of shells.

'Which?' I asked Detective Beck.

'Wow, a Benelli.' He took time out to be impressed with the gun. 'Twelve-gauge, huh? Me, I'd take the turkey loads,' he advised. 'Those target loads don't have as much stopping power.'

I popped the box he indicated into my pocket.

I carried the shotgun out to my car, Beck trailing on my heels.

'You have to lock the shotgun in your trunk and the shells in the car,' the detective informed me. I did exactly what he said, even putting the shells in the glove compartment, and then I turned to face him. He would be glad to be out of my sight, and I didn't think he would look for Jason with any enthusiasm.

'Did you check around back?' I asked.

'I had just gotten here when you pulled up.'

I jerked my head in the direction of the pond behind the house, and we circled around to the rear. My brother, aided by Hoyt Fortenberry, had put in a large deck outside the back door maybe two years ago. He'd arranged some nice outdoor furniture he'd gotten on end-of-season sale at

Wal-Mart. Jason had even put an ashtray on the wrought-iron table for his friends who went outside to smoke. Someone had used it. Hoyt smoked, I recalled. There was nothing else interesting on the deck.

The ground sloped down from the deck to the pond. While Alcee Beck checked the back door, I looked down to the pier my father had built, and I thought I could see a smear on the wood. Something in me crumpled at the sight, and I must have made a noise. Alcee came to stand by me, and I said, 'Look at the pier.'

He went on point, just like a setter. He said, 'Stay where you are,' in an unmistakably official voice. He moved carefully, looking down at the ground around his feet before he took each step. I felt like an hour passed before Alcee finally reached the pier. He squatted down on the sun-bleached boards to take a close look. He focused a little to the right of the smear, evaluating something I couldn't see, something I couldn't even make out in his mind. But then he wondered what kind of work boots my brother wore; that came in clear.

'Caterpillars,' I called. The fear built up in me till I felt I was vibrating with the intensity of it. Jason was all I had.

And I realized I'd made a mistake I hadn't done in years: I'd answered a question before it had been asked out loud. I clapped a hand over my mouth and saw the whites of Beck's eyes. He wanted away from me. And he was thinking maybe Jason was in the pond, dead. He was speculating that Jason had fallen and knocked his head against the pier, and then slid into the water. But there was a puzzling print . . .

'When can you search the pond?' I called.

He turned to look at me, terror on his face. I hadn't had

anyone look at me like that in years. I had him spooked, and I hadn't wanted to have that effect on him.

'The blood is on the dock,' I pointed out, trying to improve matters. Providing a reasonable explanation was second nature. 'I'm scared Jason went into the water.'

Beck seemed to settle down a little after that. He turned his eyes back to the water. My father had chosen the site for the house to include the pond. He'd told me when I was little that the pond was very deep and fed by a tiny stream. The area around two-thirds of the pond was mowed and maintained as yard; but the farthest edge of it was left thickly wooded, and Jason enjoyed sitting on the deck in the late evening with binoculars, watching critters come to drink.

There were fish in the pond. He kept it stocked. My stomach lurched.

Finally, the detective walked up the slope to the deck. 'I have to call around, see who can dive,' Alcee Beck said. 'It may take a while to find someone who can do it. And the chief has to okay it.'

Of course, such a thing would cost money, and that money might not be in the parish budget. I took a deep breath. 'Are you talking hours, or days?'

'Maybe a day or two,' he said at last. 'No way anyone can do it who isn't trained. It's too cold, and Jason himself told me it was deep.'

'All right,' I said, trying to suppress my impatience and anger. Anxiety gnawed at me like another kind of hunger.

'Carla Rodriguez was in town last night,' Alcee Beck told me, and after a long moment, the significance of that sank into my brain.

Carla Rodriguez, tiny and dark and electric, had been the

closest shave Jason had ever had with losing his heart. In fact, the little shifter Jason had had a date with on New Year's Eve had somewhat resembled Carla, who had moved to Houston three years ago, much to my relief. I'd been tired of the pyrotechnics surrounding her romance with my brother; their relationship had been punctuated by long and loud and public arguments, hung-up telephones, and slammed doors.

'Why? Who's she staying with?'

'Her cousin in Shreveport,' Beck said. 'You know, that Dovie.'

Dovie Rodriguez had visited Bon Temps a lot while Carla had lived here. Dovie had been the more sophisticated city cousin, down in the country to correct all our local yokel ways. Of course, we'd envied Dovie.

I thought that tackling Dovie was just what I wanted to do.

It looked like I'd be going to Shreveport after all.

Chapter 4

The detective hustled me off after that, telling me he was going to get the crime scene officer out to the house, and he'd be in touch. I got the idea, right out of his brain, that there was something he didn't want me to see, and that he'd thrown Carla Rodriguez at me to distract me.

And I thought he might take the shotgun away, since he seemed much more sure now he was dealing with a crime, and the shotgun might be part of some bit of evidence. But Alcee Beck didn't say anything, so I didn't remind him.

I was more shaken than I wanted to admit to myself. Inwardly, I'd been convinced that, though I needed to track my brother down, Jason was really okay – just misplaced. Or mislaid, more likely, ho ho ho. Possibly he was in some kind of not-too-serious trouble, I'd told myself. Now things were looking more serious.

I've never been able to squeeze my budget enough to afford a cell phone, so I began driving home. I was thinking of whom I should call, and I came up with the same answer as before. No one. There was no definite news to break. I felt as lonely as I ever have in my life. But I just didn't want to be Crisis Woman, showing up on friends' doorsteps with trouble on my shoulders.

Tears welled up in my eyes. I wanted my grandmother back. I pulled over to the side of the road and slapped myself on the cheek, hard. I called myself a few names.

Shreveport. I'd go to Shreveport and confront Dovie and Carla Rodriguez. While I was there, I'd find out if Chow and Pam knew anything about Jason's disappearance – though it was hours until they'd be up, and I'd just be kicking my heels in an empty club, assuming there'd be someone there to let me in. But I just couldn't sit at home, waiting. I could read the minds of the human employees and find out if they knew what was up.

On the one hand, if I went to Shreveport, I'd be out of touch with what was happening here. On the other hand, I'd be doing something.

While I was trying to decide if there were any more hands to consider, something else happened.

It was even odder than the preceding events of the day. There I was, parked in the middle of nowhere at the side of a parish road, when a sleek, black, brand-new Camaro pulled onto the shoulder behind me. Out of the passenger's side stepped a gorgeous woman, at least six feet tall. Of course, I remembered her; she'd been in Merlotte's on New Year's Eve. My friend Tara Thornton was in the driver's seat.

Okay, I thought blankly, staring into the rearview mirror, *this is weird*. I hadn't seen Tara in weeks, since we'd met by chance in a vampire club in Jackson, Mississippi. She'd been there with a vamp named Franklin Mott; he'd been very handsome in a senior-citizen sort of way, polished, dangerous, and sophisticated.

Tara always looks great. My high school friend has black hair, and dark eyes, and a smooth olive complexion, and she has a lot of intelligence that she uses running Tara's Togs, an upscale women's clothing store that rents space in a strip mall Bill owns. (Well, it's as upscale as Bon Temps has to offer.) Tara had become a friend of mine years before, because she came from an even sadder background than mine.

But the tall woman put even Tara in the shade. She was as dark-haired as Tara, though the new woman had reddish highlights that surprised the eye. She had dark eyes, too, but hers were huge and almond-shaped, almost abnormally large. Her skin was as pale as milk, and her legs were as long as a stepladder. She was quite gifted in the bosom department, and she was wearing fire engine red from head to toe. Her lipstick matched.

'Sookie,' Tara called. 'What's the matter?' She walked carefully up to my old car, watching her feet because she was wearing glossy, brown leather, high-heeled boots she didn't want to scuff. They'd have lasted five minutes on my feet. I spend too much of my time standing up to worry about footwear that only looks good.

Tara looked successful, attractive, and secure, in her sage green sweater and taupe pants. 'I was putting on my makeup when I heard over the police scanner that something was up at Jason's house,' she said. She slid in the passenger's seat and leaned over to hug me. 'When I got to Jason's, I saw you pulling out. What's up?' The woman in red was standing with her back to the car, tactfully looking out into the woods.

I'd adored my father, and I'd always known (and my mother herself definitely believed) that no matter what

Mother put me through, she was acting out of love. But Tara's parents had been evil, both alcoholics and abusers. Tara's older sisters and brothers had left home as fast as they could, leaving Tara, as the youngest, to foot the bill for their freedom.

Yet now that I was in trouble, here she was, ready to help.

'Well, Jason's gone missing,' I said, in a fairly level voice, but then I ruined the effect by giving one of those awful choking sobs. I turned my face so I'd be looking out my window. I was embarrassed to show such distress in front of the new woman.

Wisely ignoring my tears, Tara began asking me the logical questions: Had Jason called in to work? Had he called me the night before? Who had he been dating lately?

That reminded me of the shifter girl who'd been Jason's date New Year's Eve. I thought I could even talk about the girl's otherness, because Tara had been at Club Dead that night. Tara's tall companion was a Supe of some kind. Tara knew all about the secret world.

But she didn't, as it turned out.

Her memory had been erased. Or at least she pretended it had.

'What?' Tara asked, with almost exaggerated confusion. 'Werewolves? At that nightclub? I remember seeing you there. Honey, didn't you drink a little too much and pass out, or something?'

Since I drink very sparingly, Tara's question made me quite angry, but it was also the most unremarkable explanation Franklin Mott could have planted in Tara's head. I was so disappointed at not getting to confide in her that I closed my eyes so I wouldn't have to see the blank look on her face. I felt tears leaving little paths down my cheeks. I should have just let it go, but I said, in a low, harsh voice, 'No, I didn't.'

'Omigosh, did your date put something in your drink?' In genuine horror, Tara squeezed my hand. 'That Rohypnol? But Alcide looked like such a nice guy!'

'Forget it,' I said, trying to sound gentler. 'It doesn't really have anything to do with Jason, after all.'

Her face still troubled, Tara pressed my hand again.

All of a sudden, I was certain I didn't believe her. Tara knew vampires could remove memory, and she was pretending Franklin Mott had erased hers. I thought Tara remembered quite well what had happened at Club Dead, but she was pretending she didn't to protect herself. If she had to do that to survive, that was okay. I took a deep breath.

'Are you still dating Franklin?' I asked, to start a different conversation.

'He got me this car.'

I was a little shocked and more than a little dismayed, but I hoped I was not the kind to point fingers.

'It's a wonderful car. You don't know any witches, do you?' I asked, trying to change the subject before Tara could read my misgivings. I was sure she would laugh at me for asking her such a question, but it was a good diversion. I wouldn't hurt her for the world.

Finding a witch would be a great help. I was sure Jason's abduction – and I swore to myself it was an abduction, it was not a murder – was linked to the witches' curse on Eric. It was just too much coincidence otherwise. On the other hand, I had certainly experienced the twists and turns of a bunch of coincidences in the past few months. There, I knew I'd find a third hand.

'Sure I do,' Tara said, smiling proudly. 'Now there I can help you. That is, if a Wiccan will do?'

I had so many expressions I wasn't sure my face could fit them all in. Shock, fear, grief, and worry were tumbling around in my brain. When the spinning stopped, we would see which one was at the top.

'You're a witch?' I said weakly.

'Oh, gosh, no, not me. I'm a Catholic. But I have some friends who are Wiccan. Some of them are witches.'

'Oh, really?' I didn't think I'd ever heard the word Wiccan before, though maybe I'd read it in a mystery or romance novel. 'I'm sorry, I don't know what that means,' I said, my voice humble.

'Holly can explain it better than I can,' Tara said.

'Holly. The Holly who works with me?'

'Sure. Or you could go to Danielle, though she's not going to be as willing to talk. Holly and Danielle are in the same coven.'

I was so shocked by now I might as well get even more stunned. 'Coven,' I repeated.

'You know, a group of pagans who worship together.'

'I thought a coven had to be witches?'

'I guess not – but they have to, you know, be non-Christian. I mean, Wicca is a religion.'

'Okay,' I said. 'Okay. Do you think Holly would talk to me about this?'

'I don't know why not.' Tara went back to her car to get her cell phone, and paced back and forth between our vehicles while she talked to Holly. I appreciated a little respite to allow me to get back on my mental feet, so to speak. To be polite I got out of my car and spoke to the woman in red, who'd been very patient.

'I'm sorry to meet you on such a bad day,' I said. 'I'm Sookie Stackhouse.'

'I'm Claudine,' she said, with a beautiful smile. Her teeth were Hollywood white. Her skin had an odd quality; it looked glossy and thin, reminding me of the skin of a plum; like if you bit her, sweet juice would gush out. 'I'm here because of all the activity.'

'Oh?' I said, taken aback.

'Sure. You have vampires, and Weres, and lots of other stuff all tangled up here in Bon Temps – to say nothing of several important and powerful crossroads. I was drawn to all the possibilities.'

'Uh-huh,' I said uncertainly. 'So, do you plan on just observing all this, or what?'

'Oh, no. Just observing is not my way.' She laughed. 'You're quite the wild card, aren't you?'

'Holly's up,' Tara said, snapping her phone shut and smiling because it was hard not to with Claudine around. I realized I was smiling from ear to ear, not my usual tense grin but an expression of sunny happiness. 'She says come on over.'

'Are you coming with me?' I didn't know what to think of Tara's companion.

'Sorry, Claudine's helping me today at the shop,' Tara said. 'We're having a New Year's sale on our old inventory, and people are doing some heavy shopping. Want me to put something aside for you? I've got a few really pretty party dresses left. Didn't the one you wore in Jackson get ruined?'

Yeah, because a fanatic had driven a stake through my side. The dress had definitely suffered. 'It got stained,' I said with great restraint. 'It's real nice of you to offer, but I don't think I'll have time to try anything on. With Jason and everything, I've got so much to think about.' And precious little extra money, I told myself.

'Sure,' said Tara. She hugged me again. 'You call me if you need me, Sookie. It's funny that I don't remember that evening in Jackson any better. Maybe I had too much to drink, too. Did we dance?'

'Oh, yes, you talked me into doing that routine we did at the high school talent show.'

'I did not!' She was begging me to deny it, with a half smile on her face.

''Fraid so.' I knew damn well she remembered it.

'I wish I'd been there,' said Claudine. 'I love to dance.'

'Believe me, that night in Club Dead is one I wish I'd missed,' I said.

'Well, remind me never to go back to Jackson, if I did that dance in public,' Tara said.

'I don't think either of us better go back to Jackson.' I'd left some very irate vampires in Jackson, but the Weres were even angrier. Not that there were a lot of them left, actually. But still.

Tara hesitated a minute, obviously trying to frame something she wanted to tell me. 'Since Bill owns the building Tara's Togs is in,' she said carefully, 'I do have a number to call, a number he said he'd check in with while he was out of the country. So if you need to let him know anything . . . ?'

'Thanks,' I said, not sure if I felt thankful at all. 'He told me he left a number on a pad by the phone in his house.' There was a kind of finality to Bill's being out of the country, unreachable. I hadn't even thought of trying to get in touch with him about my predicament; out of all the people I'd considered calling, he hadn't even crossed my mind.

'It's just that he seemed pretty, you know, down.' Tara examined the toes of her boots. 'Melancholy,' she said, as if she enjoyed using a word that didn't pass her lips often. Claudine beamed with approval. What a strange gal. Her huge eyes were luminous with joy as she patted me on the shoulder.

I swallowed hard. 'Well, he's never exactly Mr. Smiley,' I said. 'I do miss him. But . . .' I shook my head emphatically. 'It was just too hard. He just . . . upset me too much. I thank you for letting me know I can call him if I need to, and I really, really appreciate your telling me about Holly.'

Tara, flushed with the deserved pleasure of having done her good deed for the day, got back in her spanky-new Camaro. After folding her long self into the passenger seat, Claudine waved at me as Tara pulled away. I sat in my car for a moment longer, trying to remember where Holly Cleary lived. I thought I remembered her complaining about the closet size in her apartment, and that meant the Kingfisher Arms.

When I got to the U-shaped building on the southern approach to Bon Temps, I checked the mailboxes to discover Holly's apartment number. She was on the ground floor, in number 4. Holly had a five-year-old son, Cody. Holly and her best friend, Danielle Gray, had both gotten married right out of high school, and both had been divorced within five years. Danielle's mom was a great help to Danielle, but Holly was not so lucky. Her long-divorced parents had both moved away, and her grandmother had died in the Alzheimer's wing of the Renard Parish nursing home. Holly had dated Detective Andy Bellefleur for a few months, but nothing had come of it. Rumor had it that old Caroline Bellefleur, Andy's grandmother, had thought Holly wasn't 'good' enough for Andy. I had no opinion on that. Neither Holly nor Andy was on my shortlist of favorite people, though I definitely felt cooler toward Andy.

When Holly answered her door, I realized all of a sudden how much she'd changed over the past few weeks. For years, her hair had been dyed a dandelion yellow. Now it was matte black and spiked. Her ears had four piercings apiece. And I noticed her hipbones pushing at the thin denim of her aged jeans.

'Hey, Sookie,' she said, pleasantly enough. 'Tara asked me if I would talk to you, but I wasn't sure if you'd show up. Sorry about Jason. Come on in.'

The apartment was small, of course, and though it had been repainted recently, it showed evidence of years of heavy use. There was a living room-dining room-kitchen combo, with a breakfast bar separating the galley kitchen from the rest of the area. There were a few toys in a basket in the corner of the room, and there was a can of Pledge and a rag on the scarred coffee table. Holly had been cleaning.

'I'm sorry to interrupt,' I said.

'That's okay. Coke? Juice?'

'No, thanks. Where's Cody?'

'He went to stay with his dad,' she said, looking down at her hands. 'I drove him over the day after Christmas.'

'Where's his dad living?'

'David's living in Springhill. He just married this girl, Allie. She already had two kids. The little girl is Cody's age, and he just loves to play with her. It's always, "Shelley this," and "Shelley that."' Holly looked kind of bleak.

David Cleary was one of a large clan. His cousin Pharr had been in my grade all through school. For Cody's genes' sake, I hoped that David was more intelligent than Pharr, which would be real easy.

'I need to talk to you about something pretty personal, Holly.'

Holly looked surprised all over again. 'Well, we haven't exactly been on those terms, have we?' she said. 'You ask, and I'll decide whether to answer.'

I tried to frame what I was going to say – to keep secret what I needed to keep secret and ask of her what I needed without offending.

'You're a witch?' I said, embarrassed at using such a dramatic word.

'I'm more of a Wiccan.'

'Would you mind explaining the difference?' I met her eyes briefly, and then decided to focus on the dried flowers in the basket on top of the television. Holly thought I could read her mind only if I was looking into her eyes. (Like physical touching, eye contact does make the reading easier, but it certainly isn't necessary.)

'I guess not.' Her voice was slow, as if she were thinking as she spoke. 'You're not one to spread gossip.'

'Whatever you tell me, I won't share with anyone.' I met her eyes again, briefly.

'Okay,' she said. 'Well, if you're a witch, of course, you practice magic rituals.'

She was using 'you' in the general sense, I thought, because saying 'I' would mean too bold a confession.

'You draw from a power that most people never tap into. Being a witch isn't being wicked, or at least it isn't supposed to be. If you're a Wiccan, you follow a religion, a pagan religion. We follow the ways of the Mother, and we have our own calendar of holy days. You can be both a

Wiccan and a witch; or more one, or more the other. It's very individualized. I practice a little witchcraft, but I'm more interested in the Wiccan life. We believe that your actions are okay if you don't hurt anyone else.'

Oddly, my first feeling was one of embarrassment, when I heard Holly tell me that she was a non-Christian. I'd never met anyone who didn't at least pretend to be a Christian or who didn't give lip service to the basic Christian precepts. I was pretty sure there was a synagogue in Shreveport, but I'd never even met a Jew, to the best of my knowledge. I was certainly on a learning curve.

'I understand. Do you know lots of witches?'

'I know a few.' Holly nodded repeatedly, still avoiding my eyes.

I spotted an old computer on the rickety table in the corner. 'Do you have, like, a chat room online, or a bulletin board, or something?'

'Oh, sure.'

'Have you heard of a group of witches that's come into Shreveport lately?'

Holly's face became very serious. Her straight dark brows drew together in a frown. 'Tell me you're not involved with them,' she said.

'Not directly. But I know someone they've hurt, and I'm afraid they might've taken Jason.'

'Then he's in bad trouble,' she said bluntly. 'The woman who leads this group is out-and-out ruthless. Her brother is just as bad. That group, they're not like the rest of us. They're not trying to find a better way to live, or a path to get in touch with the natural world, or spells to increase their inner peace. They're Wiccans. They're evil.'

'Can you give me any clues about where I might track

them down?' I was doing my best to keep my face in line. I could hear with my other sense that Holly was thinking that if the newly arrived coven had Jason, he'd be hurt badly, if not killed.

Holly, apparently in deep thought, looked out the front window of her apartment. She was afraid that they'd trace any information she gave me back to her, punish her – maybe through Cody. These weren't witches who believed in doing harm to no one else. These were witches whose lives were planned around the gathering of power of all kinds.

'They're all women?' I asked, because I could tell she was on the verge of resolving to tell me nothing.

'If you're thinking Jason would be able to charm them with his ways because he's such a looker, you can think again,' Holly told me, her face grim and somehow stripped down to basics. She wasn't trying for any effect; she wanted me to understand how dangerous these people were. 'There are some men, too. They're . . . these aren't normal witches. I mean, they weren't even normal *people*.'

I was willing to believe that. I'd had to believe stranger things since the night Bill Compton had walked into Merlotte's Bar.

Holly spoke like she knew far more about this group of witches than I'd ever suspected . . . more than the general background I'd hoped to glean from her. I prodded her a little. 'What makes them different?'

'They've had vampire blood.' Holly glanced to the side, as if she felt someone listening to her. The motion creeped me out. 'Witches – witches with a lot of power they're willing to use for evil – they're bad enough. Witches that strong who've also had vampire blood are . . . Sookie, you have no idea how dangerous they are. Some of them are Weres. Please, stay away from them.'

Werewolves? They were not only witches, but Weres? And they drank vampire blood? I was seriously scared. I didn't know how could you get any worse. 'Where are they?'

'Are you listening to me?'

'I am, but I have to know where they are!'

'They're in an old business not awful far from Pierre Bossier Mall,' she said, and I could see the picture of it in her head. She'd been there. She'd seen them. She had this all in her head, and I was getting a lot of it.

'Why were you there?' I asked, and she flinched.

'I was worried about talking to you,' Holly said, her voice angry. 'I shouldn't have even let you in. But I'd dated Jason . . . You're gonna get me killed, Sookie Stackhouse. Me and my boy.'

'No, I won't.'

'I was there because their leader sent out a call for all the witches in the area to have, like, a summit. It turned out that what she wanted to do was impose her will on all of us. Some of us were pretty impressed with her commitment and her power, but most of us smaller-town Wiccans, we didn't like her drug use – that's what drinking vampire blood amounts to – or her taste for the darker side of witch-craft. Now, that's all I want to say about it.'

'Thanks, Holly.' I tried to think of something I could tell her that would relieve her fear. But she wanted me to leave more than anything in the world, and I'd caused her enough upset. Holly's just letting me in the door had been a big concession, since she actually believed in my mind-reading ability. No matter what rumors they heard, people really wanted to believe that the contents of their heads were private, no matter what proof they had to the contrary.

I did myself.

I patted Holly on the shoulder as I left, but she didn't get up from the old couch. She stared at me with hopeless brown eyes, as if any moment someone was going to come in the door and cut off her head.

That look frightened me more than her words, more than her ideas, and I left the Kingfisher Arms as quickly as I could, trying to note the few people who saw me turn out of the parking lot. I didn't recognize any of them.

I wondered why the witches in Shreveport would want Jason, how they could have made a connection between the missing Eric and my brother. How could I approach them to find out? Would Pam and Chow help, or had they taken their own steps?

And whose blood had the witches been drinking?

Since vampires had made their presence known among us, nearly three years ago now, they'd become preyed upon in a new way. Instead of fearing getting staked through the heart by wanna-be Van Helsings, vampires dreaded modern entrepreneurs called Drainers. Drainers traveled in teams, singling out vampires by a variety of methods and binding them with silver chains (usually in a carefully planned ambush), then draining their blood into vials. Depending on the age of the vampire, a vial of blood could fetch from $200 to $400 on the black market. The effect of drinking this blood? Quite unpredictable, once the blood had left the vampire. I guess that was part of the attraction. Most commonly, for a few weeks, the drinker gained strength, visual acuity, a feeling of robust health, and enhanced attractiveness. It depended on the age of the drained vampire and the freshness of the blood.

Of course, those effects faded, unless you drank more blood.

A certain percentage of people who experienced drinking vampire blood could hardly wait to scratch up money for more. These blood junkies were extremely dangerous, of course. City police forces were glad to hire vampires to deal with them, since regular cops would simply get pulped.

Every now and then, a blood drinker simply went mad – sometimes in a quiet, gibbering kind of way, but sometimes spectacularly and murderously. There was no way to predict who would be stricken this way, and it could happen on the first drinking.

So there were men with glittering mad eyes in padded cells and there were electrifying movie stars who equally owed their condition to the Drainers. Draining was a hazardous job, of course. Sometimes the vampire got loose, with a very predictable result. A court in Florida had ruled this vampire retaliation justifiable homicide, in one celebrated case, because Drainers notoriously discarded their victims. They left a vampire, all but empty of blood, too weak to move, wherever the vamp happened to fall. The weakened vampire died when the sun came up, unless he had the good fortune to be discovered and helped to safety during the hours of darkness. It took years to recover from a draining, and that was years of help from other vamps. Bill had told me there were shelters for drained vamps, and that their location was kept very secret.

Witches with nearly the physical power of vampires – that seemed a very dangerous combination. I kept thinking of women when I thought of the coven that had moved into Shreveport, and I kept correcting myself. Men, Holly had said, were in the group.

I looked at the clock at the drive-through bank, and I saw it was just after noon. It would be full dark by a few minutes before six; Eric had gotten up a little earlier than that, at times. I could certainly go to Shreveport and come back by then. I couldn't think of another plan, and I just couldn't go home and sit and wait. Even wasting gas was better than going back to my house, though worry for Jason crawled up and down my spine. I could take the time to drop off the shotgun, but as long as it was unloaded and the shells were in a separate location, it should be legal enough to drive around with it.

For the first time in my life, I checked my rearview mirror to see if I was being followed. I am not up on spy techniques, but if someone was following me, I couldn't spot him. I stopped and got gas and an ICEE, just to see if anyone pulled into the gas station behind me, but no one did. That was real good, I decided, hoping that Holly was safe.

As I drove, I had time to review my conversation with Holly. I realized it was the first one I'd ever had with Holly in which Danielle's name had not come up once. Holly and Danielle had been joined at the hip since grade school. They probably had their periods at the same time. Danielle's parents, cradle members of the Free Will Church of God's Anointed, would have a fit if they knew, so it wasn't any wonder that Holly had been so discreet.

Our little town of Bon Temps had stretched its gates open wide enough to tolerate vampires, and gay people didn't have a very hard time of it anymore (kind of depending on how they expressed their sexual preference).

However, I thought the gates might snap shut for Wiccans.

The peculiar and beautiful Claudine had told me that she was attracted to Bon Temps for its very strangeness. I wondered what else was out there, waiting to reveal itself.

Chapter 5

Carla Rodriguez my most promising lead came first. I'd
looked up the old address I had for Dovie, with whom
I'd exchanged the odd Christmas card. I found the house
with a little difficulty. It was well away from the shopping
areas that were my only normal stops in Shreveport. The
houses were small and close together where Dovie lived,
and some of them were in bad repair.

I felt a distinct thrill of triumph when Carla herself
answered the door. She had a black eye, and she was hung-
over, both signs that she'd had a big night the night before.

'Hey, Sookie,' she said, identifying me after a moment.
'What're you doing here? I was at Merlotte's last night,
but I didn't see you there. You still working there?'

'I am. It was my night off.' Now that I was actually
looking at Carla, I wasn't sure how to explain to her what I
needed. I decided to be blunt. 'Listen, Jason's not at work
this morning, and I kind of wondered if he might be here
with you.'

'Honey, I got nothing against you, but Jason's the last
man on earth I'd sleep with,' Carla said flatly. I stared at

her, hearing that she was telling me truth. 'I ain't gonna stick my hand in the fire twice, having gotten burnt the first time. I did look around the bar a little, thinking I might see him, but if I had, I'd have turned the other way.'

I nodded. That seemed all there was to say on the subject. We exchanged a few more polite sentences, and I chatted with Dovie, who had a toddler balanced on her hip, but then it was time for me to leave. My most promising lead had just evaporated in the length of two sentences.

Trying to suppress my desperation, I drove to a busy corner filling station and parked, to check my Shreveport map. It didn't take me long to figure out how to get from Dovie's suburb to the vampire bar.

Fangtasia was in a shopping center close to Toys 'R' Us. It opened at six P.M. year-round, but of course the vampires didn't show up until full dark, which depended on the season. The front of Fangtasia was painted flat gray, and the neon writing was all in red. 'Shreveport's Premier Vampire Bar,' read the newly added, smaller writing under the exotic script of the bar's name. I winced and looked away.

Two summers before, a small group of vamps from Oklahoma had tried to set up a rival bar in adjacent Bossier City. After one particularly hot, short August night, they'd never been seen again, and the building they'd been renovating had burned to the ground.

Tourists thought stories like this were actually amusing and colorful. It added to the thrill of ordering overpriced drinks (from human waitresses dressed in trailing black 'vampire' outfits) while staring at real, honest-to-God, undead bloodsuckers. Eric made the Area Five vampires show up for this unappealing duty by giving them a set number of hours each week to present themselves at Fangtasia. Most of his underlings weren't enthusiastic about exhibiting themselves, but it did give them a chance to hook up with fang-bangers who actually yearned for the chance to be bitten. Such encounters didn't take place on the premises: Eric had rules about that. And so did the police department. The only legal biting that could take place between humans and vampires was between consenting adults, in private.

Automatically, I pulled around to the rear of the shopping center. Bill and I had almost always used the employee entrance. Back here, the door was just a gray door in a gray wall, with the name of the bar put on in stick-on letters from Wal-Mart. Right below that, a large, black, stenciled notice proclaimed STAFF ONLY. I lifted my hand to knock, and then I realized I could see that the inner dead bolt had not been employed.

The door was unlocked.

This was really, really bad.

Though it was broad daylight, the hair on the back of my neck stood up. Abruptly, I wished I had Bill at my back. I wasn't missing his tender love, either. It's probably a bad indicator of your lifestyle when you miss your ex-boyfriend because he's absolutely lethal.

Though the public face of the shopping center was fairly busy, the service side was deserted. The silence was crawling with possibilities, and none of them was pleasant. I leaned my forehead against the cold gray door. I decided to get back in my old car and get the hell out of there, which would have been amazingly smart.

And I would have gone, if I hadn't heard the moaning.

Even then, if I'd been able to spot a pay phone, I

would've just called 911 and stayed outside until someone official showed up. But there wasn't one in sight, and I couldn't stand the possibility that someone needed my help real bad, and I'd withheld it because I was chicken.

There was a heavy garbage can right by the back door, and after I'd yanked the door open – standing aside for a second to avoid anything that might dart out – I maneuvered the can to hold the door ajar. I had goose bumps all over my arms as I stepped inside.

Windowless Fangtasia requires electric light, twenty-four/seven. Since none of these lights were on, the interior was just a dark pit. Winter daylight extended weakly down the hall that led to the bar proper. On the right were the doors to Eric's office and the bookkeeper's room. On the left was the door to the large storeroom, which also contained the employee bathroom. This hall ended in a heavy door to discourage any fun lovers from penetrating to the back of the club. This door, too, was open, for the first time in my memory. Beyond it lay the black silent cavern of the bar. I wondered if anything was sitting at those tables or huddled in those booths.

I was holding my breath so I could detect the least little noise. After a few seconds, I heard a scraping movement and another sound of pain, coming from the storeroom. Its door was slightly ajar. I took four silent steps to that door. My heart was pounding all the way up in my throat as I reached into the darkness to flip the light switch.

The glare made me blink.

Belinda, the only half-intelligent fang-banger I'd ever met, was lying on the storeroom floor in a curiously contorted position. Her legs were bent double, her heels pressed against her hips. There was no blood – in fact, no visible mark – on her. Apparently, she was having a giant and perpetual leg cramp.

I knelt beside Belinda, my eyes darting glances in all directions. I saw no other movement in the room, though its corners were obscured with stacks of liquor cartons and a coffin that was used as a prop in a show the vampires sometimes put on for special parties. The employee bathroom door was shut.

'Belinda,' I whispered. 'Belinda, look at me.'

Belinda's eyes were red and swollen behind their glasses, and her cheeks were wet with tears. She blinked and focused on my face.

'Are they still here?' I asked, knowing she'd understand that I meant 'the people who did this to you.'

'Sookie,' she said hoarsely. Her voice was weak, and I wondered how long she'd lain there waiting for help. 'Oh, thank God. Tell Master Eric we tried to hold them off.' Still role-playing, you notice, even in her agony: 'Tell our chieftain we fought to the death' – you know the kind of thing.

'Who'd you try to hold off?' I asked sharply.

'The witches. They came in last night after we'd closed, after Pam and Chow had gone. Just Ginger and me . . .'

'What did they want?' I had time to notice that Belinda was still wearing her filmy black waitress outfit with the slit up the long skirt, and there were still puncture marks painted on her neck.

'They wanted to know where we'd put Master Eric. They seemed to think they'd done . . . something to him, and that we'd hidden him.' During her long pause, her face contorted, and I could tell she was in terrible pain, but I couldn't tell what was wrong with her. 'My legs,' she moaned. 'Oh . . .'

'But you didn't know, so you couldn't tell them.'

'I would never betray our master.'

And Belinda was the one with sense.

'Was anyone here besides Ginger, Belinda?' But she was so deep into a spasm of suffering that she couldn't answer. Her whole body was rigid with pain, that low moan tearing out of her throat again.

I called 911 from Eric's office, since I knew the location of the phone there. The room had been tossed, and some frisky witch had spray painted a big red pentagram on one of the walls. Eric was going to love that.

I returned to Belinda to tell her the ambulance was coming. 'What's wrong with your legs?' I asked, scared of the answer.

'They made the muscle in the back of my legs pull up, like it was half as long . . .' And she began moaning again. 'It's like one of those giant cramps you get when you're pregnant.'

It was news to me that Belinda had ever been pregnant.

'Where's Ginger?' I asked, when her pain seemed to have ebbed a little.

'She was in the bathroom.'

Ginger, a pretty strawberry blonde, as dumb as a rock, was still there. I don't think they'd meant to kill her. But they'd put a spell on her legs like they'd done to Belinda's, it looked like; her legs were drawn up double in the same peculiar and painful way, even in death. Ginger had been standing in front of the sink when she'd crumpled, and her head had hit the lip of the sink on her way down. Her eyes were sightless and her hair was matted with some clotted blood that had oozed from the depression in her temple.

There was nothing to be done. I didn't even touch

Ginger; she was so obviously dead. I didn't say anything about her to Belinda, who was in too much agony to understand, anyway. She had a couple more moments of lucidity before I took off. I asked her where to find Pam and Chow so I could warn them, and Belinda said they just showed up at the bar when it became dark.

She also said the woman who'd worked the spell was a witch named Hallow, and she was almost six feet tall, with short brown hair and a black design painted on her face.

That should make her easy to identify.

'She told me she was as strong as a vampire, too,' Belinda gasped. 'You see . . .' Belinda pointed beyond me. I whirled, expecting an attack. Nothing that alarming happened, but what I saw was almost as disturbing as what I'd imagined. It was the handle of the dolly the staff used to wheel cases of drinks around. The long metal handle had been twisted into a U.

'I know Master Eric will kill her when he returns,' Belinda said falteringly after a minute, the words coming out in jagged bursts because of the pain.

'Sure he will,' I said stoutly. I hesitated, feeling crummy beyond words. 'Belinda, I have to go because I don't want the police to keep me here for questioning. Please don't mention my name. Just say a passerby heard you, okay?'

'Where's Master Eric? Is he really missing?'

'I have no idea,' I said, forced to lie. 'I have to get out of here.'

'Go,' Belinda said, her voice ragged. 'We're lucky you came in at all.'

I had to get out of there. I knew nothing about what had happened at the bar, and being questioned for hours would cost me time I couldn't afford, with my brother missing.

Back in my car and on my way out of the shopping center, I passed the police cars and the ambulance as they headed in. I'd wiped the doorknob clean of my fingerprints. Other than that, I couldn't think of what I'd touched and what I hadn't, no matter how carefully I reviewed my actions. There'd be a million prints there, anyway; gosh, it was a bar.

After a minute, I realized I was just driving with no direction. I was overwhelmingly rattled. I pulled over into yet another filling station parking lot and looked at the pay phone longingly. I could call Alcide, ask him if he knew where Pam and Chow spent their daytime hours. Then I could go there and leave a message or something, warn them about what had happened.

I made myself take some deep breaths and think hard about what I was doing. It was extremely unlikely that the vamps would give a Were the address of their daytime resting place. This was not information that vampires passed out to anyone who asked. Alcide had no love for the vamps of Shreveport, who'd held his dad's gambling debt over Alcide's head until he complied with their wishes. I knew that if I called, he'd come, because he was just a nice guy. But his involvement could have serious consequences for his family and his business. However, if this Hallow really *was* a triple threat – a Were witch who drank vampire blood – she was very dangerous, and the Weres of Shreveport should know about her. Relieved I'd finally made up my mind, I found a pay phone that worked, and I got Alcide's card out of its slot in my billfold.

Alcide was in his office, which was a miracle. I described my location, and he gave me directions on how to reach his office. He offered to come get me, but I didn't want him to think I was an utter idiot.

I used a calling card to phone Bud Dearborn's office, to hear there was no news about Jason.

Following Alcide's directions very carefully, I arrived at Herveaux and Son in about twenty minutes. It was not too far off I-30, on the eastern edge of Shreveport, actually on my way back to Bon Temps.

The Herveauxes owned the building, and their surveying company was its sole occupant. I parked in front of the low brick building. At the rear, I spotted Alcide's Dodge Ram pickup in the large parking lot for employees. The one in front, for visitors, was much smaller. It was clear to see that the Herveauxes mostly went to their clients, rather than the clients coming to them.

Feeling shy and more than a little nervous, I pushed open the front door and glanced around. There was a desk just inside the door, with a waiting area opposite. Beyond a half wall, I could see five or six workstations, three of them occupied. The woman behind the desk was in charge of routing phone calls, too. She had short dark brown hair that was carefully cut and styled, she was wearing a beautiful sweater, and she had wonderful makeup. She was probably in her forties, but it hadn't lessened her impressiveness.

'I'm here to see Alcide,' I said, feeling embarrassed and self-conscious.

'Your name?' She was smiling at me, but she looked a little crisp around the edges, as if she didn't quite approve of a young and obviously unfashionable woman showing up at Alcide's workplace. I was wearing a bright blue-and-yellow knit top with long sleeves under my old thigh-length blue cloth coat, and aged blue jeans, and Reeboks. I'd been worried about finding my brother when

I dressed, not about standing inspection by the Fashion Police.

'Stackhouse,' I said.

'Ms. Stackhouse here to see you,' Crispy said into an intercom.

'Oh, good!' Alcide sounded very happy, which was a relief.

Crispy was saying into the intercom, 'Shall I send her back?' when Alcide burst through the door behind and to the left of her desk.

'Sookie!' he said, and he beamed at me. He stopped for a second, as if he couldn't quite decide what he should do, and then he hugged me.

I felt like I was smiling all over. I hugged him back. I was so happy to see him! I thought he looked wonderful. Alcide is a tall man, with black hair that apparently can't be tamed with a brush and comb, and he has a broad face and green eyes.

We'd dumped a body together, and that creates a bond.

He pulled gently on my braid. 'Come on back,' he said in my ear, since Ms. Crispy was looking on with an indulgent smile. I was sure the indulgent part was for Alcide's benefit. In fact, I knew it was, because she was thinking I didn't look chic enough or polished enough to date a Herveaux, and she didn't think Alcide's dad (with whom she'd been sleeping for two years) would appreciate Alcide taking up with a no-account girl like me. Oops, one of those things I didn't want to know. Obviously I wasn't shielding myself hard enough. Bill had made me practice, and now that I didn't see him anymore, I was getting sloppy. It wasn't entirely my fault; Ms. Crispy was a clear broadcaster.

Alcide was not, since he's a werewolf.

Alcide ushered me down a hall, which was nicely carpeted and hung with neutral pictures – insipid landscapes and garden scenes – which I figured some decorator (or maybe Ms. Crispy) had chosen. He showed me into his office, which had his name on the door. It was a big room, but not a grand or elegant one, because it was just chockfull of work stuff – plans and papers and hard hats and office equipment. Very utilitarian. A fax machine was humming, and set beside a stack of forms there was a calculator displaying figures.

'You're busy. I shouldn't have called,' I said, instantly cowed.

'Are you kidding? Your call is the best thing that's happened to me all day!' He sounded so sincere that I had to smile again. 'There's something I have to say to you, something I didn't tell you when I dropped your stuff off after you got hurt.' After I'd been beaten up by hired thugs. 'I felt so bad about it that I've put off coming to Bon Temps to talk to you face-to-face.'

Omigod, he'd gotten back with his nasty rotten fiancée, Debbie Pelt. I was getting Debbie's name from his brain.

'Yes?' I said, trying to look calm and open. He reached down and took my hand between his own large palms.

'I owe you a huge apology.'

Okay, that was unexpected. 'How would that be?' I asked, looking up at him with narrowed eyes. I'd come here to spill my guts, but it was Alcide who was spilling his instead.

'That last night, at Club Dead,' he began, 'when you needed my help and protection the most, I . . .'

I knew what was coming now. Alcide had changed into

a wolf rather than staying human and helping me out of the bar after I'd gotten staked. I put my free hand across his mouth. His skin was so warm. If you're used to touching vampires, you'll know just how roasty a regular human can feel, and a Were even more so, since they run a few degrees hotter.

I felt my pulse quicken, and I knew he could tell, too. Animals are good at sensing excitement. 'Alcide,' I said, 'never bring that up. You couldn't help it, and it all turned out okay, anyway.' Well, more or less – other than my heart breaking at Bill's perfidy.

'Thanks for being so understanding,' he said, after a pause during which he looked at me intently. 'I think I would have felt better if you'd been mad.' I believe he was wondering whether I was just putting a brave face on it or if I was truly sincere. I could tell he had an impulse to kiss me, but he wasn't sure if I'd welcome such a move or even allow it.

Well, I didn't know what I'd do, either, so I didn't give myself the chance to find out.

'Okay, I'm furious with you, but I'm concealing it real well,' I said. He relaxed all over when he saw me smile, though it might be the last smile we'd share all day. 'Listen, your office in the middle of day isn't a good time and place to tell you the things I need to tell you,' I said. I spoke very levelly, so he'd realize I wasn't coming on to him. Not only did I just plain old like Alcide, I thought he was one hell of a man – but until I was sure he was through with Debbie Pelt, he was off my list of guys I wanted to be around. The last I'd heard of Debbie, she'd been engaged to another shifter, though even that hadn't ended her emotional involvement with Alcide.

I was not going to get in the middle of that – not with the grief caused by Bill's infidelity still weighing heavily on my own heart.

'Let's go to the Applebee's down the road and have some coffee,' he suggested. Over the intercom, he told Crispy he was leaving. We went out through the back door.

It was about two o'clock by then, and the restaurant was almost empty. Alcide asked the young man who seated us to put us in a booth as far away from anyone else as we could get. I scooted down the bench on one side, expecting Alcide to take the other, but he slid in beside me. 'If you want to tell secrets, this is as close as we can get,' he said.

We both ordered coffee, and Alcide asked the server to bring a small pot. I inquired after his dad while the server was puttering around, and Alcide inquired after Jason. I didn't answer, because the mention of my brother's name was enough to make me feel close to crying. When our coffee had come and the young man had left, Alcide said, 'What's up?'

I took a deep breath, trying to decide where to begin. 'There's a bad witch coven in Shreveport,' I said flatly. 'They drink vampire blood, and at least a few of them are shifters.'

It was Alcide's turn to take a deep breath.

I help up a hand, indicating there was more to come. 'They're moving into Shreveport to take over the vampires' financial kingdom. They put a curse or a hex or something on Eric, and it took away his memory. They raided Fangtasia, trying to discover the day resting place of the vampires. They put some kind of spell on two of the waitresses, and one of them is in the hospital. The other one is dead.'

Alcide was already sliding his cell phone from his pocket.

'Pam and Chow have hidden Eric at my house, and I have to get back before dark to take care of him. And Jason is missing. I don't know who took him or where he is or if he's . . .' *Alive.* But I couldn't say the word.

Alcide's deep breath escaped in a whoosh, and he sat staring at me, the phone in his hand. He couldn't decide whom to call first. I didn't blame him.

'I don't like Eric being at your house,' he said. 'It puts you in danger.'

I was touched that his first thought was for my safety. 'Jason asked for a lot of money for doing it, and Pam and Chow agreed,' I said, embarrassed.

'But Jason isn't there to take the heat, and you are.'

Unanswerably true. But to give Jason credit, he certainly hadn't planned it that way. I told Alcide about the blood on the dock. 'Might be a red herring,' he said. 'If the type matches Jason's, then you can worry.' He took a sip of his coffee, his eyes focused inward. 'I've got to make some calls,' he said.

'Alcide, are you the packmaster for Shreveport?'

'No, no, I'm nowhere near important enough.'

That didn't seem possible to me, and I said as much. He took my hand.

'Packmasters are usually older than me,' he said. 'And you have to be really tough. Really, really tough.'

'Do you have to fight to get to be packmaster?'

'No, you get elected, but the candidates have to be very strong and clever. There's a sort of – well, you have a test you have to take.'

'Written? Oral?' Alcide looked relieved when he saw I was smiling. 'More like an endurance test?' I said.

He nodded. 'More like.'

'Don't you think your packmaster should know about this?'

'Yes. What else?'

'Why would they be doing this? Why pick on Shreveport? If they have that much going for them, the vampire blood and the will to do really bad things, why not set up shop in a more prosperous city?'

'That's a real good question.' Alcide was thinking hard. His green eyes squinted when he thought. 'I've never heard of a witch having this much power. I never heard of a witch being a shifter. I tend to think it's the first time this has ever happened.'

'The first time?'

'That a witch has ever tried to take control of a city, tried to take away the assets of the city's supernatural community,' he said,

'How do witches stand in the supernatural pecking order?'

'Well, they're humans who stay human.' He shrugged. 'Usually, the Supes feel like witches are just wanna-bes. The kind you have to keep an eye on, since they practice magic and we're magical creatures, but still . . .'

'Not a big threat?'

'Right. Looks like we might have to rethink that. Their leader takes vampire blood. Does she drain them herself?' He punched in a number and held the phone to his ear.

'I don't know.'

'And what does she shift into?' Shape-shifters had a choice, but there was one animal each shifter had an affinity for, her habitual animal. A shape-shifter could call herself a 'were-lynx' or a 'were-bat,' if she was out of hearing range of a werewolf. Werewolves objected very strenuously to any other two-natured creatures who termed themselves 'Were.'

'Well, she's . . . like you,' I said. The Weres considered themselves the kings of the two-natured community. They only changed into one animal, and it was the best. The rest of the two-natured community responded by calling the wolves thugs.

'Oh, no.' Alcide was appalled. At that moment, his packmaster answered the phone.

'Hello, this is Alcide.' A silence. 'I'm sorry to bother you when you were busy in the yard. Something important's come up. I need to see you as soon as possible.' Another silence. 'Yes, sir. With your permission, I'll bring someone with me.' After a second or two, Alcide pressed a button to end the conversation. 'Surely Bill knows where Pam and Chow live?' he asked me.

'I'm sure he does, but he's not here to tell me about it.' If he would.

'And where is he?' Alcide's voice was deceptively calm.

'He's in Peru.'

I'd been looking down at my napkin, which I'd pleated into a fan. I glanced up at the man next to me to see him staring down at me with an expression of incredulity.

'He's *gone*? He left you there alone?'

'Well, he didn't know anything was going to happen,' I said, trying not to sound defensive, and then I thought, *What am I saying?* 'Alcide, I haven't seen Bill since I came back from Jackson, except when he came over to tell me he was leaving the country.'

'But she told me you were back with Bill,' Alcide said in a very strange voice.

'Who told you that?'

'Debbie. Who else?'

I'm afraid my reaction was not very flattering. 'And you believed *Debbie*?'

'She said she'd stopped by Merlotte's on her way over to see me, and she'd seen you and Bill acting very, ah, friendly while she was there.'

'And you *believed* her?' Maybe if I kept shifting the emphasis, he'd tell me he was just joking.

Alcide was looking sheepish now, or as sheepish as a werewolf can look.

'Okay, that was dumb,' he admitted. 'I'll deal with her.'

'Right.' Pardon me if I didn't sound very convinced. I'd heard that before.

'Bill's really in Peru?'

'As far as I know.'

'And you're alone in the house with Eric?'

'Eric doesn't know he's Eric.'

'He doesn't remember his identity?'

'Nope. He doesn't remember his character, either, apparently.'

'That's a good thing,' Alcide said darkly. He had never viewed Eric with any sense of humor, as I did. I'd always been leery of Eric, but I'd appreciated his mischief, his single-mindedness, and his flair. If you could say a vampire had joie de vivre, Eric had it in spades.

'Let's go see the packmaster now,' Alcide said, obviously in a much grimmer mood. We slid out of the booth after he'd paid for the coffee, and without phoning in to work ('No point being the boss if I can't vanish from time to time'), he helped me up into his truck and we took off back into Shreveport. I was sure Ms. Crispy would assume we'd checked into a motel or gone to Alcide's apartment, but that was better than Ms. Crispy finding out her boss was a werewolf.

As we drove, Alcide told me that the packmaster was a retired Air Force colonel, formerly stationed at Barksdale Air Force Base in Bossier City, which flowed into Shreveport. Colonel Flood's only child, a daughter, had married a local, and Colonel Flood had settled in the city to be close to his grandchildren.

'His wife is a Were, too?' I asked. If Mrs. Flood was also a Were, their daughter would be, too. If Weres can get through the first few months, they live a good long while, barring accidents.

'She was; she passed away a few months ago.'

Alcide's packmaster lived in a modest neighborhood of ranch-style homes on smallish lots. Colonel Flood was picking up pinecones in his front yard. It seemed a very domestic and peaceable thing for a prominent werewolf to be doing. I'd pictured him in my head in an Air Force uniform, but of course he was wearing regular civilian outdoor clothes. His thick hair was white and cut very short, and he had a mustache that must have been trimmed with a ruler, it was so exact.

The colonel must have been curious after Alcide's phone call, but he asked us to come inside in a calm sort of way. He patted Alcide on the back a lot; he was very polite to me.

The house was as neat as his mustache. It could have passed inspection.

'Can I get you a drink? Coffee? Hot chocolate? Soda?' The colonel gestured toward his kitchen as if there were a servant standing there alert for our orders.

'No, thank you,' I said, since I was awash with

Applebee's coffee. Colonel Flood insisted we sit in the company living room, which was an awkwardly narrow rectangle with a formal dining area at one end. Mrs. Flood had liked porcelain birds. She had liked them a lot. I wondered how the grandchildren fared in this room, and I kept my hands tucked in my lap for fear I'd jostle something.

'So, what can I do for you?' Colonel Flood asked Alcide. 'Are you seeking permission to marry?'

'Not today,' Alcide said with a smile. I looked down at the floor to keep my expression to myself. 'My friend Sookie has some information that she shared with me. It's very important.' His smile died on the vine. 'She needs to relate what she knows to you.'

'And why do I need to listen?'

I understood that he was asking Alcide who I was – that if he was obliged to listen to me, he needed to know my bona fides. But Alcide was offended on my behalf.

'I wouldn't have brought her if it wasn't important. I wouldn't have introduced her to you if I wouldn't give my blood for her.'

I wasn't real certain what that meant, but I was interpreting it to assume Alcide was vouching for my truthfulness and offering to pay in some way if I proved false. Nothing was simple in the supernatural world.

'Let's hear your story, young woman,' said the colonel briskly.

I related all I'd told Alcide, trying to leave out the personal bits.

'Where is this coven staying?' he asked me, when I was through. I told him what I'd seen through Holly's mind.

'Not enough information,' Flood said crisply. 'Alcide, we need the trackers.'

'Yes, sir.' Alcide's eyes were gleaming at the thought of action.

'I'll call them. Everything I've heard is making me rethink something odd that happened last night. Adabelle didn't come to the planning committee meeting.'

Alcide looked startled. 'That's not good.'

They were trying to be cryptic in front of me, but I could read what was passing between the two shifters without too much difficulty. Flood and Alcide were wondering if their – hmmm, vice president? – Adabelle had missed the meeting for some innocent reason, or if the new coven had somehow inveigled her into joining them against her own pack.

'Adabelle has been chafing against the pack leadership for some time,' Colonel Flood told Alcide, with the ghost of a smile on his thin lips. 'I had hoped, when she got elected my second, that she'd consider that concession enough.'

From the bits of information I could glean from the packmaster's mind, the Shreveport pack seemed to be heavily on the patriarchal side. To Adabelle, a modern woman, Colonel Flood's leadership was stifling.

'A new regime might appeal to her,' Colonel Flood said, after a perceptible pause. 'If the invaders learned anything about our pack, it's Adabelle they'd approach.'

'I don't think Adabelle would ever betray the pack, no matter how unhappy she is with the status quo,' Alcide said. He sounded very sure. 'But if she didn't come to the meeting last night, and you can't raise her by phone this morning, I'm concerned.'

'I wish you'd go check on Adabelle while I alert the pack to action,' Colonel Flood suggested. 'If your friend wouldn't mind.'

Maybe his friend would like to get her butt back to Bon Temps and see to her paying guest. Maybe his friend would like to be searching for her brother. Though truly, I could not think of a single thing to do that would further the search for Jason, and it would be at least two hours before Eric rose.

Alcide said, 'Colonel, Sookie is not a pack member and she shouldn't have to shoulder pack responsibilities. She has her own troubles, and she's gone out of her way to let us know about a big problem we didn't even realize we had. We should have known. Someone in our pack hasn't been honest with us.'

Colonel Flood's face drew in on itself as if he'd swallowed a live eel. 'You're right about that,' he said. 'Thank you, Miss Stackhouse, for taking the time to come to Shreveport and to tell Alcide about our problem . . . which we should have known.'

I nodded to him in acknowledgment.

'And I think you're right, Alcide. One of us must have known about the presence of another pack in the city.'

'I'll call you about Adabelle,' Alcide said.

The colonel picked up the phone and consulted a red leather book before he dialed. He glanced sideways at Alcide. 'No answer at her shop.' He had as much warmth radiating from him as a little space heater. Since Colonel Flood kept his house about as cold as the great outdoors, the heat was quite welcome.

'Sookie should be named a friend of the pack.'

I could tell that was more than a recommendation. Alcide was saying something quite significant, but he sure wasn't going to explain. I was getting a little tired of the elliptical conversations going on around me.

'Excuse me, Alcide, Colonel,' I said as politely as I could. 'Maybe Alcide could run me back to my car? Since you all seem to have plans to carry out.'

'Of course,' the colonel said, and I could read that he was glad to be getting me out of the way. 'Alcide, I'll see you back here in, what? Forty minutes or so? We'll talk about it then.'

Alcide glanced at his watch and reluctantly agreed. 'I might stop by Adabelle's house while I'm taking Sookie to her car,' he said, and the colonel nodded, as if that were only pro forma.

'I don't know why Adabelle isn't answering the phone at work, and I don't believe she'd go over to the coven,' Alcide explained when we were back in his truck. 'Adabelle lives with her mother, and they don't get along too well. But we'll check there first. Adabelle's Flood's second in command, and she's also our best tracker.'

'What can the trackers do?'

'They'll go to Fangtasia and try to follow the scent trail the witches left there. That'll take them to the witches' lair. If they lose the scent, maybe we can call in help from the Shreveport covens. They have to be as worried as we are.'

'At Fangtasia, I'm afraid any scent might be obscured by all the emergency people,' I said regretfully. That would have been something to watch, a Were tracking through the city. 'And just so you know, Hallow has contacted all the witches hereabouts already. I talked to a Wiccan in Bon Temps who'd been called in to Shreveport to meet with Hallow's bunch.'

'This is bigger than I thought, but I'm sure the pack can handle it.' Alcide sounded quite confident.

Alcide backed the truck out of the colonel's driveway, and we began making our way through Shreveport once again. I was seeing more of the city this day than I'd seen in my whole life.

'Whose idea was it for Bill to go to Peru?' Alcide asked me suddenly.

'I don't know.' I was startled and puzzled. 'I think it was his queen's.'

'But he didn't tell you that directly.'

'No.'

'He might have been ordered to go.'

'I suppose.'

'Who had the power to do that?' Alcide asked, as if the answer would enlighten me.

'Eric, of course.' Since Eric was sheriff of Area Five. 'And then the queen.' That would be Eric's boss, the queen of Louisiana. Yeah, I know. It's dumb. But the vampires thought they were a marvel of modern organization.

'And now Bill's gone, and Eric's staying at your house.' Alcide's voice was coaxing me to reach an obvious conclusion.

'You think that Eric staged this whole thing? You think he ordered Bill out of the country, had witches invade Shreveport, had them curse him, began running half-naked out in the freezing cold when he supposed I might be near, and then just hoped I'd take him in and that Pam and Chow and my brother would talk to each other to arrange Eric's staying with me?'

Alcide looked properly flattened. 'You mean you'd thought of this?'

'Alcide, I'm not educated, but I'm not dumb.' Try getting educated when you can read the minds of all your classmates, not to mention your teacher. But I read a lot, and I've read lots of good stuff. Of course, now I read mostly mysteries and romances. So I've learned many curious odds and ends, and I have a great vocabulary. 'But the fact is, Eric would hardly go to this much trouble to get me to go to bed with him. Is that what you're thinking?' Of course, I knew it was. Were or not, I could see that much.

'Put that way . . .' But Alcide still didn't look satisfied. Of course, this was the man who had believed Debbie Pelt when she said that I was definitely back with Bill.

I wondered if I could get some witch to cast a truth spell on Debbie Pelt, whom I despised because she had been cruel to Alcide, insulted me grievously, burned a hole in my favorite wrap and – oh – tried to kill me by proxy. Also, she had stupid hair.

Alcide wouldn't know an honest Debbie if she came up and bit him in the ass, though backbiting was a specialty of the real Debbie.

If Alcide had known Bill and I had parted, would he have come by? Would one thing have led to another?

Well, *sure* it would have. And there I'd be, stuck with a guy who'd take the word of Debbie Pelt.

I glanced over at Alcide and sighed. This man was just about perfect in many respects. I liked the way he looked, I understood the way he thought, and he treated me with great consideration and respect. Sure, he was a werewolf, but I could give up a couple of nights of month. True, according to Alcide it would be difficult for me to carry his baby to term, but it was at least possible. Pregnancy wasn't part of the picture with a vampire.

Whoa. Alcide hadn't offered to father my babies, and he

was still seeing Debbie. What had happened to her engagement to the Clausen guy?

With the less noble side of my character – assuming my character had a noble side – I hoped that someday soon Alcide would see Debbie for the bitch she truly was, and that he'd finally take the knowledge to heart. Whether, consequently, Alcide turned to me or not, he deserved better than Debbie Pelt.

Adabelle Yancy and her mother lived in a cul-de-sac in an upper-middle-class neighborhood that wasn't too far from Fangtasia. The house was on a rolling lawn that raised it higher than the street, so the driveway mounted and went to the rear of the property. I thought Alcide might park on the street and we'd go up the brick walkway to the front door, but he seemed to want to get the truck out of sight. I scanned the cul-de-sac, but I didn't see anyone at all, much less anyone watching the house for visitors.

Attached to the rear of the house at a right angle, the three-car garage was neat as a pin. You would think cars were never parked there, that the gleaming Subaru had just strayed into the area. We climbed out of the truck.

'That's Adabelle's mother's car.' Alcide was frowning. 'She started a bridal shop. I bet you've heard of it – Verena Rose. Verena's retired from working there full-time. She drops in just often enough to make Adabelle crazy.'

I'd never been to the shop, but brides of any claim to prominence in the area made a point of shopping there. It must be a real profitable store. The brick home was in excellent shape, and no more than twenty years old. The yard was edged, raked, and landscaped.

When Alcide knocked at the back door, it flew open.

The woman who stood revealed in the opening was as put-together and neat as the house and yard. Her steel-colored hair was in a neat roll on the back of her head, and she was in a dull olive suit and low-heeled brown pumps. She looked from Alcide to me and didn't find what she was seeking. She pushed open the glass storm door.

'Alcide, how nice to see you,' she lied desperately. This was a woman in deep turmoil.

Alcide gave her a long look. 'We have trouble, Verena.'

If her daughter was a member of the pack, Verena herself was a werewolf. I looked at the woman curiously, and she seemed like one of the more fortunate friends of my grandmother's. Verena Rose Yancy was an attractive woman in her late sixties, blessed with a secure income and her own home. I could not imagine this woman down on all fours loping across a field.

And it was obvious that Verena didn't give a damn what trouble Alcide had. 'Have you seen my daughter?' she asked, and she waited for his answer with terror in her eyes. 'She can't have betrayed the pack.'

'No,' Alcide said. 'But the packmaster sent us to find her. She missed a pack officers' meeting last night.'

'She called me from the shop last night. She said she had an unexpected appointment with a stranger who'd called the shop right at closing time.' The woman literally wrung her hands. 'I thought maybe she was meeting that witch.'

'Have you heard from her since?' I said, in the gentlest voice I could manage.

'I went to bed last night mad at her,' Verena said, looking directly at me for the first time. 'I thought she'd decided to spend the night with one of her friends. One of her *girl* friends,' she explained, looking at me with eyebrows arched, so I'd get her drift. I nodded. 'She never would tell me ahead of time, she'd just say, "Expect me when you see me," or "I'll meet you at the shop tomorrow morning," or something.' A shudder rippled through Verena's slim body. 'But she hasn't come home and I can't get an answer at the shop.'

'Was she supposed to open the shop today?' Alcide asked.

'No, Wednesday's our closed day, but she always goes in to work on the books and get paperwork out of the way. She always does,' Verena repeated.

'Why don't Alcide and I drive over there and check the shop for you?' I said gently. 'Maybe she left a note.' This was not a woman you patted on the arm, so I didn't make that natural gesture, but I did push the glass door shut so she'd understand she had to stay there and she shouldn't come with us. She understood all too clearly.

Verena Rose's Bridal and Formal Shop was located in an old home on a block of similarly converted two-story houses. The building had been renovated and maintained as beautifully as the Yancys' residence, and I wasn't surprised it had such cachet. The white-painted brick, the dark green shutters, the glossy black ironwork of the railings on the steps, and the brass details on the door all spoke of elegance and attention to detail. I could see that if you had aspirations to class, this is where you'd come to get your wedding gear.

Set a little back from the street, with parking behind the store, the building featured one large bay window in front. In this window stood a faceless mannequin wearing a shining brown wig. Her arms were gracefully bent to hold a stunning bouquet. Even from the truck, I could see that the bridal dress, with its long embroidered train, was absolutely spectacular.

We parked in the driveway without pulling around back, and I jumped out of the pickup. Together we took the brick sidewalk that led from the drive to the front door, and as we got closer, Alcide cursed. For a moment, I imagined some kind of bug infestation had gotten into the store window and landed on the snowy dress. But after that moment, I knew the dark flecks were surely spatters of blood.

The blood had sprayed onto the white brocade and dried there. It was as if the mannequin had been wounded, and for a crazy second I wondered. I'd seen a lot of impossible things in the past few months.

'Adabelle,' Alcide said, as if he was praying.

We were standing at the bottom of the steps leading up to the front porch, staring into the bay window. The CLOSED sign was hanging in the middle of the glass oval inset in the door, and venetian blinds were closed behind it. There were no live brainwaves emanating from that house. I had taken the time to check. I'd discovered, the hard way, that checking was a good idea.

'Dead things,' Alcide said, his face raised to the cold breeze, his eyes shut to help him concentrate. 'Dead things inside and out.'

I took hold of the curved ironwork handrail with my left hand and went up one step. I glanced around. My eyes came to rest on something in the flowerbed under the bay window, something pale that stood out against the pine bark mulch. I nudged Alcide, and I pointed silently with my free right hand.

Lying by a pruned-back azalea, there was another hand – an unattached extra. I felt a shudder run through Alcide's body as he comprehended what he saw. There was that moment when you tried to recognize it as anything but what it was.

'Wait here,' Alcide said, his voice thick and hoarse.

That was just fine with me.

But when he opened the unlocked front door to enter the shop, I saw what lay on the floor just beyond. I had to swallow a scream.

It was lucky Alcide had his cell phone. He called Colonel Flood, told him what had happened, and asked him to go over to Mrs. Yancy's house. Then he called the police. There was just no way around it. This was a busy area, and there was a good chance someone had noticed us going to the front door.

It was surely a day for finding bodies – for me, and for the Shreveport police department. I knew there were some vampire cops on the force, but of course the vamps had to work the night shift, so we spoke to regular old human cops. There wasn't a Were or a shifter among 'em, not even a telepathic human. All these police officers were regular people who thought we were borderline suspicious.

'Why did you stop by here, buddy?' asked Detective Coughlin, who had brown hair, a weathered face, and a beer belly one of the Clydesdales would've been proud of.

Alcide looked surprised. He hadn't thought this far, which wasn't too amazing. I hadn't known Adabelle when she was alive, and I hadn't stepped inside the bridal shop as he had. I hadn't sustained the worst shock. It was up to me to pick up the reins.

'It was my idea, Detective,' I said instantly. 'My grandmother, who died last year? She always told me, "If you
need a wedding dress, Sookie, you go to Verena Rose's for
it." I didn't think to call ahead and check to see if they were
open today.'

'So, you and Mr. Herveaux are going to be married?'

'Yes,' said Alcide, pulling me against him and wrapping
his arms around me. 'We're headed for the altar.'

I smiled, but in an appropriately subdued way.

'Well, congratulations.' Detective Coughlin eyed us
thoughtfully. 'So, Miss Stackhouse, you hadn't ever met
Adabelle Yancy face-to-face?'

'I may have met the older Mrs. Yancy when I was a little
girl,' I said cautiously. 'But I don't remember her. Alcide's
family knows the Yancys, of course. He's lived here all his
life.' Of course, they're also werewolves.

Coughlin was still focused on me. 'And you didn't go in
the shop none? Just Mr. Herveaux here?'

'Alcide just stepped in while I waited out here.' I tried to
look delicate, which is not easy for me. I am healthy and
muscular, and while I am not Emme, I'm not Kate Moss
either. 'I'd seen the – the hand, so I stayed out.'

'That was a good idea,' Detective Coughlin said.
'What's in there isn't fit for people to see.' He looked
about twenty years older as he said that. I felt sorry that
his job was so tough. He was thinking that the savaged
bodies in the house were a waste of two good lives and the
work of someone he'd love to arrest. 'Would either of you
have any idea why anyone would want to rip up two ladies
like this?'

'Two,' Alcide said slowly, stunned.

'Two?' I said, less guardedly.

'Why, yes,' the detective said heavily. He had aimed to get our reactions and now he had them; what he thought of them, I would find out.

'Poor things,' I said, and I wasn't faking the tears that filled my eyes. It was kind of nice to have Alcide's chest to lean against, and as if he were reading my mind he unzipped his leather jacket so I'd be closer to him, wrapping the open sides around me to keep me warmer. 'But if one of them is Adabelle Yancy, who is the other?'

'There's not much left of the other,' Coughlin said, before he told himself to shut his mouth.

'They were kind of jumbled up,' Alcide said quietly, close to my ear. He was sickened. 'I didn't know . . . I guess if I'd analyzed what I was seeing . . .'

Though I couldn't read Alcide's thoughts clearly, I could understand that he was thinking that Adabelle had managed to take down one of her attackers. And when the rest of the group was getting away, they hadn't taken all the appropriate bits with them.

'And you're from Bon Temps, Miss Stackhouse,' the detective said, almost idly.

'Yes, sir,' I said, with a gasp. I was trying not to picture Adabelle Yancy's last moments.

'Where you work there?'

'Merlotte's Bar and Grill,' I said. 'I wait tables.'

While he registered the difference in social status between me and Alcide, I closed my eyes and laid my head against Alcide's warm chest. Detective Coughlin was wondering if I was pregnant; if Alcide's dad, a well-known and well-to-do figure in Shreveport, would approve of such a marriage. He could see why I'd want an expensive wedding dress, if I were marrying a Herveaux.

'You don't have an engagement ring, Miss Stackhouse?'

'We don't plan on a long engagement,' Alcide said. I could hear his voice rumbling in his chest. 'She'll get her diamond the day we marry.'

'You're so bad,' I said fondly, punching him in the ribs as hard as I could without being obvious.

'Ouch,' he said in protest.

Somehow this bit of byplay convinced Detective Coughlin that we were really engaged. He took down our phone numbers and addresses, then told us we could leave. Alcide was as relieved as I was.

We drove to the nearest place where we could pull over in privacy – a little park that was largely deserted in the cold weather – and Alcide called Colonel Flood again. I waited in the truck while Alcide, pacing in the dead grass, gesticulated and raised his voice, venting some of his horror and anger. I'd been able to feel it building up in him. Alcide had trouble articulating emotions, like lots of guys. It made him seem more familiar and dear.

Dear? I'd better stop thinking like that. The engagement had been drummed up strictly for Detective Coughlin's benefit. If Alcide was anyone's 'dear,' it was the perfidious Debbie's.

When Alcide climbed back into the pickup, he was scowling.

'I guess I better go back to the office and take you to your car,' he said. 'I'm sorry about all this.'

'I guess I should be saying that.'

'This is a situation neither of us created,' he said firmly. 'Neither of us would be involved if we could help it.'

'That's the God's truth.' After a minute of thinking of

the complicated supernatural world, I asked Alcide what Colonel Flood's plan was.

'We'll take care of it,' Alcide said. 'I'm sorry, Sook, I can't tell you what we're going to do.'

'Are you going to be in danger?' I asked, because I just couldn't help it.

We'd gotten to the Herveaux building by then, and Alcide parked his truck by my old car. He turned a little to face me, and he reached over to take my hand. 'I'm gonna be fine. Don't worry,' he said gently. 'I'll call you.'

'Don't forget to do that,' I said. 'And I have to tell you what the witches did about trying to find Eric.' I hadn't told Alcide about the posted pictures, the reward. He frowned even harder when he thought about the cleverness of this ploy.

'Debbie was supposed to drive over this afternoon, get here about six,' he said. He looked at his watch. 'Too late to stop her coming.'

'If you're planning a big raid, she could help,' I said.

He gave me a sharp look. Like a pointed stick he wanted to poke in my eye. 'She's a shifter, not a Were,' he reminded me defensively.

Maybe she turned into a weasel or a rat.

'Of course,' I said seriously. I literally bit my tongue so I wouldn't make any of the remarks that waited just inside my mouth, dying to be spoken. 'Alcide, do you think the other body was Adabelle's girlfriend? Someone who just got caught at the shop with Adabelle when the witches came calling?'

'Since a lot of the second body was missing, I hope that the body was one of the witches. I hope Adabelle went down fighting.'

'I hope so, too.' I nodded, putting an end to that train of thought. 'I'd better get back to Bon Temps. Eric will be waking up soon. Don't forget to tell your dad that we're engaged.'

His expression provided the only fun I'd had all day.

Chapter 6

I thought all the way home about my day in Shreveport. I'd asked Alcide to call the cops in Bon Temps from his cell phone, and he'd gotten another negative message. No, they hadn't heard any more on Jason, and no one had called to say they'd seen him. So I didn't stop by the police station on my way home, but I did have to go to the grocery to buy some margarine and bread, and I did have to go in the liquor store to pick up some blood.

The first thing I saw when I pushed open the door of Super Save-A-Bunch was a little display of bottled blood, which saved me a stop at the liquor store. The second thing I saw was the poster with the headshot of Eric. I assumed it was the photo Eric had had made when he opened Fangtasia, because it was a very nonthreatening picture. He was projecting winsome worldliness; any person in this universe would know that he'd never, ever bite. It was headed, 'HAVE YOU SEEN THIS VAMPIRE?'

I read the text carefully. Everything Jason had said about it was true. Fifty thousand dollars is a lot of money. That Hallow must be really nuts about Eric to pay that much, if all she wanted was a hump. It was hard to believe gaining control of Fangtasia (and having the bed services of Eric) would afford her a profit after paying out a reward that large. I was increasingly doubtful that I knew the whole story, and I was increasingly sure I was sticking my neck out and might get it bitten off.

Hoyt Fortenberry, Jason's big buddy, was loading pizzas into his buggy in the frozen food aisle. 'Hey, Sookie, where you think ole Jason got to?' he called as soon as he saw me. Hoyt, big and beefy and no rocket scientist, looked genuinely concerned.

'I wish I knew,' I said, coming closer so we could talk without everyone in the store recording every word. 'I'm pretty worried.'

'You don't think he's just gone off with some girl he met? That girl he was with New Year's Eve was pretty cute.'

'What was her name?'

'Crystal. Crystal Norris.'

'Where's she from?'

'From round Hotshot, out thataway.' He nodded south.

Hotshot was even smaller than Bon Temps. It was about ten miles away and had a reputation for being a strange little community. The Hotshot kids who attended the Bon Temps school always stuck together, and they were all a smidge . . . different. It didn't surprise me at all that Crystal lived in Hotshot.

'So,' Hoyt said, persisting in making his point, 'Crystal might have asked him to come stay with her.' But his brain was saying he didn't believe it, he was only trying to comfort me and himself. We both knew that Jason would have phoned by now, no matter how good a time he was having with any woman.

But I decided I'd give Crystal a call when I had a clear ten minutes, which might not be any time tonight. I asked Hoyt to pass on Crystal's name to the sheriff's department, and he said he would. He didn't seem too happy about the idea. I could tell that if the missing man had been anyone but Jason, Hoyt would have refused. But Jason had always been Hoyt's source of recreation and general amusement, since Jason was far more clever and inventive than the slow-moving, slow-thinking Hoyt: If Jason never reappeared, Hoyt would have a dull life.

We parted in the Super Save-A-Bunch parking lot, and I felt relieved that Hoyt hadn't asked me about the TrueBlood I'd purchased. Neither had the cashier, though she'd handled the bottles with distaste. As I'd paid for it, I'd thought about how much I was in the hole from hosting Eric already. Clothes and blood mounted up.

It was just dark when I got to my house and pulled the plastic grocery bags out of the car. I unlocked my back door and went in, calling to Eric as I switched on the kitchen light. I didn't hear an answer, so I put the groceries away, leaving a bottle of TrueBlood out of the refrigerator so he could have it to hand when he got hungry. I got the shotgun out of my trunk and loaded it, sticking it in the shadow of the water heater. I took a minute to call the sheriff's department again. No news of Jason, said the dispatcher.

I slumped against the kitchen wall for a long moment, feeling dejected. It wasn't a good thing to just sit around, being depressed. Maybe I'd go out to the living room and pop a movie into the VCR, as entertainment for Eric. He'd gone through all my *Buffy* tapes, and I didn't have *Angel*. I wondered if he'd like *Gone with the Wind*. (For all

I knew, he'd been around when they were filming it. On the other hand, he had amnesia. Anything should be new to him.)

But as I went down the hall, I heard some small movement. I pushed open the door of my old room gently, not wanting to make a big noise if my guest wasn't yet up. Oh, but he was. Eric was pulling on his jeans, with his back to me. He hadn't bothered with underwear, not even the itty-bitty red ones. My breath stuck in my throat. I made a sound like 'Guck,' and made myself close my eyes tight. I clenched my fists.

If there were an international butt competition, Eric would win, hands down – or cheeks up. He would get a large, large trophy. I had never realized a woman could have to struggle to keep her hands off a man, but here I was, digging my nails into my palms, staring at the inside of my eyelids as though I could maybe see through them if I peered hard enough.

It was somehow degrading, craving someone so . . . so *voraciously* – another good calendar word – just because he was physically beautiful. I hadn't thought that was something women did, either.

'Sookie, are you all right?' Eric asked. I floundered my way back to sanity through a swamp of lust. He was standing right in front of me, his hands resting on my shoulders. I looked up into his blue eyes, now focused on me and apparently full of nothing but concern. I was right on a level with his hard nipples. They were the size of pencil erasers. I bit the inside of my lip. I would *not* lean over those few inches.

'Excuse me,' I said, speaking very softly. I was scared to speak loudly, or move at all. If I did, I might knock him down. 'I didn't mean to walk in on you. I should have knocked.'

'You have seen all of me before.'

Not the rear view, bare. 'Yes, but intruding wasn't polite.'

'I don't mind. You look upset.'

You think? 'Well, I have had a very bad day,' I said, through clenched teeth. 'My brother is missing, and the Were witches in Shreveport killed the – the vice president of the Were pack there, and her hand was in the flowerbed. Well, someone's was. Belinda's in the hospital. Ginger is dead. I think I'll take a shower.' I turned on my heel and marched into my room. I went in the bathroom and shucked my clothes, tossing them into the hamper. I bit my lip until I could smile at my own streak of wildness, and then I climbed into the spray of hot water.

I know cold showers are more traditional, but I was enjoying the warmth and relaxation the heat brought. I got my hair wet and groped for the soap.

'I'll do that for you,' Eric said, pulling back the curtain to step into the shower with me.

I gasped, just short of a shriek. He had discarded the jeans. He was also in the mood, the same mood I was in. You could really tell, with Eric. His fangs were out some, too. I was embarrassed, horrified, and absolutely ready to jump him. While I stood stock-still, paralyzed by conflicting waves of emotion, Eric took the soap out of my hands and lathered up his own, set the soap back in its little niche, and began to wash my arms, raising each in turn to stroke my armpit, down my side, never touching my breasts, which were practically quivering like puppies who wanted to be petted.

'Have we ever made love?' he asked.

I shook my head, still unable to speak.

'Then I was a fool,' he said, moving one hand in a circular motion over my stomach. 'Turn around, lover.'

I turned my back to him, and he began to work on that. His fingers were very strong and very clever, and I had the most relaxed and cleanest set of shoulder blades in Louisiana by the time Eric got through.

My shoulder blades were the only thing at ease. My libido was hopping up and down. Was I really going to do this? It seemed more and more likely that I was, I thought nervously. If the man in my shower had been the real Eric, I would have had the strength to back off. I would have ordered him out the minute he stepped in. The real Eric came with a whole package of power and politics, something of which I had limited understanding and interest. This was a different Eric – without the personality that I'd grown fond of, in a perverse way – but it was beautiful Eric, who desired me, who was hungry for me, in a world that often let me know it could do very well without me. My mind was about to switch off and my body was about to take over. I could feel part of Eric pressed against my back, and he wasn't standing that close. Yikes. Yahoo. Yum.

He shampooed my hair next.

'Are you trembling because you are frightened of me?' he asked.

I considered that. Yes, and no. But I wasn't about to have a long discussion over the pros and cons. The inner debate had been tough enough. Oh, yeah, I know, there wouldn't be a better time to have a long yada-yada with Eric about the moral aspects of mating with someone you didn't love. And maybe there would never be another time to lay ground rules about being careful to be gentle with me physically. Not that I thought Eric would beat me up, but his manhood (as my romance novels called it – in this case the popular adjectives 'burgeoning' or 'throbbing' might also be applied) was a daunting prospect to a relatively inexperienced woman like me. I felt like a car that had only been operated by one driver . . . a car its new prospective buyer was determined to take to the Daytona 500.

Oh, to hell with thinking.

I took the soap from the niche and lathered up my fingers. As I stepped very close to him, I kind of folded Mr. Happy up against Eric's stomach, so I could reach around him and get my fingers on that absolutely gorgeous butt. I couldn't look him in the face, but he let me know he was delighted that I was responding. He spread his legs obligingly and I washed him very thoroughly, very meticulously. He began to make little noises, to rock forward. I began to work on his chest. I closed my lips around his right nipple and sucked. He liked that a lot. His hands pressed against the back of my head. 'Bite, a little,' he whispered, and I used my teeth. His hands began to move restlessly over whatever bit of my skin they could find, stroking and teasing. When he pulled away, he had decided to reciprocate, and he bent down. While his mouth closed over my breast, his hand glided between my legs. I gave a deep sigh, and did a little moving of my own. He had long fingers.

The next thing I knew, the water was off and he was drying me with a fluffy white towel, and I was rubbing him with another one. Then we just kissed for while, over and over.

'The bed,' he said, a little raggedly, and I nodded. He

scooped me up and then we got into a kind of tangle with me trying to pull the bedspread down while he just wanted to dump me on the bed and proceed, but I had my way because it was just too cold for the top of the bed. Once we were arranged, I turned to him and we picked back up where we'd left off, but with an escalating tempo. His fingers and his mouth were busy learning my topography, and he pressed heavily against my thigh.

I was so on fire for him I was surprised that flames didn't flicker out of my fingertips. I curled my fingers around him and stroked.

Suddenly Eric was on top of me, about to enter. I was exhilarated and very ready. I reached between us to put him at just the right spot, rubbing the tip of him over my nub as I did so.

'My lover,' he said hoarsely, and pushed.

Though I'd been sure I was prepared, and I ached with wanting him, I cried out with the shock of it.

After a moment, he said, 'Don't close your eyes. Look at me, lover.' The way he said 'lover' was like a caress, like he was calling me by a name no other man had ever used before or ever would after. His fangs were completely extended and I stretched up to run my tongue over them. I expected he would bite my neck, as Bill nearly always did.

'Watch me,' he said in my ear, and pulled out. I tried to yank him back, but he began kissing his way down my body, making strategic stops, and I was hovering on the golden edge when he got all the way down. His mouth was talented, and his fingers took the place of his penis, and then all of a sudden he looked up the length of my body to make sure I was watching – I was – and he turned his face to my inner thigh, nuzzling it, his fingers moving steadily now, faster and faster, and then he bit.

I may have made a noise, I am sure I did, but in the next second I was floating on the most powerful wave of pleasure I'd ever felt. And the minute the shining wave subsided, Eric was kissing my mouth again, and I could taste my own fluids on him, and then he was back inside me, and it happened all over again. His moment came right after, as I was still experiencing aftershocks. He shouted something in a language I'd never heard, and he closed his own eyes, and then he collapsed on top of me. After a couple of minutes, he raised his head to look down. I wished he would pretend to breathe, as Bill always had during sex. (I'd never asked him, he'd just done it, and it had been reassuring.) I pushed the thought away. I'd never had sex with anyone but Bill, and I guess it was natural to think of that, but the truth was it hurt to remember my previous one-man status, now gone for good.

I yanked myself back into The Moment, which was fine enough. I stroked Eric's hair, tucking some behind his ear. His eyes on mine were intent, and I knew he was waiting for me to speak. 'I wish,' I said, 'I could save orgasms in a jar for when I need them, because I think I had a few extra.'

Eric's eyes widened, and all of a sudden he roared with laughter. That sounded good, that sounded like the real Eric. I felt comfortable with this gorgeous but unknown stranger, after I heard that laugh. He rolled onto his back and swung me over easily until I was straddling his waist.

'If I had known you would be this gorgeous with your clothes off, I would have tried to do this sooner,' he said.

'You did try to do this sooner, about twenty times,' I said, smiling down at him.

'Then I have good taste.' He hesitated for a long minute, some of the pleasure leaving his face. 'Tell me about us. How long have I known you?'

The light from the bathroom spilled onto the right side of his face. His hair spread over my pillow, shining and golden.

'I'm cold,' I said gently, and he let me lie beside him, pulling the covers up over us. I propped myself up on one elbow and he lay on his side, so we were facing each other. 'Let me think. I met you last year at Fangtasia, the vampire bar you own in Shreveport. And by the way, the bar got attacked today. Last night. I'm sorry, I should have told you that first, but I've been so worried about my brother.'

'I want to hear about today, but give me our background first. I find myself mightily interested.'

Another little shock: The real Eric cared about his own position first, relationships down about – oh, I don't know, tenth. This was definitely odd. I told him, 'You are the sheriff of Area Five, and my former boyfriend Bill is your subordinate. He's gone, out of the country. I think I told you about Bill.'

'Your unfaithful former boyfriend? Whose maker was the vampire Lorena?'

'That's the one,' I said briefly. 'Anyway, when I met you at Fangtasia . . .'

It all took longer than I thought, and by the time I had finished with the tale, Eric's hands were busy again. He latched onto one breast with his fangs extended, drawing a little blood and a sharp gasp from me, and he sucked powerfully. It was a strange sensation, because he was getting the blood and my nipple. Painful and very exciting – I felt like he was drawing the fluid from much lower. I gasped and jerked in arousal, and suddenly he raised my leg so he could enter me.

It wasn't such a shock this time, and it was slower. Eric wanted me to be looking into his eyes; that obviously flicked his Bic.

I was exhausted when it was over, though I'd enjoyed myself immensely. I'd heard a lot about men who didn't care if the woman had her pleasure, or perhaps such men assumed that if they were happy, their partner was, too. But neither of the men I'd been with had been like that. I didn't know if that was because they were vampires, or because I'd been lucky, or both.

Eric had paid me many compliments, and I realized I hadn't said anything to him that indicated my admiration. That hardly seemed fair. He was holding me, and my head was on his shoulder. I murmured into his neck, 'You are so beautiful.'

'What?' He was clearly startled.

'You've told me you thought my body was nice.' Of course that wasn't the adjective he'd used, but I was embarrassed to repeat his actual words. 'I just wanted you to know I think the same about you.'

I could feel his chest move as he laughed, just a little. 'What part do you like best?' he asked, his voice teasing.

'Oh, your butt,' I said instantly.

'My . . . bottom?'

'Yep.'

'I would have thought of another part.'

'Well, that's certainly . . . adequate,' I told him, burying my face in his chest. I knew immediately I'd picked the wrong word.

'*Adequate?*' He took my hand, placed it on the part in

question. It immediately began to stir. He moved my hand on it, and I obligingly circled it with my fingers. 'This is *adequate*?'

'Maybe I should have said it's a gracious plenty?'

'A gracious plenty. I like that,' he said.

He was ready again, and honestly, I didn't know if I could. I was worn out to the point of wondering if I'd be walking funny the next day.

I indicated I would be pleased with an alternative by sliding down in the bed, and he seemed delighted to reciprocate. After another sublime release, I thought every muscle in my body had turned to Jell-O. I didn't talk anymore about the worry I felt about my brother, about the terrible things that had happened in Shreveport, about anything unpleasant. We whispered some heartfelt (on my part) mutual compliments, and I was just out of it. I don't know what Eric did for the rest of the night, because I fell asleep.

I had many worries waiting for me the next day; but thanks to Eric, for a few precious hours I just didn't care.

Chapter 7

The next morning the sun was shining outside when I woke. I lay in bed in a mindless pool of contentment. I was sore, but pleasantly so. I had a little bruise or two nothing that would show. And the fang marks that were a dead giveaway (har-de-har) were not on my neck, where they'd been in the past. No casual observer was going to be able to tell I'd enjoyed a vampire's company, and I didn't have an appointment with a gynecologist – the only other person who'd have a reason to check that area.

Another shower was definitely called for, so I eased out of bed and wobbled across the floor to the bathroom. We'd left it in something of a mess, with towels tossed everywhere and the shower curtain half-ripped from its plastic hoops (when had *that* happened?), but I didn't mind picking it up. I rehung the curtain with a smile on my face and a song in my heart.

As the water pounded on my back, I reflected that I must be pretty simple. It didn't take much to make me happy. A long night with a dead guy had done the trick. It wasn't just the dynamic sex that had given me so much pleasure (though that had contained moments I'd remember till the day I died); it was the companionship. Actually, the intimacy.

Call me stereotypical. I'd spent the night with a man who'd told me I was beautiful, a man who'd enjoyed me and who'd given me intense pleasure. He had touched me and held me and laughed with me. We weren't in danger of making a baby with our pleasures, because vampires just can't do that. I wasn't being disloyal to anyone (though I'll admit I'd had a few pangs when I thought of Bill), and neither was Eric. I couldn't see the harm.

As I brushed my teeth and put on some makeup, I had to admit to myself that I was sure that the Reverend Fullenwilder wouldn't agree with my viewpoint.

Well, I hadn't been going to tell him about it, anyway. It would just be between God and me. I figured God had made me with the disability of telepathy, and he could cut me a little slack on the sex thing.

I had regrets, of course. I would love to get married and have babies. I'd be faithful as can be. I'd be a good mom, too. But I couldn't marry a regular guy, because I would always know when he lied to me, when he was angry with me, every little thought he had about me. Even dating a regular guy was more than I'd been able to manage. Vampires can't marry, not yet, not legally; not that a vampire had asked me, I reminded myself, tossing a washcloth into the hamper a little forcefully. Perhaps I could stand a long association with a Were or a shifter, since their thoughts weren't clear. But there again, where was the willing Were?

I had better enjoy what I had at this moment —

something I've become quite good at doing. What I had was a handsome vampire who'd temporarily lost his memory and, along with it, a lot of his personality: a vampire who needed reassurance just as much as I did.

In fact, as I put in my earrings, I figured out that Eric had been so delighted with me for more than one reason. I could see that after days of being completely without memories of his possessions or underlings, days lacking any sense of self, last night he had gained something of his own – me. His lover.

Though I was standing in front of a mirror, I wasn't really seeing my reflection. I was seeing, very clearly, that – at the moment – I was all in the world that Eric could think of as his own.

I had better not fail him.

I was rapidly bringing myself down from 'relaxed happiness' to 'guilty grim resolution,' so I was relieved when the phone rang. It had a built-in caller ID, and I noticed Sam was calling from the bar, instead of his trailer.

'Sookie?'

'Hey, Sam.'

'I'm sorry about Jason. Any news?'

'No. I called down to the sheriff's department when I woke up, and I talked to the dispatcher. She said Alcee Beck would let me know if anything new came up. That's what she's said the last twenty times I've called.'

'Want me to get someone to take your shift?'

'No. It would be better for me to be busy, than to sit here at home. They know where to reach me if they've got anything to tell me.'

'You sure?'

'Yes. Thanks for asking, though.'

'If I can do anything to help, you let me know.'

'There is something, come to think of it.'

'Name it.'

'You remember the little shifter Jason was in the bar with New Year's Eve?'

Sam gave it thought. 'Yes,' he said hesitantly. 'One of the Norris girls? They live out in Hotshot.'

'That's what Hoyt said.'

'You have to watch out for people from out there, Sookie. That's an old settlement. An inbred settlement.'

I wasn't sure what Sam was trying to tell me. 'Could you spell that out? I'm not up to unraveling subtle hints today.'

'I can't right now.'

'Oh, not alone?'

'No. The snack delivery guy is here. Just be careful. They're really, really different.'

'Okay,' I said slowly, still in the dark. 'I'll be careful. See you at four-thirty,' I told him, and hung up, vaguely unhappy and quite puzzled.

I had plenty of time to go out to Hotshot and get back before I had to go to work. I pulled on some jeans, sneakers, a bright red long-sleeved T-shirt, and my old blue coat. I looked up Crystal Norris's address in the phone book and had to get out my chamber of commerce map to track it down. I've lived in Renard Parish my whole life, and I thought I knew it pretty well, but the Hotshot area was a black hole in my otherwise thorough knowledge.

I drove north, and when I came to the T-junction, I turned right. I passed the lumber processing plant that was Bon Temps's main employer, and I passed a reupholstering place, and I flew past the water department. There was a liquor store or two, and then a country store at a crossroads that had a prominent COLD BEER AND BAIT sign left over from the summer and propped up facing the road. I turned right again, to go south.

The deeper I went into the countryside, the worse the road seemed to grow. The mowing and maintenance crews hadn't been out here since the end of summer. Either the residents of the Hotshot community had no pull whatsoever in the parish government, or they just didn't want visitors. From time to time, the road dipped in some low-lying areas as it ran between bayous. In heavy rains, the low spots would be flooded. I wouldn't be surprised at all to hear folks out here encountered the occasional gator.

Finally I came to another crossroads, compared to which the one with the bait shop seemed like a mall. There were a few houses scattered around, maybe eight or nine. These were small houses, none of them brick. Most of them had several cars in the front yard. Some of them sported a rusty swing set or a basketball hoop, and in a couple of yards I spotted a satellite dish. Oddly, all the houses seemed pulled away from the actual crossroads; the area directly around the road intersection was bare. It was like someone had tied a rope to a stake sunk in the middle of the crossing and drawn a circle. Within it, there was nothing. Outside it, the houses crouched.

In my experience, in a little settlement like this, you had the same kind of people you had anywhere. Some of them were poor and proud and good. Some of them were poor and mean and worthless. But all of them knew each other thoroughly, and no action went unobserved.

On this chilly day, I didn't see a soul outdoors to let me know if this was a black community or a white community.

It was unlikely to be both. I wondered if I was at the right crossroads, but my doubts were washed away when I saw an imitation green road sign, the kind you can order from a novelty company, mounted on a pole in front of one of the homes. It read, HOTSHOT.

I was in the right place. Now, to find Crystal Norris's house.

With some difficulty, I spotted a number on one rusty mailbox, and then I saw another. By process of elimination, I figured the next house must be the one where Crystal Norris lived. The Norris house was little different from any of the others; it had a small front porch with an old armchair and two lawn chairs on it, and two cars parked in front, one a Ford Fiesta and the other an ancient Buick.

When I parked and got out, I realized what was so unusual about Hotshot.

No dogs.

Any other hamlet that looked like this would have at least twelve dogs milling around, and I'd be wondering if I could safely get out of the car. Here, not a single yip broke the winter silence.

I crossed over the hard, packed dirt of the yard, feeling as though eyes were on every step I took. I opened the torn screen door to knock on the heavier wooden door. Inset in it was a pattern of three glass panes. Dark eyes surveyed me through the lowest one.

The door opened, just when the pause was beginning to make me anxious.

Jason's date from New Year's Eve was less festive today, in black jeans and a cream-colored T-shirt. Her boots had come from Payless, and her short curly hair was a sort of dusty black. She was thin, intense, and though I'd carded her, she just didn't look twenty-one.

'Crystal Norris?'

'Yeah?' She didn't sound particularly unfriendly, but she did sound preoccupied.

'I'm Jason Stackhouse's sister, Sookie.'

'Oh, yeah? Come in.' She stood back, and I stepped into the tiny living room. It was crowded with furniture intended for a much larger space: two recliners and a three-cushion couch of dark brown Naugahyde, the big buttons separating the vinyl into little hillocks. You'd stick to it in the summer and slide around on it in the winter. Crumbs would collect in the depression around the buttons.

There was a stained rug in dark red and yellows and browns, and there were toys strewn in an almost solid layer over it. A picture of the Last Supper hung above the television set, and the whole house smelled pleasantly of red beans and rice and cornbread.

A toddler was experimenting with Duplos in the doorway to the kitchen. I thought it was a boy, but it was hard to be sure. Overalls and a green turtleneck weren't exactly a clue, and the baby's wispy brown hair was neither cut short nor decorated with a bow.

'Your child?' I asked, trying to make my voice pleasant and conversational.

'No, my sister's,' Crystal said. She gestured toward one of the recliners.

'Crystal, the reason I'm here . . . Did you know that Jason is missing?'

She was perched on the edge of the couch, and she'd been staring down at her thin hands. When I spoke, she looked into my eyes intently. This was not fresh news to her.

'Since when?' she asked. Her voice had a pleasantly hoarse sound to it; you'd listen to what this girl had to say, especially if you were a man.

'Since the night of January first. He left my house, and then the next morning he didn't show up for work. There was some blood on that little pier out behind the house. His pickup was still in his front yard. The door to it was hanging open.'

'I don't know nothing about it,' she said instantly.

She was lying.

'Who told you I had anything to do with this?' she asked, working up to being bitchy. 'I got rights. I don't have to talk to you.'

Sure, that was Amendment 29 to the Constitution: Shifters don't have to talk to Sookie Stackhouse.

'Yes, you do.' Suddenly, I abandoned the nice approach. She'd hit the wrong button on me. 'I'm not like you. I don't have a sister or a nephew,' and I nodded at the toddler, figuring I had a fifty-fifty chance of being right. 'I don't have a mom or a dad or anything, *anything*, except my brother.' I took a deep breath. 'I want to know where Jason is. And if you know anything, you better tell me.'

'Or you'll do what?' Her thin face was twisted into a snarl. But she genuinely wanted to know what kind of pull I had; I could read that much.

'Yeah, what?' asked a calmer voice.

I looked at the doorway to see a man who was probably on the upside of forty. He had a trimmed beard salted with gray, and his hair was cut close to his head. He was a small man, perhaps five foot seven or so, with a lithe build and muscular arms.

'Anything I have to,' I said. I looked him straight in the

eyes. They were a strange golden green. He didn't seem inimical, exactly. He seemed curious.

'Why are you here?' he asked, again in that neutral voice.

'Who are you?' I had to know who this guy was. I wasn't going to waste my time repeating my story to someone who just had some time to fill. Given his air of authority, and the fact that he wasn't opting for mindless belligerence, I was willing to bet this man was worth talking to.

'I'm Calvin Norris. I'm Crystal's uncle.' From his brain pattern, he was also a shifter of some kind. Given the absence of dogs in this settlement, I assumed they were Weres.

'Mr. Norris, I'm Sookie Stackhouse.' I wasn't imagining the increased interest in his expression. 'Your niece here went to the New Year's Eve party at Merlotte's Bar with my brother, Jason. Sometime the next night, my brother went missing. I want to know if Crystal can tell me anything that might help me find him.'

Calvin Norris bent to pat the toddler on the head, and then walked over to the couch where Crystal glowered. He sat beside her, his elbows resting on his knees, his hands dangling, relaxed, between them. His head inclined as he looked into Crystal's sullen face.

'This is reasonable, Crystal. Girl wants to know where her brother is. Tell her, if you know anything about it.'

Crystal snapped at him, 'Why should I tell her anything? She comes out here, tries to threaten me.'

'Because it's just common courtesy to help someone in trouble. You didn't exactly go to her to volunteer help, did you?'

'I didn't think he was just missing. I thought he—' And

her voice cut short as she realized her tongue had led her into trouble.

Calvin's whole body tensed. He hadn't expected that Crystal actually knew anything about Jason's disappearance. He had just wanted her to be polite to me. I could read that, but not much else. I could not decipher their relationship. He had power over the girl, I could tell that easily enough, but what kind? It was more than the authority of an uncle; it felt more like he was her ruler. He might be wearing old work clothes and safety boots, he might look like any blue-collar man in the area, but Calvin Norris was a lot more.

Packmaster, I thought. But who would be in a pack, this far out in the boondocks? Just Crystal? Then I remembered Sam's veiled warning about the unusual nature of Hotshot, and I had a revelation. *Everyone* in Hotshot was two-natured.

Was that possible? I wasn't completely certain Calvin Norris was a Were – but I knew he didn't change into any bunny. I had to struggle with an almost irresistible impulse to lean over and put my hand on his forearm, touch skin to skin to read his mind as clearly as possible.

I was completely certain about one thing: I wouldn't want to be anywhere around Hotshot on the three nights of the full moon.

'You're the barmaid at Merlotte's,' he said, looking into my eyes as intently as he'd looked into Crystal's.

'I'm *a* barmaid at Merlotte's.'

'You're a friend of Sam's.'

'Yes,' I said carefully. 'I am. I'm a friend of Alcide Herveaux's, too. And I know Colonel Flood.'

These names meant something to Calvin Norris. I wasn't

surprised that Norris would know the names of some prominent Shreveport Weres – and he'd know Sam, of course. It had taken my boss time to connect with the local two-natured community, but he'd been working on it.

Crystal had been listening with wide dark eyes, in no better mood than she had been before. A girl wearing overalls appeared from the back of the house, and she lifted the toddler from his nest of Duplos. Though her face was rounder and less distinctive and her figure was fuller, she was clearly Crystal's younger sister. She was also just as apparently pregnant again.

'You need anything, Uncle Calvin?' she asked, staring at me over the toddler's shoulder.

'No, Dawn. Take care of Matthew.' She disappeared into the back of the house with her burden. I had guessed right on the sex of the kid.

'Crystal,' said Calvin Norris, in a quiet and terrifying voice, 'you tell us now what you done.'

Crystal had believed she'd gotten away with something, and she was shocked at being ordered to confess.

But she'd obey. After a little fidgeting, she did.

'I was out with Jason on New Year's Eve,' she said. 'I'd met him at Wal-Mart in Bon Temps, when I went in to get me a purse.'

I sighed. Jason could find potential bedmates anywhere. He was going to end up with some unpleasant disease (if he hadn't already) or slapped with a paternity suit, and there was nothing I could do about it except watch it happen.

'He asked me if I'd spend New Year's Eve with him. I had the feeling the woman he'd had a date with had changed her mind, 'cause he's not the kind of guy to go without lining up a date for something big like that.'

I shrugged. Jason could have made and broken dates with five women for New Year's Eve, for all I knew. And it wasn't infrequent for women to get so exasperated by his earnest pursuit of anything with a vagina that they broke off plans with him.

'He's a cute guy, and I like to get out of Hotshot, so I said yeah. He asked me if he could come pick me up, but I knew some of my neighbors wouldn't like that, so I said I'd just meet him at the Fina station, and then we'd go in his truck. So that's what we did. And I had a real good time with him, went home with him, had a good night.' Her eyes gleamed at me. 'You want to know how he is in bed?'

There was a blur of movement, and then there was blood at the corner of her mouth. Calvin's hand was back dangling between his legs before I even realized he'd moved. 'You be polite. Don't show your worst face to this woman,' he said, and his voice was so serious I made up my mind I'd be extra polite, too, just to be safe.

'Okay. That wasn't nice, I guess,' she admitted, in a softer and chastened voice. 'Well, I wanted to see him the night after, too, and he wanted to see me again. So I snuck out and went over to his place. He had to leave to see his sister – you? You're the only sister he's got?'

I nodded.

'And he said to stay there, he'd be back in a bit. I wanted to go with him, and he said if his sister didn't have company, that woulda been fine, but she had vamp company, and he didn't want me to mix with them.'

I think Jason knew what my opinion of Crystal Norris would be, and he wanted to dodge hearing it, so he left her at his house.

'Did he come back home?' Calvin said, nudging her out of her reverie.

'Yes,' she said, and I tensed.

'What happened then?' Calvin asked, when she stopped again.

'I'm not real sure,' she said. 'I was in the house, waiting for him, and I heard his truck pull up, and I'm thinking, "Oh, good, he's here, we can party," and then I didn't hear him come up the front steps, and I'm wondering what's happening, you know? Of course all the outside lights are on, but I didn't go to the window, 'cause I knew it was him.' Of course a Were would know his step, maybe catch his smell. 'I'm listening real good,' she went on, 'and I hear him going around the outside of the house, so I'm thinking he's going to come in the back door, for some reason – muddy boots, or something.'

I took a deep breath. She'd get to the point in just a minute. I just knew she would.

'And then, to the back of the house, and farther 'way, yards away from the porch, I hear a lot of noise, and some shouting and stuff, and then nothing.'

If she hadn't been a shifter, she wouldn't have heard so much. There, I knew I'd think of a bright side if I searched hard enough.

'Did you go out and look?' Calvin asked Crystal. His worn hand stroked her black curls, as if he were petting a favorite dog.

'No sir, I didn't look.'

'Smell?'

'I didn't get close enough,' she admitted, just on the good side of sullen. 'The wind was blowing the other way.

I caught a little of Jason, and blood. Maybe a couple of other things.'

'Like what?'

Crystal looked at her own hands. 'Shifter, maybe. Some of us can change when it's not the full moon, but I can't. Otherwise, I'd have had a better chance at the scent,' she said to me in near-apology.

'Vampire?' Calvin asked.

'I never smelled a vampire before,' she said simply. 'I don't know.'

'Witch?' I asked.

'Do they smell any different from regular people?' she asked doubtfully.

I shrugged. I didn't know.

Calvin said, 'What did you do after that?'

'I knew something had carried Jason off into the woods. I just . . . I lost it. I'm not brave.' She shrugged. 'I came home after that. Nothing more I could do.'

I was trying not to cry, but tears just rolled down my cheeks. For the first time, I admitted to myself that I wasn't sure I'd ever see my brother again. But if the attacker's intention was to kill Jason, why not just leave his body in the backyard? As Crystal had pointed out, the night of New Year's Day there hadn't been a full moon. There were things that didn't have to wait for the full moon . . .

The bad thing about learning about all the creatures that existed in the world besides us is that I could imagine that there were things that might swallow Jason in one gulp. Or a few bites.

But I just couldn't let myself think about that. Though I was still weeping, I made an effort to smile. 'Thank you so much,' I said politely. 'It was real nice of you to take the time to see me. I know you have things you need to do.'

Crystal looked suspicious, but her uncle Calvin reached over and patted my hand, which seemed to surprise everyone, himself included.

He walked me out to my car. The sky was clouding over, which made it feel colder, and the wind began to toss the bare branches of the large bushes planted around the yard. I recognized yellow bells (which the nursery calls forsythia), and spirea, and even a tulip tree. Around them would be planted jonquil bulbs, and iris – the same flowers that are in my grandmother's yard, the same bushes that have grown in southern yards for generations. Right now everything looked bleak and sordid. In the spring, it would seem almost charming, picturesque; the decay of poverty gilded by Mother Nature.

Two or three houses down the road, a man emerged from a shed behind his house, glanced our way, and did a double take. After a long moment, he loped back into his house. It was too far away to make out more of his features than thick pale hair, but his grace was phenomenal. The people out here more than disliked strangers; they seemed to be allergic to them.

'That's my house over there,' Calvin offered, pointing to a much more substantial home, small but foursquare, painted white quite recently. Everything was in good repair at Calvin Norris's house. The driveway and parking area were clearly defined; the matching white toolshed stood rust-free on a neat concrete slab.

I nodded. 'It looks real nice,' I said in a voice that wasn't too wobbly.

'I want to make you an offer,' Calvin Norris said.

I tried to look interested. I half turned to face him.

'You're a woman without protection now,' he said. 'Your brother's gone. I hope he comes back, but you don't have no one to stand up for you while he's missing.'

There were a lot of things wrong with this speech, but I wasn't in any mood to debate the shifter. He'd done me a large favor, getting Crystal to talk. I stood there in the cold wind and tried to look politely receptive.

'If you need some place to hide, if you need someone to watch your back or defend you, I'll be your man,' he said. His green and golden eyes met mine directly.

I'll tell you why I didn't dismiss this with a snort: He wasn't being superior about it. According to his mores, he was being as nice as he could be, extending a shield to me if I should need it. Of course he expected to 'be my man' in every way, along with protecting me; but he wasn't being lascivious in his manner, or offensively explicit. Calvin Norris was offering to incur injury for my sake. He meant it. That's not something to get all snitty about.

'Thanks,' I said. 'I'll remember you said that.'

'I heard about you,' he said. 'Shifters and Weres, they talk to each other. I hear you're different.'

'I am.' Regular men might have found my outer package attractive, but my inner package repelled them. If I ever began to get a swelled head, after the attention paid me by Eric, or Bill, or even Alcide, all I had to do was listen to the brains of some bar patrons to have my ego deflated. I clutched my old blue coat more closely around me. Like most of the two-natured, Calvin had a system that didn't feel cold as intensely as my completely human metabolism did. 'But my difference doesn't lie in being two-natured, though I appreciate your, ah, kindness.' This was as close as I could come to asking him why he was so interested.

'I know that.' He nodded in acknowledgment of my delicacy. 'Actually, that makes you more . . . The thing is, here in Hotshot, we've inbred too much. You heard Crystal. She can only change at the moon, and frankly, even then she's not full-powered.' He pointed at his own face. 'My eyes can hardly pass for human. We need an infusion of new blood, new genes. You're not two-natured, but you're not exactly an ordinary woman. Ordinary women don't last long here.'

Well, that was an ominous and ambiguous way to put it. But I was sympathetic, and I tried to look understanding. Actually, I did understand, and I could appreciate his concern. Calvin Norris was clearly the leader of this unusual settlement, and its future was his responsibility.

He was frowning as he looked down the road at the house where I'd seen the man. But he turned to me to finish telling me what he wanted me to know. 'I think you would like the people here, and you would be a good breeder. I can tell by looking.'

That was a real unusual compliment. I couldn't quite think how to acknowledge it in an appropriate manner.

'I'm flattered that you think so, and I appreciate your offer. I'll remember what you said.' I paused to gather my thoughts. 'You know, the police will find out that Crystal was with Jason, if they haven't already. They'll come out here, too.'

'They won't find nothing,' Calvin Norris said. His golden green eyes met mine with faint amusement. 'They've been out here at other times; they'll be out here again. They never learn a thing. I hope you find your brother. You need help, you let me know. I got a job at Norcross. I'm a steady man.'

'Thank you,' I said, and got into my car with a feeling of relief. I gave Calvin a serious nod as I backed out of Crystal's driveway. So he worked at Norcross, the lumber processing plant. Norcross had good benefits, and they promoted from within. I'd had worse offers; that was for sure.

As I drove to work, I wondered if Crystal had been trying to get pregnant during her nights with Jason. It hadn't seemed to bother Calvin at all to hear that his niece had had sex with a strange man. Alcide had told me that Were had to breed with Were to produce a baby that had the same trait, so the inhabitants of this little community were trying to diversify, apparently. Maybe these lesser Weres were trying to breed out; that is, have children by regular humans. That would be better than having a generation of Weres whose powers were so weak they couldn't function successfully in their second nature, but who also couldn't be content as regular people.

Getting to Merlotte's was like driving from one century into another. I wondered how long the people of Hotshot had been clustered around the crossroads, what significance it had originally held for them. Though I couldn't help but be a little curious, I found it was a real relief to discard these wonderings and return to the world as I knew it.

That afternoon, the little world of Merlotte's Bar was very quiet. I changed, tied on my black apron, smoothed my hair, and washed my hands. Sam was behind the bar with his arms crossed over his chest, staring into space. Holly was carrying a pitcher of beer to a table where a lone stranger sat.

'How was Hotshot?' Sam asked, since we were alone at the bar.

'Very strange.'

He patted me on the shoulder. 'Did you find out anything useful?'

'Actually, I did. I'm just not sure what it means.' Sam needed a haircut, I noticed; his curly red-gold hair formed an arc around his face in a kind of Renaissance-angel effect.

'Did you meet Calvin Norris?'

'I did. He got Crystal to talk to me, and he made me a most unusual offer.'

'What's that?'

'I'll tell you some other time.' For the life of me, I couldn't figure out how to phrase it. I looked down at my hands, which were busy rinsing out a beer mug, and I could feel my cheeks burning.

'Calvin's an okay guy, as far as I know,' Sam said slowly. 'He works at Norcross, and he's a crew leader. Good insurance, retirement package, everything. Some of the other guys from Hotshot own a welding shop. I hear they do good work. But I don't know what goes on in Hotshot after they go home at night, and I don't think anyone else does, either. Did you know Sheriff Dowdy, John Dowdy? He was sheriff before I moved here, I think.'

'Yeah, I remember him. He hauled Jason in one time for vandalism. Gran had to go get him out of jail. Sheriff Dowdy read Jason a lecture that had him scared straight, at least for a while.'

'Sid Matt told me a story one night. It seems that one spring, John Dowdy went out to Hotshot to arrest Calvin Norris's oldest brother, Carlton.'

'For what?' Sid Matt Lancaster was an old and well-known lawyer.

'Statutory rape. The girl was willing, and she was even experienced, but she was underage. She had a new stepdad, and he decided Carlton had disrespected him.'

No politically correct stance could cover all those circumstances. 'So what happened?'

'No one knows. Late that night, John Dowdy's patrol car was found halfway back into town from Hotshot. No one in it. No blood, no fingerprints. He hasn't ever been seen since. No one in Hotshot remembered seeing him that day, they said.'

'Like Jason,' I said bleakly. 'He just vanished.'

'But Jason was at his own house, and according to you, Crystal didn't seem to be involved.'

I threw off the grip of the strange little story. 'You're right. Did anyone ever find out what happened to Sheriff Dowdy?'

'No. But no one ever saw Carlton Norris again, either.'

Now, that was the interesting part. 'And the moral of this story is?'

'That the people of Hotshot take care of their own justice.'

'Then you want them on your side.' I extracted my own moral from the story.

'Yes,' Sam said. 'You definitely want them on your side. You don't remember this? It was around fifteen years ago.'

'I was coping with my own troubles then,' I explained. I'd been an orphaned nine-year-old, coping with my growing telepathic powers.

Shortly after that, people began to stop by the bar on their way home from work. Sam and I didn't get a chance to talk the rest of the evening, which was fine with me. I was very fond of Sam, who'd often had a starring role in some of my most private fantasies, but at this point, I had so much to worry about I just couldn't take on any more.

That night, I discovered that some people thought Jason's disappearance improved Bon Temps society. Among these were Andy Bellefleur and his sister, Portia, who stopped by Merlotte's for supper, since their grandmother Caroline was having a dinner party and they were staying out of the way. Andy was a police detective and Portia was a lawyer, and they were both not on my list of favorite people. For one thing (a kind of sour-grapey thing), when Bill had found out they were his descendants, he'd made an elaborate plan to give the Bellefleurs money anonymously, and they'd really enjoyed their mysterious legacy to the hilt. But they couldn't stand Bill himself, and it made me constantly irritated to see their new cars and expensive clothes and the new roof on the Bellefleur mansion, when they dissed Bill all the time – and me, too, for being Bill's girlfriend.

Andy had been pretty nice to me before I started dating Bill. At least he'd been civil and left a decent tip. I'd just been invisible to Portia, who had her own share of personal woes. She'd come up with a suitor, I'd heard, and I wondered maliciously if that might not be due to the sudden upsurge in the Bellefleur family fortunes. I also wondered, at times, if Andy and Portia got happy in direct proportion to my misery. They were in fine fettle this winter evening, both tucking into their hamburgers with great zest.

'Sorry about your brother, Sookie,' Andy said, as I refilled his tea glass.

I looked down at him, my face expressionless. *Liar*, I

thought. After a second, Andy's eyes darted uneasily away from mine to light on the saltshaker, which seemed to have become peculiarly fascinating.

'Have you seen Bill lately?' Portia asked, patting her mouth with a napkin. She was trying to break the uneasy silence with a pleasant query, but I just got angrier.

'No,' I said. 'Can I get you all anything else?'

'No, thanks, we're just fine,' she said quickly. I spun on my heel and walked away. Then my mouth puckered in a smile. Just as I was thinking, *Bitch*, Portia was thinking, *What a bitch.*

Her ass is hot, Andy chimed in. Gosh, telepathy. What a blast. I wouldn't wish it on my worst enemy. I envied people who only heard with their ears.

Kevin and Kenya came in, too, very carefully not drinking. Theirs was a partnership that had given the people of Bon Temps much hilarity. Lily white Kevin was thin and reedy, a long-distance runner; all the equipment he had to wear on his uniform belt seemed almost too much for him to carry. His partner, Kenya, was two inches taller, pounds heavier, and fifteen shades darker. The men at the bar had been putting bets down for two years on whether or not they'd become lovers – of course, the guys at the bar didn't put it as nicely as that.

I was unwillingly aware that Kenya (and her handcuffs and nightstick) featured in all too many patrons' daydreams, and I also knew that the men who teased and derided Kevin the most mercilessly were the ones who had the most lurid fantasies. As I carried hamburger baskets over to Kevin and Kenya's table, I could tell that Kenya was wondering whether she should suggest to Bud Dearborn that he call in the tracking dogs from a neighboring parish in the search for Jason, while Kevin was worried about his mother's heart, which had been acting up more than usual lately.

'Sookie,' Kevin said, after I'd brought them a bottle of ketchup, 'I meant to tell you, some people came by the police department today putting out posters about a vampire.'

'I saw one at the grocery,' I said.

'I realize that just because you were dating a vampire, you aren't an expert,' Kevin said carefully, because Kevin always did his best to be nice to me, 'but I wondered if you'd seen this vamp. Before he disappeared, I mean.'

Kenya was looking up at me, too, her dark eyes examining me with great interest. Kenya was thinking I always seemed to be on the fringes of bad things that happened in Bon Temps, without being bad myself (thanks, Kenya). She was hoping for my sake that Jason was alive. Kevin was thinking I'd always been nice to him and Kenya; and he was thinking he wouldn't touch me with a ten-foot pole. I sighed, I hoped imperceptibly. They were waiting for an answer. I hesitated, wondering what my best choice was. The truth is always easiest to remember.

'Sure, I've seen him before. Eric owns the vampire bar in Shreveport,' I said. 'I saw him when I went there with Bill.'

'You haven't seen him recently?'

'I sure didn't abduct him from Fangtasia,' I said, with quite a lot of sarcasm in my voice.

Kenya gave me a sour look, and I didn't blame her. 'No one said you did,' she told me, in a 'Don't give me any trouble' kind of voice. I shrugged and drifted away.

I had plenty to do, since some people were still eating supper (and some were drinking it), and some regulars were drifting in after eating at home. Holly was equally busy, and when one of the men who worked for the phone company spilled his beer on the floor, she had to go get the mop and bucket. She was running behind on her tables when the door opened. I saw her putting Sid Matt Lancaster's order in front of him, with her back to the door. So she missed the next entrance, but I didn't. The young man Sam had hired to bus the tables during our busy hour was occupied with clearing two tables pulled together that had held a large party of parish workers, and so I was clearing off the Bellefleurs' table. Andy was chatting with Sam while he waited for Portia, who'd visited the ladies' room. I'd just pocketed my tip, which was fifteen percent of the bill to the penny. The Bellefleur tipping habits had improved – slightly – with the Bellefleur fortunes. I glanced up when the door was held open long enough for a cold gust of air to chill me.

The woman coming in was tall and so slim and broad-shouldered that I checked her chest, just to be sure I'd registered her gender correctly. Her hair was short and thick and brown, and she was wearing absolutely no makeup. There was a man with her, but I didn't see him until she stepped to one side. He was no slouch in the size department himself, and his tight T-shirt revealed arms more developed than any I'd ever seen. Hours in the gym; no, years in the gym. His chestnut hair trailed down to his shoulders in tight curls, and his beard and mustache were perceptibly redder. Neither of the two wore coats, though it was definitely coat weather. The newcomers walked over to me.

'Where's the owner?' the woman asked.

'Sam. He's behind the bar,' I said, looking down as soon

as I could and wiping the table all over again. The man had looked at me curiously; that was normal. As they brushed past me, I saw that he carried some posters under his arm and a staple gun. He'd stuck his hand through a roll of masking tape, so it bounced on his left wrist.

I glanced over at Holly. She'd frozen, the cup of coffee in her hand halfway down on its way to Sid Matt Lancaster's placemat. The old lawyer looked up at her, followed her stare to the couple making their way between the tables to the bar. Merlotte's, which had been on the quiet and peaceful side, was suddenly awash in tension. Holly set down the cup without burning Mr. Lancaster and spun on her heel, going through the swinging door to the kitchen at warp speed.

I didn't need any more confirmation on the identity of the woman.

The two reached Sam and began a low-voiced conversation with him, with Andy listening in just because he was in the vicinity. I passed by on my way to take the dirty dishes to the hatch, and I heard the woman say (in a deep, alto voice) '. . . put up these posters in town, just in case anyone spots him.'

This was Hallow, the witch whose pursuit of Eric had caused such an upset. She, or a member of her coven, was probably the murderer of Adabelle Yancy. This was the woman who might have taken my brother, Jason. My head began pounding as if there were a little demon inside trying to break out with a hammer.

No wonder Holly was in such a state and didn't want Hallow to glimpse her. She'd been to Hallow's little meeting in Shreveport, and her coven had rejected Hallow's invitation.

'Of course,' Sam said. 'Put up one on this wall.' He indicated a blank spot by the door that led back to the bathrooms and his office.

Holly stuck her head out the kitchen door, glimpsed Hallow, ducked back in. Hallow's eyes flicked over to the door, but not in time to glimpse Holly, I hoped.

I thought of jumping Hallow, beating on her until she told me what I wanted to know about my brother. That was what the pounding in my head was urging me to do – initiate action, any action. But I had a streak of common sense, and luckily for me it came to the fore. Hallow was big, and she had a sidekick who could crush me – plus, Kevin and Kenya would make me stop before I could get her to talk.

It was horribly frustrating to have her right in front of me and at the same time be unable to discover what she knew. I dropped all my shields, and I listened in as hard as I could.

But she suspected something when I touched inside her head.

She looked vaguely puzzled and glanced around. That was enough warning for me. I scrambled back into my own head as quickly as I could. I continued back behind the bar, passing within a couple of feet of the witch as she tried to figure out who'd brushed at her brain.

This had never happened to me before. No one, *no one*, had ever suspected I was listening in. I squatted behind the bar to get the big container of Morton Salt, straightened, and carefully refilled the shaker I'd snatched from Kevin and Kenya's table. I concentrated on this as hard as anyone can focus on performing such a nothing little task, and when I was through, the poster had been mounted with the staple gun. Hallow was lingering, prolonging her talk with Sam so she could figure out who had touched the inside of her head, and Mr. Muscles was eyeing me — but only like a man looks at a woman — as I returned the shaker to its table. Holly hadn't reappeared.

'Sookie,' Sam called.

Oh, for goodness sake. I had to respond. He was my boss.

I went over to the three of them, dread in my heart and a smile on my face.

'Hey,' I said, by way of greeting, giving the tall witch and her stalwart sidekick a neutral smile. I raised my eyebrows at Sam to ask him what he'd wanted.

'Marnie Stonebrook, Mark Stonebrook,' he said.

I nodded to each of them. *Hallow, indeed*, I thought, half-amused. 'Hallow' was just a tad more spiritual than 'Marnie.'

'They're looking for this guy,' Sam said, indicating the poster. 'You know him?'

Of course Sam knew that I knew Eric. I was glad I'd had years of concealing my feelings and thoughts from the eyes of others. I looked the poster over deliberately.

'Sure, I've seen him,' I said. 'When I went to that bar in Shreveport? He's kind of unforgettable, isn't he?' I gave Hallow — Marnie — a smile. We were just gals together, Marnie and Sookie, sharing a gal moment.

'Handsome guy,' she agreed in her throaty voice. 'He's missing now, and we're offering a reward for anyone who can give us information.'

'I see that from the poster,' I said, letting a tiny hint of irritation show in my voice. 'Is there any particular reason you think he might be around here? I can't imagine what a Shreveport vampire would be doing in Bon Temps.' I looked at her questioningly. Surely I wasn't out of line in asking that?

'Good question, Sookie,' Sam said. 'Not that I mind having the poster up, but how come you two are searching this area for the guy? Why would he be here? Nothing happens in Bon Temps.'

'This town has a vampire in residence, doesn't it?' Mark Stonebrook said suddenly. His voice was almost a twin of his sister's. He was so buff you expected to hear a bass, and even an alto as deep as Marnie's sounded strange coming from his throat. Actually, from Mark Stonebrook's appearance, you'd think he'd just grunt and growl to communicate.

'Yeah, Bill Compton lives here,' Sam said. 'But he's out of town.'

'Gone to Peru, I heard,' I said.

'Oh, yes, I'd heard of Bill Compton. Where does he live?' Hallow asked, trying to keep the excitement out of her voice.

'Well, he lives out across the cemetery from my place,' I said, because I had no choice. If the two asked someone else and got a different answer than the one I gave them, they'd know I had something (or in this case, someone) to conceal. 'Out off Hummingbird Road.' I gave them directions, not very clear directions, and hoped they got lost out in somewhere like Hotshot.

'Well, we might drop by Compton's house, just in case Eric went to visit him,' Hallow said. Her eyes cut to her brother Mark, and they nodded at us and left the bar. They didn't care whether this made sense or not.

'They're sending witches to visit all the vamps,' Sam said softly. Of course. The Stonebrooks were going to the residences of all vampires who owed allegiance to Eric – the vamps of Area Five. They suspected that one of these vamps might be hiding Eric. Since Eric hadn't turned up, he was being hidden. Hallow had to be confident that her spell had worked, but she might not know exactly how it had worked.

I let the smile fade off my face, and I leaned against the bar on my elbows, trying to think real hard.

Sam said, 'This is big trouble, right?' His face was serious.

'Yes, this is big trouble.'

'Do you need to leave? There's not too much happening here. Holly can come out of the kitchen now that they're gone, and I can always see to the tables myself, if you need to get home . . .' Sam wasn't sure where Eric was, but he suspected, and he'd noticed Holly's abrupt bolt into the kitchen.

Sam had earned my loyalty and respect a hundred times over.

'I'll give them five minutes to get out of the parking lot.'

'Do you think they might have something to do with Jason's disappearance?'

'Sam, I just don't know.' I automatically dialed the sheriff's department and got the same answer I'd gotten all day – 'No news, we'll call you when we know something.' But after she said that, the dispatcher told me that the pond was going to be searched the next day; the police had managed to get hold of two search-and-rescue divers. I didn't know how to feel about this information. Mostly, I was relieved that Jason's disappearance was being taken seriously.

When I hung up the phone, I told Sam the news. After a second, I said, 'It seems too much to believe that two men could disappear in the Bon Temps area at the same time. At least, the Stonebrooks seem to think Eric's around here. I have to think that there's a connection.'

'Those Stonebrooks are Weres,' Sam muttered.

'*And* witches. You be careful, Sam. She's a killer. The Weres of Shreveport are out after her, and the vamps, too. Watch your step.'

'Why is she so scary? Why would the Shreveport pack have any trouble handling her?'

'She's drinking vampire blood,' I said, as close to his ear as I could get without kissing him. I glanced around the room, to see that Kevin was watching our exchange with a lot of interest.

'What does she want with Eric?'

'His business. All his businesses. And him.'

Sam's eyes widened. 'So it's business, and personal.'

'Yep.'

'Do you know where Eric is?' He'd avoided asking me directly until now.

I smiled at him. 'Why would I know that? But I confess, I'm worried about those two being right down the road from my house. I have a feeling they're going to break into Bill's place. They might figure Eric's hiding with Bill, or in Bill's house. I'm sure he's got a safe hole for Eric to sleep in and blood on hand.' That was pretty much all a vampire required, blood and a dark place.

'So you're going over to guard Bill's property? Not a good idea, Sookie. Let Bill's homeowners insurance take care of whatever damage they do searching. I think he told me he went with State Farm. Bill wouldn't want you hurt in defense of plants and bricks.'

'I don't plan on doing anything that dangerous,' I said,

and truly, I didn't plan it. 'But I do think I'll run home. Just in case. When I see their car lights leaving Bill's house, I'll go over and check it out.'

'You need me to come with you?'

'Nah, I'm just going to do damage assessment, that's all. Holly'll be enough help here?' She'd popped out of the kitchen the minute the Stonebrooks had left.

'Sure.'

'Okay, I'm gone. Thanks so much.' My conscience didn't twinge as much when I noticed that the place wasn't nearly as busy as it'd been an hour ago. You got nights like that, when people just cleared out all of a sudden.

I had an itchy feeling between my shoulder blades, and maybe all our patrons had, too. It was that feeling that something was prowling that shouldn't be: that Halloween feeling, I call it, when you kind of picture something bad is easing around the corner of your house, to peer into your windows.

By the time I grabbed my purse, unlocked my car, and drove back to my house, I was almost twitching from uneasiness. Everything was going to hell in a handbasket, seemed to me. Jason was missing, the witch was here instead of Shreveport, and now she was within a half mile of Eric.

As I turned from the parish road onto my long, meandering driveway and braked for the deer crossing it from the woods on the south side to the woods on the north – moving away from Bill's house, I noticed – I had worked myself into a state. Pulling around to the back door, I leaped from the car and bounded up the back steps.

I was caught in midbound by a pair of arms like steel bands. Lifted and whirled, I was wrapped around Eric's waist before I knew it.

'Eric,' I said, 'you shouldn't be out—'

My words were cut off by his mouth over mine.

For a minute, going along with this program seemed like a viable alternative. I'd just forget all the badness and screw his brains out on my back porch, cold as it was. But sanity seeped back in past my overloaded emotional state, and I pulled a little away. He was wearing the jeans and Louisiana Tech Bulldogs sweatshirt Jason had bought for him at Wal-Mart. Eric's big hands supported my bottom, and my legs circled him as if they were used to it.

'Listen, Eric,' I said, when his mouth moved down to my neck.

'Ssshh,' he whispered.

'No, you have to let me speak. We have to hide.'

That got his attention. 'From whom?' he said into my ear, and I shivered. The shiver was unrelated to the temperature.

'The bad witch, the one that's after you,' I scrambled to explain. 'She came into the bar with her brother and they put up that poster.'

'So?' His voice was careless.

'They asked what other vampires lived locally, and of course we had to say Bill did. So they asked for directions to Bill's house, and I guess they're over there looking for you.'

'And?'

'That's right across the cemetery from here! What if they come over here?'

'You advise me to hide? To get back in that black hole below your house?' He sounded uncertain, but it was clear to me his pride was piqued.

'Oh, yes. Just for a little while! You're my responsibility; I have to keep you safe.' But I had a sinking feeling I'd expressed my fears in the wrong way. This tentative stranger, however uninterested he seemed in vampire concerns, however little he seemed to remember of his power and possessions, still had the vein of pride and curiosity Eric had always shown at the oddest moments. I'd tapped right into it. I wondered if maybe I could talk him into at least getting into my house, rather than standing out on the porch, exposed.

But it was too late. You just never could tell Eric anything.

Chapter 8

'Come on, lover, let's have a look,' Eric said, giving me a quick kiss. He jumped off the back porch with me still attached to him – like a large barnacle – and he landed silently, which seemed amazing. I was the noisy one, with my breathing and little sounds of surprise. With a dexterity that argued long practice, Eric slung me around so that I was riding his back. I hadn't done this since I was a child and my father had carried me piggyback, so I was considerably startled.

Oh, I was doing one great job of hiding Eric. Here we were, bounding through the cemetery, going *toward* the Wicked Witch of the West, instead of hiding in a dark hole where she couldn't find us. This was *so* smart.

At the same time, I had to admit that I was kind of having fun, despite the difficulties of keeping a grip on Eric in this gently rolling country. The graveyard was somewhat downhill from my house. Bill's house, the Compton house, was quite a bit more uphill from Sweet Home Cemetery. The journey downhill, mild as the slope was, was exhilarating, though I glimpsed two or three parked cars on the narrow blacktop that wound through the graves. That startled me. Teenagers sometimes chose the cemetery for privacy, but not in groups. But before I could think it through, we had passed them, swiftly and silently. Eric managed the uphill portion more slowly, but with no evidence of exhaustion.

We were next to a tree when Eric stopped. It was a huge oak, and when I touched it I became more or less oriented. There was an oak this size maybe twenty yards to the north of Bill's house.

Eric loosened my hands so I'd slide down his back, and then he put me between him and the tree trunk. I didn't know if he was trying to trap me or protect me. I gripped both his wrists in a fairly futile attempt to keep him beside me. I froze when I heard a voice drifting over from Bill's house.

'This car hasn't moved in a while,' a woman said. Hallow. She was in Bill's carport, which was on this side of the house. She was close. I could feel Eric's body stiffen. Did the sound of her voice evoke an echo in his memory?

'The house is locked up tight,' called Mark Stonebrook, from farther away.

'Well, we can take care of that.' From the sound of her voice, she was on the move to the front door. She sounded amused.

They were going to break into Bill's house! Surely I should prevent that? I must have made some sudden move, because Eric's body flattened mine against the trunk of the tree. My coat was worked up around my waist, and the bark bit into my butt through the thin material of my black pants.

I could hear Hallow. She was chanting, her voice low and

somehow ominous. She was actually casting a spell. That should have been exciting and I should have been curious: a real magic spell, cast by a real witch. But I felt scared, anxious to get away. The darkness seemed to thicken.

'I smell someone,' Mark Stonebrook said.

Fee, fie, foe, fum.

'What? Here and now?' Hallow stopped her chant, sounding a little breathless.

I began to tremble.

'Yeah.' His voice came out deeper, almost a growl.

'Change,' she ordered, just like that. I heard a sound I knew I'd heard before, though I couldn't trace the memory. It was a sort of gloppy sound. Sticky. Like stirring a stiff spoon through some thick liquid that had hard things in it, maybe peanuts or toffee bits. Or bone chips.

Then I heard a real howl. It wasn't human at all. Mark had changed, and it wasn't the full moon. This was real power. The night suddenly seemed full of life. Snuffling. Yipping. Tiny movements all around us.

I was some great guardian for Eric, huh? I'd let him sweep me over here. We were about to be discovered by a vampire-blood drinking Were witch, and who knows what all else, and I didn't even have Jason's shotgun. I put my arms around Eric and hugged him in apology.

'Sorry,' I whispered, as tiny as a bee would whisper. But then I felt something brush against us, something large and furry, while I was hearing Mark's wolfy sounds from a few feet away on the other side of the tree. I bit my lip hard to keep from giving a yip myself.

Listening intently, I became sure there were more than two animals. I would have given almost anything for a floodlight. From maybe ten yards away came a short, sharp bark. Another wolf? A plain old dog, in the wrong place at the wrong time?

Suddenly, Eric left me. One minute, he was pressing me against the tree in the pitch-black dark, and the next minute, cold air hit me from top to bottom (so much for my holding on to his wrists). I flung my arms out, trying to discover where he was, and touched only air. Had he just stepped away so he could investigate what was happening? Had he decided to join in?

Though my hands didn't encounter any vampires, something big and warm pressed against my legs. I used my fingers to better purpose by reaching down to explore the animal. I touched lots of fur: a pair of upright ears, a long muzzle, a warm tongue. I tried to move, to step away from the oak, but the dog (wolf?) wouldn't let me. Though it was smaller than I and weighed less, it leaned against me with such pressure that there was no way I could move. When I listened to what was going on in the darkness – a lot of growling and snarling – I decided I was actually pretty glad about that. I sank to my knees and put one arm across the canine's back. It licked my face.

I heard a chorus of howls, which rose eerily into the cold night. The hair on my neck stood up, and I buried my face in the neck fur of my companion and prayed. Suddenly, over all the lesser noises, there was a howl of pain and a series of yips.

I heard a car start up, and headlights cut cones into the night. My side of the tree was away from the light, but I could see that I was huddled by a dog, not a wolf. Then the lights moved and gravel sprayed from Bill's driveway as the car reversed. There was a moment's pause, I presumed while the driver shifted into drive, and then the car screeched and I heard it going at high speed down the hill to the turnoff onto Hummingbird Road. There was a terrible thud and a high shrieking sound that made my heart hammer even harder. It was the sound of a pain a dog makes when it's been hit by a car.

'Oh, Jesus,' I said miserably, and clutched my furry friend. I thought of something I could do to help, now that it seemed the witches had left.

I got up and ran for the front door of Bill's house before the dog could stop me. I pulled my keys out of my pocket as I ran. They'd been in my hand when Eric had seized me at my back door, and I'd stuffed them into my coat, where a handkerchief had kept them from jingling. I felt around for the lock, counted my keys until I arrived at Bill's – the third on the ring – and opened his front door. I reached in and flipped the outside light switch, and abruptly the yard was illuminated.

It was full of wolves.

I didn't know how scared I should be. Pretty scared, I guessed. I was just assuming both of the Were witches had been in the car. What if one of them was among the wolves present? And where was my vampire?

That question got answered almost immediately. There was a sort of *whump* as Eric landed in the yard.

'I followed them to the road, but they went too fast for me there,' he said, grinning at me as if we'd been playing a game.

A dog – a collie – went up to Eric, looked up at his face and growled.

'Shoo,' Eric said, making an imperious gesture with his hand.

My boss trotted over to me and sat against my legs

again. Even in the darkness, I had suspected that my guardian was Sam. The first time I'd encountered him in this transformation, I'd thought he was a stray, and I'd named him Dean, after a man I knew with the same eye color. Now it was a habit to call him Dean when he went on four legs. I sat on Bill's front steps and the collie cuddled against me. I said, 'You are one great dog.' He wagged his tail. The wolves were sniffing Eric, who was standing stock-still.

A big wolf trotted over to me, the biggest wolf I'd ever seen. Weres turn into large wolves, I guess; I haven't seen that many. Living in Louisiana, I've never seen a standard wolf at all. This Were was almost pure black, which I thought was unusual. The rest of the wolves were more sil-very, except for one that was smaller and reddish.

The wolf gripped my coat sleeve with its long white teeth and tugged. I rose immediately and went over to the spot where most of the other wolves were milling. We were at the outer edge of the light, so I hadn't noticed the clus-ter right away. There was blood on the ground, and in the middle of the spreading pool lay a young dark-haired woman. She was naked.

She was obviously and terribly injured.

Her legs were broken, and maybe one arm.

'Go get my car,' I told Eric, in the kind of voice that has to be obeyed.

I tossed him my keys, and he took to the air again. In one available corner of my brain, I hoped that he remem-bered how to drive. I'd noted that though he'd forgotten his personal history, his modern skills were apparently intact.

I was trying not to think about the poor injured girl right in front of me. The wolves circled and paced, whining. Then the big black one raised his head to the dark sky and howled again. This was a signal to all the others, who did the same thing. I glanced back to be sure that Dean was keeping away, since he was the outsider. I wasn't sure how much human personality was left after these two-natured people trans-formed, and I didn't want anything to happen to him. He was sitting on the small porch, out of the way, his eyes fixed on me.

I was the only creature with opposable thumbs on the scene, and I was suddenly aware that that gave me a lot of responsibility.

First thing to check? Breathing. Yes, she was! She had a pulse. I was no paramedic, but it didn't seem like a normal pulse to me – which would be no wonder. Her skin felt hot, maybe from the changeover back to human. I didn't see a terrifying amount of fresh blood, so I hoped that no major arteries had been ruptured.

I slid a hand beneath the girl's head, very carefully, and touched the dusty dark hair, trying to see if her scalp was lacerated. No.

Sometime during the process of this examination, I began shaking all over. Her injuries were really frightening. Everything I could see of her looked beaten, battered, broken. Her eyes opened. She shuddered. Blankets – she'd need to be kept warm. I glanced around. All the wolves were still wolves.

'It would be great if one or two of you could change back,' I told them. 'I have to get her to a hospital in my car, and she needs blankets from inside this house.'

One of the wolves, a silvery gray, rolled onto its side – okay, male wolf – and I heard the same gloppy noise again. A haze wrapped around the writhing figure, and when it dispersed, Colonel Flood was curled up in place of the wolf. Of course, he was naked, too, but I chose to rise above my natural embarrassment. He had to lie still for at least a minute or two, and it was obviously a great effort for him to sit up.

He crawled over to the injured girl. 'Maria-Star,' he said hoarsely. He bent to smell her, which looked very weird when he was in human form. He whined in distress.

He turned his head to look at me. He said, 'Where?' and I understood he meant the blankets.

'Go in the house, go up the stairs. There's a bedroom at the head of the stairs. There's a blanket chest at the foot of the bed. Get two blankets out of there.'

He staggered to his feet, apparently having to deal with some disorientation from his rapid change, before he began striding toward the house.

The girl – Maria-Star – followed him with her eyes.

'Can you talk?' I asked.

'Yes,' she said, barely audibly.

'Where does it hurt worst?'

'I think my hips and legs are broken,' she said. 'The car hit me.'

'Did it throw you up in the air?'

'Yes.'

'The wheels didn't pass over you?'

She shuddered. 'No, it was the impact that hurt me.'

'What's your full name? Maria-Star what?' I'd need to know for the hospital. She might not be conscious by then.

'Cooper,' she whispered.

By then, I could hear a car coming up Bill's drive.

The colonel, moving more smoothly now, sped out of the house with the blankets, and all the wolves and the one human instantly arrayed themselves around me and their wounded pack member. The car was obviously a threat until they learned likewise. I admired the colonel. It took quite a man to face an approaching enemy stark naked.

The new arrival was Eric, in my old car. He pulled up to Maria-Star and me with considerable panache and squealing brakes. The wolves circled restlessly, their glowing yellow eyes fixed on the driver's door. Calvin Norris's eyes had looked quite different; fleetingly, I wondered why.

'It's my car; it's okay,' I said, when one of the Weres began growling. Several pairs of eyes turned to fix on me consideringly. Did I look suspicious, or tasty?

As I finished wrapping Maria-Star in the blankets, I wondered which one of the wolves was Alcide. I suspected he was the largest, darkest one, the one that just that moment turned to look me in the eyes. Yes, Alcide. This was the wolf I'd seen at Club Dead a few weeks ago, when Alcide had been my date on a night that had ended cata-strophically – for me and a few other people.

I tried to smile at him, but my face was stiff with cold and shock.

Eric leaped out of the driver's seat, leaving the car run-ning. He opened the back door. 'I'll put her in,' he called, and the wolves began barking. They didn't want their pack sister handled by a vampire, and they didn't want Eric to be anywhere close to Maria-Star.

Colonel Flood said, 'I'll lift her.' Eric looked at the older man's slight physique and lifted a doubtful eyebrow, but had the sense to stand aside. I'd wrapped the girl as well as I could without jarring her, but the colonel knew this was going to hurt her even worse. At the last minute, he hesi-tated.

'Maybe we should call the ambulance,' he muttered.

'And explain this how?' I asked. 'A bunch of wolves and a naked guy, and her being up here next to a private home where the owner's absent? I don't think so!'

'Of course.' He nodded, accepting the inevitable. Without even a hitch in his breathing, he stood with the bundle that was the girl and went to the car. Eric did run to the other side, open that door, and reach in to help pull her farther onto the backseat. The colonel permitted that. The girl shrieked once, and I scrambled behind the wheel as fast as I could. Eric got in the passenger side, and I said, 'You can't go.'

'Why not?' He sounded amazed and affronted.

'I'll have twice the explaining to do if I have a vampire with me!' It took most people a few minutes to decide Eric was dead, but of course they would figure it out eventually. Eric stubbornly stayed put. 'And everyone's seeing your face on the damn posters,' I said, working to keep my voice reasonable but urgent. 'I live among pretty good people, but there's no one in this parish who couldn't use that much money.'

He got out, not happily, and I yelled, 'Turn off the lights and relock the house, okay?'

'Meet us at the bar when you have word about Maria-Star!' Colonel Flood yelled back. 'We've got to get our cars and clothes out of the cemetery.' Okay, that explained the glimpse I'd caught on the way over.

As I steered slowly down the driveway, the wolves watched me go, Alcide standing apart from the rest, his black furry face turning to follow my progress. I wondered what wolfy thoughts he was thinking.

The closest hospital was not in Bon Temps, which is way too small to have its own (we're lucky to have a Wal-Mart), but in nearby Clarice, the parish seat. Luckily, it's on the outskirts of the town, on the side nearest Bon Temps. The ride to the Renard Parish Hospital only seemed to take years; actually, I got there in about twenty minutes. My passenger moaned for the first ten minutes, and then fell ominously silent. I talked to her, begged her to talk to me, asked her to tell me how old she was, and turned on the radio in attempt to spark some response from Maria-Star.

I didn't want to take the time to pull over and check on her, and I wouldn't have known what to do if I had, so I drove like a bat out of hell. By the time I pulled up to the emergency entrance and called to the two nurses standing outside smoking, I was sure the poor Were was dead.

She wasn't, judging from the activity that surrounded her in the next couple of minutes. Our parish hospital is a little one, of course, and it doesn't have the facilities that a city hospital can boast. We counted ourselves lucky to have a hospital at all. That night, they saved the Were's life.

The doctor, a thin woman with graying spiked hair and huge black-rimmed glasses, asked me a few pointed questions that I couldn't answer, though I'd been working on my basic story all the way to the hospital. After finding me clueless, the doctor made it clear I was to get the hell out of the way and let her team work. So I sat in a chair in the hall and waited, and worked on my story some more.

There was no way I could be useful here, and the glaring fluorescent lights and the gleaming linoleum made a harsh, unfriendly environment. I tried to read a magazine, and tossed it on the table after a couple of minutes. For the seventh or eighth time, I thought of skipping out. But there was a woman stationed at the night reception desk, and she was keeping a close eye on me. After a few more minutes, I decided to visit the women's room to wash the blood off my hands. While I was in there, I took a few swipes at my coat with a wet paper towel, which was largely a wasted effort.

When I emerged from the women's room, there were two cops waiting for me. They were big men, both of them. They rustled with their synthetic padded jackets, and they creaked with the leather of their belts and equipment. I couldn't imagine them sneaking up on anyone.

The taller man was the older. His steel gray hair was clipped close to his scalp. His face was carved with a few deep wrinkles, like ravines. His gut overhung his belt. His partner was a younger man, maybe thirty, with light brown hair and light brown eyes and light brown skin – a curiously monochromatic guy. I gave them a quick but comprehensive scan with all my senses.

I could tell the two were both prepared to find out I'd had a hand in the injuries of the girl I'd brought in, or that I at least knew more than I was saying.

Of course, they were partially right.

'Miss Stackhouse? You brought in the young woman Dr. Skinner is treating?' the younger man said gently.

'Maria-Star,' I said. 'Cooper.'

'Tell us how you came to do that,' the older cop said.

It was definitely an order, though his tone was moderate. Neither man knew me or knew of me, I 'heard.' Good.

I took a deep breath and dove into the waters of mendacity. 'I was driving home from work,' I said. 'I work at Merlotte's Bar – you know where that is?'

They both nodded. Of course, police would know the location of every bar in the parish.

'I saw a body lying by the side of the road, on the gravel of the shoulder,' I said carefully, thinking ahead so I wouldn't say something I couldn't take back. 'So I stopped. There wasn't anyone else in sight. When I found out she was still alive, I knew I had to get to help. It took me a long time to get her into the car by myself.' I was trying to account for the passage of time since I'd left work and the gravel from Bill's driveway that I knew would be in her skin. I couldn't gauge how much care I needed to take in putting my story together, but more care was better than less.

'Did you notice any skid marks on the road?' The light brown policeman couldn't go long without asking a question.

'No, I didn't notice. They may have been there. I was just – after I saw her, all I thought about was her.'

'So?' the older man prompted.

'I could tell she was hurt real bad, so I got her here as fast as I could.' I shrugged. End of my story.

'You didn't think about calling an ambulance?'

'I don't have a cell phone.'

'Woman who comes home from work that late, by herself, really ought to have a cell phone, ma'am.'

I opened my mouth to tell him that if he felt like paying the bill, I'd be glad to have one, when I restrained myself. Yes, it *would* be handy to have a cell phone, but I could barely afford my regular phone. My only extravagance was cable TV, and I justified that by telling myself it was my only recreational spending. 'I hear you,' I said briefly.

'And your full name is?' This from the younger man. I looked up, met his eyes.

'Sookie Stackhouse,' I said. He'd been thinking I seemed kind of shy and sweet.

'You the sister of the man who's missing?' The gray-haired man bent down to look in my face.

'Yes, sir.' I looked down at my toes again.

'You're sure having a streak of bad luck, Miss Stackhouse.'

'Tell me about it,' I said, my voice shaking with sincerity.

'Have you ever seen this woman, the woman you brought in, before tonight?' The older officer was scribbling in a little notepad he'd produced from a pocket. His name was Curlew, the little pin on his pocket said.

I shook my head.

'You think your brother might have known her?'

I looked up, startled. I met the eyes of the brown man again. His name was Stans. 'How the heck would I know?' I asked. I knew in the next second that he'd just wanted me to look up again. He didn't know what to make of me. The monochromatic Stans thought I was pretty and seemed like a good little Samaritan. On the other hand, my job was one educated nice girls didn't often take, and my brother was well known as a brawler, though many of the patrol officers liked him.

'How is she doing?' I asked.

They both glanced at the door behind which the struggle to save the young woman went on.

'She's still alive,' Stans said.

'Poor thing,' I said. Tears rolled down my cheeks, and I began fumbling in my pockets for a tissue.

'Did she say anything to you, Miss Stackhouse?'

I had to think about that. 'Yes,' I said. 'She did.' The truth was safe, in this instance.

They both brightened at the news.

'She told me her name. She said her legs hurt worst, when I asked her,' I said. 'And she said that the car had hit her, but not run her over.'

The two men looked at each other.

'Did she describe the car?' Stans asked.

It was incredibly tempting to describe the witches' car. But I mistrusted the glee that bubbled up inside me at the idea. And I was glad I had, the next second, when I realized that the trace evidence they'd get off the car would be wolf fur. Good thinking, Sook.

'No, she didn't,' I said, trying to look as though I'd been groping through my memory. 'She didn't really talk much after that, just moaning. It was awful.' And the upholstery on my backseat was probably ruined, too. I immediately wished I hadn't thought of something so selfish.

'And you didn't see any other cars, trucks, any other vehicles on your way to your house from the bar, or even when you were coming back to town?'

That was a slightly different question. 'Not on my road,' I said hesitantly. 'I probably saw a few cars when I got closer to Bon Temps and went through town. And of course I saw more between Bon Temps and Clarice. But I don't recall any in particular.'

'Can you take us to the spot where you picked her up? The exact place?'

'I doubt it. There wasn't anything to mark it besides her,' I said. My coherence level was falling by the minute. 'No big tree, or road, or mile marker. Maybe tomorrow? In the daytime?'

Stans patted me on the shoulder. 'I know you're shook up, miss,' he said consolingly. 'You done the best you could for this girl. Now we gotta leave it up to the doctors and the Lord.'

I nodded emphatically, because I certainly agreed. The older Curlew still looked at me a little skeptically, but he thanked me as a matter of form, and they strode out of the hospital into the blackness. I stepped back a little, though I remained looking out into the parking lot. In a second or two, they reached my car and shone their big flashlights through the windows, checking out the interior. I keep the inside of my car spanky-clean, so they wouldn't see a thing but bloodstains in the backseat. I noticed that they checked out the front grille, too, and I didn't blame them one little bit.

They examined my car over and over, and finally they stood under one of the big lights, making notes on clipboards.

Not too long after that, the doctor came out to find me. She pulled her mask down and rubbed the back of her neck with a long, thin hand. 'Miss Cooper is doing better. She's stable,' she said.

I nodded, and then I closed my eyes for a moment with sheer relief. 'Thank you,' I croaked.

'We're going to airlift her to Schumpert in Shreveport. The helicopter'll be here any second.'

I blinked, trying to decide if that were a good thing or a bad thing. No matter what my opinion was, the Were had to go to the best and closest hospital. When she became able to talk, she'd have to tell them something. How could I ensure that her story jibed with mine?

'Is she conscious?' I asked.

'Just barely,' the doctor said, almost angrily, as if such injuries were an insult to her personally. 'You can speak to her briefly, but I can't guarantee she'll remember, or understand. I have to go talk to the cops.' The two officers were striding back into the hospital, I saw from my place at the window.

'Thank you,' I said, and followed her gesture to her left. I pushed open the door into the grim glaring room where they'd been working on the girl.

It was a mess. There were a couple of nurses in there even now, chatting about this or that and packing away some of the unused packages of bandages and tubes. A man with a bucket and mop stood waiting in a corner. He would clean the room when the Were – the girl – had been wheeled out to the helicopter. I went to the side of the narrow bed and took her hand.

I bent down close.

'Maria-Star, you know my voice?' I asked quietly. Her face was swollen from its impact with the ground, and it was covered with scratches and scrapes. These were the smallest of her injuries, but they looked very painful to me.

'Yes,' she breathed.

'I'm the one that found you by the *side of the road*,' I said. 'On the way to my house, south of Bon Temps. You were lying by the parish road.'

'Understand,' she murmured.

'I guess,' I continued carefully, 'that someone made you get out of his car, and that someone then hit you with the car. But you know how it is after a trauma, sometimes people don't remember *anything*.' One of the nurses turned to me, her face curious. She'd caught the last part of my sentence. 'So don't worry if you don't remember.'

'I'll try,' she said ambiguously, still in that hushed, far-away voice.

There was nothing more I could do here, and a lot more that could go wrong, so I whispered 'Good-bye,' told the nurses I appreciated them, and went out to my car. Thanks to the blankets (which I supposed I'd have to replace for Bill), my backseat wasn't messed up too bad.

I was glad to find something to be pleased about.

I wondered about the blankets. Did the police have them? Would the hospital call me about them? Or had they been pitched in the garbage? I shrugged. There was no point worrying about two rectangles of material anymore, when I had so much else crammed on my worry list. For one thing, I didn't like the Weres congregating at Merlotte's. That pulled Sam way too far into Were concerns. He was a shifter, after all, and shifters were much more loosely involved with the supernatural world. Shifters tended to be more 'every shifter for himself,' while the Weres were always organized. Now they were using Merlotte's for a meeting place, after hours.

And then there was Eric. Oh, Lord, Eric would be waiting for me at the house.

I found myself wondering what time it was in Peru. Bill had to be having more fun than I was. It seemed like I'd gotten worn out on New Year's Eve and never caught up; I'd never felt this exhausted.

I was just past the intersection where I'd turned left, the road that eventually passed Merlotte's. The headlights illuminated flashes of trees and bushes. At least there were no more vampires running down the side . . .

'Wake up,' said the woman sitting by me on the front seat.

'What?' My eyelids popped open. The car swerved violently.

'You were falling asleep.'

By this time, I wouldn't have been surprised if a beached whale had lain across the road.

'You're who?' I asked, when I felt my voice might be under my control.

'Claudine.'

It was hard to recognize her in the dashboard light, but sure enough, it seemed to be the tall and beautiful woman who'd been in Merlotte's New Year's Eve, who'd been with Tara the previous morning. 'How did you get in my car? Why are you here?'

'Because there's been an unusual amount of supernatural activity in this area in the past week or two. I'm the go-between.'

'Go between what?'

'Between the two worlds. Or, more accurately, between the three worlds.'

Sometimes life just hands you more than you take. Then you just accept.

'So, you're like an angel? That's how come you woke me up when I was falling asleep at the wheel?'

'No, I haven't gotten that far yet. You're too tired to take this in. You have to ignore the mythology and just accept me for what I am.'

I felt a funny jolt in my chest.

'Look,' Claudine pointed out. 'That man's waving to you.'

Sure enough, in Merlotte's parking lot there stood a semaphoring vampire. It was Chow.

'Oh, just great,' I said, in the grumpiest voice I could manage. 'Well, I hope you don't mind us stopping, Claudine. I need to go in.'

'Sure, I wouldn't miss it.'

Chow waved me to the rear of the bar, and I was aston-ished to find the employee parking area jam-packed with cars that had been invisible from the road.

'Oh, boy!' Claudine said. 'A party!' She got out of my car as if she could hardly restrain her glee, and I had the satisfaction of seeing that Chow was absolutely stupefied when he took in all six feet of her. It's hard to surprise a vampire.

'Let's go in,' Claudine said gaily, and took my hand.

Chapter 9

Every Supe I'd ever met was in Merlotte's. Or maybe it just seemed like that, since I was dead tired and wanted to be by myself. The Were pack was there, all in human form and all more or less dressed, to my relief.

Alcide was in khakis and an unbuttoned shirt in green and blue plaid. It was hard to believe he could run on four legs. The Weres were drinking coffee or soft drinks, and Eric (looking happy and healthy) was having some TrueBlood. Pam was sitting on a barstool, wearing an ash green tracksuit, which she managed to make prim-but-sexy. She had a bow in her hair and beaded sneakers on her feet. She'd brought Gerald with her, a vampire I'd met once or twice at Fangtasia. Gerald looked about thirty, but I'd heard him refer to Prohibition once as if he'd lived through it. What little I knew of Gerald didn't predispose me to getting closer to him.

Even in such a company, my entrance with Claudine was nothing short of sensational. In the improved lighting of the bar, I could see that Claudine's strategically rounded body was packed into an orange knit dress, and her long legs ended in the highest of high heels. She looked like a scrumptious slut, super-sized.

Nope, she couldn't be an angel – at least, as I understood angels.

Looking from Claudine to Pam, I decided it was massively unfair that they looked so clean and appealing. Like I needed to feel unattractive, in addition to being worn out and scared and confused! Doesn't every gal want to walk into a room side by side with a gorgeous woman who practically has 'I want to fuck' tattooed on her forehead? If I hadn't caught a glimpse of Sam, whom I'd dragged into this whole thing, I would've turned around and walked right out.

'Claudine,' said Colonel Flood. 'What brings you here?'

Pam and Gerald were both staring at the woman in orange intently, as if they expected her to take off her clothes any second.

'My girl, here' – and Claudine inclined her head toward me – 'fell asleep at the wheel. How come you aren't watching out for her better?'

The colonel, as dignified in his civvies as he had been in his skin, looked a little startled, as if it was news to him that he was supposed to provide protection for me. 'Ah,' he said. 'Uh . . .'

'Should have sent someone to the hospital with her,' Claudine said, shaking her waterfall of black hair.

'I offered to go with her,' Eric said indignantly. 'She said it would be too suspicious if she went to the hospital with a vampire.'

'Well, hel-lo, tall, blond, and *dead*,' Claudine said. She looked Eric up and down, admiring what she saw. 'You in the habit of doing what human women ask of you?'

Thanks a lot, Claudine, I told her silently. I was supposed to be guarding Eric, and now he wouldn't even shut the door if I told him to. Gerald was still ogling her in the same stunned way. I wondered if anyone would notice if I stretched out on one of the tables and went to sleep. Suddenly, just as Pam's and Gerald's had done, Eric's gaze sharpened and he seemed fixed on Claudine. I had time to think it was like watching cats that'd suddenly spotted something skittering along the baseboards before big hands spun me around and Alcide gathered me to him. He'd maneuvered through the crowd in the bar until he'd reached me. Since his shirt wasn't buttoned, I found my face pressed against his warm chest, and I was glad to be there. The curly black hair did smell faintly of dog, true, but otherwise I was comforted at being hugged and cherished. It felt delightful.

'Who are you?' Alcide asked Claudine. I had my ear against his chest and I could hear him from inside and outside, a strange sensation.

'I'm Claudine, the fairy,' the huge woman said. 'See?'

I had to turn to see what she was doing. She'd lifted her long hair to show her ears, which were delicately pointed.

'Fairy,' Alcide repeated. He sounded as astonished as I felt.

'Sweet,' said one of the younger Weres, a spiky-haired male who might be nineteen. He looked intrigued with the turn of events, and he glanced around at the other Weres seated at his table as if inviting them to share his pleasure. 'For real?'

'For a while,' Claudine said. 'Sooner or later, I'll go one way or another.' No one understood that, with the possible exception of the colonel.

'You are one mouthwatering woman,' said the young Were. To back up the fashion statement of the spiked hair, he wore jeans and a ragged Fallen Angel T-shirt; he was barefoot, though Merlotte's was cool, since the thermostat was turned down for the rest of the night. He was wearing toe rings.

'Thanks!' Claudine smiled down at him. She snapped her fingers, and there was the same kind of haze around her that enveloped the Weres when they shifted. It was the haze of thick magic. When the air cleared, Claudine was wearing a spangled white evening gown.

'Sweet,' the boy repeated in a dazed way, and Claudine basked in his admiration. I noticed she was keeping a certain distance from the vampires.

'Claudine, now that you've shown off, could we please talk about something besides you?' Colonel Flood sounded as tired as I felt.

'Of course,' Claudine said in an appropriately chastened voice. 'Just ask away.'

'First things first. Miss Stackhouse, how is Maria-Star?'

'She survived the ride to the hospital in Clarice. They're airlifting her to Shreveport, to Schumpert hospital. She may already be on her way. The doctor sounded pretty positive about her chances.'

The Weres all looked at one another, and most of them let out gusty noises of relief. One woman, about thirty years old, actually did a little happy dance. The vampires, by now almost totally fixated on the fairy, didn't react at all.

'What did you tell the emergency room doctor?' Colonel Flood asked. 'I have to let her parents know what the official line is.' Maria-Star would be their first-born, and their only Were child.

'I told the police that I found her by the side of the road, that I didn't see any signs of a car braking or anything. I told them she was lying on the gravel, so we won't have to worry about grass that isn't pressed down when it ought to be . . . I hope she got it. She was pretty doped up when I talked to her.'

'Very good thinking,' Colonel Flood said. 'Thanks, Miss Stackhouse. Our pack is indebted to you.'

I waved my hand to disclaim any debt. 'How did you come to show up at Bill's house at the right time?'

'Emilio and Sid tracked the witches to the right area.' Emilio must be the small, dark man with huge brown eyes. There was a growing immigrant Mexican population in our area, and Emilio was apparently a part of that community. The spike-haired boy gave me a little wave, and I assumed he must be Sid. 'Anyway, after dark, we started keeping an eye on the building where Hallow and her coven are holed up. It's hard to do; it's a residential neighborhood that's mostly black.' African-American twins, both girls, grinned at each other. They were young enough to find this exciting, like Sid. 'When Hallow and her brother left for Bon Temps, we followed them in our cars. We called Sam, too, to warn him.'

I looked at Sam reproachfully. He hadn't warned me, hadn't mentioned the Weres were heading our way, too.

Colonel Flood went on, 'Sam called me on my cell to tell me where he figured they were heading when they walked out of his bar. I decided an isolated place like the Compton house would be a good place to get them. We were able to park our cars in the cemetery and change, so we got there just in time. But they caught our scent early.' The colonel glared at Sid. Apparently, the younger Were had jumped the gun.

'So they got away,' I said, trying to sound neutral. 'And now they know you're on to them.'

'Yes, they got away. The murderers of Adabelle Yancy. The leaders of a group trying to take over not only the vamps' territory, but ours.' Colonel Flood had been sweeping the assembled Weres with a cold gaze, and they wilted under his stare, even Alcide. 'And now the witches'll be on their guard, since they know we're after them.'

Their attention momentarily pulled from the radiant fairy Claudine, Pam and Gerald seemed discreetly amused by the colonel's speech. Eric, as always these days, looked as confused as if the colonel were speaking in Sanskrit.

'The Stonebrooks went back to Shreveport when they left Bill's?' I asked.

'We assume so. We had to change back very quickly – no easy matter – and then get to our cars. A few of us went one way, a few another, but we caught no glimpse of them.'

'And now we're here. Why?' Alcide's voice was harsh.

'We're here for several reasons,' the packmaster said. 'First, we wanted to know about Maria-Star. Also, we wanted to recover for a bit before we drive back to Shreveport ourselves.'

The Weres, who seemed to have pulled their clothes on pretty hastily, did look a little ragged. The dark-moon transformation and the rapid change back to two-legged form had taken a toll on all of them.

'And why are you here?' I asked Pam.

'We have something to report, too,' she said. 'Evidently, we have the same goals as the Weres – on this matter, anyway.' She tore her gaze away from Claudine with an effort. She and Gerald exchanged glances, and as one, they turned to Eric, who looked back at them blankly. Pam sighed, and Gerald looked down at his booted feet.

'Our nest mate Clancy didn't return to us last night,' Pam said. Hard on this startling announcement, she focused once again on the fairy. Claudine seemed to have some overwhelming allure for the vampires.

Most of the Weres looked like they were thinking that one less vampire was a step in the right direction. But Alcide said, 'What do you think has happened?'

'We got a note,' Gerald said, one of the few times I'd ever heard him speak out loud. He had a faint English accent. 'The note said that the witches plan to drain one of our vampires for each day they have to search for Eric.'

All eyes went to Eric, who looked stunned. 'But why?' he asked. 'I can't understand what makes me such a prize.'

One of the Were girls, a tan blonde in her late twenties, took silent issue with that. She rolled her eyes toward me, and I could only grin back. But no matter how good Eric looked, and what ideas interested parties might have about the fun to be had with him in bed (and on top of that, the control he had over various vampire enterprises in Shreveport), this single-minded pursuit of Eric rang the 'Excessive' alarm. Even if Hallow had sex with Eric, and then drained him dry and consumed all his blood – Wait, there was an idea.

'How much blood can be got from one of you?' I asked Pam.

She stared at me, as close to surprised as I'd ever seen her. 'Let me see,' she said. She stared into space, and her fingers wiggled. It looked like Pam was translating from one unit of measurement to another. 'Six quarts,' she said at last.

'And how much blood do they sell in those little vials?'

'That's . . .' She did some more figuring. 'Well, that would be less than a fourth of a cup.' She anticipated where I was heading. 'So Eric contains over ninety-six saleable units of blood.'

'How much you reckon they could charge for that?'

'Well, on the street, the price has reached $225 for regular vampire blood,' Pam said, her eyes as cold as winter frost. 'For Eric's blood . . . He is so old . . .'

'Maybe $425 a vial?'

'Conservatively.'

'So, on the hoof, Eric's worth . . .'

'Over forty thousand dollars.'

The whole crowd stared at Eric with heightened interest – except for Pam and Gerald, who along with Eric had resumed their contemplation of Claudine. They appeared to have inched closer to the fairy.

'So, do you think that's enough motivation?' I asked. 'Eric spurned her. She wants him, she wants his stuff, and she wants to sell his blood.'

'That's a lot of motivation,' agreed a Were woman, a pretty brunette in her late forties.

'Plus, Hallow's nuts,' Claudine said cheerfully.

I didn't think the fairy had stopped smiling since she'd appeared in my car. 'How do you know that, Claudine?' I asked.

'I've been to her headquarters,' she said.

We all regarded her in silence for a long moment, but not as raptly as the three vampires did.

'Claudine, have you gone over?' Colonel Flood asked. He sounded more tired than anything else.

'James,' Claudine said. 'Shame on you! She thought I was an area witch.'

Maybe I wasn't the only one who was thinking that such overflowing cheer was a little weird. Most of the fifteen or so Weres in the bar didn't seem too comfortable around the fairy. 'It would have saved us a lot of trouble if you'd told us that earlier than tonight, Claudine,' the colonel said, his tone frosty.

'A real fairy,' Gerald said. 'I've only had one before.'

'They're hard to catch,' Pam said, her voice dreamy. She edged a little closer.

Even Eric had lost his blank and frustrated mien and took a step toward Claudine. The three vamps looked like chocaholics at the Hershey factory.

'Now, now,' Claudine said, a little anxiously. 'Anything with fangs, take a step back!'

Pam looked a bit embarrassed, and she tried to relax. Gerald subsided unwillingly. Eric kept creeping forward.

Neither of the vampires nor any of the Weres looked willing to take Eric on. I mentally girded my loins. After all, Claudine had awakened me before I could crash my car.

'Eric,' I said, taking three quick steps to stand between Eric and the fairy. 'Snap out of it!'

'What?' Eric paid no more attention to me than he would to a fly buzzing around his head.

'She's off limits, Eric,' I said, and Eric's eyes did flicker down to my face.

'Hi, remember me?' I put my hand on his chest to slow him down. 'I don't know why you're in such a lather, fella, but you need to hold your horses.'

'I want her,' Eric said, his blue eyes blazing down into mine.

'Well, she's gorgeous,' I said, striving for reasonable,

though actually I was a little hurt. 'But she's not available. Right, Claudine?' I aimed my voice back over my shoulder.

'Not available to a vampire,' the fairy said. 'My blood is intoxicating to a vampire. You don't want to know what they'd be like after they had me.' But she still sounded cheerful.

So I hadn't been too far wrong with the chocolate metaphor. Probably this was why I hadn't encountered any fairies before; I was too much in the company of the undead.

When you have thoughts like that, you know you're in trouble.

'Claudine, I guess we need you to step outside now,' I said a little desperately. Eric was pushing against me, not testing me seriously yet (or I'd be flat on my back), but I'd had to retreat a step already. I wanted to hear what Claudine had to tell the Weres, but I realized separating the vamps from the fairy was top priority.

'Just like a big petit four,' Pam sighed, watching Claudine twitch her white-spangled butt all the way out the front door with Colonel Flood close behind her. Eric seemed to snap to once Claudine was out of sight, and I breathed a sigh of relief.

'Vamps really like fairies, huh?' I said nervously.

'Oh, yeah,' they said simultaneously.

'You know, she saved my life, and she's apparently help-ing us out on this witch thing,' I reminded them.

They looked sulky.

'Claudine was actually quite helpful,' Colonel Flood said as he reentered, sounding surprised. The door swung shut behind him.

Eric's arm went around me, and I could feel one kind of hunger being morphed into another.

'Why was she in their coven headquarters?' Alcide asked, more angrily than was warranted.

'You know fairies. They love to flirt with disaster, they love to role-play.' The packmaster sighed heavily. 'Even Claudine, and she's one of the good ones. Definitely on her way up. What she tells me is this: This Hallow has a coven of about twenty witches. All of them are Weres or the larger shifters. They are all vampire blood users, maybe addicts.'

'Will the Wiccans help us fight them?' asked a middle-aged woman with dyed red hair and a couple of chins.

'They haven't committed to it yet.' A young man with a military haircut – I wondered if he was stationed at Barksdale Air Force Base – seemed to know the story on the Wiccans. 'Acting on our packmaster's orders, I called or otherwise contacted every Wiccan coven or individual Wiccan in the area, and they are all doing their best to hide from these creatures. But I saw signs that most of them were heading for a meeting tonight, though I don't know where. I think they are going to discuss the situation on their own. If they could mount an attack as well, it would help us.'

'Good work, Portugal,' said Colonel Flood, and the young man looked gratified.

Since we had our backs to the wall, Eric had felt free to let his hand roam over my bottom. I didn't object to the sensation, which was very pleasant, but I did object to the venue, which was too darn public.

'Claudine didn't say anything about prisoners who might have been there?' I asked, taking a step away from Eric.

'No, I'm sorry, Miss Stackhouse. She didn't see anyone

answering your brother's description, and she didn't see the vampire Clancy.'

I wasn't exactly surprised, but I was very disappointed. Sam said, 'I'm sorry, Sookie. If Hallow doesn't have him, where can he be?'

'Of course, just because she didn't see him, doesn't mean he's not there for sure,' the colonel said. 'We're sure she took Clancy, and Claudine didn't catch sight of him.'

'Back to the Wiccans,' suggested the red-haired Were. 'What should we do about them?'

'Tomorrow, Portugal, call all your Wiccan contacts again,' Colonel Flood said. 'Get Culpepper to help you.'

Culpepper was a young woman with a strong, handsome face and a no-nonsense haircut. She looked pleased to be included in something Portugal was doing. He looked pleased, too, but he tried to mask it under a brusque manner. 'Yes, sir,' he said snappily. Culpepper thought that was cute as hell; I was lifting that directly from her brain. Were she might be, but you couldn't disguise an admiration that intense. 'Uh, why am I calling them again?' Portugal asked after a long moment.

'We need to know what they plan to do, if they'll share that with us,' Colonel Flood said. 'If they're not with us, they can at least stay out of the way.'

'So, we're going to war?' This was from an older man, who seemed to be a pair with the red-haired woman.

'It was the vampires that started it,' the redheaded woman said.

'That is *so* untrue,' I said indignantly.

'Vamp humper,' she said.

I'd had worse things said about me, but not to my face, and not from people who intended me to hear them.

Eric had left the floor before I could decide if I was more hurt or more enraged. He had instantly opted for enraged, and it made him very effective. She was on the ground on her back and he was on top of her with fangs extended before anyone could even be alarmed. It was lucky for the red-haired woman that Pam and Gerald were equally swift, though it took both of them to lift Eric off the redheaded Were. She was bleeding only a little, but she was yelping nonstop.

For a long second, I thought the whole room was going to erupt into battle, but Colonel Flood roared, 'SILENCE!' and you didn't disobey that voice.

'Amanda,' he said to the red-haired woman, who was whimpering as though Eric had removed a limb, and whose companion was busy checking out her injuries in a wholly unnecessary panic, 'you will be polite to our allies, and you will keep your damn opinions to yourself. Your offense cancels out the blood he spilled. No retaliation, Parnell!' The male Were snarled at the colonel, but finally gave a grudging nod.

'Miss Stackhouse, I apologize for the poor manners of the pack,' Colonel Flood said to me. Though I was still upset, I made myself nod. I couldn't help but notice that Alcide was looking from me to Eric, and he looked – well, he looked appalled. Sam had the sense to be quite expressionless. My back stiffened, and I ran a quick hand over my eyes to dash away the tears.

Eric was calming down, but it was with an effort. Pam was murmuring in his ear, and Gerald was keeping a good grip on his arm.

To make my evening perfect, the back door to Merlotte's opened once again, and Debbie Pelt walked in.

'Y'all are having a party without me.' She looked at the odd assemblage and raised her eyebrows. 'Hey, baby,' she said directly to Alcide, and ran a possessive hand down his arm, twining her fingers with his. Alcide had an odd expression on his face. It was as though he was simultaneously happy and miserable.

Debbie was a striking woman, tall and lean, with a long face. She had black hair, but it wasn't curly and disheveled like Alcide's. It was cut in asymmetrical tiny clumps, and it was straight and swung with her movement. It was the dumbest haircut I'd ever seen, and it had undoubtedly cost an arm and a leg. Somehow, men didn't seem to be interested in her haircut.

It would have been hypocritical of me to greet her. Debbie and I were beyond that. She'd tried to kill me, a fact that Alcide knew; and yet she still seemed to exercise some fascination for him, though he'd thrown her out when he first learned of it. For a smart and practical and hardworking man, he had a great big blind spot, and here it was, in tight Cruel Girl jeans and a thin orange sweater that hugged every inch of skin. What was she doing here, so far from her own stomping grounds?

I felt a sudden impulse to turn to Eric and tell him that Debbie had made a serious attempt on my life, just to see what would happen. But I restrained myself yet again. All this restraint was plain painful. My fingers were curled under, transforming my hands into tight fists.

'We'll call you if anything more happens in this meeting,' Gerald said. It took me a minute to understand I was being dismissed, and that it was because I had to take Eric back to my house lest he erupt again. From the look on his face, it wouldn't take much. His eyes were glowing blue, and his fangs were at least half extended. I was more than ever tempted to . . . no, I was *not*. I would leave.

'Bye, bitch,' Debbie said, as I went out the door. I caught a glimpse of Alcide turning to her, his expression appalled, but Pam grabbed me by the arm and hustled me out into the parking lot. Gerald had a hold of Eric, which was a good thing, too.

As the two vampires handed us out to Chow, I was seething.

Chow thrust Eric into the passenger's seat, so it appeared I was the designated driver. The Asian vamp said, 'We'll call you later, go home,' and I was about to snap back at him. But I glanced over at my passenger and decided to be smart instead and get out of there quickly. Eric's belligerence was dissolving into a muddle. He looked confused and lost, as unlike the hair-trigger avenger he'd been only a few minutes before as you can imagine.

We were halfway home before Eric said anything. 'Why are vampires so hated by Weres?' he asked.

'I don't know,' I answered, slowing down because two deer bounded across the road. You see the first one, you always wait: There'll be another one, most often. 'Vamps feel the same about Weres and shifters. The supernatural community seems to band together against humans, but other than that, you guys squabble a lot, at least as far as I can tell.' I took a deep breath and considered phraseology. 'Um, Eric, I appreciate your taking my part, when that Amanda called me a name. But I'm pretty used to speaking up for myself when I think it's called for. If I were a vampire, you wouldn't feel you had to hit people on my behalf, right?'

'But you're not as strong as a vampire, not even as strong as a Were,' Eric objected.

'No argument there, honey. But I also wouldn't have even thought of hitting her, because that would give her a reason to hit me back.'

'You're saying I made it come to blows when I didn't need to.'

'That's exactly what I'm saying.'

'I embarrassed you.'

'No,' I said instantly. Then I wondered if that wasn't exactly the case. 'No,' I repeated with more conviction, 'you didn't embarrass me. Actually, it made me feel good, that you felt, ah, fond enough of me to be angry when Amanda acted like I was something stuck to her shoe. But I'm used to that treatment, and I can handle it. Though Debbie's taking it to a whole different level.'

The new, thoughtful Eric gave that a mental chewing over.

'Why are you used to that?' he asked.

It wasn't the reaction I'd expected. By that time we were at the house, and I checked out the surrounding clearing before I got out of the car to unlock the back door. When we were safely inside with the dead bolt shot, I said, 'Because I'm used to people not thinking much of barmaids. Uneducated barmaids. Uneducated telepathic barmaids. I'm used to people thinking I'm crazy, or at least off mentally. I'm not trying to sound like I think I'm Poor Pitiful Pearl, but I don't have a lot of fans, and I'm used to that.'

'That confirms my bad opinion of humans in general,' Eric said. He pulled my coat off my shoulders, looked at it with distaste, hung it on the back of one of the chairs pushed in under the kitchen table. 'You are beautiful.'

No one had ever looked me in the eyes and said that. I

found I had to lower my head. 'You are smart, and you are loyal,' he said relentlessly, though I waved a hand to ask him to quit. 'You have a sense of fun and adventure.'

'Cut it out,' I said.

'Make me,' he said. 'You have the most beautiful breasts I've ever seen. You're brave.' I put my fingers across his mouth, and his tongue darted out to give them a quick lick. I relaxed against him, feeling the tingle down to my toes. 'You're responsible and hardworking,' he continued. Before he could tell me that I was good about replacing the garbage can liner when I took the garbage out, I replaced my fingers with my lips.

'There,' he said softly, after a long moment. 'You're creative, too.'

For the next hour, he showed me that he, too, was creative.

It was the only hour in an extremely long day that I hadn't been consumed with fear: for the fate of my brother, about Hallow's malevolence, about the horrible death of Adabelle Yancy. There were probably a few more things that made me fearful, but in such a long day it was impossible to pick any one thing that was more awful than the other.

As I lay wrapped up in Eric's arms, humming a little wordless tune as I traced the line of his shoulder with an idle finger, I was bone-deep grateful for the pleasure he'd given me. A piece of happiness should never be taken as due.

'Thank you,' I said, my face pressed to his silent chest.

He put a finger under my chin so I would raise my eyes to his. 'No,' he said quietly. 'You took me in off the road and kept me safe. You're ready to fight for me. I can tell this about you. I can't believe my luck. When this witch is defeated, I would bring you to my side. I will share every-thing I have with you. Every vampire who owes me fealty will honor you.'

Was this medieval, or what? Bless Eric's heart, none of that was going to happen. At least I was smart enough, and realistic enough, not to deceive myself for a minute, though it was a wonderful fantasy. He was thinking like a chieftain with thralls at his disposal, not like a ruthless head vampire who owned a tourist bar in Shreveport.

'You've made me very happy,' I said, which was certainly the truth.

Chapter 10

The pond behind Jason's house had already been searched by the time I got up the next morning. Alcee Beck pounded on my door about ten o'clock, and since it sounded exactly like a lawman knocking, I pulled on my jeans and a sweatshirt before I went to the door.

'He's not in the pond,' Beck said, without preamble.

I sagged against the doorway. 'Oh, thank God.' I closed my eyes for a minute to do just that. 'Please come in.' Alcee Beck stepped over the threshold like a vampire, looking around him silently and with a certain wariness.

'Would you like some coffee?' I asked politely, when he was seated on the old couch.

'No, thank you,' he said stiffly, as uncomfortable with me as I was with him. I spotted Eric's shirt hanging on the doorknob of my bedroom, not quite visible from where Detective Beck was sitting. Lots of women wear men's shirts, and I told myself not to be paranoid about its presence. Though I tried not to listen to the detective's mind, I could tell that he was uneasy being alone in the house of a white woman, and he was wishing that Andy Bellefleur would get there.

'Excuse me for a minute,' I said, before I yielded to temptation and asked him why Andy was due to arrive. That would shake Alcee Beck to the core. I grabbed the shirt as I went into my room, folded it, and tucked it in a drawer before I brushed my teeth and washed my face. By the time I returned to the living room, Andy had made his appearance. Jason's boss, Catfish Hennessey, was with him. I could feel the blood leaving my head and I sat down very heavily on the ottoman sitting by the couch.

'What?' I said. I couldn't have uttered another word.

'The blood on the dock is probably feline blood, and there's a print in it, besides Jason's boot print,' said Andy. 'We've kept this quiet, because we didn't want those woods crawling with idiots.' I could feel myself swaying in an invisible wind. I would have laughed, if I hadn't had the 'gift' of telepathy. He wasn't thinking tabby or calico when he said feline; he was thinking panther.

Panthers were what we called mountain lions. Sure, there aren't mountains around here, but panthers – the oldest men hereabouts called them 'painters' – live in low bottomland, too. To the best of my knowledge, the only place panthers could be found in the wild was in Florida, and their numbers were dwindling to the brink of extinction. No solid evidence had been produced to prove that any live native panthers had been living in Louisiana in the past fifty years, give or take a decade.

But of course, there were stories. And our woods and streams could produce no end of alligators, nutria, possums, coons, and even the occasional black bear or wildcat. Coyotes, too. But there were no pictures, or scat, or print casts, to prove the presence of panthers . . . until now.

Andy Bellefleur's eyes were hot with longing, but not for

me. Any red-blooded male who'd ever gone hunting, or even any P.C. guy who photographed nature, would give almost anything to see a real wild panther. Despite the fact that these large predators were deeply anxious to avoid humans, humans would not return the favor.

'What are you thinking?' I asked, though I knew damn good and well what they were thinking. But to keep them on an even keel, I had to pretend not to; they'd feel better, and they might let something slip. Catfish was just thinking that Jason was most likely dead. The two lawmen kept fixing me in their gaze, but Catfish, who knew me better than they did, was sitting forward on the edge of Gran's old recliner, his big red hands clasped to each other so hard the knuckles were white.

'Maybe Jason spotted the panther when he came home that night,' Andy said carefully. 'You know he'd run and get his rifle and try to track it.'

'They're endangered,' I said. 'You think Jason doesn't know that panthers are endangered?' Of course, they thought Jason was so impulsive and brainless that he just wouldn't care.

'Are you sure that would be at the top of his list?' Alcee Beck asked, with an attempt at gentleness.

'So you think Jason shot the panther,' I said, having a little difficulty getting the words out of my mouth.

'It's a possibility.'

'And then what?' I crossed my arms over my chest.

All three men exchanged a glance. 'Maybe Jason followed the panther into the woods,' Andy said. 'Maybe the panther wasn't so badly wounded after all, and it got him.'

'You think my brother would trail a wounded and dangerous animal into the woods – at night, by himself.' Sure they did. I could read it loud and clear. They thought that would be absolutely typical Jason Stackhouse behavior. What they didn't get was that (reckless and wild as my brother was) Jason's favorite person in the entire universe was Jason Stackhouse, and he would not endanger that person in such an obvious way.

Andy Bellefleur had some misgivings about this theory, but Alcee Beck sure didn't. He thought I'd outlined Jason's procedure that night exactly. What the two lawmen didn't know, and what I couldn't tell them, was that if Jason had seen a panther at his house that night, the chances were good the panther was actually a shape-shifting human. Hadn't Claudine said that the witches had gathered some of the larger shifters into their fold? A panther would be a valuable animal to have at your side if you were contemplating a hostile takeover.

'Jay Stans, from Clarice, called me this morning,' Andy said. His round face turned toward me and his brown eyes locked on me. 'He was telling me about this gal you found by the side of the road last night.'

I nodded, not seeing the connection, and too preoccupied with speculation about the panther to guess what was coming.

'This girl have any connection to Jason?'

'What?' I was stunned. 'What are you talking about?'

'You find this girl, this Maria-Star Cooper, by the side of the road. They searched, but they didn't find any trace of an accident.'

I shrugged. 'I told them I wasn't sure I could pin the spot down, and they didn't ask me to go looking, after I offered. I'm not real surprised they couldn't find any evidence, not knowing the exact spot. I tried to pin it down, but it was at night, and I was pretty scared. Or she could have just been dumped where I found her.' I don't watch the Discovery Channel for nothing.

'See, what we were thinking,' Alcee Beck rumbled, 'is that this girl was one of Jason's discards, and maybe he was keeping her somewhere secret? But you let her go when Jason disappeared.'

'Huh?' It was like they were speaking Urdu or something. I couldn't make any sense out of it.

'With Jason getting arrested under suspicion of those murders last year and all, we wondered if there wasn't some fire under all that smoke.'

'You know who did those killings. He's in jail, unless something's happened that I don't know about. And he confessed.' Catfish met my eyes, and his were very uneasy. This line of questioning had my brother's boss all twitchy. Granted, my brother was a little kinky in the sex department (though none of the women he'd kinked with seemed to mind), but the idea of him keeping a sex slave that I had to deal with when he vanished? Oh, come on!

'He did confess, and he's still in jail,' Andy said. Since Andy had taken the confession, I should hope so. 'But what if Jason was his accomplice?'

'Wait a damn minute now,' I said. My pot was beginning to boil over. 'You can't have it both ways. If my brother is dead out in the woods after chasing a mythical wounded panther, how could he have been holding, what's her name, Maria-Star Cooper, hostage somewhere? You're thinking I've been in on my brother's supposed bondage activities, too? You think I hit her with my car? And then I loaded her in and drove her to the emergency room?'

We all glared at each other for a long moment. The men

were tossing out waves of tension and confusion like they were necklaces at Mardi Gras.

Then Catfish launched himself off the couch like a bottle rocket. 'No,' he bellowed. 'You guys asked me to come along to break this bad news about the panther to Sookie. No one said anything about this stuff about some girl that got hit by a car! This here is a nice girl.' Catfish pointed at me. 'No one's going to call her different! Not only did Jason Stackhouse never have to do more than crook his little finger at a girl for her to come running, much less take one hostage and do weird stuff to her, but if you're saying Sookie let this Cooper girl free when Jason didn't come home, and then tried to run over her, well, all I got to say is, you can go straight to hell!'

God bless Catfish Hennessey is all *I* had to say.

Alcee and Andy left soon after, and Catfish and I had a disjointed talk consisting mostly of him cursing the lawmen. When he ran down, he glanced at his watch.

'Come on, Sookie. You and me got to get to Jason's.'

'Why?' I was willing but bewildered.

'We got us a search party together, and I know you'll want to be there.'

I stared at him with my mouth open, while Catfish fumed about Alcee and Andy's allegations. I tried real hard to think of some way to cancel a search party. I hated to think of those men and women putting on all their winter gear to plow through the underbrush, now bare and brown, that made the woods so difficult to navigate. But there was no way to stop them, when they meant so well; and there was every reason to join them.

There was the remote chance that Jason *was* out there in the woods somewhere. Catfish told me he'd gotten together as many men as he could, and Kevin Pryor had agreed to be the coordinator, though off-duty. Maxine Fortenberry and her churchwomen were bringing out coffee and doughnuts from the Bon Temps Bakery. I began crying, because this was just overwhelming, and Catfish turned even redder. Weeping women were way high on Catfish's long list of things that made him uncomfortable.

I eased his situation by telling him I had to get ready. I threw the bed together, washed my face clean of tears, and yanked my hair back into a ponytail. I found a pair of ear-muffs that I used maybe once a year, and pulled on my old coat and stuck my yard work gloves in my pocket, along with a wad of Kleenex in case I got weepy again.

The search party was the popular activity for the day in Bon Temps. Not only do people like to help in our small town – but also rumors had inevitably begun circulating about the mysterious wild animal footprint. As far as I could tell, the word 'panther' was not yet currency; if it had been, the crowd would have been even larger. Most of the men had come armed – well, actually, most of the men were always armed. Hunting is a way of life around here, the NRA provides most of the bumper stickers, and deer season is like a holy holiday. There are special times for hunting deer with a bow and arrow, with a muzzleloader, or with a rifle. (There may be a spear season, for all I know.) There must have been fifty people at Jason's house, quite a party on a workday for such a small community.

Sam was there, and I was so glad to see him I almost began crying again. Sam was the best boss I'd ever had, and a friend, and he always came when I was in trouble. His red-gold hair was covered with a bright orange knit cap, and he wore bright orange gloves, too. His heavy brown jacket looked somber in contrast, and like all of the men, he was wearing work boots. You didn't go out in the woods, even in winter, with ankles unprotected. Snakes were slow and sluggish, but they were there, and they'd retaliate if you stepped on them.

Somehow the presence of all these people made Jason's disappearance seem that much more terrifying. If all these people believed Jason might be out in the woods, dead or badly wounded, he might be. Despite every sensible thing I could tell myself, I grew more and more afraid. I had a few minutes of blanking out on the scene entirely while I imagined all the things that could have happened to Jason, for maybe the hundredth go-round.

Sam was standing beside me, when I could hear and see again. He'd pulled off a glove, and his hand found mine and clasped it. His felt warm and hard, and I was glad to be holding on to him. Sam, though a shifter, knew how to aim his thoughts at me, though he couldn't 'hear' mine in return. *Do you really believe he's out there?* he asked me.

I shook my head. Our eyes met and held.

Do you think he's still alive?

That was a lot harder. Finally, I just shrugged. He kept hold of my hand, and I was glad of it.

Arlene and Tack scrambled out of Arlene's car and came toward us. Arlene's hair was as bright red as ever, but quite a bit more snarled than she usually wore it, and the short-order cook needed to shave. So he hadn't started keeping a razor at Arlene's yet, was the way I read it.

'Did you see Tara?' Arlene asked.

'No.'

'Look.' She pointed, as surreptitiously as you can, and I saw Tara in jeans and rubber boots that came up to her knees. She looked as unlike the meticulously groomed clothing-store proprietor as I could imagine, though she was wearing an adorable fake-fur hat of white and brown that made you want to go up and stroke her head. Her coat matched the hat. So did her gloves. But from the waist down, Tara was ready for the woods. Jason's friend Dago was staring at Tara with the stunned look of the newly smitten. Holly and Danielle had come, too, and since Danielle's boyfriend wasn't around, the search party was turning out to have an unexpected social side.

Maxine Fortenberry and two other women from her church had let down the tailgate of Maxine's husband's old pickup, and there were several thermoses containing coffee set up there, along with disposable cups, plastic spoons, and packages of sugar. Six dozen doughnuts steamed up the long boxes they'd been packed in. A large plastic trash can, already lined with a black bag, stood ready. These ladies knew how to throw a search party.

I couldn't believe all this had been organized in the space of a few hours. I had to take my hand from Sam's to fish out a tissue and mop my face with it. I would have expected Arlene to come, but the presence of Holly and Danielle was just about stunning, and Tara's attendance was even more surprising. She wasn't a search-the-woods kind of woman. Kevin Pryor didn't have much use for Jason, but here he was, with a map and pad and pencil, organizing away.

I caught Holly's eye, and she gave me a sad sort of smile, the kind of little smile you gave someone at a funeral.

Just then Kevin banged the plastic trash can lid against the tailgate of the truck, and when everyone's attention was on him, he began to give directions for the search. I hadn't realized Kevin could be so authoritative; on most occasions, he was overshadowed by his clingy mother, Jeneen, or his oversized partner, Kenya. You wouldn't catch Kenya out in the woods looking for Jason, I reflected, and just then I spotted her and had to swallow my own thoughts. In sensible gear, she was leaning against the Fortenberrys' pickup, her brown face absolutely expressionless. Her stance suggested that she was Kevin's enforcer – that she'd move or speak only if he were challenged in some way. Kenya knew how to project silent menace; I'll give her that. She would throw a bucket of water on Jason if he were on fire, but her feelings for my brother were certainly not overwhelmingly positive. She'd come because Kevin was volunteering. As Kevin divided people up into teams, her dark eyes left him only to scan the faces of the searchers, including mine. She gave me a slight nod, and I gave her the same.

'Each group of five has to have a rifleman,' Kevin called. 'That can't be just anybody. It has to be someone who's spent time out in the woods hunting.' The excitement level rose to the boiling point with this directive. But after that, I didn't listen to the rest of Kevin's instructions. I was still tired from the day before, for one thing; what an exceptionally full day it had been. And the whole time, in the background, my fear for my brother had been nagging and eating at me. I'd been woken early this morning after a long night, and here I was standing in the cold outside my childhood home, waiting to participate in a touching wild goose chase – or at least I hoped it was a wild goose chase. I was too dazed to judge any more. A chill wind began to gust through the clearing around the house, making the tears on my cheeks unbearably cold.

Sam put his arms around me, though in our coats it was quite awkward. It seemed to me I could feel the warmth of him even through all the material.

'You know we won't find him out there,' he whispered to me.

'I'm pretty sure we won't,' I said, sounding anything but certain.

Sam said, 'I'll smell him if he's out there.'

That was so practical.

I looked up at him. I didn't have to look far, because Sam's not a real tall man. Right now, his face was very serious. Sam has more fun with his shifter self than most of the two-natured, but I could tell he was intent on easing my fear. When he was in his second nature, he had the dog's keen sense of smell; when he was in his human form, that sense was still superior to that of a one-natured man. Sam would be able to smell a fairly recent corpse.

'You're going out in the woods,' I said.

'Sure. I'll do my best. If he's there, I think I'll know.'

Kevin had told me the sheriff had tried to hire the tracking dogs trained by a Shreveport police officer, but the officer had said they were booked for the day. I wondered if that were true, or if the man just hadn't wanted to risk his dogs in the woods with a panther. Truthfully, I couldn't blame him. And here was a better offer, right in front of me.

'Sam,' I said, my eyes filling with tears. I tried to thank him, but the words wouldn't come. I was lucky to have a friend like Sam, and well I knew it.

'Hush, Sookie,' he said. 'Don't cry. We'll find out what happened to Jason, and we'll find a way to restore Eric to his mind.' He rubbed the tears off my cheeks with his thumb.

No one was close enough to hear, but I couldn't help glancing around to make sure.

'Then,' Sam said, a distinctly grim edge to his voice, 'we can get him out of your house and back to Shreveport where he belongs.'

I decided no reply was the best policy.

'What was your word for the day?' he asked, standing back.

I gave him a watery smile. Sam always asked about the daily offering of my Word a Day calendar. 'I didn't check this morning. Yesterday was "farrago,"' I said.

He raised his brows inquiringly.

'A confused mess,' I said.

'Sookie, we'll find a way out of this.'

When the searchers divided up into groups, I discovered that Sam was not the only two-natured creature out in Jason's yard that day. I was astonished to see a contingent from Hotshot. Calvin Norris, his niece Crystal, and a second man who seemed vaguely familiar were standing by themselves. After a moment of stirring the sludge of my memory, I realized that the second man was the one I'd seen emerging from the shed behind the house down from Crystal's. His thick pale hair triggered the memory, and I was sure of it when I saw the graceful way he moved. Kevin assigned the Reverend Jimmy Fullenwilder to the trio as their armed man. The combination of the three Weres with the reverend would have made me laugh under other circumstances.

Since they lacked a fifth, I joined them.

The three Weres from Hotshot gave me sober nods, Calvin's golden green eyes fixed on me thoughtfully. 'This here's Felton Norris,' he said, by way of introduction.

I nodded back to Felton, and Jimmy Fullenwilder, a gray-haired man of about sixty, shook hands. 'Of course I know Miss Sookie, but the rest of you I'm not sure of. I'm Jimmy Fullenwilder, pastor of Greater Love Baptist,' he said, smiling all around. Calvin absorbed this information with a polite smile, Crystal sneered, and Felton Norris (had they run out of last names in Hotshot?) grew colder. Felton was an odd one, even for an inbred werewolf. His eyes were remarkably dark, set under straight thick brown brows, which contrasted sharply with his pale hair. His face was broad at the eyes, narrowing a little too abruptly to a thin-lipped mouth. Though he was a bulky man, he moved lightly and quietly, and as we began to move out into the woods, I realized that all the Hotshot residents had that in common. In comparison with the Norrises, Jimmy Fullenwilder and I were blundering elephants.

At least the minister carried his 30-30 like he knew how to use it.

Following our instructions, we stood in a row, stretching out our arms at shoulder height so we were fingertip to fingertip. Crystal was on my right, and Calvin was on my left. The other groups did the same. We began the search in the fanlike shape determined by the curve of the pond.

'Remember who's in your group,' Kevin bellowed. 'We don't want to leave people out here! Now, start.'

We began scanning the ground ahead of us, moving at a steady pace. Jimmy Fullenwilder was a couple of steps ahead, since he was armed. It was apparent right away that there were woodcraft disparities between the Hotshot folks, the reverend, and me. Crystal seemed to flow through the undergrowth, without having to wade through it or push it aside, though I could hear her progress. Jimmy

Fullenwilder, an avid hunter, was at home in the woods and an experienced outdoorsman, and I could tell he was getting much more information from his surroundings than I was, but he wasn't able to move like Calvin and Felton. They glided through the woods like ghosts, making about as much noise.

Once, when I ran into a particularly dense thicket of thorny vines, I felt two hands clamp on either side of my waist, and I was just lifted over it before I had a chance to react. Calvin Norris put me down very gently and went right back to his position. I don't think anyone else noticed. Jimmy Fullenwilder, the only one who would have been startled, had gotten a little ahead.

Our team found nothing: not a shred of cloth or flesh, not a boot print or panther print, not a smell or a trace or a drop of blood. One of the other teams yelled over that they'd found a chewed-up possum corpse, but there was no immediate way to tell what had caused its death.

The going got tougher. My brother had hunted in these woods, allowed some friends of his to hunt there, but otherwise had not interfered with nature in the twenty acres around the house. That meant he hadn't cleared away fallen branches or pulled up seedlings, which compounded the difficulty of our movement.

My team happened to be the one that found his deer stand, which he and Hoyt had built together about five years ago.

Though the stand faced a natural clearing running roughly north-south, the woods were so thick around it that we were temporarily out of sight of the other searchers, which I would not have thought possible in winter, with the branches bare. Every now and then a human voice, raised in a distant call, would make its way through the pines and the bushes and the branches of the oaks and gum trees, but the sense of isolation was overwhelming.

Felton Norris swarmed up the deer stand ladder in such an unhuman way that I had to distract Reverend Fullenwilder by asking him if he'd mind praying in church for my brother's return. Of course, he told me he already had, and furthermore, he notified me he'd be glad to see me in his church on Sunday to add my voice to those lifted in prayer. Though I missed a lot of churchgoing because of my job, and when I did go I attended the Methodist church (which Jimmy Fullenwilder well knew), I pretty much had to say yes. Just then Felton called down that the stand was empty. 'Come down careful, this ladder's not too steady,' Calvin called back, and I realized Calvin was warning Felton to look human when he descended. As the shifter descended slowly and clumsily, I met Calvin's eyes, and he looked amused.

Bored by the wait at the foot of the deer stand, Crystal had flitted ahead of our point man, the Reverend Fullenwilder, something Kevin had warned us not to do. Just as I was thinking, *I can't see her*, I heard her scream.

In the space of a couple of seconds, Calvin and Felton had bounded over the clearing toward the sound of Crystal's voice, and the Reverend Jimmy and I were left to run behind. I hoped the agitation of the moment would obscure his perception of the way Calvin and Felton were moving. Up ahead of us, we heard an indescribable noise, a loud chorus of squeals and frenetic movement coming from the undergrowth. Then a hoarse shout and another shrill scream came to us muffled by the cold thickness of the woods.

We heard yelling from all directions as the other searchers responded, hurrying toward the alarming sounds.

My heel caught in a snarl of vines and I went down, ass over teacup. Though I rolled to my feet and began running again, Jimmy Fullenwilder had gotten ahead of me, and as I plunged through a stand of low pines, each no bigger around than a mailing tube, I heard the boom of the rifle.

Oh, my God, I thought. *Oh, my God.*

The little clearing was filled with blood and tumult. A huge animal was thrashing in the dead leaves, spraying scarlet drops on everything in its vicinity. But it was no panther. For the second time in my life, I was seeing a razorback hog, that ferocious feral pig that grows to a huge size.

In the time it took me to realize what was in front of me, the sow collapsed and died. She reeked of pig and blood. A crashing and squealing in the undergrowth around us indicated she hadn't been alone when Crystal stumbled upon her.

But not all the blood was the sow's.

Crystal Norris was swearing a blue streak as she sat with her back against an old oak, her hands clamped over her gored thigh. Her jeans were wet with her own blood, and her uncle and her – well, I didn't know what relationship Felton bore to Crystal, but I was sure there was one – kinsman were bending over her. Jimmy Fullenwilder was standing with his rifle still pointed at the beast, and he had an expression on his face that I can only describe as shell-shocked.

'How is she?' I asked the two men, and only Calvin looked up. His eyes had gone very peculiar, and I realized they'd gotten more yellow, rounder. He cast an unmistakable look at the huge carcass, a look of sheer desire. There was blood around his mouth. There was a patch of fur on the back of his hand, kind of buff-colored. He must make a strange-looking wolf. I pointed silently at this evidence of his nature, and he shivered with longing as he nodded acknowledgment. I yanked a handkerchief out of my coat pocket, spat on it, and wiped his face with it before Jimmy Fullenwilder could fall out of his fascination with his kill and observe his strange companions. When Calvin's mouth wasn't stained anymore, I knotted the handkerchief around his hand to conceal the fur.

Felton seemed to be normal, until I observed what was at the end of his arms. They weren't really hands anymore . . . but not really wolf paws, either. They were something very odd, something big and flat and clawed.

I couldn't read the men's thoughts, but I could feel their desires, and most of those desires had to do with raw red pig meat, and lots of it. Felton actually rocked back and forth once or twice with the force of his desire. Their silent struggle was painful to endure, even secondhand. I felt the change when the two men began to force their brains into human patterns. In a few seconds, Calvin managed to speak.

'She's losing blood fast, but if we get her to the hospital she'll be all right.' His voice was thick, and he spoke with an effort. Felton, his eyes still downcast, began tearing clumsily at his flannel shirt. With his hands misshapen, he couldn't manage the job, and I took it over. When Crystal's wound was bound as tightly as the makeshift bandage could compress it, the two men lifted the now white and silent Crystal and began to carry her rapidly out of the woods. The position of Felton's hands hid them from sight, thank God.

This all occurred so quickly that the other searchers converging on the clearing were just beginning to absorb what had happened, and react.

'I shot a hog,' Jimmy Fullenwilder was saying, shaking his head from side to side, as Kevin and Kenya burst into the clearing from the east. 'I can't believe it. It just threw her over and the other sows and little ones scattered and then the two men were on it, and then they got out of the way and I shot it in the throat.' He didn't know if he was a hero or if he was in big trouble with the Department of Wildlife. He'd had more to fear than he would ever realize. Felton and Calvin had almost gone into full Were mode at the threat to Crystal and the arousal of their own hunting instincts, and the fact that they'd thrown themselves away from the pig rather than change utterly proved they were very strong, indeed. But the fact that they'd begun to change, hadn't been able to stop it, seemed to argue the opposite. The line between the two natures of some of the denizens of Hotshot seemed be growing very blurred.

In fact, there were bite marks on the hog. I was so overwhelmed with anxiety that I couldn't keep up my guard, and all the excitement of all the searchers poured into my head – all the revulsion/fear/panic at the sight of the blood, the knowledge that a searcher had been seriously injured, the envy of other hunters at Jimmy Fullenwilder's coup. It was all too much, and I wanted to get away more than I've ever wanted anything.

'Let's go. This'll be the end of the search, at least for today,' Sam said at my elbow. We walked out of the woods together, very slowly. I told Maxine what had happened, and after I'd thanked her for her wonderful contribution and accepted a box of doughnuts, I drove home. Sam followed me. I was a little more myself by the time we got there.

As I unlocked the back door, it felt quite strange knowing that there was actually someone else already in the house. Was Eric conscious on some level of my footsteps on the floor above his head – or was he as dead as an ordinary dead person? But the wondering ran through my head and out the other side, because I was just too overloaded to consider it.

Sam began to make coffee. He was somewhat at home in the kitchen, as he'd dropped in a time or two when my Gran was alive, and he'd visited on other occasions.

As I hung up our coats, I said, 'That was a disaster.'

Sam didn't disagree.

'Not only did we not find Jason, which I truly never expected we would, but the guys from Hotshot almost got outed, and Crystal got hurt. I don't know why they thought they should be there anyway, frankly.' I know it wasn't nice of me to say that, but I was with Sam, who'd seen enough of my bad side to be under no illusions.

'I talked to them before you got there. Calvin wanted to show he was willing to court you, in a Hotshot kind of way,' Sam said, his voice quiet and even. 'Felton is their best tracker, so he made Felton come, and Crystal just wanted to find Jason.'

Instantly I felt ashamed of myself. 'I'm sorry,' I said, holding my head in my hands and dropping into a chair. 'I'm sorry.'

Sam knelt in front of me and put his hands on my knees. 'You're entitled to be cranky,' he said.

I bent over him and kissed the top of his head. 'I don't

know what I'd do without you,' I said, without any thought at all.

He looked up at me, and there was a long, odd moment, when the light in the room seemed to dance and shiver. 'You'd call Arlene,' he said with a smile. 'She'd come over with the kids, and she'd try to spike your coffee, and she'd tell you about Tack's angled dick, and she'd get you to laughing, and you'd feel better.'

I blessed him for letting the moment pass. 'You know, that kind of makes me curious, that bit about Tack, but it probably falls into the category of "too much information,"' I said.

'I thought so, too, but that didn't prevent me from hearing it when she was telling Charlsie Tooten.'

I poured us each a cup of coffee and put the half-empty sugar bowl within Sam's reach, along with a spoon. I glanced over at the kitchen counter to see how full the clear sugar canister was, and I noticed that the message light on the answering machine was blinking. I only had to get up and take a step to press the button. The message had been recorded at 5:01 A.M. Oh. I'd turned the phone ringer off when I'd gone to bed exhausted. Almost invariably my messages were real mundane – Arlene asking me if I'd heard a piece of gossip, Tara passing the time of day during a slow hour at the store – but this one was a real doozy.

Pam's clear voice said, 'Tonight we attack the witch and her coven. The Weres have persuaded the local Wiccans to join us. We need you to bring Eric. He can fight, even if he doesn't know who he is. He will be useless to us if we can't break the spell, anyway.' That Pam, ever practical. She was willing to use Eric for cannon fodder, since we might not be able to restore him to full Eric leadership mode. After a

DEAD TO THE WORLD 231

little pause, she continued, 'The Weres of Shreveport are allying with vampires in battle. You can watch history being made, my telepathic friend.'

The sound of the phone being put back in the cradle. The click that heralded the next message, which came in two minutes after the first.

'Thinking of that,' Pam said, as if she'd never hung up, 'there is the idea that your unusual ability can help us in our fight, and we want to explore that. Isn't that the right buzzword now? Explore? So get here as close to first dark as possible.' She hung up again.

Click. '"Here" is 714 Parchman Avenue,' Pam said. Hung up.

'How can I do that, with Jason still missing?' I asked, when it became clear Pam hadn't called again.

'You're going to sleep now,' Sam said. 'Come on.' He pulled me to my feet, led me to my room. 'You're going to take off your boots and jeans, crawl back in the bed, and take a long nap. When you get up, you'll feel better. You leave Pam's number so I can reach you. Tell the cops to call the bar if they learn anything, and I'll phone you if I hear from Bud Dearborn.'

'So you think I should do this?' I was bewildered.

'No, I'd give anything if you wouldn't. But I think you have to. It's not my fight; I wasn't invited.' Sam gave me a kiss on the forehead and left to go back to Merlotte's.

His attitude was kind of interesting, after all the vampire insistence (both Bill's and Eric's) that I was a possession to be guarded. I felt pretty empowered and gung-ho for about thirty seconds, until I remembered my New Year's resolution: *no getting beaten up.* If I went to Shreveport with Eric, then I was sure to see things I didn't want to see, learn things I didn't want to know, and get my ass whipped, too.

On the other hand, my brother Jason had made a deal with the vampires, and I had to uphold it. Sometimes I felt that my whole life had been spent stuck between a rock and a hard place. But then, lots of people had complicated lives.

I thought of Eric, a powerful vampire whose mind had been stripped clean of his identity. I thought of the carnage I'd seen in the bridal shop, the white lace and brocade speckled with dried blood and matter. I thought of poor Maria-Star, in the hospital in Shreveport. These witches were bad, and bad should be stopped; bad should be overcome. That's the American model.

It seemed kind of strange to think that I was on the side of vampires and werewolves, and that was the good side. That made me laugh a little, all to myself. Oh, yes, we good guys would save the day.

Chapter 11

Amazingly, I did sleep. I woke with Eric on the bed beside me. He was smelling me.

'Sookie, what is this?' he asked in a very quiet voice. He knew, of course, when I woke. 'You smell of the woods, and you smell of shifter. And something even wilder.'

I supposed the shifter he smelled was Sam. 'And Were,' I prompted, not wanting him to miss out on anything.

'No, not Were,' he said.

I was puzzled. Calvin had lifted me over the brambles, and his scent should still have been on me.

'More than one kind of shifter,' Eric said in the near-dark of my room. 'What have you been doing, my lover?'

He didn't exactly sound angry, but he didn't sound happy, either. Vampires. They wrote the book on possessive.

'I was in the search party for my brother, in the woods behind his home,' I said.

Eric was still for a minute. Then he wrapped his arms around me and hauled me up against him. 'I'm sorry,' he said. 'I know you are worried.'

'Let me ask you something,' I said, willing to test a theory of mine.

'Of course.'

'Look inside yourself, Eric. Are you really, really sorry? Worried about Jason?' Because the real Eric, in his right mind, would not have cared one little bit.

'Of course,' he protested. Then, after a long moment – I wished I could see his face – he said, 'Not really.' He sounded surprised. 'I know I should be. I should be concerned about your brother, because I love having sex with you, and I should want you to think well of me so you'll want sex, too.'

You just had to like the honesty. This was the closest to the real Eric I'd seen in days.

'But you'll listen, right? If I need to talk? For the same reason?'

'Of course, my lover.'

'Because you want to have sex with me.'

'That, of course. But also because I find I really do . . .' He paused, as if he were about to say something outrageous. 'I find I have feelings for you.'

'Oh,' I said into his chest, sounding as astonished as Eric had. His chest was bare, as I suspected the rest of him was. I felt the light sprinkling of curly blond hair against my cheek.

'Eric,' I said, after a long pause, 'I almost hate to say this, but I have feelings for you, too.' There was a lot I needed to tell Eric, and we should be in the car on our way to Shreveport already. But I was taking this moment to savor this little bit of happiness.

'Not love, exactly,' he said. His fingers were busy trying to find out how best to get my clothes off.

'No, but something close.' I helped him. 'We don't have much time, Eric,' I said, reaching down, touching him, making him gasp. 'Let's make it good.'

'Kiss me,' he said, and he wasn't talking about his mouth. 'Turn this way,' he whispered. 'I want to kiss you, too.'

It didn't take long, after all, for us to be holding each other, sated and happy.

'What's happened?' he asked. 'I can tell something is frightening you.'

'We have to go to Shreveport now,' I said. 'We're already past the time Pam said on the phone. Tonight's the night we face off against Hallow and her witches.'

'Then you must stay here,' he said immediately.

'No,' I said gently, putting my hand on his cheek. 'No, baby, I have to go with you.' I didn't tell him Pam thought using me in the battle would be a good idea. I didn't tell him he was going to be used as a fighting machine. I didn't tell him I was sure someone was going to die tonight; maybe quite a few someones, human and Were and vampire. It was probably the last time I would use an endearment when I addressed Eric. It was perhaps the last time Eric would wake up in my house. One of us might not survive this night, and if we did, there was no way to know how we'd be changed.

The drive to Shreveport was silent. We'd washed up and dressed without talking much, either. At least seven times, I thought of heading back to Bon Temps, with or without Eric.

But I didn't.

Eric's skills did not include map reading, so I had to pull over to check my Shreveport map to plot our course to

714 Parchman, something I hadn't foreseen before we got to the city. (I'd somehow expected Eric to remember the directions, but of course, he didn't.)

'Your word of the day was "annihilate,"' he told me cheerfully.

'Oh. Thanks for checking.' I probably didn't sound very thankful. 'You're sounding pretty excited about all this.'

'Sookie, there's nothing like a good fight,' he said defensively.

'That depends on who wins, I would think.'

That kept him quiet for a few minutes, which was fine. I was having trouble negotiating the strange streets in the darkness, with so much on my mind. But we finally got to the right street, and the right house on that street. I had always pictured Pam and Chow living in a mansion, but the vampires had a large ranch-style house in an upper-middle-class suburb. It was a trimmed-lawn, bike-riding, lawn-sprinkling street, from what I could tell.

The light by the driveway was on at 714, and the three-car garage around at the rear was full. I drove up the slope to the concrete apron that was placed for overflow parking. I recognized Alcide's truck and the compact car that had been parked in Colonel Flood's carport.

Before we got out of my old car, Eric leaned over to kiss me. We looked at each other, his eyes wide and blue, the whites so white you could hardly look away, his golden hair neatly brushed. He'd tied it back with one of my elastic bands, a bright blue one. He was wearing a pair of jeans and a new flannel shirt.

'We could go back,' he said. In the dome light of the car, his face looked hard as stone. 'We could go back to your house. I can stay with you always. We can know each other's bodies in every way, night after night. I could love you.' His nostrils flared, and he looked suddenly proud. 'I could work. You would not be poor. I would help you.'

'Sounds like a marriage,' I said, trying to lighten the atmosphere. But my voice was too shaky.

'Yes,' he said.

And he would never be himself again. He would be a false version of Eric, an Eric cheated out of his true life. Providing our relationship (such as it was) lasted, he would stay the same; but I wouldn't.

Enough with the negative thinking, Sookie, I told myself. I would be a total idiot to pass up living with this gorgeous creature for however long. We actually had a good time together, and I enjoyed Eric's sense of humor and his company, to say nothing of his lovemaking. Now that he'd lost his memory, he was lots of uncomplicated fun.

And that was the fly in the ointment. We would have a counterfeit relationship, because this was the counterfeit Eric. I'd come full loop.

I slid out of the car with a sigh. 'I'm a total idiot,' I said as he came around the back of the car to walk with me to the house.

Eric didn't say anything. I guess he agreed with me.

'Hello,' I called, pushing open the door after my knock brought no response. The garage door led into the laundry room and from there into the kitchen.

As you would expect in a vampire home, the kitchen was absolutely clean, because it wasn't used. This kitchen was small for a house the size of this one. I guess the real estate agent had thought it was her lucky day – her lucky night – when she'd shown it to vampires, since a real family who cooked at home would have trouble dealing with a kitchen the size of a king bed. The house had an open floor plan, so you could see over the breakfast bar into the 'family' room – in this case, the main room for a mighty odd family. There were three open doorways that probably led into the formal living room, the dining room, and the bedroom area.

Right at the moment, this family room was crammed with people. I got the impression, from the glimpses of feet and arms, that more people were standing in the open doorways into the other rooms.

The vampires were there: Pam, Chow, Gerald, and at least two more I recognized from Fangtasia. The two-natured were represented by Colonel Flood, red-haired Amanda (my big fan), the teenage boy with spiked brown hair (Sid), Alcide, Culpepper, and (to my disgust) Debbie Pelt. Debbie was dressed in the height of fashion – at least her version of fashion – which seemed a little out of place for a meeting of this kind. Maybe she wanted to remind me that she had a very good job working at an advertising agency.

Oh, good. Debbie's presence made the night just about perfect.

The group I didn't recognize had to be the local witches, by the process of elimination. I assumed that the dignified woman sitting on the couch was their leader. I didn't know what her correct title would be – coven master? Mistress? She was in her sixties, and she had iron gray hair. An African American with skin the color of coffee, she had brown eyes that looked infinitely wise and also skeptical. She'd brought a pale young man with glasses, who wore pressed khakis with a striped shirt and polished loafers. He might work in Office Depot or Super One Foods in some kind of managerial position, and his kids would think that he was out bowling or attending some church meeting on this cold January night. Instead, he and the young female witch beside him were about to embark on a fight to the death.

The remaining two empty chairs were clearly intended for Eric and me.

'We expected you earlier,' Pam said crisply.

'Hi, good to see you, too, thanks for coming on such short notice,' I muttered. For one long moment, everyone in the room looked at Eric, waiting for him to take charge of the action, as he had for years. And Eric looked back at them blankly. The long pause began to be awkward.

'Well, let's lay this out,' Pam said. All the assembled Supes turned their faces to her. Pam seemed to have taken the leadership bit between her teeth, and she was ready to run with it.

'Thanks to the Were trackers, we know the location of the building Hallow is using for her headquarters,' Pam told me. She seemed to be ignoring Eric, but I sensed it was because she didn't know what else to do. Sid grinned at me; I remembered he and Emilio had tracked the killers from the bridal shop to the house. Then I realized he was showing me he'd filed his teeth to points. Ick.

I could understand the presence of the vamps, the witches, and the Weres, but why was Debbie Pelt at this meeting? She was a shifter, not a Were. The Weres had always been so snobby about the shifters, and here was one; furthermore, one out of her own territory. I loathed and distrusted her. She must have insisted on being here, and that made me trust her even less, if that was possible.

If she was so determined to join in, put Debbie in the first line of fire, would be my advice. You wouldn't have to worry about what she was doing behind your back.

My grandmother would certainly have been ashamed of my vindictiveness; but then (like Alcide) she would have found it almost impossible to believe that Debbie had really tried to kill me.

'We'll infiltrate the neighborhood slowly,' Pam said. I wondered if she'd been reading a commando manual. 'The witches have already broadcast a lot of magic in the area, so there aren't too many people out on the streets. Some of the Weres are already in place. We won't be so obvious. Sookie will go in first.'

The assembled Supes turned their eyes to me at the same moment. That was pretty disconcerting: like being in a ring of pickup trucks at night, when they all turn on their headlights to illuminate the center.

'Why?' Alcide asked. His big hands gripped his knees. Debbie, who'd slumped down to sit on the floor beside the couch, smiled at me, knowing Alcide couldn't see her.

'Because Sookie is human,' Pam pointed out. 'And she's more of a natural phenomenon than a true Supe. They won't detect her.'

Eric had taken my hand. He was gripping it so hard that I thought I could hear my bones grinding together. Prior to his enchantment, he would have nipped Pam's plan in the bud, or maybe he would've enthusiastically endorsed it. Now he was too cowed to comment, which he clearly wanted to do.

'What am I supposed to do when I get there?' I was proud of myself for sounding so calm and practical. I'd rather be taking a complicated drink order from a table of drunken tree-trimmers than be first in the line of battle.

'Read the minds of the witches inside while we get into

position. If they detect us approaching, we lose the surprise of it, and we stand a greater chance of sustaining serious injury.' When she got excited, Pam had a slight accent, though I'd never been able to figure out what it was. I thought it might just be English as it had been spoken three hundred years ago. Or whatever. 'Can you count them? Is that possible?'

I thought for a second. 'Yes, I can do that.'

'That would be a big help, too.'

'What do we do when we get in the building?' asked Sid. Jittery with the thrill of it all, he was grinning, his pointed teeth showing.

Pam looked mildly astonished. 'We kill them all,' she said.

Sid's grin faded. I flinched. I wasn't the only one.

Pam seemed to realize she'd said something unpalatable. 'What else would we do?' she asked, genuinely amazed.

That was a stumper.

'They'll do their best to kill *us*,' Chow pointed out. 'They only made one attempt at negotiation, and it cost Eric his memory and Clancy his life. They delivered Clancy's clothes to Fangtasia this morning.' People glanced away from Eric, embarrassed. He looked stricken, and I patted his hand with my free one. His grip on my right hand relaxed a little. My circulation resumed in that hand, and it tingled. That was a relief.

'Someone needs to go with Sookie,' Alcide said. He glowered at Pam. 'She can't go close to that house by herself.'

'I'll go with her,' said a familiar voice from the corner of the room, and I leaned forward, searching the faces.

'Bubba!' I said, pleased to see the vampire. Eric stared in

wonder at the famous face. The glistening black hair was combed back in a pompadour, and the pouty lower lip was stretched in the trademark smile. His current keeper must have dressed him for the evening, because instead of a jumpsuit decked with rhinestones, or jeans and a T-shirt, Bubba was wearing camo.

'Pleased to see ya, Miss Sookie,' Bubba said. 'I'm wearing my Army duds.'

'I see that. Looking good, Bubba.'

'Thank you, ma'am.'

Pam considered. 'That might be a good idea,' she said. 'His, ah – the mental broadcast, the signature, you all get what I'm telling you? – is so, ah, atypical that they won't discover a vampire is near.' Pam was being very tactful.

Bubba made a terrible vampire. Though stealthy and obedient, he couldn't reason very clearly, and he liked cat blood better than human blood.

'Where's Bill, Miss Sookie?' he asked, as I could have predicted he would. Bubba had always been very fond of Bill.

'He's in Peru, Bubba. That's way down in South America.'

'No, I'm not,' said a cool voice, and my heart flip-flopped. 'I'm back.' Out of an open doorway stepped my former flame.

This was just an evening for surprises. I hoped some of them would be pleasant.

Seeing Bill so unexpectedly gave me a heavier jolt than I'd figured. I'd never had an ex-boyfriend before, my life having been pretty devoid of boyfriends alto- gether, so I didn't have much experience in handling my emotions about being in his presence, especially with

Eric gripping my hand like I was Mary Poppins and he was my charge.

Bill looked good in his khakis. He was wearing a Calvin Klein dress shirt I'd picked out for him, a muted plaid in shades of brown and gold. Not that I noticed.

'Good, we need you tonight,' Pam said. Ms. Businesslike. 'You'll have to tell me how the ruins were, the ones everyone talks about. You know the rest of the people here?'

Bill glanced around. 'Colonel Flood,' he said, nodding. 'Alcide.' His nod to Alcide had less cordiality. 'I haven't met these new allies,' he said, indicating the witches. Bill waited until the introductions were complete to ask, 'What is Debbie Pelt doing here?'

I tried not to gape at having my innermost thoughts spoken aloud. My question exactly! And how did Bill know Debbie? I tried to remember if their paths had crossed in Jackson, if they'd actually met face-to-face; and I couldn't recall such a meeting, though of course Bill knew what she'd done.

'She's Alcide's woman,' Pam said, in a cautious, puzzled sort of way.

I raised my eyebrows, looking at Alcide, and he turned a dusky red.

'She's here for a visit, and she decided to come along with him,' Pam went on. 'You object to her presence?'

'She joined in while I was being tortured in the king of Mississippi's compound,' Bill said. 'She enjoyed my pain.'

Alcide stood, looking as shocked as I'd ever seen him. 'Debbie, is this true?'

Debbie Pelt tried not to flinch, now that every eye was on her, and every eye was unfriendly. 'I just happened to be visiting a Were friend who lived there, one of the guards,' she said. Her voice didn't sound calm enough to match the words. 'Obviously, there was nothing I could do to free you. I would have been ripped to shreds. I can't believe you remember me being there very clearly. You were certainly out of it.' There was a hint of contempt in her words.

'You joined in the torture,' Bill said, his voice still impersonal and all the more convincing for it. 'You liked the pincers best.'

'You didn't tell anyone he was there?' Alcide asked Debbie. His voice was not impersonal at all. It held grief, and anger, and betrayal. 'You knew someone from another kingdom was being tortured at Russell's, and you didn't do anything?'

'He's a *vamp*, for God's sake,' Debbie said, sounding no more than irritated. 'When I found out later that you'd been taking Sookie around to hunt for him so you could get your dad out of hock with the vamps, I felt terrible. But at the time, it was just vamp business. Why should I interfere?'

'But why would any decent person join in torture?' Alcide's voice was strained.

There was a long silence.

'And of course, she tried to kill Sookie,' Bill said. He still managed to sound quite dispassionate.

'I didn't know you were in the trunk of the car when I pushed her in! I didn't know I was closing her in with a hungry vampire!' Debbie protested.

I don't know about anyone else, but I wasn't convinced for a second.

Alcide bent his rough black head to look down into his hands as if they held an oracle. He raised his face to look at Debbie. He was a man unable to dodge the bullet of truth any longer. I felt sorrier for him than I'd felt for anyone in a long, long time.

'I abjure you,' Alcide said. Colonel Flood winced, and young Sid, Amanda, and Culpepper looked both astonished and impressed, as if this were a ceremony they'd never thought to witness. 'I see you no longer. I hunt with you no longer. I share flesh with you no longer.'

This was obviously a ritual of great significance among the two-natured. Debbie stared at Alcide, aghast at his pronouncement. The witches murmured to one another, but otherwise the room remained silent. Even Bubba was wide-eyed, and most things went right over his shiny head.

'No,' Debbie said in a strangled voice, waving a hand in front of her, as if she could erase what had passed. 'No, Alcide!'

But he stared right through her. He saw her no longer.

Even though I loathed Debbie, her face was painful to see. Like most of the others present, as soon as I could, I looked anywhere else but at the shifter. Facing Hallow's coven seemed like a snap compared to witnessing this episode.

Pam seemed to agree. 'All right then,' she said briskly. 'Bubba will lead the way with Sookie. She will do her best to do whatever it is that she does – and she'll signal us.' Pam pondered for a moment. 'Sookie, a recap: We need to know the number of people in the house, whether or not they are all witches, and any other tidbit you can glean. Send Bubba back to us with whatever information you find and stand guard in case the situation changes while we move up. Once we're in position, you can retire to the cars, where you'll be safer.'

I had no problem with that whatsoever. In a crowd of witches, vampires, and Weres, I was no kind of combatant.

'This sounds okay, if I have to be involved at all,' I said. A tug on my hand drew my eyes to Eric's. He looked pleased at the prospect of fighting, but there was still uncertainty in his face and posture. 'But what will happen to Eric?'

'What do you mean?'

'If you go in and kill everyone, who'll un-curse him?' I turned slightly to face the experts, the Wiccan contingent. 'If Hallow's coven dies, do their spells die with them? Or will Eric still be without a memory?'

'The spell must be removed,' said the oldest witch, the calm African-American woman. 'If it is removed by the one who laid it in the first place, that's best. It can be lifted by someone else, but it will take more time, more effort, since we don't know what went into the making of the spell.'

I was trying to avoid looking at Alcide, because he was still shaking with the violence of the emotions that had led him to cast out Debbie. Though I hadn't known such an action was possible, my first reaction was to feel a little bitter about his *not* casting her out right after I'd told him a month ago she'd tried to kill me. However, he could have told himself I'd been mistaken, that it hadn't been Debbie I'd sensed near me before she'd pushed me into the Cadillac's trunk.

As far as I knew, this was the first time Debbie had admitted she had done it. And she'd protested she hadn't known Bill was in the trunk, unconscious. But shoving a person into a car trunk and shutting the lid was no kind of amusing prank, right?

Maybe Debbie had been lying to herself some, too.

I needed to listen to what was happening now. I'd have lots of time to think about the human ego's capacity to deceive itself, if I survived the night.

Pam was saying, 'So you're thinking we need to save Hallow? To take the spell off Eric?' She didn't sound happy at the prospect. I swallowed my painful feelings and made myself listen. This was no time to start brooding.

'No,' the witch said instantly. 'Her brother, Mark. There is too much danger in leaving Hallow alive. She must die as quickly as we can reach her.'

'What will you be doing?' Pam asked. 'How will you help us in this attack?'

'We will be outside, but within two blocks,' the man said. 'We'll be winding spells around the building to make the witches weak and indecisive. And we have a few tricks up our sleeves.' He and the young woman, who had on a huge amount of black eye makeup, looked pretty pleased at a chance to use those tricks.

Pam nodded as if winding spells was sufficient aid. I thought waiting outside with a flamethrower would have been better.

All this time, Debbie Pelt had been standing as if she'd been paralyzed. Now she began to pick her way through to the back door. Bubba leaped up to grab her arm. She hissed at him, but he didn't falter, though I would have.

None of the Weres reacted to this occurrence. It really was as though she were invisible to them.

'Let me leave. I'm not wanted,' she said to Bubba, fury and misery fighting for control of her face.

Bubba shrugged. He just held on to her, waiting for Pam's judgment.

'If we let you go, you might run to the witches and let them know we are coming,' Pam said. 'That would be of a piece with your character, apparently.'

Debbie had the gall to look outraged. Alcide looked as if he were watching the Weather Channel.

'Bill, you take charge of her,' Chow suggested. 'If she turns on us, kill her.'

'That sounds wonderful,' Bill said, smiling in a fangy way.

After a few more arrangements about transportation, and some more quiet consultation among the witches, who were facing a completely different kind of fight, Pam said, 'All right, let's go.' Pam, who looked more than ever like Alice in Wonderland in her pale pink sweater and darker pink slacks, stood up and checked her lipstick in the mirror on the wall close to where I'd been sitting. She gave her reflection an experimental smile, as I've seen women do a thousand times.

'Sookie, my friend,' she said, turning to aim the smile at me. 'Tonight is a great night.'

'It is?'

'Yes.' Pam put her arm around my shoulders. 'We defend what is ours! We fight for the restoration of our leader!' She grinned past me at Eric. 'Tomorrow, Sheriff, you will be back at your desk at Fangtasia. You'll be able to go to your own house, your own bedroom. We've kept it clean for you.'

I checked Eric's reaction. I'd never heard Pam address Eric by his title before. Though the head vampire for each section was called a sheriff, and I should have been used to that by now, I couldn't help but picture Eric in a cowboy outfit with a star pinned to his chest, or (my favorite) in black tights as the villainous sheriff of Nottingham. I found it interesting, too, that he didn't live here with Pam and Chow.

Eric gave Pam such a serious look that the grin faded right off her face. 'If I die tonight,' he said, 'pay this woman the money that was promised her.' He gripped my shoulder. I was just draped in vampires.

'I swear,' Pam said. 'Chow and Gerald will know, too.'

Eric said, 'Do you know where her brother is?'

Startled, I stepped away from Pam.

Pam looked equally taken aback. 'No, Sheriff.'

'It occurred to me that you might have taken him hostage to ensure she didn't betray me.'

The idea had never crossed my mind, but it should have. Obviously, I had a lot to learn about being devious.

'I wish I'd thought of that,' Pam said admiringly, echoing my thoughts with her own twist. 'I wouldn't have minded spending some time with Jason as my hostage.' I couldn't understand it: Jason's allure just seemed universal. 'But I didn't take him,' Pam said. 'If we get through this, Sookie, I'll look for him myself. Could it be Hallow's witches have him?'

'It's possible,' I said. 'Claudine said she didn't see any hostages, but she also said there were rooms she didn't look into. Though I don't know why they would have taken Jason, unless Hallow knows I have Eric? Then they might have used him to make me talk, just the way you would have used him to make me keep silent. But they haven't approached me. You can't use blackmail on someone who doesn't know anything about the hold you have on them.'

'Nonetheless, I'll remind all those who are going to enter the building to watch out for him,' Pam said.

'How is Belinda?' I asked. 'Have you made arrangements to pay her hospital bills?'

She looked at me blankly.

'The waitress who was hurt defending Fangtasia,' I reminded her, a little dryly. 'You remember? The friend of Ginger, who *died*?'

'Of course,' said Chow, from his place against the wall. 'She is recovering. We sent her flowers and candy,' he told Pam. Then he focused on me. 'Plus, we have a group insurance policy.' He was proud as a new father about that.

Pam looked pleased with Chow's report. 'Good,' she said. 'You have to keep them happy. Are we ready to go?'

I shrugged. 'I guess so. No point in waiting.'

Bill stepped in front of me as Chow and Pam consulted about which vehicle to take. Gerald had gone out to make sure everyone was on the same page as far as the plan of battle.

'How was Peru?' I asked Bill. I was very conscious of Eric, a huge blond shadow at my elbow.

'I made a lot of notes for my book,' Bill said. 'South America hasn't been good to vampires as a whole, but Peru is not as hostile as the other countries, and I was able to talk to a few vampires I hadn't heard of before.' For months, Bill had been compiling a vampire directory at the behest of the queen of Louisiana, who thought having such an item would be very handy. Her opinion was certainly not the universal opinion of the vampire community, some of whom had very strong objections to being outed, even among their own kind. I guess secrecy could be almost impossible to give up, if you'd clung to it for centuries.

There were vampires who still lived in graveyards, hunting every night, refusing to recognize the change in their status; it was like the stories about the Japanese soldiers who'd held out on Pacific islands long after World War II was over.

'Did you get to see those ruins you talked about?'

'Machu Picchu? Yes, I climbed up to them by myself. It was a great experience.'

I tried to picture Bill going up a mountain at night, seeing the ruins of an ancient civilization in the moonlight. I couldn't even imagine what that must have been like. I'd never been out of the country. I hadn't often been out of the state, for that matter.

'This is Bill, your former mate?' Eric's voice sounded a little . . . strained.

'Ah, this is – well, yes, sort of,' I said unhappily. The 'former' was correct; the 'mate' was a little off.

Eric placed both his hands on my shoulders and moved in close to me. I had no doubt he was staring over the top of my head at Bill, who was staring right back. Eric might as well have stuck a SHE'S MINE sign on top of my head. Arlene had told me that she loved moments like this, when her ex saw plainly that someone else valued her even if he didn't. All I can say is, my taste in satisfaction runs completely different. I hated it. I felt awkward and ridiculous.

'You really don't remember me,' Bill said to Eric, as if he'd doubted it up until this moment. My suspicion was confirmed when he told me, as if Eric wasn't standing there, 'Truly, I thought this was an elaborate scheme on Eric's part to stay in your house so he could talk his way into your bed.'

Since the same thought had occurred to me, though I'd discarded it pretty quickly, I couldn't protest; but I could feel myself turning red.

'We need to get in the car,' I told Eric, turning to catch a glimpse of his face. It was rock hard and expressionless, which usually signaled he was in a dangerous state of mind. But he came with me when I moved toward the door, and the whole house slowly emptied its inhabitants into the narrow suburban street. I wondered what the neighbors thought. Of course, they knew the house was inhabited by vampires – no one around during the day, all the yard work done by human hirelings, the people who came and went at night being so very pale. This sudden activity had to invite neighborhood attention.

I drove in silence, Eric beside me on the front seat. Every now and then he reached over to touch me. I don't know who Bill had caught a ride with, but I was glad it wasn't me. The testosterone level would have been too high in the car, and I might have been smothered.

Bubba was sitting in the backseat, humming to himself. It sounded like 'Love Me Tender.'

'This is a crappy car,' Eric said, out of the blue, as far as I was concerned.

'Yes,' I agreed.

'Are you afraid?'

'I am.'

'If this whole thing works, will you still see me?'

'Sure,' I said, to make him happy. I was convinced that after this confrontation, nothing would be the same. But without the true Eric's conviction of his own prowess and intelligence and ruthlessness, this Eric was pretty shaky. He'd be up for the actual battle, but right now he needed a boost.

Pam had plotted out where everyone should park, to prevent Hallow's coven from becoming alarmed by the sudden appearance of a lot of cars. We had a map with our spot marked on it. That turned out to be an E-Z Mart on the corner of a couple of larger roads in a down-sliding area that was changing over from residential to commercial. We parked in the most out-of-the-way corner the E-Z Mart afforded. Without further discussion, we set out to our appointed locations.

About half the houses on the quiet street had real-estate signs in the front lawn, and the ones that remained in private hands were not well maintained. Cars were as battered as mine, and big bare patches indicated that the grass wasn't fertilized or watered in the summer. Every lighted window seemed to show the flickering of a television screen.

I was glad it was winter so the people who lived here were all inside. Two white vampires and a blond woman would excite comment, if not aggression, in this neighborhood. Plus, one of the vampires was pretty recognizable, despite the rigors of his changeover – which was why Bubba was almost always kept out of sight.

Soon we were at the corner where Eric was supposed to part from us so he could rendezvous with the other vampires. I would have continued on to my appointed post without a word; by now I was keyed up to such a pitch of tension I felt I could vibrate if you tapped me with a finger. But Eric wasn't content with a silent separation. He gripped my arms and kissed me for all he was worth, and believe me, that was plenty.

Bubba made a sound of disapproval. 'You're not supposed to be kissing on anybody else, Miss Sookie,' he said. 'Bill said it was okay, but I don't like it.'

After one more second, Eric released me. 'I'm sorry if we

offended you,' he said coldly. He looked back down at me. 'I'll see you later, my lover,' he said very quietly.

I laid my hand against his cheek. 'Later,' I said, and I turned and walked away with Bubba at my heels.

'You ain't mad at me, are you, Miss Sookie?' he asked anxiously.

'No,' I said. I made myself smile at him, since I knew he could see me far more clearly than I could see him. It was a cold night, and though I was wearing my coat, it didn't seem to be as warm as it used to be. My bare hands were quivering with cold, and my nose felt numb. I could just detect a whiff of wood smoke from a fireplace, and automobile exhaust, and gasoline, and oil, and all the other car odors that combine to make City Smell.

But there was another smell permeating the neighborhood, an aroma that indicated this neighborhood was contaminated by more than urban blight. I sniffed, and the odor curled through the air in almost visible flourishes. After a moment's thought, I realized this must be the smell of magic, thick and stomach-clenching. Magic smells like I imagine a bazaar in some exotic foreign country might. It reeks of the strange, the different. The scent of a lot of magic can be quite overwhelming. Why weren't the residents complaining to the police about it? Couldn't everyone pick up on that odor?

'Bubba, do you smell something unusual?' I asked in a very low voice. A dog or two barked as we walked past in the black night, but they quickly quieted when they caught the scent of vampire. (To them, I guess, Bubba was the something unusual.) Dogs are almost always frightened of vampires, though their reaction to Weres and shifters is more unpredictable.

I found myself convinced I wanted nothing more than to go back to the car and leave. It was a conscious effort to make my feet move in the correct direction.

'Yeah, I sure do,' he whispered back. 'Someone's been laying some spells. Stay-away magic.' I didn't know if the Wiccans on our side, or the witches on Hallow's, had been responsible for this pervasive piece of craft, but it was effective.

The night seemed almost unnaturally silent. Maybe three cars passed us as we walked the maze of suburban streets. Bubba and I saw no other pedestrians, and the sense of ominous isolation grew. The stay-away intensified as we came closer to what we were supposed to stay away from.

The darkness between the pools of light below the street-lamps seemed darker, and the light didn't seem to reach as far. When Bubba took my hand, I didn't pull away. My feet seemed to drag at each step.

I'd caught a whiff of this smell before, at Fangtasia. Maybe the Were tracker had had an easier job than I'd thought.

'We're there, Miss Sookie,' Bubba said, his voice just a quiet thread in the night. We'd come around a corner. Since I knew there was a spell, and I knew I could keep walking, I did; but if I'd been a resident of the area, I would have found an alternative route, and I wouldn't have thought twice about it. The impulse to avoid this spot was so strong that I wondered if the people who lived on this block had been able to come home from their jobs. Maybe they were eating out, going to movies, drinking in bars – anything to avoid returning to their homes. Every house on the street looked suspiciously dark and untenanted.

Across the road, and at the opposite end of the block, was the center of the magic.

Hallow's coven had found a good place to hole up: a business up for lease, a large building that had held a combination florist shop-bakery. Minnie's Flowers and Cakes stood in a lonely position, the largest store in a strip of three that had, one by one, faded and gone out like flames on a candelabra. The building had apparently been empty for years. The big plate-glass windows were plastered with posters for events long past and political candidates long since defeated. Plywood nailed over the glass doors was proof that vandals had broken in more than once.

Even in the winter chill, weeds pushed up through cracks in the parking area. A big Dumpster stood to the right side of the parking lot. I viewed it from across the street, getting as much of a picture of the outside as I could before closing my eyes to concentrate on my other senses. I took a moment to be rueful.

If you'd asked me, I would've had a hard time tracing the steps that had led me to this dangerous place at this dangerous time. I was on the edges of a battle in which both sides were pretty dubious. If I'd fallen in with Hallow's witches first, I would probably have been convinced that the Weres and the vampires deserved to be eradicated.

At this time a year ago, no one in the world really understood what I was, or cared. I was just Crazy Sookie, the one with the wild brother, a woman others pitied and avoided, to varying degrees. Now here I was, on a freezing street in Shreveport, gripping the hand of a vampire whose face was legendary and whose brain was mush. Was this betterment?

And I was here not for amusement, or improvement, but to reconnoiter for a bunch of supernatural creatures, gathering information on a group of homicidal, blood-drinking, shape-changing witches.

I sighed, I hoped inaudibly. Oh, well. At least no one had hit me.

My eyes closed, and I dropped my shields and reached out with my mind to the building across the street.

Brains, busy busy busy. I was startled at the bundle of impressions I was receiving. Maybe the absence of other humans in the vicinity, or the overwhelming pervasion of magic, was responsible; but some factor had sharpened my other sense to the point of pain. Almost stunned by the flow of information, I realized I had to sort through it and organize it. First, I counted brains. Not literally ('One temporal lobe, two temporal lobes . . .'), but as a thought cluster. I came up with fifteen. Five were in the front room, which had been the showroom of the store, of course. One was in the smallest space, which was most likely the bathroom, and the rest were in the third and largest room, which lay to the rear. I figured it had been the work area.

Everyone in the building was awake. A sleeping brain still gives me a low mumble of a thought or two, in dreaming, but it's not the same as a waking brain. It's like the difference between a dog twitching in its sleep and an alert puppy.

To get as much information as possible, I had to get closer. I had never attempted to pick through a group to get details as specific as guilt or innocence, and I wasn't even sure that was possible. But if any of the people in the building were not evil witches, I didn't want them to be in the thick of what was to come.

'Closer,' I breathed to Bubba. 'But under cover.'

'Yes'm,' he whispered back. 'You gonna keep your eyes closed?'

I nodded, and he led me very carefully across the street and into the shadow of the Dumpster that stood about five yards south of the building. I was glad it was cold, because that kept the garbage smell at an acceptable level. The ghosts of the scents of doughnuts and blossoms lay on top of the funk of spoiled things and old diapers that passersby had tossed into the handy receptacle. It didn't blend happily with the magic smell.

I adjusted, blocked out the assault on my nose, and began listening. Though I'd gotten better at this, it was still like trying to hear twelve phone conversations at once. Some of them were Weres, too, which complicated matters. I could only get bits and pieces.

. . . hope that's not a vaginal infection I feel coming on . . .
She won't listen to me, she doesn't think men can do the job.
If I turned her into a toad, who could tell the difference?
. . . wish we'd gotten some diet Coke . . .
I'll find that damn vamp and kill him . . .
Mother of the Earth, listen to my pleas.
I'm in too deep . . .
I better get a new nail file.

This was not decisive, but no one had been thinking, 'Oh, these demonic witches have trapped me, won't somebody help?' or 'I hear the vampires approaching!' or anything dramatic like that. This sounded like a band of people who knew each other, were at least relaxed in each other's company, and therefore held the same goals. Even the one who was praying was not in any state of urgency or need. I hoped Hallow wouldn't sense the crush of my mind, but everyone I'd touched had seemed preoccupied.

'Bubba,' I said, just a little louder than a thought, 'you

go tell Pam there are fifteen people in there, and as far as I can tell, they're all witches.'

'Yes'm.'

'You remember how to get to Pam?'

'Yes'm.'

'So you can let go my hand, okay?'

'Oh. Okay.'

'Be silent and careful,' I whispered.

And he was gone. I crouched in the shadow that was darker than the night, beside the smells and cold metal, listening to the witches. Three brains were male, the rest female. Hallow was in there, because one of the women was looking at her and thinking of her . . . dreading her, which kind of made me uneasy. I wondered where they'd parked their cars – unless they flew around on broomsticks, ha ha. Then I wondered about something that should already have crossed my mind.

If they were so darn wary and dangerous, where were their sentries?

At that moment, I was seized from behind.

Chapter 12

'Who are you?' asked a thin voice.

Since she had one hand clapped over my mouth and the other was holding a knife to my neck, I couldn't answer. She seemed to grasp that after a second, because she told me, 'We're going in,' and began to push me toward the back of the building.

I couldn't have that. If she'd been one of the witches in the building, one of the blood-drinking witches, I couldn't have gotten away with this, but she was a plain old witch, and she hadn't watched Sam break up as many bar fights as I had. With both hands, I reached up and grabbed her knife wrist, and I twisted it as hard as I could while I hit her hard with my lower body. Over she went, onto the filthy cold pavement, and I landed right on top of her, pounding her hand against the ground until she released the knife. She was sobbing, the will seeping out of her.

'You're a lousy lookout,' I said to Holly, keeping my voice low.

'Sookie?' Holly's big eyes peered out from under a knit

watch cap. She'd dressed for utility tonight, but she still had on bright pink lipstick.

'What the hell are you doing here?'

'They told me they'd get my boy if I didn't help them.'

I felt sick. 'How long have you been helping them? Before I came to your apartment, asking for help? How long?' I shook her as hard as I could.

'When she came to the bar with her brother, she knew there was another witch there. And she knew it wasn't you or Sam, after she'd talked to you. Hallow can do anything. She knows everything. Late that night, she and Mark came to my apartment. They'd been in a fight; they were all messed up, and they were mad. Mark held me down while Hallow punched me. She liked that. She saw my picture of my son; she took it and said she could curse him long distance, all the way from Shreveport – make him run out in the traffic or load his daddy's gun . . .' Holly was crying by now. I didn't blame her. It made me sick to think of it, and he wasn't even my child. 'I had to say I'd help her,' Holly whimpered.

'Are there others like you in there?'

'Forced to do this? A few of them.'

That made some thoughts I'd heard more understandable.

'And Jason? He in there?' Though I'd looked at all three of the male brains in the building, I still had to ask.

'Jason is a Wiccan? For real?' She pulled off the watch cap and ran her fingers through her hair.

'No, no, no. Is she holding him hostage?'

'I haven't seen him. Why on earth would Hallow have Jason?'

I'd been fooling myself all along. A hunter would find

my brother's remains someday: it's always hunters, or people walking their dogs, isn't it? I felt a falling away beneath my feet, as if the ground had literally dropped out from under me, but I called myself back to the here and now, away from emotions I couldn't afford to feel until I was in a safer place.

'You have to get out of here,' I said in the lowest voice I could manage. 'You have to get out of this area now.'

'She'll get my son!'

'I guarantee she won't.'

Holly seemed to read something in the dim view she had of my face. 'I hope you kill them all,' she said as passionately as you can in a whisper. 'The only ones worth saving are Parton and Chelsea and Jane. They got blackmailed into this just like I did. Normally, they're just Wiccans who like to live real quiet, like me. We don't want to do no one no harm.'

'What do they look like?'

'Parton's a guy about twenty-five, brown hair, short, birthmark on his cheek. Chelsea is about seventeen, her hair's dyed that bright red. Jane, um, well – Jane's just an old woman, you know? White hair, pants, blouse with flowers on it. Glasses.' My grandmother would have reamed Holly for lumping all old women together, but God bless her, she wasn't around anymore, and I didn't have the time.

'Why didn't Hallow put one of her toughest people out here on guard duty?' I asked, out of sheer curiosity.

'They got a big ritual spell thing set up for tonight. I can't believe the stay-away spell didn't work on you. You must be resistant.' Then Holly whispered, with a little rill of laughter in her voice, 'Plus, none of 'em wanted to get cold.'

'Go on, get out of here,' I said almost inaudibly, and helped her up. 'It doesn't matter where you parked your car, go north out of here.' In case she didn't know which direction was north, I pointed.

Holly took off, her Nikes making almost no sound on the cracked sidewalk. Her dull dyed black hair seemed to soak up the light from the streetlamp as she passed beneath it. The smell around the house, the smell of magic, seemed to intensify. I wondered what to do now. Somehow I had to make sure that the three local Wiccans within the dilapidated building, the ones who'd been forced to serve Hallow, wouldn't be harmed. I couldn't think of a way in hell to do that. Could I even save one of them?

I had a whole collection of half thoughts and abortive impulses in the next sixty seconds. They all led to a dead end.

If I ran inside and yelled, 'Parton, Chelsea, Jane – out!' that would alert the coven to the impending attack. Some of my friends – or at least my allies – would die.

If I hung around and tried to tell the vampires that three of the people in the building were innocent, they would (most likely) ignore me. Or, if a bolt of mercy struck them, they'd have to save all the witches and then cull the innocent ones out, which would give the coven witches time to counterattack. Witches didn't need physical weapons.

Too late, I realized I should have kept a hold of Holly and used her as my entrée into the building. But endangering a frightened mother was not a good option, either.

Something large and warm pressed against my side. Eyes and teeth gleamed in the city's night light. I almost screamed until I recognized the wolf as Alcide. He was very large. The silver fur around his eyes made the rest of his coat seem even darker.

I put an arm across his back. 'There are three in there who mustn't die,' I said. 'I don't know what to do.'

Since he was a wolf, Alcide didn't know what to do, either. He looked into my face. He whined, just a little. I was supposed to be back at the cars by now; but here I was, smack in the danger zone. I could feel movement in the dark all around me. Alcide slunk away to his appointed position at the rear door of the building.

'What are you doing here?' Bill said furiously, though it sounded strange coming out in a tiny thread of a whisper. 'Pam told you to leave once you'd counted.'

'Three in there are innocent,' I whispered back. 'They're locals. They were forced.'

Bill said something under his breath, and it wasn't a happy something.

I passed along the sketchy descriptions Holly had given me.

I could feel the tension in Bill's body, and then Debbie joined us in our foxhole. What was she thinking, to pack herself in so closely with the vampire and the human who hated her most?

'I told you to stay back,' Bill said, and his voice was frightening.

'Alcide abjured me,' she told me, just as if I hadn't been there when it happened.

'What did you expect?' I was exasperated at her timing and her wounded attitude. Hadn't she ever heard of consequences?

'I have to do something to earn back his trust.'

She'd come to the wrong shop, if she wanted to buy some self-respect.

'Then help me save the three in there who are innocent.'
I recounted my problem again. 'Why haven't you changed
into your animal?'

'Oh, I can't,' she said bitterly. 'I've been abjured. I can't
change with Alcide's pack anymore. They have license to
kill me, if I do.'

'What did you shift into, anyway?'

'Lynx.'

That was appropriate.

'Come on,' I said. I began to wriggle toward the building. I loathed this woman, but if she could be of use to me,
I had to ally with her.

'Wait, I'm supposed to go to the back door with the
Were,' Bill hissed. 'Eric's already back there.'

'So go!'

I sensed that someone else was at my back and risked a
quick glance to see that it was Pam. She smiled at me, and
her fangs were out, so that was a little unnerving.

Maybe if the witches inside hadn't been involved in a
ritual, and hadn't been relying on their less-than-dedicated
sentry and their magic, we wouldn't have made it to the
door undetected. But fortune favored us for those few minutes. We got to the front door of the building, Pam and
Debbie and I, and there met up with the young Were, Sid.
I could recognize him even in his wolf body. Bubba was
with him.

I was struck with a sudden inspiration. I moved a few
feet away with Bubba.

'Can you run back to the Wiccans, the ones on our side?
You know where they are?' I whispered.

Bubba nodded his head vigorously.

'You tell them there are three local Wiccans inside

who're being forced into this. Ask if they can make up some spell to get the three innocent ones to stand out.'

'I'll tell them, Miss Sookie. They're real sweet to me.'

'Good fella. Be quick, be quiet.'

He nodded, and was gone into the darkness.

The smell around the building was intensifying to such a degree that I was having trouble breathing. The air was so permeated with scent, I was reminded of passing a candle shop in a mall.

Pam said, 'Where have you sent Bubba?'

'Back to our Wiccans. They need to make three innocent people stand out somehow so we won't kill 'em.'

'But he has to come back now. He has to break down the door for me!'

'But . . .' I was disconcerted at Pam's reaction. 'He can't go in without an invitation, like you.'

'Bubba is brain damaged, degraded. He's not altogether a true vampire. He can enter without an express invitation.'

I gaped at Pam. 'Why didn't you tell me?' She just raised her eyebrows. When I thought back, it was true that I could remember at least twice that Bubba had entered dwellings without an invitation. I'd never put two and two together.

'So I'll have to be the first through the door,' I said, more matter-of-factly than I was really feeling. 'Then I invite you all in?'

'Yes. Your invitation will be enough. The building doesn't belong to them.'

'Should we do this now?'

Pam gave an almost inaudible snort. She was smiling in the glow of the streetlight, suddenly exhilarated. 'You waiting for an engraved invite?'

Lord save me from sarcastic vampires. 'You think Bubba's had enough time to get to the Wiccans?'

'Sure. Let's nail some witch butt,' she said happily. I could tell the fate of the local Wiccans was very low on her list of priorities. Everyone seemed to be looking forward to this but me. Even the young Were was showing a lot of fang.

'I kick, you go in,' Pam said. She gave me a quick peck on the cheek, utterly surprising me.

I thought, *I* so *don't want to be here.*

Then I got up from my crouch, stood behind Pam, and watched in awe while she cocked a leg and kicked with the force of four or five mules. The lock shattered, the door sprang inward while the old wood nailed over it splintered and cracked, and I leaped inside and screamed 'Come in!' to the vampire behind me and the ones at the back door. For an odd moment, I was in the lair of the witches by myself, and they'd all turned to look at me in utter astonishment.

The room was full of candles and people sitting on cushions on the floor; during the time we'd waited outside, all the others in the building seemed to have come into this front room, and they were sitting cross-legged in a circle, each with a candle burning before her, and a bowl, and a knife.

Of the three I'd try to save, 'old woman' was easiest to recognize. There was only one white-haired woman in the circle. She was wearing bright pink lipstick, a little skewed and smeared, and there was dried blood on her cheek. I grabbed her arm and pushed her into a corner, while all about me was chaos. There were only three human men in the room. Hallow's brother, Mark, now being attacked by a pack of wolves, was one of them. The second male was a middle-aged man with concave cheeks and suspicious black hair, and he not only was muttering some kind of spell but pulling a switchblade from the jacket lying on the floor to his right. He was too far away for me to do anything about it; I had to rely on the others to protect themselves. Then I spotted the third man, birthmark on cheek – must be Parton. He was cowering with his hands over his head. I knew how he felt.

I grabbed his arm and pulled up, and he came up punching, of course. But I wasn't having any of that, no one was going to hit me, so I aimed my fist through his ineffectually flailing arms and got him right on the nose. He shrieked, adding another layer of noise to the already cacophonous room, and I yanked him over to the same corner where I'd stashed Jane. Then I saw that the older woman and the young man were both shining. Okay, the Wiccans had come through with a spell and it was working, though just a tad late. Now I had to find a shining young woman with dyed red hair, the third local.

But my luck ran out then; hers already had. She was shining, but she was dead. Her throat had been torn out by one of the wolves: one of ours, or one of theirs, it didn't really matter.

I scrambled though the melee back to the corner and seized both of the surviving Wiccans by the arm. Debbie Pelt came rushing up. 'Get out of here,' I said to them. 'Find the other Wiccans out there, or go home now. Walk, get a cab, whatever.'

'It's a bad neighborhood out there,' quavered Jane.

I stared at her. 'And this isn't?' The last I saw of the two, Debbie was pointing and giving them instructions. She had stepped out the doorway with them. I was about to take off after them, since I wasn't supposed to be here anyway, when one of the Were witches snapped at my leg. Its teeth missed flesh but snagged my pants leg, and that was enough to yank me back. I stumbled and nearly fell to the floor, but managed to grasp the doorjamb in time to regain my feet. At that moment, the second wave of Weres and vamps came through from the back room, and the wolf darted off to meet the new assault from the rear.

The room was full of flying bodies and spraying blood and screams.

The witches were fighting for all they were worth, and the ones who could shift had done so. Hallow had changed, and she was a snarling mass of snapping teeth. Her brother was trying to work some kind of magic, which required him to be in his human form, and he was trying to hold off the Weres and the vampires long enough to complete the spell.

He was chanting something, he and the concave-cheeked man, even as Mark Stonebrook drove a fist into Eric's stomach.

A heavy mist began to crawl through the room. The witches, who were fighting with knives or wolf teeth, got the idea, and those who could speak began to add to whatever Mark was saying. The cloud of mist in the room began to get thicker and thicker, until it was impossible to tell friend from foe.

I leaped for the door to escape from the suffocating cloud. This stuff made breathing a real effort. It was like trying to inhale and exhale cotton balls. I extended my hand, but the bit of wall I touched didn't include a door. It had been right there! I felt a curl of panic in my stomach as I patted frantically, trying to trace the outline of the exit.

Not only did I fail to find the doorjamb, I lost touch with the wall altogether on my next sideways step. I stumbled over a wolf's body. I couldn't see a wound, so I got hold of its shoulders and dragged, trying to rescue it from the thick smoke.

The wolf began to writhe and change under my hands, which was pretty disconcerting. Even worse, it changed into a naked Hallow. I didn't know anyone could change that fast. Terrified, I let go of her immediately and backed away into the cloud. I'd been trying to be a good Samaritan with the wrong victim. A nameless woman, one of the witches, grabbed me from behind with superhuman strength. She tried to grip my neck with one hand while holding my arm with the other, but her hand kept slipping, and I bit her as hard as I could. She might be a witch, and she might be a Were, and she might have drunk a gallon of vamp blood, but she was no warrior. She screamed and released me.

By now I was completely disoriented. Which way was out? I was coughing and my eyes were streaming. The only sense I was sure of was gravity. Sight, hearing, touch: all were affected by the thick white billows, which were getting ever denser. The vampires had an advantage in this situation; they didn't need to breathe. All the rest of us did. Compared to the thickening atmosphere in the old bakery, the polluted city air outside had been pure and delicious.

Gasping and weeping, I flung my arms out in front of me and tried to find a wall or a doorway, any sort of landmark. A room that had not seemed so large now seemed cavernous. I felt I'd stumbled through yards of nothingness, but that wasn't possible unless the witches had changed the dimensions of the room, and my prosaic mind just couldn't accept the possibility. From around me I heard screams and sounds that were muffled in the cloud, but no less frightening. A spray of blood suddenly appeared down the front of my coat. I felt the spatter hit my face. I made a noise of distress that I couldn't form into words. I knew it wasn't my blood, and I knew I hadn't been hurt, but somehow that was hard for me to believe.

Then something fell past me, and as it was on its way to the floor I glimpsed a face. It was the face of Mark Stonebrook, and he was in the process of dying. The smoke closed in around him, and he might as well have been in another city.

Maybe I should crouch, too? The air might be better close to the floor. But Mark's body was down there, and other things. So much for Mark removing the spell on Eric, I thought wildly. Now we'll need Hallow. 'The best-laid plans of mice and men . . .' Where'd my grandmother gotten that quote? Gerald knocked me sideways as he pushed past in pursuit of something I couldn't see.

I told myself I was brave and resourceful, but the words rang hollow. I blundered ahead, trying not trip over the debris on the floor. The witches' paraphernalia, bowls and knives and bits of bone and vegetation that I couldn't identify, had been scattered in the scuffle. A clear spot opened up unexpectedly, and I could see an overturned bowl and one of the knives on the floor at my feet. I scooped up the knife just before the cloud rolled back over it. I was sure the knife was supposed to be used for some ritual – but I wasn't a witch, and I needed it to defend myself. I felt better when I had the knife, which was real pretty and felt very sharp.

I wondered what our Wiccans were doing. Could they be responsible for the cloud? I wished I'd gotten to vote.

Our witches, as it turned out, were getting a live feed from the scene of the fight from one of their coven sisters, who was a scryer. (Though she was physically with them, she could see what was happening on the surface of a bowl of water, I learned later.) She could make out more using that method than we could, though why she didn't see just a bunch of white smoke billowing on the surface of that water, I don't know.

Anyway, our witches made it rain . . . in the building. Somehow the rain slowly cut back on the cloud cover, and though I felt damp and extremely cold, I also discovered I was close to the inner door, the one leading into the second, large room. Gradually, I became aware that I could see; the room had started to glow with light, and I could discern shapes. One bounded toward me on legs that seemed not-quite-human, and Debbie Pelt's face snarled at me. What was she doing here? She'd stepped out the door to show the Wiccans which way to find safety, and now she was back in the room.

I don't know if she could help it or not, or if she'd just gotten swept up in the madness of battle, but Debbie had partially changed. Her face was sprouting fur, and her teeth had begun to lengthen and sharpen. She snapped at my throat, but a convulsion caused by the change made her teeth fall short. I tried to step back, but I stumbled over something on the floor and took a precious second or two to regain my footing. She began to lunge again, her intent unmistakable, and I recalled that I had a knife in my hand. I slashed at her, and she hesitated, snarling.

She was going to use the confusion to settle our score. I

wasn't strong enough to fight a shape-shifter. I'd have to use the knife, though something inside me cringed at the thought.

Then from the tags and tatters of the mist came a big hand stained with blood, and that big hand grabbed Debbie Pelt's throat and squeezed. And squeezed. Before I could track the hand up the arm to the face of its owner, a wolf leaped from the floor to knock me down.

And sniff my face.

Okay, that was . . . then the wolf on top of me was knocked off and rolling on the floor, snarling and snapping at another wolf. I couldn't help, because the two were moving so quickly I couldn't be sure I'd help the right party.

The mist was dispersing at a good rate now, and I could see the room as a whole, though there were still patches of opaque fog. Though I'd been desperate for this moment, I was almost sorry now that it'd arrived. Bodies, both dead and wounded, littered the floor among the paraphernalia of the coven, and blood spattered the walls. Portugal, the handsome young Were from the air force base, lay sprawled in front of me. He was dead. Culpepper crouched beside him, keening. This was a small piece of war, and I hated it.

Hallow was still standing and completely in her human form, bare and smeared with blood. She picked up a wolf and slung it at the wall as I watched. She was magnificent and horrible. Pam was creeping up behind her, and Pam was disheveled and dirty. I'd never seen the vampire so much as ruffled, and I almost didn't recognize her. Pam launched herself, catching Hallow at the hips and knocking her to the floor. It was as good a tackle as I'd ever seen in years of Friday night football, and if Pam had caught

Hallow a little higher up and could have gotten a grip on her, it would have been all over. But Hallow was slippery with the misty rain and with blood, and her arms were free. She twisted in Pam's grasp and seized Pam's long straight hair in both hands and pulled, and clumps of the hair came off, attached to a good bit of scalp.

Pam shrieked like a giant teakettle. I'd never heard a noise that loud come out of a throat – in this case not a human throat, but a throat nonetheless. Since Pam was definitely of the 'get even' school, she pinned Hallow to the floor by gripping both her upper arms and pressing, pressing, until Hallow was flattened. Since the witch was so strong, it was a terrible struggle, and Pam was hampered by the blood streaming down her face. But Hallow was human, and Pam was not. Pam was winning until one of the witches, the hollow-cheeked man, crawled over to the two woman and bit into Pam's neck. Both her arms were occupied, and she couldn't stop him. He didn't just bite, he drank, and as he drank, his strength increased, as if his battery was getting charged. He was draining right from the source. No one seemed to be watching but me. I scrambled across the limp, furry body of a wolf and one of the vampires to pummel on the hollow-cheeked man, who simply ignored me.

I would have to use the knife. I'd never done something like this; when I'd struck back at someone, it had always been a life-or-death situation, and the life and the death had been mine. This was different. I hesitated, but I had to do something quick. Pam was weakening before my eyes, and she would not be able to restrain Hallow much longer. I took the black-bladed knife with its black handle, and I held it to his throat; I jabbed him, a little.

'Let go of her,' I said. He ignored me.

I jabbed harder, and a stream of scarlet ran down the skin of his neck. He let go of Pam then. His mouth was all covered in her blood. But before I could rejoice that he'd freed her, he spun over while he was still underneath me and came after me, his eyes absolutely insane and his mouth open to drink from me, too. I could feel the yearning in his brain, the *want, want, want.* I put the knife to his neck again, and just as I was steeling myself, he lunged forward and pushed the blade into his own neck.

His eyes went dull almost instantly.

He'd killed himself by way of me. I don't think he'd ever realized the knife was there.

This was a close killing, a right-in-my-face killing, and I'd been the instrument of death, however inadvertently.

When I could look up, Pam was sitting on Hallow's chest, her knees pinning Hallow's arms, and she was smiling. This was so bizarre that I looked around the room to find the reason, and I saw that the battle appeared to be over. I couldn't imagine how long it had lasted, that loud but invisible struggle in the thick mist, but now I could see the results all too clearly.

Vampires don't kill neat, they kill messy. Wolves, too, are not known for their table manners. Witches seemed to manage to splash a little less blood, but the end result was really horrible, like a very bad movie, the kind you were ashamed you'd paid to see.

We appeared to have won.

At the moment, I hardly cared. I was really tired, mentally and physically, and that meant all the thoughts of the humans, and some of the thoughts of the Weres, rolled around in my brain like clothes in a dryer. There was nothing I could do about it, so I let the tag ends drift around in my head while, using the last of my strength, I pushed off of the corpse. I lay on my back and stared up at the ceiling. Since I had no thoughts, I filled up with everyone else's. Almost everyone was thinking the same kind of thing I was: how tired they were, how bloody the room was, how hard it was to believe they'd gone through a fight like this and survived. The spiky-haired boy had reverted to his human form, and he was thinking how much more he'd enjoyed it than he thought he should. In fact, his unclothed body was showing visible evidence of how much he'd enjoyed it, and he was trying to feel embarrassed about that. Mostly, he wanted to track down that cute young Wiccan and find a quiet corner. Hallow was hating Pam, she was hating me, she was hating Eric, she was hating everyone. She began to try to mumble a spell to make us all sick, but Pam gave her an elbow in the neck, and that shut her right up.

Debbie Pelt got up from the floor in the door and surveyed the scene. She looked amazingly pristine and energetic, as if she'd never had a furry face and wouldn't even begin to know how to kill someone. She picked her way through the bodies strewn on the floor, some living and some not, until she found Alcide, still in his wolf form. She squatted down to check him over for wounds, and he growled at her in clear warning. Maybe she didn't believe he would attack, or maybe she just fooled herself into believing it, but she laid her hand on his shoulder, and he bit her savagely enough to draw blood. She shrieked and scrambled back. For a few seconds, she crouched there, cradling her bleeding hand and crying. Her eyes met mine and almost glowed with hatred. She would never forgive me. She would blame me the rest of her life for Alcide's discovery of her dark nature. She'd toyed with him for two years, pulling him to her, pushing him back, concealing from him the elements of her nature he would never accept, but wanting him with her nonetheless. Now it was all over.

And this was my fault?

But I wasn't thinking in Debbie terms, I was thinking like a rational human being, and of course Debbie Pelt was not. I wished the hand that had caught her neck during the struggle in the cloud had choked her to death. I watched her back as she pushed open the door and strode into the night, and at that moment I knew Debbie Pelt would be out to get me for the rest of her life. Maybe Alcide's bite would get infected and she'd get blood poisoning?

In reflex action, I chastised myself: That was an evil thought; God didn't want us to wish ill on anyone. I just hoped He was listening in to Debbie, too, the way you hope the highway patrolman who stopped you for a ticket is also going to stop the guy behind you who was trying to pass you on the double yellow line.

The redheaded Were, Amanda, came over to me. She was bitten here and there, and she had a swollen lump on her forehead, but she was quietly beaming. 'While I'm in a good mood, I want to apologize for insulting you,' she said directly. 'You came through in this fight. Even if you can tolerate vamps, I won't hold that against you anymore. Maybe you'll see the light.' I nodded, and she strolled away to check on her packmates.

Pam had tied up Hallow, and Pam, Eric, and Gerald had gone to kneel beside someone on the other side of the room. I wondered vaguely what was happening over there, but Alcide was shimmering back into human form, and when he'd oriented himself, he crawled over to me. I was too exhausted to care that he was naked, but I had a floating idea that I should try to remember the sight, since I'd want to recall it at my leisure later.

He had some grazes and bloody spots, and one deep laceration, but overall he looked pretty good.

'There's blood on your face,' he said, with an effort.

'Not mine.'

'Thank God,' he said, and he lay on the floor beside me. 'How bad are you hurt?'

'I'm not hurt, not really,' I said. 'I mean, I got shoved around a lot, and choked a little maybe, and snapped at, but no one hit me!' By golly, I was going to make my New Year's resolution come true, after all.

'I'm sorry we didn't find Jason here,' he said.

'Eric asked Pam and Gerald if the vampires were holding him, and they said no,' I remarked. 'He'd thought of a real good reason for the vamps to have him. But they didn't.'

'Chow is dead.'

'How?' I asked, sounding as calm as if it hardly mattered. Truthfully, I had never been very partial to the bartender, but I would have shown a decent concern if I hadn't been so tired.

'One of Hallow's group had a wooden knife.'

'I never saw one before,' I said after a moment, and that was all I could think to say about the death of Chow.

'Me, neither.'

After a long moment, I said, 'I'm sorry about Debbie.' What I meant was, I was sorry Debbie had hurt him so badly, had proved to be such a dreadful person that he'd had to take a drastic step to get her out of his life.

'Debbie who?' he asked, and rolled to his feet and padded away across the filthy floor strewn with blood, bodies, and supernatural debris.

Chapter 13

The aftermath of a battle is melancholy and nasty. I guess you could call what we'd had a battle . . . maybe more like a supernatural skirmish? The wounded have to be tended, the blood has to be cleaned up, the bodies have to be buried. Or, in this case, disposed of – Pam decided to burn the store down, leaving the bodies of Hallow's coven inside.

They hadn't all died. Hallow, of course, was still alive. One other witch survived, though she was badly hurt and very low on blood. Of the Weres, Colonel Flood was gravely wounded; Portugal had been killed by Mark Stonebrook. The others were more or less okay. Only Chow had died, out of the vampire contingent. The others had wounds, some very horrible, but vampires will heal.

It surprised me that the witches hadn't made a better showing.

'They were probably good witches, but they weren't good fighters,' Pam said. 'They were picked for their magical ability and their willingness to follow Hallow, not for their battle skills. She shouldn't have tried to take over Shreveport with such a following.'

'Why Shreveport?' I asked Pam.

'I'm going to find out,' Pam said, smiling.

I shuddered. I didn't want to consider Pam's methods. 'How are you going to keep her from doing a spell on you while you question her?'

Pam said, 'I'll think of something.' She was still smiling.

'Sorry about Chow,' I said, a little hesitantly.

'The job of bartender at Fangtasia doesn't seem to be a good-luck job,' she admitted. 'I don't know if I'll be able to find someone to replace Chow. After all, he and Long Shadow both perished within a year of starting work.'

'What are you going to do about un-hexing Eric?'

Pam seemed glad enough to talk to me, even if I was only a human, since she'd lost her sidekick. 'We'll make Hallow do it, sooner or later. And she'll tell us why she did it.'

'If Hallow just gives up the general outline of the spell, will that be enough? Or will she have to perform it herself?' I tried to rephrase that in my head so it was clearer, but Pam seemed to understand me.

'I don't know. We'll have to ask our friendly Wiccans. The ones you saved should be grateful enough to give us any help we need,' Pam said, while she tossed some more gasoline around the room. She'd already checked the building to remove the few things she might want from it, and the local coven had gathered up the magical paraphernalia, in case one of the cops who came to investigate this fire could recognize the remnants.

I glanced at my watch. I hoped that Holly had made it safely home by now. I would tell her that her son was safe.

I kept my eyes averted from the job the youngest witch was doing on Colonel Flood's left leg. He'd sustained an ugly gash in the quadriceps. It was a serious wound. He made light of it, and after Alcide fetched their clothes, the colonel limped around with a smile on his face. But when blood seeped through the bandage, the packmaster had to allow his Weres to take him to a doctor who happened to be two-natured and willing to help off the books, since no one could think of a good story that would explain such a wound. Before he left, Colonel Flood shook hands ceremoniously with the head witch and with Pam, though I could see the sweat beading on his forehead even in the frigid air of the old building.

I asked Eric if he felt any different, but he was still oblivious to his past. He looked upset and on the verge of terror. Mark Stonebrook's death hadn't made a bit of difference, so Hallow was in for a few dreadful hours, courtesy of Pam. I just accepted that. I didn't want to think about it closely. Or at all.

As for me, I was feeling completely at a loss. Should I go home to Bon Temps, taking Eric with me? (Was I in charge of him anymore?) Should I try to find a place to spend the remaining hours of the night here in the city? Shreveport was home for everyone but Bill and me, and Bill was planning on using Chow's empty bed (or whatever it was) for the coming day, at Pam's suggestion.

I dithered around indecisively for a few minutes, trying to make up my mind. But no one seemed to need me for anything specific, and no one sought me out for conversation. So when Pam got involved in giving the other vampires directions about Hallow's transportation, I just walked out. The night was quite as still as it had been, but a few dogs did bark as I walked down the street. The smell of magic had lessened. The night was just as dark, and even colder, and I was at low ebb. I didn't know what I'd say if a policeman stopped me; I was blood-spattered and tattered, and I had no explanation. At the moment, I found it hard to care.

I'd gotten maybe a block when Eric caught up with me. He was very anxious – almost fearful. 'You weren't there. I just looked around and you weren't there,' he said accusingly. 'Where are you going? Why didn't you tell me?'

'Please,' I said, and held up a hand to beg him to be silent. 'Please.' I was too tired to be strong for him, and I had to fight an overwhelming depression, though I couldn't have told you exactly why; after all, no one had hit me. I should be happy, right? The goals of the evening had been met. Hallow was conquered and in captivity; though Eric hadn't been restored to himself, he soon would be, because Pam was sure to bring Hallow around to the vampire way of thinking, in a painful and terminal way.

Undoubtedly, Pam would also discover why Hallow had begun this whole course of action. And Fangtasia would acquire a new bartender, some fangy hunk who would bring in the tourist bucks. She and Eric would open the strip club they'd been considering, or the all-night dry-cleaners, or the bodyguard service.

My brother would still be missing.

'Let me go home with you. I don't know them,' Eric said, his voice low and almost pleading. I hurt inside when Eric said something that was so contrary to his normal personality. Or was I seeing Eric's true nature? Was his flash and assurance something he'd assumed, like another skin, over the years?

'Sure, come on,' I said, as desperate as Eric was, but in my own way. I just wanted him to be quiet, and strong.

I'd settle for quiet.

He loaned me his physical strength, at least. He picked me up and carried me back to the car. I was surprised to find that my cheeks were wet with tears.

'You have blood all over you,' he said into my ear.

'Yes, but don't get excited about it,' I warned. 'It doesn't do a thing for me. I just want to shower.' I was at the hic-cupping-sob stage of crying, almost done.

'You'll have to get rid of this coat now,' he said, with some satisfaction.

'I'll get it cleaned.' I was too tired to respond to disparaging comments about my coat.

Getting away from the weight and smell of the magic was almost as good as a big cup of coffee and a hit of oxygen. By the time I got close to Bon Temps, I wasn't feeling so ragged, and I was calm as I let us in the back door. Eric came in behind me and took a step to my right to go around the kitchen table, as I leaned left to flick on the light switch.

When I turned on the light, Debbie Pelt was smiling at me.

She had been sitting in the dark at my kitchen table, and she had a gun in her hand.

Without saying a word, she fired at me.

But she'd reckoned without Eric, who was so fast, faster than any human. He took the bullet meant for me, and he took it right in the chest. He went down in front of me.

She hadn't had time to search the house, which was lucky. From behind the water heater, I yanked the shotgun I'd taken from Jason's house. I pumped it – one of the scari-est sounds in the world – and I shot Debbie Pelt while she was still staring, shocked, at Eric, who was on his knees and coughing up blood. I racked another shell, but I didn't need to shoot her again. Her fingers relaxed and her gun fell to the floor.

I sat on the floor myself, because I couldn't stay upright anymore.

Eric was now full length on the floor, gasping and twitching in a pool of blood.

There wasn't much left of Debbie's upper chest and neck.

My kitchen looked like I'd been dismembering pigs, pigs that'd put up a good fight.

I started to reach up to scrabble for the telephone at the end of the counter. My hand dropped back to the floor when I wondered whom I was going to call.

The law? Ha.

Sam? And mire him down further in my troubles? I didn't think so.

Pam? Let her see how close I'd come to letting my charge get killed? Uh-uh.

Alcide? Sure, he'd love seeing what I'd done with his fiancée, abjure or no abjure.

Arlene? She had her living to make, and two little kids. She didn't need to be around something illegal.

Tara? Too queasy.

This is when I would have called my brother, if I'd known where he was. When you have to clean the blood out of the kitchen, it's family you want.

I'd have to do this by myself.

Eric came first. I scrambled over to him, reclined by him with one elbow to prop me up.

'Eric,' I said loudly. His blue eyes opened. They were bright with pain.

The hole in his chest bubbled blood. I hated to think

what the exit wound looked like. Maybe it had been a twenty-two? Maybe the bullet was still inside? I looked at the wall behind where he'd been standing, and I couldn't see a spray of blood or a bullet hole. Actually, I realized, if the bullet had gone through him, it would have struck me. I looked down at myself, fumbled the coat off. No, no fresh blood.

As I watched Eric, he began to look a little better. 'Drink,' he said, and I almost put my wrist to his lips, when I reconsidered. I managed to get some TrueBlood out of the refrigerator and heat it up, though the front of the microwave was less than pristine.

I knelt to give it to him. 'Why not you?' he asked painfully.

'I'm sorry,' I apologized. 'I know you earned it, sweetie. But I have to have all my energy. I've got more work ahead.'

Eric downed the drink in a few big gulps. I'd unbuttoned his coat and his flannel shirt, and as I looked at his chest to mark the progression of his bleeding, I saw an amazing thing. The bullet that had hit him popped out of the wound. In another three minutes, or perhaps less, the hole had closed. The blood was still drying on his chest hair, and the bullet wound was gone.

'Another drink?' Eric asked.

'Sure. How do you feel?' I was numb myself.

His smile was crooked. 'Weak.'

I got him more blood and he drank this bottle more slowly. Wincing, he pulled himself to a full sitting position. He looked at the mess on the other side of the table.

Then he looked at me.

'I know, I know, I did terrible!' I said. 'I'm so sorry!' I could feel tears – again – trailing down my cheeks. I could hardly feel more miserable. I'd done a dreadful thing. I'd failed in my job. I had a massive cleanup ahead of me. And I looked awful.

Eric looked mildly surprised at my outburst. 'You might have died of the bullet, and I knew I wouldn't,' he pointed out. 'I kept the bullet from you in the most expedient way, and then you defended me effectively.'

That was certainly a skewed way to look at it, but oddly enough, I did feel less horrible.

'I killed another human,' I said. That made two in one night; but in my opinion, the hollow-cheeked witch had killed himself by pushing down on the knife.

I'd definitely fired the shotgun all by myself.

I shuddered and turned away from the ragged shell of bone and flesh that had once held Debbie Pelt.

'You didn't,' he said sharply. 'You killed a shifter who was a treacherous, murderous bitch, a shifter who had tried to kill you twice already.' So it had been Eric's hand that had squeezed her throat and made her let go of me. 'I should have finished the job when I had her earlier,' he said, by way of confirmation. 'It would have saved us both some heartache; in my case, literally.'

I had a feeling this was not what the Reverend Fullenwilder would be saying. I muttered something to that effect.

'I was never a Christian,' Eric said. Now, that didn't surprise me. 'But I can't imagine a belief system that would tell you to sit still and get slaughtered.'

I blinked, wondering if that wasn't exactly what Christianity taught. But I am no theologian or Bible scholar, and I would have to leave the judgment on my action to God, who was also no theologian.

Somehow I felt better, and I was in fact grateful to be alive.

'Thank you, Eric,' I said. I kissed him on the cheek. 'Now you go clean up in the bathroom while I start in here.'

But he was not having any of that. God bless him, he helped me with great zeal. Since he could handle the most disgusting things with no apparent qualms, I was delighted to let him.

You don't want to know how awful it was, or all the details. But we got Debbie together and bagged up, and Eric took her way out into the woods and buried her and concealed the grave, he swore, while I cleaned. I had to take down the curtains over the sink and soak them in the washing machine in cold water, and I stuck my coat in with them, though without much hope of its being wearable again. I pulled on rubber gloves and used bleach-soaked wipes to go over and over the chair and table and floor, and I sprayed the front of the cabinets with wood soap and wiped and wiped.

You just wouldn't believe where specks of blood had landed.

I realized that attention to these tiny details was helping me keep my mind off of the main event, and that the longer I avoided looking at it squarely – the longer I let Eric's practical words sink into my awareness – the better off I'd be. There was nothing I could undo. There was no way I could mend what I had done. I'd had a limited number of choices, and I had to live with the choice I'd made. My Gran had always told me that a woman – any woman worth her salt – could do whatever she had to. If you'd called Gran a liberated woman, she would have denied it vigorously, but she'd been the strongest woman I'd ever known, and if she believed I could complete this grisly task just because I had to, I would do it.

When I was through, the kitchen reeked of cleaning products, and to the naked eye it was literally spotless. I was sure a crime scene expert would be able to find trace evidence (a tip of the hat to the Learning Channel), but I didn't intend that a crime scene expert would ever have reason to come into my kitchen.

She'd broken in the front door. It had never occurred to me to check it before I came in the back. So much for my career as a bodyguard. I wedged a chair under the doorknob to keep it blocked for the remainder of the night.

Eric, returned from his burial detail, seemed to be high on excitement, so I asked him to go scouting for Debbie's car. She had a Mazda Miata, and she'd hidden it on a four-wheeler trail right across the parish road from the turnoff to my place. Eric had had the foresight to retain her keys, and he volunteered to drive her car somewhere else. I should have followed him, to bring him back to my house, but he insisted he could do the job by himself, and I was too exhausted to boss him around. I stood under a stream of water and scrubbed myself clean while he was gone. I was glad to be alone, and I washed myself over and over. When I was as clean as I could get on the outside, I pulled on a pink nylon nightgown and crawled in the bed. It was close to dawn, and I hoped Eric would be back soon. I had opened the closet and the hole for him, and put an extra pillow in it.

I heard him come in just as I was falling asleep, and he kissed me on the cheek. 'All done,' he said, and I mumbled, 'Thanks, baby.'

'Anything for you,' he said, his voice gentle. 'Good night, my lover.'

It occurred to me that I was lethal for exes. I'd dusted Bill's big love (and his mom); now I'd killed Alcide's off-and-on-again sweetie. I knew hundreds of men. I'd never gone homicidal on their exes. But creatures I cared about, well, that seemed to be different. I wondered if Eric had any old girlfriends around. Probably about a hundred or so. Well, they'd better beware of me.

After that, whether I willed it or not, I was sucked down into a black hole of exhaustion.

Chapter 14

I guess Pam worked on Hallow right up until dawn was peeking over the horizon. I myself was so heavily asleep, so in need of both physical and mental healing, I didn't wake until four in the afternoon. It was a gloomy winter day, the kind that makes you switch on the radio to see if an ice storm is coming. I checked to make sure I had three or four days' worth of firewood moved up onto the back porch.

Eric would be up early today.

I dressed and ate at the speed of a snail, trying to get a handle on my state of being.

Physically, I was fine. A bruise here or there, a little muscle soreness – that was nothing. It was the second week of January and I was sticking to my New Year's resolution just great.

On the other hand – and there's always another hand – mentally, or maybe emotionally, I was less than rock-steady. No matter how practical you are, no matter how strong-stomached you are, you can't do something like I'd done without suffering some consequences.

That's the way it should be.

When I thought of Eric getting up, I thought of maybe doing some snuggling before I had to go to work. And I thought of the pleasure of being with someone who thought I was so important.

I hadn't anticipated that the spell would have been broken.

Eric got up at five-thirty. When I heard movement in the guest bedroom, I tapped on the door and opened it. He whirled, his fangs running out and his hands clawing in front of him.

I'd almost said, 'Hi, honey,' but caution kept me mute.

'Sookie,' he said slowly. 'Am I in your house?'

I was glad I'd gotten dressed. 'Yes,' I said, regrouping like crazy. 'You've been here for safekeeping. Do you know what happened?'

'I went to a meeting with some new people,' he said, doubt in his voice. 'Didn't I?' He looked down at his Wal-Mart clothes with some surprise. 'When did I buy these?'

'I had to get those for you,' I said.

'Did you dress me, too?' he asked, running his hands down his chest and lower. He gave me a very Eric smile.

He didn't remember. Anything.

'No,' I said. I flashed on Eric in the shower with me. The kitchen table. The bed.

'Where is Pam?' he asked.

'You should call her,' I said. 'Do you recall anything about yesterday?'

'Yesterday I had the meeting with the witches,' he said, as if that was indisputable.

I shook my head. 'That was days ago,' I told him, unable to add the number of them up in my head. My heart sank even lower.

'You don't remember last night, after we came back from Shreveport,' I pressed him, suddenly seeing a gleam of light in all this.

'Did we make love?' he asked hopefully. 'Did you finally yield to me, Sookie? It's only a matter of time, of course.' He grinned at me.

No, last night we cleaned up a body, I thought.

I was the only one who knew. And even I didn't know where Debbie's remains were buried, or what had happened to her car.

I sat down on the edge of my old narrow bed. Eric looked at me closely. 'Something's wrong, Sookie? What happened while I was – Why don't I remember what happened?'

Least said, soonest mended.

All's well that ends well.

Out of sight, out of mind. (Oh, I wished that were true.)

'I bet Pam will be here any minute,' I said. 'I think I'll let her tell you all about it.'

'And Chow?'

'No, he won't be here. He died last night. Fangtasia seems to have a bad effect on bartenders.'

'Who killed him? I'll have vengeance.'

'You've already had.'

'Something more is wrong with you,' Eric said. He'd always been astute.

'Yes, lots of stuff is wrong with me.' I would've enjoyed hugging him right then, but it would just complicate everything. 'And I think it's going to snow.'

'Snow, here?' Eric was as delighted as a child. 'I love snow!'

Why was I not surprised?

'Maybe we will get snowed in together,' he said suggestively, waggling his blond eyebrows.

I laughed. I just couldn't help it. And it was a hell of a lot better than crying, which I'd done quite enough of lately. 'As if you'd ever let the weather stop you from doing what you wanted to do,' I said, and stood. 'Come on, I'll heat you up some blood.'

Even a few nights of intimacy had softened me enough that I had to watch my actions. Once I almost stroked his hair as I passed him; and once I bent to give him a kiss, and had to pretend I'd dropped something on the floor.

When Pam knocked on my front door thirty minutes later, I was ready for work, and Eric was antsy as hell.

Pam was no sooner seated opposite him than he began bombarding her with questions. I told them quietly that I was leaving, and I don't think they even noticed when I went out the kitchen door.

Merlotte's wasn't too busy that night, after we dealt with a rather large supper crowd. A few flakes of snow had convinced most of the regulars that going home sober might be a very good idea. There were enough customers left to keep Arlene and me moderately busy. Sam caught me as I was loading my tray with seven mugs of beer and wanted to be filled in on the night before.

'I'll tell you later,' I promised, thinking I'd have to edit my narrative pretty carefully.

'Any trace of Jason?' he asked.

'No,' I said, and felt sadder than ever. The dispatcher at the law enforcement complex had sounded almost snappish when I'd called to ask if there was any news.

Kevin and Kenya came in that night after they'd gotten off duty. When I took their drinks to the table (a bourbon and Coke and a gin and tonic), Kenya said, 'We've been looking for your brother, Sookie. I'm sorry.'

'I know you all have been trying,' I said. 'I appreciate you all organizing the search party so much! I just wish . . .' And then I couldn't think of anything else to say. Thanks to my disability, I knew something about each of them that the other didn't know. They loved each other. But Kevin knew his mother would stick her head in the oven before she'd see him married to a black woman, and Kenya knew her brothers would rather ram Kevin through a wall than see him walk down the aisle with her.

And I knew this, despite the fact that neither of them did; and I hated having this personal knowledge, this intimate knowledge, that I just couldn't help knowing.

Worse than knowing, even, was the temptation to interfere. I told myself very sternly that I had enough problems of my own without causing problems for other people. Luckily, I was busy enough the rest of the night to erase the temptation from my mind. Though I couldn't reveal those kinds of secrets, I reminded myself that I owed the two officers, big-time. If I heard of something I could let them know, I would.

When the bar closed, I helped Sam put the chairs up on the tables so Terry Bellefleur could come in and mop and clean the toilets early in the morning. Arlene and Tack had left, singing 'Let It Snow' while they went out the back door. Sure enough, the flakes were drifting down outside, though I didn't think they'd stick past morning. I thought of the creatures out in the woods tonight, trying to keep warm and dry. I knew that in some spot in the forest, Debbie Pelt lay in a hole, cold forever.

I wondered how long I'd think of her like that, and I

hoped very much I could remember just as clearly what an awful person she'd been, how vindictive and murderous.

In fact, I'd stood staring out the window for a couple of minutes when Sam came up behind me.

'What's on your mind?' he asked. He gripped my elbow, and I could feel the strength in his fingers.

I sighed, not for the first time. 'Just wondering about Jason,' I said. That was close enough to the truth.

He patted me in a consoling way. 'Tell me about last night,' he said, and for one second I thought he was asking me about Debbie. Then, of course, I knew he referred to the battle with the witches, and I was able to give him an account.

'So Pam showed up tonight at your place.' Sam sounded pleased about that. 'She must have cracked Hallow, made her undo the spell. Eric was himself again?'

'As far as I could tell.'

'What did he have to say about the experience?'

'He didn't remember anything about it,' I said slowly. 'He didn't seem to have a clue.'

Sam looked away from me when he said, 'How are you, with that?'

'I think it's for the best,' I told him. 'Definitely.' But I would be going home to an empty house again. The knowledge skittered at the edges of my awareness, but I wouldn't look at it directly.

'Too bad you weren't working the afternoon shift,' he said, somehow following a similar train of thought. 'Calvin Norris was in here.'

'And?'

'I think he came in hopes of seeing you.'

I looked at Sam skeptically. 'Right.'

'I think he's serious, Sookie.'

'Sam,' I said, feeling unaccountably wounded, 'I'm on my own, and sometimes that's no fun, but I don't have to take up with a werewolf just because he offers.'

Sam looked mildly puzzled. 'You wouldn't have to. The people in Hotshot aren't Weres.'

'He said they were.'

'No, not Weres with a capital W. They're too proud to call themselves shifters, but that's what they are. They're were-panthers.'

'What?' I swear I saw dots floating in the air around my eyes.

'Sookie? What's wrong?'

'Panthers? Didn't you know that the print on Jason's dock was the print of a panther?'

'No, no one told me about any print! Are you sure?'

I gave him an exasperated look. 'Of course, I'm sure. And he vanished the night Crystal Norris was waiting for him in his house. You're the only bartender in the world who doesn't know all the town gossip.'

'Crystal – *she's* the Hotshot girl he was with New Year's Eve? The skinny black-headed girl at the search?'

I nodded.

'The one Felton loves so much?'

'He what?'

'Felton, you know, the one who came along on the search. She's been his big love his whole life.'

'And you know this how?' Since I, the mind reader, didn't, I was distinctly piqued.

'He told me one night when he'd had too much to drink. These guys from Hotshot, they don't come in much, but when they do, they drink serious.'

'So why would he join in the search?'

'I think maybe we'd better go ask a few questions.'

'This late?'

'You got something better to do?'

He had a point, and I sure wanted to know if they had my brother or could tell me what had happened to him. But in a way, I was scared of finding out.

'That jacket's too light for this weather, Sookie,' Sam said, as we bundled up.

'My coat is at the cleaner's,' I said. Actually, I hadn't had a chance to put it in the dryer, or even to check to make sure all the blood had come out. And it had holes in it.

'Hmmm' was all Sam said, before he loaned me a green pullover sweater to wear under my jacket. We got in Sam's pickup because the snow was really coming down, and like all men, Sam was convinced he could drive in the snow, though he'd almost never done so.

The drive out to Hotshot seemed even longer in the dark night, with the snow swirling down in the headlights.

'I thank you for taking me out here, but I'm beginning to think we're crazy,' I said, when we were halfway there.

'Is your seat belt on?' Sam asked.

'Sure.'

'Good,' he said, and we kept on our way.

Finally we reached the little community. There weren't any streetlights out here, of course, but a couple of the residents had paid to have security lights put up on the electric poles. Windows were glowing in some of the houses.

'Where do you think we should go?'

'Calvin's. He's the one with the power,' Sam said, sounding certain.

I remembered how proud Calvin had been of his house, and I was a little curious to see the inside. His lights were on, and his pickup was parked in front of the house. Stepping out of the warm truck into the snowy night was like walking through a chilly wet curtain to reach the front door. I knocked, and after a long pause, the door came open. Calvin looked pleased until he saw Sam behind me.

'Come in,' he said, not too warmly, and stood aside. We stamped our feet politely before we entered.

The house was plain and clean, decorated with inexpensive but carefully arranged furniture and pictures. None of the pictures had people in them, which I thought interesting. Landscapes. Wildlife.

'This is a bad night to be out driving around,' Calvin observed.

I knew I'd have to tread carefully, as much as I wanted to grab the front of his flannel shirt and scream in his face. This man was a ruler. The size of the kingdom didn't really matter.

'Calvin,' I said, as calmly as I could, 'did you know that the police found a panther print on the dock, by Jason's bootprint?'

'No,' he said, after a long moment. I could see the anger building behind his eyes. 'We don't hear a lot of town gossip out here. I wondered why the search party had men with guns, but we make other people kind of nervous, and no one was talking to us much. Panther print. Huh.'

'I didn't know that was your, um, other identity, until tonight.'

He looked at me steadily. 'You think that one of us made off with your brother.'

I stood silent, not shifting my eyes from his. Sam was equally still beside me.

'You think Crystal got mad at your brother and did him harm?'

'No,' I said. His golden eyes were getting wider and rounder as I spoke to him.

'Are you afraid of me?' he asked suddenly.

'No,' I said. 'I'm not.'

'Felton,' he said.

I nodded.

'Let's go see,' he said.

Back out into the snow and darkness. I could feel the sting of the flakes on my cheeks, and I was glad my jacket had a hood. Sam's gloved hand took mine as I stumbled over some discarded tool or toy in the yard of the house next to Felton's. As we trailed up to the concrete slab that formed Felton's front porch, Calvin was already knocking at the door.

'Who is it?' Felton demanded.

'Open,' said Calvin.

Recognizing his voice, Felton opened the door immediately. He didn't have the same cleanliness bug as Calvin, and his furniture was not so much arranged as shoved up against whatever wall was handiest. The way he moved was not human, and tonight that seemed even more pronounced than it had at the search. Felton, I thought, was closer to reverting to his animal nature. Inbreeding had definitely left its mark on him.

'Where is the man?' Calvin asked without preamble.

Felton's eyes flared wide, and he twitched, as if he was thinking about running. He didn't speak.

'Where?' Calvin demanded again, and then his hand

changed into a paw and he swiped it across Felton's face. 'Does he live?'

I clapped my hands across my mouth so I wouldn't scream. Felton sank to his knees, his face crossed with parallel slashes filling with blood.

'In the shed in back,' he said indistinctly.

I went back out the front door so quickly that Sam barely caught up with me. Around the corner of the house I flew, and I fell full-length over a woodpile. Though I knew it would hurt later, I jumped up and found myself supported by Calvin Norris, who, as he had in the woods, lifted me over the pile before I knew what he intended. He vaulted it himself with easy grace, and then we were at the door of the shed, which was one of those you order from Sears or Penney's. You have your neighbors come help put it up, when the concrete truck comes to pour your slab.

The door was padlocked, but these sheds aren't meant to repel determined intruders, and Calvin was very strong. He broke the lock, and pushed back the door, and turned on the light. It was amazing to me that there was electricity out here, because that's certainly not the norm.

At first I wasn't sure I was looking at my brother, because this creature looked nothing like Jason. He was blond, sure, but he was so filthy and smelly that I flinched, even in the freezing air. And he was blue with the cold, since he had only pants on. He was lying on a single blanket on the concrete floor.

I was on my knees beside him, gathering him up as best I could in my arms, and his eyelids fluttered open. 'Sookie?' he said, and I could hear the disbelief in his voice. 'Sookie? Am I saved?'

'Yes,' I said, though I was by no means so sure. I remember what had happened to the sheriff who'd come out here and found something amiss. 'We're going to take you home.'

He'd been bitten.

He'd been bitten a lot.

'Oh, no,' I said softly, the significance of the bites sinking in.

'I didn't kill him,' Felton said defensively, from outside.

'You bit him,' I said, and my voice sounded like another person's. 'You wanted him to be like you.'

'So Crystal wouldn't like him better. She knows we need to breed outside, but she really likes me best,' Felton said.

'So you grabbed him, and you kept him, and you bit him.'

Jason was too weak to stand.

'Please carry him to the truck,' I said stiffly, unable to meet the eyes of anyone around me. I could feel the fury rising in me like a black wave, and I knew I had to restrain it until we were out of here. I had just enough control to do this. I knew I did.

Jason cried out when Calvin and Sam lifted him. They got the blanket, too, and sort of tucked it around him. I stumbled after them as they made their way back to Calvin's and the truck.

I had my brother back. There was a chance he was going to turn into a panther from time to time, but I had him back. I didn't know if the rules for all shifters were the same, but Alcide had told me that Weres who were bitten, not born – created Weres, rather than genetic Weres – changed into the half-man, half-beast creatures who populated horror movies. I forced myself to get off that track, to think of the joy of having my brother back, alive.

Calvin got Jason into the truck and slid him over, and Sam climbed into the driver's seat. Jason would be between us after I climbed into the truck. But Calvin had to tell me something first.

'Felton will be punished,' he said. 'Right now.'

Punishing Felton hadn't been at the top of my list of things to think about, but I nodded, because I wanted to get the hell out of there.

'If we're taking care of Felton, are you going to go to the police?' he asked. He was standing stiffly, as if he was trying to be casual about the question. But this was a dangerous moment. I knew what happened to people who drew attention to the Hotshot community.

'No,' I said. 'It was just Felton.' Though, of course, Crystal had to have known, at least on some level. She'd told me she'd smelled an animal that night at Jason's. How could she have mistaken the smell of panther, when she was one? And she had probably known all along that that panther had been Felton. His smell would be familiar to her. But it just wasn't the time to go into that; Calvin would know that as well as I, when he'd had a moment to think. 'And my brother may be one of you now. He'll need you,' I added, in the most even voice I could manage. It wasn't very even, at that.

'I'll come get Jason, next full moon.'

I nodded again. 'Thank you,' I told him, because I knew we would never have found Jason if he'd stonewalled us. 'I have to get my brother home now.' I knew Calvin wanted me to touch him, wanted me to connect with him somehow, but I just couldn't do it.

'Sure,' he said, after a long moment. The shape-shifter stepped back while I scrambled up into the cab. He seemed to know I wouldn't want any help from him right now.

I'd thought I'd gotten unusual brain patterns from the Hotshot people because they were inbred. It had never occurred to me they were something other than wolves. I'd assumed. I know what my high school volleyball coach always said about 'assume.' Of course, he'd also told us that we had to leave everything out on the court so it would be there when we came back, which I had yet to figure out.

But he'd been right about assumptions.

Sam had already gotten the heater in the truck going, but not at full blast. Too much heat too soon would be bad for Jason, I was sure. As it was, the second Jason began to warm up, his smell was pretty evident, and I nearly apologized to Sam, but sparing Jason any further humiliation was more important.

'Aside from the bites, and being so cold, are you okay?' I asked, when I thought Jason had stopped shivering and could speak.

'Yes,' he said. 'Yes. Every night, every damn night, he'd come in the shed, and he'd change in front of me, and I'd think, Tonight he's going to kill me and eat me. And every night, he'd bite me. And then he'd just change back and leave. I could tell it was hard for him, after he'd smelled the blood . . . but he never did more than bite.'

'They'll kill him tonight,' I said. 'In return for us not going to the police.'

'Good deal,' said Jason, and he meant it.

Chapter 15

Jason was able to stand on his own long enough to take a shower, which he said was the best one he'd taken in his life. When he was clean and smelled like every scented thing in my bathroom, and he was modestly draped with a big towel, I went all over him with Neosporin. I used up a whole tube on the bites. They seemed to be healing clean already, but I could not stop myself from trying to think of things to do for him. He'd had hot chocolate, and he'd eaten some hot oatmeal (which I thought was an odd choice, but he said all Felton had brought him to eat had been barely cooked meat), and he'd put on the sleeping pants I'd bought for Eric (too big, but the drawstring waist helped), and he'd put on a baggy old T-shirt I'd gotten when I'd done the Walk for Life two years before. He kept touching the material as if he was delighted to be dressed.

He seemed to want to be warm and to sleep, more than anything. I put him in my old room. With a sad glance at the closet, which Eric had left all askew, I told my brother good night. He asked me to turn the hall light on and leave the door cracked a little. It cost Jason to ask that, so I didn't say a word. I just did as he'd requested.

Sam was sitting in the kitchen, drinking a cup of hot tea.

He looked up from watching the steam of it and smiled at me. 'How is he?'

I sank down into my usual spot. 'He's better than I thought he would be,' I said. 'Considering he spent the whole time in the shed with no heat and being bitten every day.'

'I wonder how long Felton would have kept him?'

'Until the full moon, I guess. Then Felton would've found out if he'd succeeded or not.' I felt a little sick.

'I checked your calendar. He's got a couple of weeks.'

'Good. Give Jason time to get his strength back before he has something else to face.' I rested my head in my hands for a minute. 'I have to call the police.'

'To let them know to stop searching?'

'Yep.'

'Have you made up your mind what to say? Did Jason mention any ideas?'

'Maybe that the male relatives of some girl had kidnapped him?' Actually, that was sort of true.

'The cops would want to know where he'd been held. If he'd gotten away on his own, they'd want to know how, and they'd be sure he'd have more information for them.'

I wondered if I had enough brainpower left to think. I stared blankly at the table: the familiar napkin holder that my grandmother had bought at a craft fair, and the sugar bowl, and the salt- and peppershakers shaped like a rooster and a hen. I noticed something had been tucked under the saltshaker.

It was a check for $50,000, signed by Eric Northman.

Eric had not only paid me, he had given me the biggest tip of my career.

'Oh,' I said, very gently. 'Oh, boy.' I looked at it for a minute more, to make sure I was reading it correctly. I passed it across the table to Sam.

'Wow. Payment for keeping Eric?' Sam looked up at me, and I nodded. 'What will you do with it?'

'Put it through the bank, first thing tomorrow morning.'

He smiled. 'I guess I was thinking longer term than that.'

'Just relax. It'll just relax me to have it. To know that . . .' To my embarrassment, here came tears. Again. *Damn.* 'So I won't have to *worry* all the time.'

'Things have been tight recently, I take it.' I nodded, and Sam's mouth compressed. 'You . . .' he began, and then couldn't finish his sentence.

'Thanks, but I can't do that to people,' I said firmly. 'Gran always said that was the surest way to end a friendship.'

'You could sell this land, buy a house in town, have neighbors,' Sam suggested, as if he'd been dying to say that for months.

'Move out of this house?' Some member of my family had lived in this house continuously for over a hundred and fifty years. Of course, that didn't make it sacred or anything, and the house had been added to and modernized many times. I thought of living in a small modern house with level floors and up-to-date bathrooms and a convenient kitchen with lots of plugs. No exposed water heater. Lots of blown-in insulation in the attic. A carport!

Dazzled at the vision, I swallowed. 'I'll consider it,' I said, feeling greatly daring to even entertain the idea. 'But

I can't think of anything much right now. Just getting through tomorrow will be hard enough.'

I thought of the police man-hours that had been put into searching for Jason. Suddenly I was so tired, I just couldn't make an attempt to fashion a story for the law.

'You need to go to bed,' Sam said astutely.

I could only nod. 'Thank you, Sam. Thank you so much.' We stood and I gave him a hug. It turned into a longer hug than I'd planned, because hugging him was unexpectedly restful and comfortable. 'Good night,' I said. 'Please drive careful going back.' I thought briefly of offering him one of the beds upstairs, but I kept that floor shut off and it would be awfully cold up there; and I'd have to go up and make the bed. He'd be more comfortable making the short drive home, even in the snow.

'I will,' he said, and released me. 'Call me in the morning.

'Thanks again.'

'Enough thank-yous,' he said. Eric had put a couple of nails in the front door to hold it shut, until I could get a dead bolt put on. I locked the back door behind Sam, and I barely managed to brush my teeth and change into a night-gown before I crawled in my bed.

The first thing I did the next morning was check on my brother. Jason was still deeply asleep, and in the light of day, I could clearly see the effects of his imprisonment. His face had a coating of stubble. Even in his sleep, he looked older. There were bruises here and there, and that was just on his face and arms. His eyes opened as I sat by the bed, looking at him. Without moving, he rolled his eyes around, taking in the room. They stopped when they came to my face.

'I didn't dream it,' he said. His voice was hoarse. 'You and Sam came and got me. They let me go. The panther let me go.'

'Yes.'

'So what's been happening while I was gone?' he asked next. 'Wait, can I go to the bathroom and get a cup of coffee before you tell me?'

I liked his asking instead of telling (a Jason trait, telling), and I was glad to tell him yes and even volunteer to get the coffee. Jason seemed happy enough to crawl back in bed with the mug of coffee and sugar, and prop himself up on the pillows while we talked.

I told him about Catfish's phone call, our to-and-fro with the police, the search of the yard and my conscription of his Benelli shotgun, which he immediately demanded to see.

'You fired it!' he said indignantly, after checking it over.

I just stared at him.

He flinched first. 'I guess it worked like a shotgun is 'spose to,' he said slowly. 'Since you're sitting here looking pretty much okay.'

'Thanks, and don't ask me again,' I said.

He nodded.

'Now we have to think of a story for the police.'

'I guess we can't just tell them the truth.'

'Sure, Jason, let's tell them that the village of Hotshot is full of were-panthers, and that since you slept with one, her boyfriend wanted to make you a were-panther, too, so she wouldn't prefer you over him. That's why he changed into a panther and bit you every day.'

There was a long pause.

'I can just see Andy Bellefleur's face,' Jason said in a

subdued kind of way. 'He still can't get over me being innocent of murdering those girls last year. He'd love to get me
committed as being delusional. Catfish would have to fire
me, and I don't think I'd like it at the mental hospital.'

'Well, your dating opportunities would sure be limited.'

'Crystal – God, that girl! You warned me. But I was so
bowled over by her. And she turns out to be a . . . you
know.'

'Oh, for goodness sake, Jason, she's a shape-shifter. Don't
go on like she's the creature from the Black Lagoon, or
Freddy Krueger, or something.'

'Sook, you know a lot of stuff we don't know, don't you?
I'm getting that picture.'

'Yes, I guess so.'

'Besides vampires.'

'Right.'

'There's lots else.'

'I tried to tell you.'

'I believed what you said, but I just didn't get it. Some
people I know – I mean besides Crystal – they're not always
people, huh?'

'That's right.'

'Like how many?'

I counted up the two-natured I'd seen in the bar: Sam,
Alcide, that little were-fox who'd been standing Jason and
Hoyt drinks a couple of weeks ago . . . 'At least three,' I
said.

'How do you know all this?'

I just stared at him.

'Right,' he said, after a long moment. 'I don't want to
know.'

'And now, you,' I said gently.

'Are you sure?'

'No, and we won't be sure for a couple of weeks,' I said. 'But Calvin'll help you if you need it.'

'I won't take help from them!' Jason's eyes were blazing, and he looked positively feverish.

'You don't have a choice,' I said, trying not to snap. 'And Calvin didn't know you were there. He's an okay guy. But it's not even time to talk about it yet. We have to figure out what to tell the police right now.'

For at least an hour we went over and over our stories, trying to find threads of truth to help us stitch together a fabrication.

Finally, I called the police station. The day-shift dispatcher was tired of hearing my voice, but she was still trying to be nice. 'Sookie, like I told you yesterday, hon, we'll call you when we find out something about Jason,' she said, trying to suppress the note of exasperation beneath her soothing tone.

'I've got him,' I said.

'You – WHAT?' The shriek came over loud and clear. Even Jason winced.

'I've got him.'

'I'll send someone right over.'

'Good,' I said, though I didn't mean it.

I had the foresight to get the nails out of the front door before the police got there. I didn't want them asking what had happened to it. Jason had looked at me oddly when I got out the hammer, but he didn't say a word.

'Where's your car?' Andy Bellefleur asked first thing.

'It's at Merlotte's.'

'Why?'

'Can I just tell you and Alcee, together, one time?' Alcee

Beck was coming up the front steps. He and Andy came in the house together, and at the sight of Jason lying wrapped up on my couch, they both stopped dead in their tracks. I knew then that they'd never expected to see Jason alive again.

'Glad to see you safe and sound, man,' Andy said, and shook Jason's hand. Alcee Beck followed on his heels. They sat down, Andy in Gran's recliner and Alcee in the armchair I usually took, and I perched on the couch beside Jason's feet. 'We're glad you're in the land of the living, Jason, but we need to know where you've been and what happened to you.'

'I have no idea,' Jason said.

And he stuck to it for hours.

There had been no believable story Jason could tell that could account for everything: his absence, his poor physical condition, the bite marks, his sudden reappearance. The only possible line he could take was to say the last thing he remembered, he'd heard a funny noise outside while he was entertaining Crystal, and when he'd gone to investigate, he'd been hit on the head. He didn't remember anything until somehow he'd felt himself pushed from a vehicle to land in my yard the night before. I'd found him there when Sam brought me home from work. I'd ridden home with Sam because I was scared to drive in the snow.

Of course, we'd cleared this with Sam ahead of time, and he'd agreed, reluctantly, that it was the best we could come up with. I knew Sam didn't like to lie, and I didn't either, but we had to keep that particular can of worms closed.

The beauty of this story was its simplicity. As long as Jason could resist the temptation to embroider, he'd be safe. I'd known that would be hard for Jason; he loved to talk, and he loved to talk big. But as long as I was sitting there, reminding him of the consequences, my brother managed to restrain himself. I had to get up to get him another cup of coffee – the lawmen didn't want any more – and as I was coming back in the living room, Jason was saying he thought he remembered a cold dark room. I gave him a very plain look, and he said, 'But you know, my head is so confused, that may just be something I dreamed.'

Andy looked from Jason to me, clearly getting angrier and angrier. 'I just can't understand you two,' he said. His voice was almost a growl. 'Sookie, I know you worried about him. I'm not making that up, am I?'

'No, I am so glad to have him back.' I patted my brother's foot under the blanket.

'And you, you didn't want to be wherever you were, right? You missed work, you cost the parish thousands of dollars from our budget to search for you, and you disrupted the lives of hundreds of people. And you're sitting here lying to us!' Andy's voice was almost a shout as he finished. 'Now, the same night you show up, this missing vampire on all the posters called the police in Shreveport to say he's recovering from memory loss, too! And there's a strange fire in Shreveport with all kinds of bodies recovered! And you're trying to tell me there's no connection!'

Jason and I gaped at each other. Actually, there *was* no connection between Jason and Eric. It just hadn't occurred to me how strange that would look.

'What vampire?' Jason asked. It was so good, I almost believed him myself.

'Let's leave, Alcee,' Andy said. He slapped his notebook shut. He put his pen back in his shirt pocket with such an emphatic thrust that I was surprised he had a pocket left. 'This bastard won't even tell us the truth.'

'Don't you think I'd tell you if I could?' Jason said. 'Don't you think I'd like to lay hands on whoever did this to me?' He sounded absolutely, one hundred percent sincere, because he was. The two detectives were shaken in their disbelief, especially Alcee Beck. But they still left unhappy with the two of us. I felt sorry for it, but there was nothing I could do.

Later that day, Arlene picked me up so I could fetch my car from Merlotte's. She was happy to see Jason, and she gave him a big hug. 'You had your sister some kind of worried, you rascal,' she said, with mock ferocity. 'Don't you ever scare Sookie like that again.'

'I'll do my best,' Jason said, with a good approximation of his old roguish smile. 'She's been a good sister to me.'

'Now, that's God's truth,' I said, a little sourly. 'When I bring my car back, I think I might just run you home, big brother.'

Jason looked scared for a minute. Being alone had never been his favorite thing, and after hours by himself in the cold of the shed, it might be even harder.

'I bet girls all over Bon Temps are making food to bring to your place now that they heard you're back,' Arlene said, and Jason brightened perceptibly. ' 'Specially since I've been telling everyone what an invalid you are.'

'Thanks, Arlene,' Jason said, looking much more like himself.

I echoed that on the way into town. 'I really appreciate you cheering him up. I don't know what all he went through, but he's going to have a rough time getting over it, I think.'

'Honey, you don't need to worry about Jason. He's the original survivor. I don't know why he didn't try out for the show.'

We laughed all the way into town at the idea of staging a *Survivor* episode in Bon Temps.

'What with the razorbacks in the woods, and that panther print, they might have an exciting time of it if we had *Survivor: Bon Temps*,' Arlene said. 'Tack and me would just sit back and laugh at them.'

That gave me a nice opening to tease her about Tack, which she enjoyed, and altogether she cheered up me just as much as Jason. Arlene was good about stuff like that. I had a brief conversation with Sam in the storeroom of Merlotte's, and he told me Andy and Alcee had already been by to see if his story meshed with mine.

He hushed me before I could thank him again.

I took Jason home, though he hinted broadly he'd like to stay with me one more night. I took the Benelli with us, and I told him to clean it that evening. He promised he would, and when he looked at me, I could tell he wanted to ask me again why I'd had to use it. But he didn't. Jason had learned some things in the past few days, himself.

I was working the late shift again, so I would have a little time on my hands when I got home before I had to go in to work. The prospect felt good. I didn't see any running men on my way back to my house, and no one phoned or popped in with a crisis for a whole two hours. I was able to change the sheets on both beds, wash them, and sweep the kitchen and straighten up the closet concealing the hidey-hole, before the knock came at the front door.

I knew who it would be. It was full dark outside, and sure enough, Eric stood on my front porch.

He looked down at me with no very happy face. 'I find myself troubled,' he said without preamble.

'Then I've got to drop everything so I can help you out,' I said, going instantly on the offensive.

He cocked an eyebrow. 'I'll be polite and ask if I can come in.' I hadn't rescinded his invitation, but he didn't want to just stroll into my house. Tactful.

'Yes, you can.' I stepped back.

'Hallow is dead, having been forced to counter the curse on me, obviously.'

'Pam did a good job.'

He nodded. 'It was Hallow or me,' he said. 'I like me better.'

'Why'd she pick Shreveport?'

'Her parents were jailed in Shreveport. They were witches, too, but they also ran confidence games of some kind, using their craft to make their victims more convinced of their sincerity. In Shreveport, their luck ran out. The supernatural community refused to make any effort to get the older Stonebrooks out of jail. The woman ran afoul of a voodoo priestess while she was incarcerated, and the man ran afoul of a knife in some bathroom brawl.'

'Pretty good reason to have it in for the supernaturals of Shreveport.'

'They say I was here for several nights.' Eric had decided to change the subject.

'Yes,' I said. I tried to look agreeably interested in what he had to say.

'And in that time, we never . . . ?'

I didn't pretend to misunderstand him.

'Eric, does that seem likely?' I asked.

He hadn't sat down, and he moved closer to me, as if

looking at me hard would reveal the truth. It would have been easy to take a step, be even closer.

'I just don't know,' he said. 'And it's making me a little aggravated.'

I smiled. 'Are you enjoying being back at work?'

'Yes. But Pam ran everything well during my absence. I'm sending lots of flowers to the hospital. Belinda, and a wolf named Maria-Comet or something.'

'Maria-Star Cooper. You didn't send any to me,' I pointed out tartly.

'No, but I left you something more meaningful under the saltshaker,' he said, with much the same edge. 'You'll have to pay taxes on it. If I know you, you'll give your brother some of it. I hear you got him back.'

'I did,' I said briefly. I knew I was getting closer to bursting out with something, and I knew he should leave soon. I'd given Jason such good advice about being quiet, but it was hard to follow it myself. 'And your point is?'

'It won't last for long.'

I don't think Eric realized how much money fifty thousand dollars was, by my standards. 'What's your point? I can tell you have one, but I don't have an idea what it might be.'

'Was there a reason I found brain tissue on my coat sleeve?'

I felt all the blood drain from my face, the way it does when you're on the edge of passing out. The next thing I knew, I was on the couch and Eric was beside me.

'I think there are some things you're not telling me, Sookie, my dear,' he said. His voice was gentler, though.

The temptation was almost overwhelming.

But I thought of the power Eric would have over me, even more power than he had now; he would know I had slept with him, and he would know that I had killed a woman and he was the only one who'd witnessed it. He would know that not only did he owe me his life (most likely), I certainly owed him mine.

'I liked you a lot better when you didn't remember who you were,' I said, and with that truth forefront in my mind, I knew I had to keep quiet.

'Harsh words,' he said, and I almost believed he was really hurt.

Luckily for me, someone else came to my door. The knock was loud and peremptory, and I felt a jolt of alarm.

The caller was Amanda, the insulting redheaded female Were from Shreveport. 'I'm on official business today,' she said, 'so I'll be polite.'

That would be a nice change.

She nodded to Eric and said, 'Glad to have you back in your right mind, vampire,' in a completely unconcerned tone. I could see that the Weres and vampires of Shreveport had reverted to their old relationship.

'And good to see you, too, Amanda,' I said.

'Sure,' she said, but hardly as if she cared. 'Miss Stackhouse, we're making inquiries for the shifters of Jackson.'

Oh, no. 'Really? Won't you please sit down? Eric was just leaving.'

'No, I'd love to stay and hear Amanda's questions,' Eric said, beaming.

Amanda looked at me, eyebrows raised.

There wasn't a hell of a lot I could do about it.

'Oh, by all means, stay,' I said. 'Please sit down, both of you. I'm sorry, but I don't have a lot of time before I'm due at work.'

'Then I'll get right to the point,' Amanda said. 'Two nights ago, the woman that Alcide abjured – the shifter from Jackson, the one with the weird haircut?'

I nodded, to show I was on the same page. Eric looked pleasantly blank. He wouldn't in a minute.

'Debbie,' the Were recalled. 'Debbie Pelt.'

Eric's eyes widened. Now, that name he did know. He began to smile.

'Alcide abjured her?' he said.

'You were sitting right there,' snapped Amanda. 'Oh, wait, I forgot. That was while you were *under a curse.*'

She enjoyed the hell out of saying that.

'Anyway, Debbie didn't make it back to Jackson. Her family is worried about her, especially since they heard that Alcide abjured her, and they're afraid something might have happened to her.'

'Why do you think she would have said anything to me?'

Amanda made a face. 'Well, actually, I think she would rather have eaten glass than talked to you again. But we're obliged to check with everyone who was there.'

So this was just routine. I wasn't being singled out. I could feel myself relax. Unfortunately, so could Eric. I'd had his blood; he could tell things about me. He got up and wandered back to the kitchen. I wondered what he was doing.

'I haven't seen her since that night,' I said, which was true, since I didn't specify what time. 'I have no idea where she is now.' That was even truer.

Amanda told me, 'No one admits to having seen Debbie after she left the area of the battle. She drove off in her own car.'

Eric strolled back into the living room. I glanced at him, worried about what he was up to.

'Has her car been seen?' Eric asked.

He didn't know he'd been the one who'd hidden it.

'No, neither hide nor hair,' Amanda said, which was a strange image to use for a car. 'I'm sure she just ran off somewhere to get over her rage and humiliation. Being abjured; that's pretty awful. It's been years since I've heard the words said.'

'Her family doesn't think that's the case? That's she's gone somewhere to, ah, think things over?'

'They're afraid she's done something to herself.' Amanda snorted. We exchanged glances, showing we agreed perfectly about the likelihood of Debbie committing suicide. 'She wouldn't do anything that convenient,' Amanda said, since she had the nerve to say it out loud and I didn't.

'How's Alcide taking this?' I asked anxiously.

'He can hardly join in the search,' she pointed out, 'since he's the one who abjured her. He acts like he doesn't care, but I notice the colonel calls him to let him know what's happening. Which, so far, is nothing.' Amanda heaved herself to her feet, and I got up to walk her to the door. 'This sure has been a bad season for people going missing,' she said. 'But I hear through the grapevine that you got your brother back, and Eric's returned to his normal self, looks like.' She cast him a glance to make sure he knew how little she liked that normal self. 'Now Debbie has gone missing, but maybe she'll turn up, too. Sorry I had to bother you.'

'That's all right. Good luck,' I said, which was meaningless under the circumstances. The door closed behind her, and I wished desperately that I could just walk out and get in my car and drive to work.

I made myself turn around. Eric was standing.

'You're going?' I said, unable to keep from sounding startled and relieved.

'Yes, you said you had to get to work,' he said blandly.

'I do.'

'I suggest you wear that jacket, the one that's too light for the weather,' he said. 'Since your coat is still in bad shape.'

I'd run it through the washer on cold water wash, but I guess I hadn't checked it well enough to be sure everything had come off. That's where he'd been, searching for my coat. He'd found it on its hanger on the back porch, and examined it.

'In fact,' Eric said, as he went to the front door, 'I'd throw it away entirely. Maybe burn it.'

He left, closing the door behind him very quietly.

I knew, as sure as I knew my name, that tomorrow he would send me another coat, in a big fancy box, with a big bow on it. It would be the right size, it would be a top brand, and it would be warm.

It was cranberry red, with a removable liner, a detachable hood, and tortoiseshell buttons.